ONE MAGIC MOMENT

LYNN KURLAND

JOVE BOOKS, NEW YORK

THE BERKLEY PUBLISHING GROUP
Published by the Penguin Group
Penguin Group (USA) Inc.
375 Hudson Street, New York, New York 10014, USA
Penguin Group (Canada), 90 Eglinton Avenue East, Suite 700, Toronto, Ontario M4P 2Y3, Canada
(a division of Pearson Penguin Canada Inc.)
Penguin Books Ltd., 80 Strand, London WC2R 0RL, England
Penguin Group Ireland, 25 St. Stephen's Green, Dublin 2, Ireland (a division of Penguin Books Ltd.)
Penguin Group (Australia), 250 Camberwell Road, Camberwell, Victoria 3124, Australia
(a division of Pearson Australia Group Pty. Ltd.)
Penguin Books India Pvt. Ltd., 11 Community Centre, Panchsheel Park, New Delhi—110 017, India
Penguin Group (NZ), 67 Apollo Drive, Rosedale, Auckland 0632, New Zealand
(a division of Pearson New Zealand Ltd.)
Penguin Books (South Africa) (Pty.) Ltd., 24 Sturdee Avenue, Rosebank, Johannesburg 2196,
South Africa

Penguin Books Ltd., Registered Offices: 80 Strand, London WC2R 0RL, England

This is a work of fiction. Names, characters, places, and incidents either are the product of the author's
imagination or are used fictitiously, and any resemblance to actual persons, living or dead, business
establishments, events, or locales is entirely coincidental. The publisher does not have control over and
does not have any responsibility for author or third-party websites or their content.

ONE MAGIC MOMENT

A Jove Book / published by arrangement with Kurland Book Productions, Inc.

PRINTING HISTORY
Jove mass-market edition / May 2011

Copyright © 2011 by Kurland Book Productions, Inc.
Cover art by Jim Griffin.
Cover handlettering by Ron Zinn.
Cover design by George Long.

ISBN: 978-0-515-14951-7

JOVE®
Jove Books are published by The Berkley Publishing Group,
a division of Penguin Group (USA) Inc.,
375 Hudson Street, New York, New York 10014.
JOVE® is a registered trademark of Penguin Group (USA) Inc.
The "J" design is a trademark of Penguin Group (USA) Inc.

PRINTED IN THE UNITED STATES OF AMERICA

10 9 8 7 6 5 4 3 2 1

To my cousin-in-law, H. H.-B., PhD

Prologue

CHEVINGTON CASTLE, ENGLAND
PRESENT DAY

The castle was crawling with the past.

The man stood on the edge of the forest and looked at the keep in front of him, considering the spectacle that greeted his eyes. He was no ghost hunter, to be sure, but even he could bear witness to the paranormal activity going on under his nose. The air was full of the sounds of shouts of men in battle, the whinnies of horses, the ringing of swords. None of it was surprising, given the number of skirmishes the keep had seen over the years. It had sat squarely between London and the Scottish border for centuries, hosted queens and their lovers, been a refuge for noblemen and villains alike.

And the last had been just the lads in his family.

It was, or so he'd heard, a favorite destination for all manner of paranormal investigators, which he could easily understand. The bloody place gave him the willies, and he'd been born there.

Several years ago, as it happened.

He tucked his hands into the pockets of his very modern though stylishly rustic barn jacket and leaned against an acceptably sturdy tree so he could continue to watch the goings-on and rest his old bones at the same time. Along with the allure it seemed to have for ghost hunters, Chevington also seemed to draw a fair number of reenactment troupes. There was, he would freely admit, ample room on the grounds for the holding of mock tourneys and entertainments, and there were certainly enough otherworldly players milling about to lend the scene a certain air of authenticity.

The National Trust had taken over the place many years earlier and done a credible job of preserving its history and keeping it from being overrun by nutters in tights. The only slight irritation was that even though he'd trotted out his finest gentlemanly manners, he'd left the old woman manning the ticket booth unwilling to accept his most charming smile as entrance fee. Nay, twelve quid it had been to merely walk over the grounds of his own bloody home.

Not that he'd lived there in years, of course. How many years was something he'd shared with only a pair of souls, souls he had trusted implicitly. The bulk of his time had been spent on his private business: popping in here and there; dashing back out when things became tedious; living a life he never could have imagined in his youth—

He frowned as something unusual caught his eye—and considering where he was, that was saying something indeed. The living history enthusiasts were dressed in their usual garb, doing their usual things, save one lad who seemed to hold himself aloof and apart, pacing along the ridge of an earthen bulwark as if he had done the same many times before. The lad wasn't overly tall and his hood obscured all but a flash of fair hair, but still, there was something about the way he moved that seemed familiar somehow.

The old man blinked, but the hooded figure had suddenly disappeared into the crowd and thereby become lost to his view. He frowned thoughtfully. He had returned to England because he'd felt—how to put it?—as if Fate had been tapping him on the shoulder, then pointing to where he should be looking. He scanned the group in front of him again for possible clues, then shook his head slowly. Perhaps age had rendered him foolish and imaginative. Obviously he needed a bit of a rest. Perhaps he would indulge in a restorative weekender in the south of France where he would find superior fare to ingest and beautiful women to admire. Aye, that was just the thing for him.

Besides, what was there left for him to do in damp, chilly England? He'd put into motion all the things he could and watched as a fortuitous circumstance or two had done what he could not. All that was left for him to do was wait and see how Fate carried on.

Of course, he wasn't above sticking a pole in her spokes, as it were, to put her off her course and onto his if necessary, but he didn't imagine there was a need for that quite yet.

He saw again that flash of blond hair, which bothered him. He almost considered marching off into the fray, as it were, but good sense prevailed. Many Englishmen had fair hair and many others a fondness for the history of their ancestors. There was nothing unusual about the sight.

Which didn't explain why the hair on the back of his neck was standing up, but perhaps he could consider that later, when he wasn't standing out in a light drizzle that had quite suddenly turned into a bit of sleeting rain that stung where it struck his cheeks.

He turned his collar up against the weather. Perhaps he would follow the instinct that had brought him to England and put off his holiday in order to do a little snooping in the current environs. He ignored an intense desire for a proper afternoon's tea and a hot fire and kept his attention on what was in front of him. He could safely say that he wasn't orchestrating the affairs of those around him for merely altruistic reasons.

His life, as it happened, depended on it.

Chapter 1

SEDGWICK CASTLE, ENGLAND
PRESENT DAY

It wasn't every day that the daughter of rootless hippies held the key to an honest-to-goodness medieval castle.

Tess Alexander stood at the end of the bridge that spanned the moat in which sat that spectacular, honest-to-goodness medieval castle and had to pause for a moment and contemplate the irony of her situation. Unlike her sisters who had either openly spurned fairy tales and all their trappings or embraced them fully, she had remained out of the fray. She had listened to her siblings argue the merits of possible castle life, but never offered her own opinion on whether or not the possession of a romantically medieval habitation and a knight in shining armor to go with it was a good thing.

There was something of a karmic nature going on that out of all her sisters, she was the one with the key to a castle that boasted running water.

She crossed the bridge that spanned her moat, having to remind herself that she was in the twenty-first century, not the twelfth. She walked under the barbican gate and looked up at what actually might keep bad guys at bay. The steel spikes of the portcullises—all three of them—hung above her head like metal icicles. She'd never had occasion to lower any of them, though she'd been assured they were still fully functional. As long as they stayed up where they were supposed to instead of falling down on her head, she was satisfied with their condition.

The courtyard was, she supposed, much as it had been over the centuries: cobblestones in paths surrounded by swaths of grass that had no doubt been dirt in the old days. She wasn't unhappy for a bit of green, though she supposed all she had to do to enjoy that was look out the window at the forest that surrounded her castle.

She walked up the steps to the great hall, then simply stood there with the key in her hand for far longer than she should have. Her hand was trembling, something she tried without success to ignore. It was ridiculous. This was her home, and she could walk inside and still breathe normally. The fact that she'd been hyperventilating the last time she'd come out the door was something she didn't need to think about—

A sudden growling behind her—a noise that belonged to the sort of dog that could stand up and put its paws on her shoulders before it made a snack of her nose—almost sent her lurching face-first into the heavy wooden door. She whirled around on the top step, desperately wishing she had something more to use as a defensive weapon than harsh language. She took a firmer grip on her backpack strap just in case she was afforded the opportunity to offer it as meal instead of her face, then looked at her would-be attacker.

Mr. Beagle, the guard dog of the gift shop's proprietress.

Mrs. Tippets stood just behind her tiny terrier, wearing a frown that bespoke serious irritation indeed. Tess would have smiled in relief, but she didn't imagine smiling would improve matters any. She had no idea what she'd done to inspire such antipathy in Mrs. Tippets, but she'd definitely done something.

Mrs. Tippets ran the castle's gift shop with an iron fist and a dour expression, not even cracking a smile at the delivery of her paycheck. Tess supposed it was a wonder anyone left the premises with any sort of souvenir. Tess didn't open the castle every day for visitors and she did limit even those excursions into her home to the lower floor and the outside, but the gift shop was open five days a week. When it came to keeping Sedgwick in the black, every bit pence helped.

"You're back," Mrs. Tippets said, her frown not dissipating.

"Well, yes," Tess said faintly, trying to look less unnerved than she was. She attempted a wave at the dog but only had another growl in return. "I don't suppose you could call off Mr. Beagle—"

"And I suppose you'll be holding another of those hoity-toity *events* soon," Mrs. Tippets continued, with no small bit of suspicion and disapproval. "All those people eyeing my wares more closely than I like."

Tess bit her tongue, because her aunt had pounded into her the adage that if she didn't have anything pleasant to say, she should confine herself to comments on her companion's health and the weather.

And yes, she held *events* because it kept the lights on. And given that Mrs. Tippets's job was to keep the gift shop open so the attendees at those events could splash out for a few souvenirs, the woman should have perhaps been a little more interested in when those events would be indeed happening and how many people would be indeed looking at her wares. But since Tess couldn't think of a polite way to say as much, she settled for a deep breath.

"Lovely weather we're having," she said politely.

Mrs. Tippets looked at her as if she'd lost her mind, then without another word took her yipping terrier and turned away.

"Your sister came back this morning," she threw over her shoulder as she marched off toward the gates. "Without a key, of course."

Tess nodded, then turned back to the door and put her key into the lock. She turned it, then froze.

Her sister was back?

She found it difficult to breathe all of the sudden. She'd just talked to Peaches in Seattle that morning. Cinderella was also stateside, busy being Botoxed and writing a book about adventures Tess was sure she was making up, and Moonbeam and Valerie were both employed in very useful work of their own across the Pond.

That left just Pippa . . .

Tess pushed the door open, dropped her backpack, and was halfway across the hall before she realized that the sister coming toward her was not her younger sister, but her twin.

"Tess," Peaches said, breaking into a run suddenly and catching Tess by the arms, "what is it?"

"I narrowly escaped . . . an assault . . . by Mr. Beagle," Tess said, hoping that would be enough to justify how she couldn't seem to catch her breath. "And when I talked to you this morning, you were in Seattle. So I thought Mrs. Tippets might have been talking about—well, never mind what I thought."

"I called you from your kitchen," Peaches said with a faint frown. "I said as much."

Tess pushed away from her sister. "I wasn't listening."

"Apparently."

"And I'm fine," Tess said, trying to sound as if she hadn't just had the wind knocked out of her.

"I didn't say you weren't," Peaches said, her frown deepening. "But now that you bring it up—"

"I'm okay," Tess repeated. "Really."

"Then where have you been for the last month when you led me to believe you were here at the castle?"

"I was at Cambridge," Tess said. "Doing, ah, research. Important, time-sensitive research."

Peaches's frown turned into an expression of profound skepticism. "Tess—"

"I just needed to get away for a few days," Tess interrupted, pasting a bright smile on her face. "That's all. So I went and passed many delightful hours in a musty old library."

"If you say so. I'll go make you some green juice."

Tess thought she might have needed something a little stronger than one of her sister's ultra-healthy concoctions, but she wasn't going to argue. She retrieved her backpack from where she'd dropped it by the front door, then made it halfway across the great hall before she found herself standing in one place, unable to go any farther. That had happened to her regularly over the past year of owning the castle, so she didn't suppose anyone would think it strange if she just stood there and gaped.

Sedgwick was, she had to admit, spectacular. The hall wasn't an enormous thing such as one might have found in a more substantial castle such as Artane, but its height made her feel small and fragile just the same. The tapestries that lined the walls and the enormous fireplaces were enough to convince her that she'd walked back in time hundreds of years.

Only in her castle there were rugs on the floors, a fridge big enough to hold all her party platters, and a lovely Aga stove to warm her toes by in the kitchen. She didn't want to think about the fact that while she had a glorious castle that had been lovingly restored decades ago thanks to a man with buckets of money and enormous amounts of time on his hands, her sister Pippa had a castle that wasn't in such nice shape.

Never mind that Pippa also had a knight with spurs on his heels to keep her safe in that castle and that the only thing running in her sister's castle was men away from her husband's very sharp sword. It was tempting to stand on the edge of that great hall and wonder if Pippa might be at that very moment standing on that very spot eight hundred years in the past—

But she refrained because the thought was just too ridiculous to take seriously. People didn't travel through time, sisters didn't fall in love with men who were centuries older than they were, and England was not full of paranormal happenings she couldn't explain.

She studiously ignored the fact that she'd seen ghosts in her hall—particularly a red-haired, bekilted Scotsman who seemed to be most often found lingering near the little room near the gatehouse she used as a prop room for those who wanted to take the experience of walking around her castle to new and dangerous levels of authenticity—or that she had, with her own eyes, seen more paranormal activity of other kinds than any Kansas-born Yank should ever have had to be witness to.

Like Fate and Karma currently standing with their arms linked there near a fire that some enterprising soul had apparently started earlier that morning, watching her to see what she would do.

Ignore them, that's what she would do, because she wasn't going to think any more about her sister, or ghosts, or time travel. And if her walk across the hall was more of a run and her sudden enthusiasm for whatever nastiness Peaches could pour into a glass was unusual, who could blame her?

The truth was, she hadn't intended to let the events of the past few weeks get to her as they had. She had sent Pippa off into the unknown and apparently unrestrainable ether one morning five weeks earlier, then returned to her castle in the south, sure in the knowledge that her sister was happily wed to the man she loved.

She'd been convinced that her pleasure in her sister's happiness would be enough to override any small twinge of sadness she felt over having lost the company of that beloved younger sister. She'd had no trouble putting on a happy face long enough to put her other sister Peaches on a plane back to Seattle and sing jaunty medieval tunes on her way back to her keep.

That had lasted only until she'd walked in her front door and promptly fallen apart.

She'd done the only thing she could: she'd fled to Cambridge, lucking into a gig house-sitting for a colleague on sabbatical who'd had his house sitter flake out on him. It should have continued at least through the middle of December, but the man's sister had shown up and announced she was taking over, leaving Tess with the choice of either bumming couch space off friends or returning to Sedgwick.

Well, actually, the decision had been a bit more clear-cut than that. Her series of autumn events was heading into full swing, and she'd needed to be home to see to them. Could she be blamed if she'd put off getting on the train until the very last moment possible, giving herself time to convince herself that she could actually go inside her hall and breathe?

She thought not.

She set her backpack on a chair in front of the hearth and dug inside for her wallet. She needed to get out; that was the ticket. She could go someplace less, ah, *old*, like Knole House, or maybe even just down to the local pub. That was a lovely seventeenth-century building full of dark wood and even more modern amenities like bangers and mash. Yes, something more on the current side was just what she needed—

"Hey, where are you going?" Peaches called from the top of the passageway that led to the kitchen. "I haven't gotten to your juice yet."

"I'll drink it later," Tess said, shoving her wallet into her jacket pocket. "I'm going out."

Peaches was silent in such a meaningful sort of way that Tess found she had to stop in mid-flight and turn to look at her. She took a deep breath and attempted a smile.

"I just need a few minutes in a more modern place. But save me some juice."

Peaches only watched her, her expression one of understanding.

Tess nodded, then turned and fled out the front door before she opened her mouth and a terrible noise of grief came out. So Pippa had gotten married and moved a bit out of cell phone range. Lots of people did that and their families survived. Tess was sure she'd be counting herself in that latter group very soon.

Within minutes, she was backing out of what served as the castle's car park, happy to be doing something constructive with her time. She drove along the small road leading away from her castle, slowed down, considered, then swerved expertly and sideswiped an ancient and fortunately quite sturdy oak. She stopped, hopped out of the car and went to look for the mirror she'd knocked off.

It had fallen more or less where they usually fell, which saved her the time she would have otherwise spent looking for it. She tossed the latest victim into the pile of mirrors languishing behind the tree, then got back in her car and started off again. The village was small, and any business she could provide for it, she went out of her way to see to. She'd been knocking off side mirrors for almost a year, because it gave her an excuse to go to town, and it gave Grant, the owner of the local garage, something to fix. He'd been the first local to be pleasant to her as the new owner of the hall up the way, and she'd shown her gratitude as she could.

But he wasn't there any longer. He'd sold his shop at the end of the summer so he could retire to France. Tess imagined that the new owner, no doubt as dour and crusty as Grant had been, would welcome a friendly hand extended. Giving him a little business was the least she could do. It might take her mind off the things she wasn't allowing to bother her.

She turned onto the main road and started toward the village. She had been in England for several years, so the vagaries of driving on the left had long since ceased to be anything she even thought about. Narrow roads didn't bother her, nor did passing trucks that took up more space than they should have.

Of course, trying to pass trucks with expensive black sports cars keeping a safe following distance of approximately six inches from her back bumper was a novelty, but she was nothing if not flexible.

She passed the lorry, fully expecting the black car to speed past her after she did so. He didn't. He merely swung in behind her as if his front bumper had been magnetically attracted to the back of hers. What was it about guys in sports cars? She suspected the bill of sale came with detailed instructions on how to tail little runabouts to intimidate and unnerve their innocent drivers. Tess was tempted to slam on the brakes to get him to back off, but she had money in her budget for side mirrors, not rear-end restorations.

She finally had had enough. She rolled down her window and motioned politely for the gentleman to pass her. Could she be blamed if she'd felt compelled to use an extended middle finger to do the like?

He took the hint, then blew past her so quickly she barely had the time to get her window back up before bits of road hit her in the face.

She rolled her eyes, then put the encounter behind her. She had more important things to do, like support her new mechanic.

The village wasn't a large place, as villages in her part of southern England went, and it was fortunately far enough off the beaten path that the traffic was light. And while that likely didn't do much for the local economy, it certainly contributed to a rustic, step-back-in-time sort of charm.

But not *too* far, thankfully.

Tess pulled into the front of the mechanic's shop, turned off the engine, then crawled out of her car. She wrapped her intentions to do good around her like a cloak and walked into the garage. A guy who couldn't have been more than about twenty popped up from behind a car and walked toward her with a welcoming expression.

"Oh, hello," he said, smiling. "Need a tune-up?"

Tess gestured back toward her car. "I'm afraid I've lost a mirror," she said. "It happens with surprisingly regularity, so I imagine I'll be in again soon." She smiled. "I don't think we've met, though. Are you the one who bought the shop—"

"Me?" he interrupted with a laugh. "Oh, nay, miss, I'm not the owner. He's in the—"

"Enough, Bobby," a voice said curtly.

Tess turned in time to see a shadow detach itself from the back of the shop. She had the impression of broad shoulders, long legs, and a lithe grace that seemed somehow completely out of character for an old geezer who'd taken on a shop where he could work on his vintage whatever it was he loved. She was half tempted to readjust her intimidation chignon, but she didn't dare attract any more of Karma's attention than she had already by just getting out of bed. She watched the man remain in the shadows for a moment or two before he ducked into what was probably his office and shut the door firmly behind him.

Bobby smiled awkwardly. "I'll have it done in a blink, miss. Why don't you take your ease in the pub? It looks like rain."

She handed him the keys. "I have an extra mirror in the boot," she said slowly. Actually, she had a box full of them, but he would figure that out soon enough.

"Even better, then," Bobby said with a smile.

Tess left the shop before she got herself in any more trouble, then wondered how it had gone from a fairly fallish day to the depths of winter in such a short time.

And why had the shop owner not been an old geezer, like she'd been expecting?

There was something else about him that bothered her, but she couldn't lay her finger on it. She supposed it would either come to her or it wouldn't. For the moment, the best thing she could do was try to ground herself in her own century.

She sought refuge in the pub, then settled for a high-backed bench near the window. It seemed like a very reasonable thing to drink tea and watch the occasional car go by. There was no activity across the street, except Bobby, who didn't waste any time in getting to work on her car.

She considered the shop's owner. The truth was, she hadn't expected to find a young man—young being a relative term, of course, when used to compare a man of eighty to a man of perhaps thirty—as the owner of that shop, but she couldn't believe that hulking shadow to be anything else. Odd, though, that such a young man had decided on such a sleepy town so far away from anywhere else.

Then again, she supposed she could wonder the same thing about herself, but at least she headed up to the university now and then—

"Cheers, ducks," said a rather sloppy voice. "Want some companies?"

Tess looked up from her tea to find a man sliding into the bench across from her. She didn't recognize him, but she supposed that wasn't unusual. Even after a year, she couldn't say she knew more than half the villagers by sight and even fewer of them by name. The guy now leering at her from across the table might have been a local, but he wasn't one she wanted to know better.

"I'm just finishing," she said, vowing to stand outside in the rain if necessary to avoid any of the proffered companies.

He put his foot up on the end of her bench, effectively blocking her exit. "I think you should stay and have another cuppa."

Tess finished the last sip of her tea, then set her cup down. "And I think you should move your foot while you still can."

"A woman with a bit of vim," he said with an indulgent chuckle. "I like that."

Tess looked pointedly at his foot until he put it back on the floor, then grabbed her purse and shifted toward the end of the bench. She started to stand up only to find his hand suddenly on her arm in a grip that was, to put it mildly, unpleasantly firm.

"You're hurting me," she said loudly.

"You need a bit of taming," he said in return.

Tess tried to pull her arm away, but he was having none of that. She was just contemplating how best to grab the teapot so she could slosh the still-very-hot innards on him, then clobber him with the pot itself, when she realized none of that was going to be necessary.

A hand was suddenly holding on to Mr. Friendly's forearm in a way that made the aforementioned groper squeak before he covered it up with a very manly "no need to get testy, mate."

Tess found herself freed from all unwanted advances. She looked up to find that her rescuer was tall, dark-haired, and very well built. She realized with equal clarity that she had just seen him, hovering in the back of the shop across the street.

She would have thanked him, or gaped at him, or blurted out a question about his name, but she was too busy being shepherded out of the pub by a man who would have put Ireland's finest sheepdog to shame.

She managed to stop outside the pub only because she dug her heels in. She looked up at her rescuer, thanks on the tip of her tongue, only to have her mouth fall open.

It was her sister Pippa's husband, Montgomery de Piaget.

Only it couldn't be, because the man next to her was dressed in modern clothes and, she soon found, speaking in modern English.

"Your car's finished," he said, taking her by the arm and leading her off the sidewalk. "Looks like rain."

It was December; of course it looked like rain. Actually, it looked like snow from where she was standing given the sudden chill that had washed over her. She wished she could have shut her mouth, but she couldn't.

She looked around herself to make sure she was still in the twenty-first century, looked at the comforting tarmac under her feet, looked at the shop that rose up in front of her with her little red Ford sitting in front of it. She looked at the fingers curled around her arm in a way that wasn't at all uncomfortable but definitely supportive, as if she'd been a woman of questionable balance who couldn't be counted on to make it across the street on her own.

She took a moment or two to get hold of her rampaging and apparently quite unreliable imagination as she was escorted into the garage's office. She didn't see her escort's face again because he kept it turned away from her as he held out his hand.

"Charge card," he said briskly.

Tess fumbled in her purse for it, feeling not flustered, but floored. She was having a hallucination; that was it. It was broad daylight and she was having a hallucination. Or a paranormal, um, something. And it all involved that man standing on the other side of the counter from her, the one who looked like . . .

Well, never mind who he looked like. The truth was, he might have looked like someone she knew, but he couldn't possibly be that someone because that man was safely locked away eight hundred years in the past.

Her delusion—and she was perfectly happy to term him that and be done—didn't seem at all inclined to look at her, which was just fine with her. Maybe he'd seen how the first sight of himself had freaked her out and decided that one view of his admittedly gorgeous face was enough.

She watched his back as he ran her credit card, then at the dark hair that shadowed his face as he pushed the slip across his counter for her to sign. The moment she'd finished, he shoved her keys at her as if he couldn't wait to be out of her presence, then ushered her out of his office.

He pointed in the direction he wanted her to go, then disappeared into the darkness at the back of the garage. She looked at the door where she'd last seen the man who definitely wasn't Montgomery de Piaget but couldn't have looked any more like him if he *had* been him, then turned and stumbled out of the shop.

She ran bodily into Bobby before she realized he was giving her new mirror a last-minute polish. She looked at him and wondered what he thought of his boss, how long he'd worked for him, if he knew any pertinent details about him.

"All ready to go, then?" Bobby asked with a friendly smile.

"Sure," Tess managed. She stepped back as Bobby opened the door but hesitated before she got in. "Could I ask you a question?"

Bobby shrugged. "As you will, miss."

She nodded toward the back of the shop. "Is that your boss?"

"Aye, miss."

"Does he have a name?" she managed.

"John," Bobby said simply, "and just John. He don't like to be talked about so I don't unless he says to. I fancy you can imagine why."

Yes, because he would probably draw his sword and skewer you on it, was the first thing she thought, but that thought was so ridiculous, wild horses couldn't have dragged it out of her. Of course she hadn't seen what she'd just seen because Montgomery de Piaget was safely tucked away with her sister in 1241. He wasn't hanging around a garage in the village ten miles from her castle.

"And you won't tell me his last name?" she managed.

Bobby shifted. "As I said, miss, he don't care to be forthcomin' about details, if you—"

"Bobby!"

Tess jumped at the call, which wasn't quite a shout but was definitely a warning. Bobby snapped a salute at her, grinned, then hurried back into the shop to see to who knew what. Maybe the whole thing had been a serious deviation from reality and she was operating under rules she didn't understand. Bobby's boss, John, was perhaps a ghost and Bobby his undead servant. For all she knew, they were vampires, or werewolves, or whatever other paranormal things the south of England could conjure up.

Perhaps she needed a little lie-down before she lost it completely.

She let out her breath slowly, then got into her car. She had to have a few more bracing breaths before she took hold of herself, put the keys into the ignition, and got herself out of the parking lot.

Half an hour later, she was walking back across her bridge to her very own castle where she could lower the portcullises, bar the door in her great hall, then lock herself in her solar and not have to face anything that made her uncomfortable.

Peaches looked up as she stumbled finally into the solar and managed to get herself into a chair in front of the fire without looking as if she'd fallen there.

"You look like you've seen a ghost—wait a minute." She turned back to her phone call. "Tiffany? Hang on for just a second, would you? I have a situation here." Peaches put her thumb back over the phone. "What happened?"

"Nothing," Tess managed. "I'm good."

"You don't look good," Peaches said. "Maybe you should go upstairs and lie down."

"I had a nap last week."

"Have another one today."

Tess took a deep breath. "I can't. I have clients coming today."

"That's tomorrow. I checked your schedule."

"Then I have phone calls to make."

Peaches frowned at her, then shrugged slightly and turned back to her conversation.

Tess checked her calendar, then realized she did indeed have a phone call to make. She decided she was grateful she hadn't blown off what could be a potentially large party after the new year. She would have to trot out all her best manners and coherent conversation.

It would keep her from thinking about things that *really* made her crazy. There were people who resembled their ancestors to such a degree that it was spooky, weren't there? She'd seen it countless times in history books. Maybe John the garage owner was somehow related to the de Piagets and all their good genes had found home in him.

It could happen.

It could also happen that there were strange and mysterious things going on within a twenty-mile radius of her house.

She knew she shouldn't have been surprised.

Chapter 2

He'd always known it would be steel to kill him.

John de Piaget kept the engine balanced on the hoist long enough to look to his right to make certain he had enough space to roll out from underneath it before it slipped its moorings and crushed him. Finding that side of his garage floor comfortingly empty, he took a deep breath, then flung himself to his right the split second before the engine overbalanced and landed on the floor where his empty head had recently been.

He pushed himself up until he was merely sitting on the floor, shaking like a woman, instead of lying there, shaking like the fool he was. He never made mistakes like the one he'd just made. Fortunately, he knew just at whose feet to lay the blame.

That wench who had interrupted the peace of his shop not an hour earlier.

He looked at Bobby, who had been talking to him just before he'd almost killed himself. "She forgot what?"

"Her credit card." Bobby paused. "Want help with the engine?"

John looked at his lone employee, an experienced mechanic who Grant had taken on just before he'd sold John the shop. He didn't like to ask for aid, but in this case he couldn't do anything else. He nodded, then accepted help with righting the block and settling things as he should have to start with.

It took less than two hours to put the entire Jaguar back together. He thanked Bobby briskly for his aid, cleaned his hands, then went into his office to phone the owner to tell her she could send someone for her car anytime she liked. He fished her husband's card she'd given him out of his wallet, then froze.

Geoffrey Segrave, Segrave & Kingsley, LLP.

John pursed his lips. A solicitor amongst a clutch of lawyerly types, no doubt. He was tempted to wallow in the irony of doing business with a man bearing that last name, but he didn't do irony any longer. In fact, there were several things he didn't do any longer, beginning and ending with looking at anything that might have loitered in his past—

He cut his thoughts off before they migrated to points forbidden and uncomfortable. He arranged for one of the man's flunkies to come pick up the Jag the next day for his lady wife, then hung up and considered the rest of his afternoon. He looked at the credit card on his counter, then at the garage. There were times, he supposed, when what looked like a bad idea from the start was exactly what it seemed.

Hadn't he told himself that setting up shop in a small village might be less than desirable? Hadn't he reminded himself that if one wanted to avoid standing out, losing oneself in a city of decent size was the wisest course of action? Had he not fought with a good deal of determination what had felt like the hand of Fate in each step that had led him from a rather comfortable, if nomadic, life in the north to a far-too-exposed existence in the south?

He was going to have to fight harder next time, that was obvious.

"Oy, boss," Bobby said from behind him, "what about the young miss's card?"

John suppressed the urge to flinch. 'Twas his fault she'd left it behind, of course, because he'd stopped just short of shoving her out of his shop. He would have vastly preferred to have been able to say that it was because he'd been distracted, or irritated that he'd had to rescue her in the pub, or anxious to get her out of his office so he could see to other things.

But none of that was true.

The truth was, he'd watched her walk over to the pub, then followed her there just to have another look at her. Could he be blamed for ordering for himself a Lilt, neat, to be enjoyed whilst leaning against the wall watching a young woman who seemed to have trouble judging the distance between her passenger door and the nearest unyielding surface? Grant had told him he would have some regular customers with peculiar mechanical issues. He'd never expected that one of them would take his breath away just to look at her.

He supposed she would have gotten away from Frank's lecherous advances soon enough on her own, but he'd been across the tavern, brandishing his chivalry, almost before he'd known he was going to.

He sighed, then turned and took the credit card from Bobby. "I'll get it back to her. What's left on your list for the day?"

"I'm finished," Bobby said. "Unless you'd like me to pop the bonnet on that old Jag of yours—"

"I'll see to that one myself," John said without hesitation, "though your generosity is much appreciated." He couldn't bring himself to thank Bobby again for the earlier rescue. Once had been more than enough.

"I'll tidy up, then," Bobby said, then trudged past him out into the garage, already humming some mindless tune that was popular in the current day.

John had hummed enough mindless things in recent years that he thought he might safely leave them behind for the afternoon and see to a few other things.

"Lock up for me after you're through, would you?" John called. "I've an errand to run."

"She's a bit o' alright," Bobby agreed.

"I'm taking groceries to Mrs. Winston," John said darkly.

"Old Doris?" Bobby asked with a laugh. "Aye, she's a bit o' alright as well."

John cursed him under his breath and left the shop. He did indeed intend to be about a bit of good-deed-doing, though he couldn't say it was completely altruistic. Doris Winston was every day of eighty and managed her own grocery visits with ease, but she happened to have an ear to the ground on a daily basis.

If there was anything to be known about that dark-haired beauty who'd come into his shop and knocked the breath from him, it would be Doris.

John hated to think what she'd dredged up about him.

The tale he'd noised about himself was an innocuous one about his having left home early, then having bummed about various garages by day and bands by night until he'd come into a bit of money, which had allowed him to buy old Grant's garage when the man's rheumatism had necessitated a decamping for France. All of which, for the most part, was true.

Well, except the part about limiting himself to bands. It wouldn't have done his reputation as a gearhead any good for anyone to have known he far preferred classical guitar to grunge, jazz to pop, and that he could be, when he'd occasionally indulged in a pint too many, prevailed upon to dredge up a ballad or two of a less modern vintage. Fortunately for him, the women he'd been stupid enough to play them for had been completely clueless as to their origin.

And his, for that matter.

He had to admit, he found himself longing, just once, to meet a gel who looked at him, then looked away, instead of looking, then boldly looking a bit more until he'd understood the invitation. He'd become just as adept at the look that said he wasn't at all interested.

He hadn't been able to muster up even a hint of that sort of look that afternoon. He'd been too damn flustered, something he had never once in his life experienced.

Perhaps that should have been a sign of some sort.

Aye, one that said he should ask old Mrs. Winston where the poor driver in question might be found so he could return her card to her and have done as quickly as possible. He turned up the collar of his leather jacket and quickened his pace toward the local green grocer.

Half an hour later, he was standing under the awning of Doris Winston's front stoop. The door opened and he was greeted with almost as much enthusiasm as she used when he arrived to pay his rent on the little cottage behind his shop that she owned. He'd offered to buy it—indeed he would have preferred that—but she had insisted that for as long as she was alive she wanted to see him every month. Not being one to argue with old women, he'd acquiesced without complaint. The grocery runs were made simply because he liked her.

"Ah, Johnny," she said, holding open her door, "you've come for tea."

"I wouldn't want to put you to any trouble," he said politely.

"You know it's no trouble, lad. Come and sit, and fill an old woman's ears with village gossip. I heard you rescued a pretty thing from unwanted advances in the pub a few minutes ago."

"Three hours ago," John corrected, following her into her kitchen. "Who passed on those tidings?"

"I never reveal my sources," Doris said airily. "Just leave the things there, love, and come sit. We'll have a little chat over my famous black currant jam."

He imagined they would.

She graciously allowed him to hold out her chair at her tea table. He sat across from her, indulged for a quarter hour in a ritual he had come to quite enjoy over the years, then pushed his cup aside and looked at his landlady.

"I'm curious," he said in as offhand a manner as he could manage. "Mildly."

"Her name's Tess Alexander."

He suppressed a smirk. He'd known that already from a casual glance at her credit card.

"And she's a Yank."

He felt his jaw slip down. "She's not. She didn't have an accent."

"And how much conversation did you have with her, my lad?"

John pursed his lips. "Enough to listen to her threaten to do damage to Frank Rivers if he didn't keep his hands to himself."

"Thought she needed a rescue, did you?"

"I was being gentlemanly."

Doris only smiled. "I imagine you were. First gentlemanly, then curious. Where will it lead?"

"To my returning her charge card to her and resuming my own very sensible existence whilst she goes about her own," John said grimly. "Pray give me details to aid me in that."

Doris pushed her teacup aside as well. "She's an academic, or so I understand, and has a PhD in medieval studies of some sort."

John supposed he would look less than dignified to have his

mouth continually hanging open, so he decided it was best to just grit his teeth.

Medieval studies. His least favorite topic of conversation, as it happened. He'd known just looking at her that the relationship was doomed from the start.

"She was offered Sedgwick by Roland, the last Earl of Sedgwick," Doris continued, "though it's my understanding she didn't have a clue who he was at first. Thought him the caretaker, I daresay. You know he wasn't one for carrying on with his title."

John hadn't known Sedgwick had *had* a last earl, so he supposed the current owner, the possessor of those astonishingly pretty green eyes, might be forgiven as well.

"I believe he'd been looking for the proper person to bequeath his keep to," Doris continued with a faint shrug, "which took a bit of doing. He'd learned of her through some symposium on medieval life and liked what he'd heard. He up and gave her the castle without hesitation. She doesn't seem to lack for funds, so I'm assuming he gave her a few quid as well to keep the lights on. She runs parties there of all sorts, mostly reenactment things. Those seem particularly suited to a castle still boasting a roof, don't they?"

He grunted, because that was all he could do.

"I think she teaches still, some. I imagine you might find her lectures interesting."

"I much prefer the nineteenth century," he commented as nonchalantly as possible. "The music was sublime, don't you agree?"

She looked at him over her spectacles. "I agree. Perhaps you should play something from that era for me sometime."

He agreed that he would, thanked her profusely for tea, then made for the door before she could ask any more questions or delve any further into her list of things she possibly knew about him. He'd unbent far enough the month before to tell her he'd been born in the north, grown to manhood in the north, then left home to seek his fortune. He'd admitted to a former employment at a garage, but he hadn't elaborated. He never elaborated.

"You'll come play for me this week," she announced. "I'll expect something tolerable to listen to."

"I'll attempt it," he promised before he escaped out her front door.

He walked quickly back toward his shop only to realize that he was walking quickly toward something he didn't want to. He didn't care for otherworldly sensations. The fact that he'd had Fate tap him smartly on the shoulder when Mistress Tess Alexander had pulled into his car park had unnerved him more than he wanted to admit. He didn't know her and wasn't entirely sure he wanted to rectify that. He liked his pleasant, unremarkable life where he merely passed his days enjoying the comforts modern times could provide. Anything else made him supremely uncomfortable.

Nay, it was more than that. As far as he was concerned, his life had begun eight years ago when he'd left home with nothing but the clothes on his back, a bag full of coins, and his wits to keep himself alive. Thinking about anything that had come before was something he absolutely refused to do. If an acquaintance began to pry into those years, he or she was pointedly discouraged from prying any further. Blunt questions were answered with an absolute severing of all contact. As far as he was concerned, he had no past.

It was safer that way.

He almost ploughed into a bairn of some sort who had come flying out his mother's gates toward the street. He caught the little brat out of habit—damn that chivalry and all its incarnations—and put him back into his mother's frantically outstretched arms without comment.

Bairns, he noted with a knowing nod. Yet another thing to avoid like the plague. He had more than enough to keep himself occupied with without the burdens of a wife and children and a place to put them and keep them safe. It was all he could do to keep others from dinging his car. He wasn't interested in taking on anything else.

He put his head down and continued on his way, praying he wouldn't encounter anything else unsettling before he'd done his duty and could retreat to his cozy cottage where he could keep the world at bay.

He walked behind the shop and opened one of the garages there. In times past, he knew old Grant had stored his prized collection of vintage Jaguars in those bays. He'd filled those slots with his own collection of things he'd had shipped down from the north: two Jaguars, a sweet little MG, and a rather less-than-discreet black Aston Martin. He considered, then decided that perhaps discreet was more the order of the day. He chose the Jag that was running, then managed to get himself out of the village without losing a hubcap or running afoul of any overzealous traffic wardens.

He'd never driven to Sedgwick, as it happened, and he missed the turnoff—to his disgust. He flipped a U-turn in an appropriate place, then retraced his steps. He forced himself to simply watch the road without putting any thought into the watching. He would have preferred to avoid looking at the castle in time as well, but he couldn't. He turned off his car in the car park, leaned his head back against the seat, then let out a slow, unsteady breath.

The keep was spectacular.

He hadn't paid attention to many castles over the past few years. He'd lived and worked in the shadow of Edinburgh Castle for a pair of years, true, but he was an Englishman, not a Scot, so their puny bit of stone perched up atop that bluff had troubled him not at all. He had avoided, again like the plague, visits to any other keeps of note.

He wondered, briefly, if he might have been a bit hasty about that.

The last time he'd seen Sedgwick, it had been overrun by Denys of Sedgwick's ill-bred and mannerless children who had seemingly taken great pleasure at crawling in and out of the holes in their father's foundations—

He opened the car door abruptly, putting an end to thoughts he wouldn't have allowed on his mind's stage if he'd been thinking clearly. He crawled out of his car before he could think too much about what he was doing, then locked the door and walked toward the bridge that spanned what looked less like a cesspit and more like a lovely, serene lake.

He hesitated at the end of the bridge, though he wondered why. It was a private house, true, but there had been no sign that he could see telling him that only certain hours were maintained and would he mind keeping his sorry arse off the property outside those hours.

He continued across the bridge, realizing only as he was doing so that he was keeping a wary eye out for lads leaning over the parapet with unfriendly arrows pointed his way. He resisted the urge to clap his hand to his forehead to hopefully dislodge what good sense he'd started the day with and continued on into the barbican gate with its trio of portcullises that were no doubt still hiding in their nooks thanks only to prayers and a bit of duct tape. He was happy to leave them behind—

Until he walked into the courtyard.

He stumbled to a halt, then simply looked at the woman who was standing there with her arms wrapped around herself, staring off at things he couldn't see. She was so still, she might have been made of stone. He froze, lest he disturb her.

She was dressed as she had been earlier that morning, in jeans and a sweater. Her hair was either very short, or caught up in some sort of business at the back of her head. There was a light rain falling, but she didn't seem to notice. What she was thinking, he couldn't have said, but it seemingly occupied all her energies.

He had the feeling it was a melancholy sort of subject, which struck him as particularly wrong. She should have been waiting in the courtyard for the man who was hers, waiting to be loved, cherished, protected—

She turned her head suddenly and looked at him, as if she'd known he'd been standing there.

His first instinct was to make an abrupt dash for the nearest exit, but he didn't run from things that were dangerous.

He paused. He might have not been faulted for scampering away when his heart might have been involved, but since that happened so rarely, he wasn't sure he could use that excuse at present.

Immediately on the heels of those thoughts came the one that he was truly going to look like an idiot if he simply stood there and gaped at one of the most beautiful women he'd ever seen. Not beautiful in a gaudy, flashy, expensive sort of way. Beautiful in a quiet, lingering sort of way that had him almost turning in truth and fleeing indeed whilst what was left of his good sense remained.

That he didn't might have been, he conceded reluctantly, the hand of Fate clutching the back of his coat so he couldn't do aught but walk forward, but he wasn't going to examine that closely enough to find out.

Tess Alexander only stood there, watching him with enormous eyes, as if she'd just seen a ghost.

He suppressed the urge to look over his shoulder in truth that time, on the off chance that she had it aright. He wasn't unaccustomed to things of a paranormal nature, though he preferred to keep them behind him where he needn't look at them. He continued on toward her until he was standing but a foot away.

"You forgot your charge card," he said, his voice sounding hoarse in his ears.

"You shoved me out of your office," she said faintly.

He paused. "I can be a bit of an arse."

She held out her hand.

John was halfway to taking her hand in his before he realized she was merely waiting for him to put her card into it. He fumbled in his coat pocket for it, then handed it to her. She took it, then clutched it as if it were some sort of lifeline.

"Thank you . . ." She trailed off.

"John," he supplied.

"John?"

"John de Piaget," he said, though he rarely gave his last name unless it was required. He had, actually, given a few false names over the years, when he'd been working under the table in the north and hadn't particularly cared for anyone to know who he was.

Not that anyone would have cared, surely. It wasn't as if his family was notorious or noteworthy. He knew his father's hall was still standing because he'd seen a picture of it in a newspaper once. He hadn't seen the castle itself since he'd put it behind him years ago, and he'd had no interest in finding out who lived there or if the whole place had been turned over to the National Trust because his father's descendants hadn't managed to hold on to it. In the end, his name would mean nothing to anyone. Still, old habits died hard, which was why he generally just went by John and left the rest to the imagination.

Tess didn't react to his name; she merely nodded and remained where she was. John supposed she would have stood there all day if he hadn't taken her by the elbow and drawn her away from the spot she seemed to be rooted to.

"'Tis raining out," he said, guiding her toward the great hall.

"I don't mind the rain."

"You will when you catch cold," he said.

She didn't argue. She simply walked with him across the

courtyard and up the steps to the hall door. It opened, as if they'd
been expected, and John looked up.

And gasped.

He realized immediately that Tess not only had a sister, but
a twin sister at that, only the woman standing there looking at
him—again as if she'd seen a ghost—could not have been more
different. Tess had obviously walked the hallowed halls of University long enough to take on its conservative mores. Her sister had apparently been frequenting more—how could he say it
politely?—unbuttoned venues.

"Peaches, move."

John watched Tess's sister step back unsteadily and hold the
door open. Tess looked up at him.

"Care to come in?"

"I've things to do," he said, then he released her and backed
away before he could find himself sucked into that hall and into
something he could tell already he didn't want to get involved in.
He had a sense about that sort of thing.

"Thank you for bringing me my card," Tess said quietly.

He nodded but didn't look at her again. He turned and strode
purposefully across her courtyard and out the gates, forcing himself to merely walk calmly, though with definite purpose. He had
things to do, important things, things that didn't involve looking
at a woman who made him want to run like hell the other way.

He hurried back toward the life he'd been so comfortable in
that morning.

Odd how it didn't seem as welcoming as it had before.

Chapter 3

T ess rubbed her arms as she stood in front of the roaring fire in her great hall. She'd built that fire herself an hour ago, which she imagined the former owners of Sedgwick hadn't needed to do, but her staff hadn't arrived yet and she was freezing.

Paranormal activity did that to a woman, she supposed.

She didn't like to get lost in the past unless it was the *past* past where some Plantagenet or other was king, but she found herself powerless to stop herself from reliving the events of the previous afternoon.

There she'd been, standing innocently in her courtyard, getting rained on, when she'd realized someone was watching her. She'd known without looking just who it was, but that hadn't made it any easier to face him and not feel a little faint.

And that hadn't exactly come from his good looks, truth be told.

She remembered taking her card from him, remembered asking him his name—an unnecessary and unsurprising exercise if ever there had been one—then listening to his car drive off into the distance. Then she had simply stood at the door of her hall, watching the rain fall softly onto the grass, dirt, and cobblestones of her courtyard. She had wondered, very briefly, if her sister Pippa had ever stood in just that spot and watched another de Piaget lad walk away with all due haste.

She imagined that that de Piaget brother had walked away with a great deal more reluctance.

Peaches had, quite wisely, said nothing, but that could have been because her cell phone had chosen that moment to ring and she'd gone off to do business. By the time she'd finished, Tess had been on her way to bed. Peaches had given her a hug and said nothing.

Tess had known that wouldn't last. She looked to her right to find Peaches standing next to her, clad in yoga gear. She cleared her throat, but that didn't go very well. She tried again.

"That's the new owner of the garage in the village," she croaked.

"Was it?" Peaches asked. "I don't suppose you got his name."

"John de Piaget."

Peaches nodded thoughtfully, not looking terribly surprised. She glanced at Tess. "You're shaking."

Tess couldn't argue with that. "Can you blame me?"

"Nope."

"I think I'm either hallucinating or having a nervous breakdown."

Peaches put her hand on Tess's forehead. "Well, you're not feverish."

"I don't think a fever's part of either."

"You're probably right." She shivered. "He can't be who he looks like."

"That was my first thought as well, but I'm not sure how long we'll manage to cling to it."

Peaches looked at Tess assessingly. "Are you heading back to the village for another look?"

"When hell freezes over," Tess said without hesitation. She had to take a deep breath. "I'm going to go into London to pick up a book or two Andrew found for me."

"Taking the first train available?"

"When escaping uncomfortable things, it's always best to get an early start."

"Things will look better when you get back," Peaches offered, "or they might just look different." She shrugged. "Sometimes, that's all you can hope for."

Tess turned and looked at her sister steadily. "Do you think that things are going to look any different later? With him, I mean?"

"I doubt it, but what are you going to do about it? Ask him a few pointed questions about when he was born? Let him know that his brother Montgomery married your younger sister?"

"We don't know he's Montgomery's brother."

Peaches rolled her eyes. "He couldn't look any more like our charming brother-in-law if he *were* Montgomery, which we know he isn't. They have to be twins."

"You and I could be having a joint hallucination," Tess said, grasping desperately for any excuse—reasonable or not—to discount what was staring her in the face.

Peaches only looked at her steadily.

Tess shivered in spite of herself. "I don't think I want to see him again."

"Then either find a different mechanic or stop knocking mirrors off your car," Peaches advised. She paused, then spoke carefully. "You know, we could solve this mystery quite easily if I rifled through that book in your gift shop on de Piaget genealogy—"

"No."

Peaches blew her bangs out of her eyes. "Tess, be reasonable."

"I don't want to know," Tess said firmly.

Peaches shrugged. "Well, you probably don't have anything to worry about anyway. It's not like you're going to start running into him everywhere you go. I'm sure he has other interests besides medieval geopolitical studies."

Tess shot her a sharp look. "Don't."

"Don't what?" Peaches asked, obviously unimpressed. "Don't talk about things that make you uncomfortable? Please, Tess. It's facing the things that make you uncomfortable that are generally most necessary for your growth. And just so you know, people pay me big bucks for that kind of advice."

"Have any of your clients had a sister—and I can hardly believe I'm saying this—time travel back to the thirteenth century to marry a guy whose twin looks to be living down the road—" She held up her hand. "Never mind. You don't have to answer that." She took a deep breath, then stepped forward and put her arms around her sister. "She loved you more than she loved me, but in spite of that, this is killing me."

"She loved us both equally," Peaches said. "And if it makes you feel any better, it's killing me, too."

Tess released her sister in surprise. "You haven't said anything."

"I've been too worried about you."

Tess could only shake her head. "I haven't even managed to ask you why you came back to England or what you'll do with your business in the States while you're here."

"I thought I might like an extended stay in your luxurious castle. I think I can force myself to take care of business over the phone while I'm fondling your tapestries. But mostly," she said with a grave smile, "I just came to make sure you weren't losing it."

"Thank you," Tess said quietly. "And forgive me. I've been incredibly selfish to worry more about myself than you."

"And yet I still love you," Peaches said. She turned Tess toward the door and gave her a little push. "Go to London and forget about him. I'll answer the phones and keep the marauders at bay for you."

"I owe you," Tess managed.

"And the price will be very high," Peaches promised.

Tess doubted that, but she would have paid it just the same without hesitation. She went to get her coat and keys, grateful for a reason to get out of the castle for a bit and think about something besides medieval things.

Or medieval men.

Not that she needed to worry about those sorts of guys. Not really. The odds of again seeing John de Piaget—who despite another set of odds she didn't want to calculate couldn't possibly be the medieval brother of Montgomery de Piaget—were indeed very slim. She could conduct all her business in the village by phone and she could certainly manage to avoid losing any more side mirrors for a while. Maybe John would get tired of the provincial nature of the village and decide he should move somewhere else with fancier cars to fix. She was perfectly safe.

Within minutes, she was on her way toward the station. Unfortunately, she'd only been on the main road for a couple of minutes before she discovered that someone was tailing her. It was that black sports car again. She was tempted to give the guy the finger, since that's what he was accustomed to from her—

Her tire blowing startled her so badly, she yelped. She looked quickly for a place to pull over. She'd never been more grateful for anything than she was for a little farmer's turnout that allowed her to get herself off the road.

She jumped again when she realized her friend had pulled in so tightly next to her that the driver was going to have to crawl out his passenger door to get out—though why he'd stopped she couldn't have said. It wasn't possible that some rich guy in a suit would want to help her. Maybe he was going to scold her for her bad behavior earlier in the week. Well, she had a thing or two to say to him about his driving habits, so maybe they could just have it out right there in a patch of nettles. She girded herself for battle and crawled out of her car.

She watched the Aston Martin's far door open, then saw a dark head emerge. And she thought she just might have to sit down.

John de Piaget straightened, then walked around the back of what was apparently his car and then hers.

"Ah," she attempted.

"Spare tyre?" he asked briskly.

"In the boot," she managed, clutching her keys as if they'd been all that kept her from falling into some bottomless abyss. And when he held out his hand for those keys, she had to force herself to surrender them. "I can fix it myself," she said in a last-ditch attempt to save herself and her sanity.

"I imagine you can," he agreed, walking around to the trunk of her car, "but I'll do it instead."

She pulled the hood of her slicker up over her head to ward off what was less of a rain than it was an early morning mist and went to see what he would find to use. Her car wasn't new and it hadn't been hers until she'd moved into the castle, but it had served her well enough. The truth was, she'd never had to look in the trunk for rescue tools.

John was simply staring down into her trunk. She peeked around the trunk lid and saw that there was definitely no spare tire inside. There was, however, her box of new side mirrors. He stared at them for another minute or two, shook his head, then looked at her.

"Need anything from inside your car?"

She had a hard time concentrating on his words. She was just too darn distracted by his face. "What?"

"Your gear from inside your car," he said, sounding as if he were dredging up a fair amount of patience.

"Why?"

"Because I don't think you want to wait here until I can get a new tyre for you. What do you need for the day?"

"Ah, my bag," she began.

He only waited, as if her next move should have been obvious. It might have been, if she could have done something besides stand there and stare at him, mute.

He sighed, then eased past her to rummage about in her car. He handed her bag to her, then took her car key off her ring and locked the door with it. He then tossed the key into the trunk.

"Wait—" she blurted out as he shut the trunk lid. She looked at him in surprise. "I needed that."

He handed her the remaining keys, took her by the elbow and led her over to the passenger side of his car. He opened the door and got in.

"Are you going to leave me here?" she asked in surprise. "Without my car key?"

He looked up from where he was sitting in the passenger seat. "I hadn't intended to, no."

"You can't mean to take me with you," she said, realizing as the words were out there that she'd attached a look of horror to them.

He lifted a shoulder in a half shrug. "It seemed polite."

"But I don't want to go with you," she said, feeling slightly alarmed at the thought of being in an enclosed space with him.

He shot her a look. "I don't think you have much choice, unless you want to stand out in the rain all morning." He slid over the gearshift into the driver's seat, then leaned back over and looked up at her. "Get in."

Tess felt her mouth fall open. "You . . . rude . . ." She was obviously not at her best because she couldn't come up with a single truly cutting thing to call him. "You're bossy."

He blinked, then smiled so quickly she would have thought

she'd imagined it if the very sight of that knee-weakening smile hadn't been burned onto her retinas.

"Please, Miss Alexander, do me the courtesy of getting into my humble carriage before you catch your death either from the inclement weather we're experiencing or from the fool who will no doubt eventually come along behind us and plow first into my boot and then into your very fetching self and cause us all a great deal of unnecessary trauma."

"Well," she said, feeling a very uncomfortable heat in her cheeks, "that's a little better." She sat with as much dignity as possible on a seat that was better suited to a luxury mansion than a stupid car. When John leaned over her and pulled the door shut, she realized she was in deep trouble. "I have places to go," she said quickly, because it made her feel more in charge to say it.

"Anywhere in particular?" he asked.

"The train station."

"Going to London?"

"Yes, actually, I was."

She made the grave mistake of looking at him. He had gray eyes. She supposed she should have known that given that his brother did as well, but she realized that she hadn't really done all that much looking into Montgomery de Piaget's eyes.

She wished she could call Pippa, just once. Just to tell her that she wasn't the only one Karma had been gunning for. To ask her how she was, if she was happy, if Montgomery had turned to fat and turned his swordsman's duties over to her.

She supposed Pippa would have only laughed at the last.

"Are you unwell, Miss Alexander?"

The kindness in John's voice, damn him, almost undid her right there on the spot.

"I'm fine," she said, more hoarsely than she'd intended. "Just late." She had to pause and dig for something nice to say. "I appreciate the rescue."

"I'm for London as well," he began slowly, "if you'd rather not take the train."

Heaven help her, that was the very last thing she needed. It was going to be bad enough to be in the same car with him for the five minutes it would take to get to the station. "No," she managed, "I'll be fine. Thanks just the same."

He shrugged and pulled out his mobile. A very brief conversation with Bobby resulted in a promise that her car would be waiting for her at her castle, good as new, when she was finished with her business.

"But you locked my car key in the trunk," Tess reminded him.

"Bobby won't need it, but he'll fetch it out for you and leave it at the keep."

"I'm not sure I want to know the details."

John almost smiled again, she was sure of it. She was very glad he hadn't. She was still trying to erase the memory of the last one.

She managed to get herself buckled, then leaned her head back against the seat and tried to ignore the fact that she was in a car that had to have cost a cool quarter million pounds if it'd been a hundred quid. She couldn't say she was up on too many current events—it wasn't her preferred century, after all—but she did love cars, and she had found over the years of teaching that a little knowledge of what a college-aged boy might be interested in had tended to earn her a few brownie points.

The question was, how had John de Piaget possibly afforded the kind of car she was riding in?

And how was it he was driving as easily as if he'd been doing it his entire adult life?

She looked out the window, watching the dark gray of the morning give way to something only slightly less gloomy. She waited until John had stopped outside the station, then put on her most polite, uninterested expression.

"Thank you very much," she said, not caring that it sounded rather more prim than it should have. "I appreciate the rescue."

He looked at his hands on the wheel. "My business will take a good part of the day," he said slowly, "but I'll ferry you home, if you like."

"Peaches can come get me," she said, then she stopped when she realized that wasn't true. Her sister was booked again for the whole of the afternoon and into the evening with more client consultations. The perils of doing business with people living eight hours behind her.

Well, it didn't matter. She would call a cab, or take a bus, or walk. If worst came to worst, she could hike across country and get home as the crow flew. She didn't have to allow the man sitting next to her to give her any help.

All in keeping with her determination to avoid him at all costs, of course.

He pulled out his wallet, removed a card from it, then wrote something on the back. He looked at it for several excruciatingly long moments, then held it out toward her, not looking at her.

"If you wrap up your business early and are up for a bit of explore, come find me here," he said. "If all goes well, I'll be finished about three. My mobile number's on the front. "

"Are you in class?" she asked, taking the card as if it had been a live thing.

"Something like that," he said abruptly. He turned away and immediately got out of the car.

Well, he obviously wasn't much for personal questions. She didn't bother to wonder why not because the answer was staring her fully in the face. Beyond reason, beyond any sane rationalization, beyond anything reasonable, she was having her door currently opened by a man who she absolutely knew wasn't what he was pretending to be.

He held out his hand to help her out of the car.

And time stopped.

She wasn't one to indulge in thoughts of magical moments or slices of time where Karma was doing what she did, but she was left with no choice but to acknowledge that she was, unwillingly and with a good deal of unease, facing one of those moments. The world had gone still and quiet, as if it along with time held its breath for something monumental to happen.

Tess didn't dare look at John to see if he was wrapped up in the same bit of stardusty sort of stuff she was. She simply took a very careful breath and put her hand into his.

As if she'd done it a million unthinking, unremarkable times before.

Only she hadn't.

Time sighed.

She took a deep breath, then allowed John de Piaget to help her from the car. And as she did so, she reminded herself that she wasn't unaccustomed to dating powerful, intelligent, or important men. She was equally practiced in encountering on a business level extremely intimidating, brilliant, and famous men. If she could handle all that, she could surely deal with the touch of John's hand. It didn't have to mean anything.

A pity that, despite her protests, it did.

She pulled her hand away quickly, and the moment was gone. If John felt anything, he didn't show it. He merely stood back, looked anywhere but at her, then shut the door when she'd moved away from it.

"Thank you again," she managed.

"You're welcome," he said politely, but he didn't move. He simply stood there, waiting, not watching her, until she'd managed to get herself moving forward. She walked into the train station without looking back. She waited for her train without allowing herself to think about anything at all. It was only as she sat down by a window and the train began to move that she looked at the card she still held in her hand.

The business side had the name of Grant's garage, then nothing more than the shop number and John's cell number under it with just his first name.

Odd.

She turned it over and found an address written there in a rather lovely hand, all things considered. Then again, he was a lord's son. She imagined his education had been extensive and consisted of quite a bit more than just swordplay.

She shook her head. She hadn't considered that part of his life. Was he as skilled as his brother?

Did she care?

She wasn't sure she could bear to even begin to think about that.

She put the card into her bag, shut it purposefully, then concentrated on the lovely English countryside passing by her, countryside that was full of farmland, the occasional groupings of oasts, and not a single castle for miles.

Thankfully.

Chapter 4

John cursed his way to London.

It was perhaps the first time in what seemed at the moment to be an exceptionally long life that he found himself grateful for all the languages he'd taken the time to learn—or been forced to learn by his father. He'd started his current tour of curses in tatty old English, worked his way through French, German, Italian, then ventured into Portuguese and Russian. The last gave him a bit of a headache, so he'd turned to things a bit more familiar like Old English and Norman French.

And the Latin he'd conjugated during mass every morning of his first nineteen years of life to keep himself awake.

That hadn't but gotten him to the M25 where he unfortunately needed the foul language the most. He usually had enough patience to negotiate morning traffic, but he wasn't at his best presently. He settled for news on the radio and a deliberate and purposeful dredging up of the last of his reserves of patience.

Damn that Tess Alexander.

He knew his present discomfort wasn't *entirely* her fault, but a decent bit of it was and he was fully prepared to blame her for it. If she hadn't come into his shop, if she hadn't blown a tyre, if she hadn't with every breath she took left him dazzled and distracted . . . well, actually it *was* entirely her fault that he was affected.

He paused, then blew his hair out of his eyes. To be entirely fair, he could have done something besides follow her so closely that morning. He'd known it was her car, which should have left him whipping his own car about and taking a different route north. By nay, he'd had to follow her, then he'd had to help her, then he'd done the most irrational thing of all by giving her one of his cards and telling her to come find him.

And then he'd touched her hand and been lost.

He cursed feebly, because that was now all he could manage. He was daft, that was it. He'd suffered a momentary weakness, but he might not pay for it too dearly. Perhaps she wouldn't use his card, which would save him from more discomfort. He would make sure to duck out the back when she came into his shop in the village, which would finish the tale once and for all.

A pity the memory of the feel of her hand in his was something he couldn't seem to put behind him.

He snapped back to himself just before he plowed into the car in front of him, then forced himself to concentrate on what he should have been doing in the first place, which was driving.

It took him almost two hours to get into the city, which he supposed was better than it would have been if he'd been using just his feet. He pulled into the car park of the studio, leaned his head back against the seat and let out his breath slowly.

Truly, he loathed London.

If he hadn't had business there that he enjoyed, he never would have ventured into its innards again. There were too many people, too much noise, too much confusion. He hadn't particularly enjoyed it as a lad, either, though he was the first to admit things had changed a bit over the years. His dislike of the place, however, had remained steady.

It was comforting somehow that some things didn't change.

He pushed himself out of his car and went to fetch his guitar out of the boot. He reached in and started to shove aside the mail he'd tossed atop the case that morning, then sighed and reached for it. No sense in not at least seeing what sort of rubbish his new shop was entitling him to.

He tossed aside the junk mailings, then froze with a thin letter in his hands.

His suddenly unsteady hands, as it happened.

He recognized the handwriting, though he'd only seen it a few times. There was no return address, but that didn't surprise him. There was only one way to get hold of the writer of the letter and that wasn't through the Royal Mail.

He blew out his breath, then opened the letter, steeling himself for all sorts of things he wouldn't care to read. The scrawl there was as illegible as it always had been.

John,

Thought you'd be interested in this bloke Ian MacLeod's contact info. He's Cameron's cousin by marriage and specializes in swords and that sort of rot.

Cheers,
Oliver

John leaned—gingerly, of course—against the fender of his car. Well, he might have sat down, but since he'd done it so carefully, perhaps no one would notice how unsteady beneath him his knees had suddenly become.

Something untoward was at work in his life.

If he'd been a more superstitious sort of lad, he might have thought Fate was stalking him. First a woman who had spent her academic life wallowing in the Middle Ages, then an unexpected note from a man he hadn't talked to in months. He wasn't sure he wanted to think about why he'd become acquainted with Oliver, but perhaps there was no harm in it now there was no danger of his falling upon his arse from undue stress over the memory.

He had, a year or so into his current life, found himself a bit more strapped financially than he had supposed he might be, which had necessitated the relinquishing of a bit of his inheritance. He'd heard tell of a group, Cameron Antiquities, that specialized in very discreet purchases and sales of, ah, antiquities. Since that was what he'd had to sell, he'd made contact, then eventually made a friend of sorts of Oliver who had been the go-between between him and Robert Cameron. He'd pre-

ferred to keep his anonymity for his own reasons—and Cameron
had been a Scot, which had been yet another reason to keep his
distance—so he'd simply dealt with Oliver as the occasion arose.

Oliver had never asked him where he'd come by his apparently never-ending stash of medieval gold coins and he hadn't
volunteered the information. He'd simply wanted his assets converted into modern sterling as quickly and discreetly as possible,
and Oliver had obliged.

Obviously, Oliver had been thinking a bit more diligently
about why John had come by his inheritance than John had
feared he might.

Ordinarily, John would have done as he always did when
dealing with nosy souls; he would have immediately severed all
contact with Oliver and left him to his ruminations. But something stopped him. It wasn't that he still had a decent amount of
medieval gold stashed in a safe-deposit box in Zurich, or that
he'd had a nagging suspicion that at some point in the future, he
might actually want to have a brief chat with Robert Cameron
over a pint.

He supposed it was that he had found, beyond reason, something of a friend who treated the unacknowledged oddities of his
past without so much as a lifting of an eyebrow.

Which was a maudlin bit of business that should have had
him taking something firm to his forehead until good sense returned. He scowled. 'Twas obviously a weakness brought on by
a bit too much contact with a certain wench. All the more reason
to hope he never saw *her* again.

He looked again at Ian MacLeod's phone number. He'd heard
of him, of course, because when one had a Claymore hiding in
one's closet, hearing about others with that sort of preference
seemed to come along with the territory—even if he did his best
to keep it a secret. Well, a Claymore and two medieval swords of
varying adornment but equally superior quality.

His two concessions to the past he never thought about.

He'd also heard rumors about Ian MacLeod's cousin, who
was reputedly the laird of a particular branch of the clan Mac-
Leod loitering in the Highlands, though he couldn't bring the
blighter's given name to mind at the moment.

It was odd how the name MacLeod continued to come up
when he didn't expect it. He'd been able to ignore it easily

enough in the past, but to be reminded of it now by virtue of a reference to Ian MacLeod? When he was doing his damndest to avoid a woman who knew all about a time period he was doing *his* damndest to forget?

He folded the letter up and shoved it in his pocket. He didn't have time to think about it at the moment. He imagined he wouldn't have the occasion to think about it later. He would probably keep the information for purely academic reasons, but it would be a cold day in hell before he used it.

Surely.

He pulled his guitar out of the boot of his car, then took himself and his shaking knees into the studio. At least here he wouldn't be faced with things he didn't like. He had developed a reputation through a very fortuitous chain of events as a respectable studio musician. He'd done quite a bit of recording in Scotland; eventually word had spread and he'd found himself in London more often than not. In fact, that was one of the reasons he'd looked for a business to buy in the south. Finding Grant's shop had been a marvelous stroke of good fortune.

Or so he'd thought.

Now, as he found himself faced with his past thanks to two different souls, he was beginning to think his purchase of that shop could be credited to a less savory source. Perhaps he should have stayed in Scotland or decamped for somewhere completely different, like the Colonies. Or perhaps Germany where he could have actually gotten his Vanquish out of first gear on a regular basis.

And to think he'd actually given Tess Alexander his business card with his mobile number scrawled on it in his own hand.

He was, again, daft.

He walked inside, grateful for the rush of warmth that would do his unpleasantly cold hands some good. Janet, the receptionist, smiled when she saw him.

"You're early," she noted. "As usual."

"Just trying to keep Kenneth from sacking me," John said easily.

She laughed. "He would never do that. Too many people bothering him for your time." She nodded to her left. "The main studio's empty and waiting for you."

"I appreciate that," he said.

"Coffee?"

He grimaced. "Can't stand the stuff," he said, which was what he said every time she offered him some. He started to walk away, then turned back. "I might be having a guest this afternoon."

"What's her name?" Janet asked, her eyes twinkling.

He pursed his lips. "Why should it be a she?"

"Because you have a very long list of would-be groupies who all happen to be female. Who am I looking for?"

"A neighbor," he said as casually as possible. "Tess Alexander is her name. I'm not sure she'll bother, but you never know."

"I'll watch for her," she said easily.

He nodded his thanks, snagged a bottle of water from the kitchen, then made his way to the studio. He found himself a comfortable chair, pulled out the music he'd been charged with playing, then tuned his guitar and prepared to warm up a bit.

Unbidden and certainly unwelcome memories of his past washed over him without warning. Commanding them to leave him be was useless. It had been, he could admit with all frankness, that sort of day.

Playing the guitar hadn't been the first job he'd had after leaving home; that had been mucking out stables. His skill with horses and, truth be told, his inordinate fondness for them had earned him room and board for a pair of months until he'd gotten on his feet a bit and been able to look for something that paid better. It had been listening to modern music whilst about his work that had given him the idea that perhaps he might make a go of that sort of thing.

A year, two different stables, and a restaurant dishwashing job or two later—he hadn't dared convert any of his gold at that point—he'd had a guitar and himself in Edinburgh at the same time. He'd performed at the Festival for a lark that first time, absolutely clueless as to who might have been in the audience. After all, what had it mattered? He'd given himself a year to see what another world was like before he'd fully intended to return to his own, wiser, more seasoned, and ready to settle down into the rather pedestrian life of a lord's fourth son. He'd had no intention of loitering about in present-day England to see who might have wanted his musical services.

He deftly circumvented the memories of a particular fortnight that had left him realizing he was rather more wedded to the present day than he'd anticipated he might be.

It had been at that point that he'd made more definite plans, found a lad to put him legally in the current century, and run across a fortuitous and random mention of Cameron Antiquities, Ltd. A discreet inquiry had resulted in that cautious friendship with Oliver and even an offer of an introduction to Lord Robert Cameron. John had declined the latter because at the time he'd had enough of nobility to last him a bit.

He'd continued on with his life, continued to play, forced himself to acclimatize to his circumstances, and flown under the radar, as the saying went. He'd gone from being a grubby, overwhelmed stable boy to being a reclusive, several-times-over millionaire. He dabbled with cars because he'd always fancied unraveling how mechanical things worked. He played whatever stringed instrument he could lay his hands on—some rather badly, as it happened—because he had inherited his grandmother's love for music. He'd moved from day to day, ignoring who he had been and contenting himself with who he was.

Until Tess Alexander had walked into his shop and forced his world to grind to a halt.

A doctor of medieval studies.

The irony of it was enough to do him in.

And now that bloody note from Oliver, whom he hadn't seen since the first of the year when he'd first begun to investigate a move south. John pursed his lips. Of course, he'd heard of Ian MacLeod's school of swordplay, but he'd dismissed it as a Highlander taking his heritage far too seriously for his own good.

It was as he'd thought before: Oliver had obviously spent too much time wondering why it was John had such a large supply of rare medieval gold coins and that had led him to speculating on other things he shouldn't have.

John didn't particularly want to think about that.

He didn't want to think about anything else that made him uncomfortable, either, so he turned his mind back to the music in front of him. He would have a decent day, pick up a few quid for his trouble, then hopefully escape before Tess Alexander did the unthinkable and called him.

He felt fairly safe in assuming she wouldn't. He wasn't sure what he'd done to irritate her, but she seemed to want as little to do with him as he did her. His damnable chivalry would have been trotted out and exercised, then put away where it could trouble him no further for the day. He would return home to relative obscurity and that would be the end of it. Perhaps he would find a driving instructor and mail her the man's business card so she didn't carry on with leaving what he was sure were monumental dings in an innocent oak tree.

He would also never curse himself for missing the turnoff to Sedgwick because he would never have a need to go there again.

He felt better already, having put his life back in order, all the pieces back in place.

He put that beautiful, haunting woman out of his mind and got to work.

Chapter 5

Tess looked at the address on the card John had given her
and wondered if she had lost her mind. She'd been wondering that for the better part of the day, actually, ever since she'd
gotten on the train.

She'd arrived in London too early to conduct any business,
so she'd killed a couple of hours in her favorite coffee shop, pretending to look out the window and watch humanity hurry by.

She'd eventually made her way to pick up the two rare and
pricey books on medieval warfare her preferred dealer had found
for her, then spent a useless hour in his shop, poking around in
piles of things that hadn't been dusted in at least a year. She'd
loitered in Victorian England for a bit, which had been a decent
distraction, though perhaps not enough of one.

She'd wandered the streets for a good half an hour before she
made herself at least go and order something for an early lunch.
She tried to eat, but she'd been less successful at it than she
would have liked to have been. She had managed part of a salad
and some juice, then taken her knitting out and tried to work on
a sock. That resulted half an hour later in the necessity of ripping
out everything she'd managed to do. She had shoved everything

back into her bag, ignored her instinct for self-preservation, and gone to look for a Tube station.

She realized as she now stood in front of the appropriate address that she was looking at a recording studio. She frowned, then opened the door and walked inside. It wasn't an enormous place from what she could tell, but the receptionist was dressed nicely and the client list Tess glanced at while she was waiting for the girl to get off the phone was downright impressive.

The girl hung up and smiled at her. "You must be Miss Alexander."

Tess smiled uncomfortably. "Yes, well—"

"John said you might be coming." She stood. "Come on. I'll take you back."

Tess followed her because she couldn't on such short notice invent a good reason why she shouldn't. Within moments, she found herself standing in the darkest part of a mixing room listening to John playing the acoustic guitar.

She was provided with a chair, which she sank down into gratefully. A dozen questions immediately clamored for attention, but she ignored them all in favor of simply sitting there and listening. She had no idea he was accompanying a jazz vocal group until the tracks were played back together. He listened with a frown, then requested some sort of do-over. She wasn't a picky listener; she honestly couldn't tell the difference, but he seemed to be happier with the subsequent effort.

She continued to sit in the dark and listen as he recorded another two songs. It was so far from what she'd expected to find him doing, she could hardly take it in.

It unfortunately gave her the chance to look at him from the safety and comfort of knowing he had no idea she was sitting there gaping at him.

He was gorgeous. There was no other way to say it. She supposed she shouldn't have expected anything else. She'd had a good look at his brother for several days and almost grown accustomed to being startled at the sight. Worse still, she just happened to know John and Montgomery's, ah, nephew, Stephen de Piaget, who was almost as handsome as they were.

But there was something about John . . .

Maybe it was the perfection of his face with his chiseled cheekbones and strong jaw, or enviable physique that a T-shirt and jeans did nothing to hide, or his long fingers that flew over strings as if he'd done nothing else with those hands for the whole of his life but practice.

Or it could have been the fact that she knew she was looking at a medieval knight who somehow, beyond all reason, found himself masquerading as something quite different in the twenty-first century.

He finished before she'd finished the cataloging of his perfections. She'd really hoped she might get past them quickly so she could get back to listing all the reasons why she never wanted to lay eyes on him again. Too bad she just wasn't going to have time for that. She watched as a man in slacks and a sweater came into the studio and chatted with him for a bit. The producer turned on the mic when John directed a few questions his way. Tess knew she was sitting too far back to be seen, but she found herself unaccountably nervous just the same.

"Dave's been nagging me again," the man in the sweater said, sounding as if he was fully prepared to engage in a bit of it himself. "He's pretty determined."

"No," John said stiffly. "Still no."

Tess was marginally satisfied to see he could be as unyielding with others as he had been with her.

"It would just be a demo now, but it could be a career direction."

"*This* isn't a career, Kenneth. It's a diversion."

Kenneth looked at him calculatingly. "I have a lute."

Tess found herself sitting on the edge of her seat. A *lute*? She couldn't imagine that John would ever admit to playing such a thing, but what did she know? Maybe he was more in touch with his past than he'd let on and didn't mind demonstrating that for others.

Which didn't adequately explain why he seemed so perfectly at home in jeans and a pricey black sports car, but she would think about that later, when she could think straight again.

She couldn't say she knew enough about John de Piaget to predict what he was going to do, but she had to admit he looked almost as ready to bolt as he had when she'd asked him if he wanted to come inside her great hall.

He sat back in his chair and looked up at Kenneth with absolutely no expression on his face. "Absolutely not."

Kenneth looked at him, obviously amused. "I'm not asking you to cut out a major organ and hand it over, John. It's just a lute."

Tess found herself unaccountably nervous. It was one thing for her to know who John was and, more to the point, *what* he was; it was another thing entirely for someone else to know. Kenneth, whoever he was and whatever sort of sway he held over John, was likely completely oblivious to John's past. She could only imagine how zealously John guarded that past.

Actually, she didn't have to imagine much. She could see it on his face.

Briefly. As quickly as the shutters had come down, they disappeared and the moment was gone. John simply looked up at his tormentor.

"Don't tell me," he drawled, "Dave just *happened* to leave it behind the last time he was here."

"He's forgetful."

"Why in the hell would he think *I* could play it?"

"He heard you in Edinburgh last year at the Festival."

John looked heavenward briefly, then back at Kenneth. "I was drunk."

Kenneth only smiled. "Were you?"

"No," John said shortly, "but I wish I had been. I absolutely wish I were now."

"But you aren't, and I have a very lovely reproduction instrument in my office." He smiled encouragingly. "One song, sung soberly."

"I only *know* one song."

Tess doubted that, but she didn't suppose she should offer that observation.

"Then play that one," Kenneth said smoothly. "Five minutes of your time and I stop having to avoid his calls. Do it for me as thanks for all the lovely gigs I've gotten you over the years."

John dragged his hand through his hair. "Damn you."

Kenneth rubbed his hands together. "I'll be right back." He looked over his shoulder on his way out the door. "Don't go anywhere."

John sent him a dark look, then put away his guitar and began to pace around the studio. He stopped at one point, then turned and looked into the booth.

Tess was sure he couldn't possibly see her. She was sitting so far back in the shadows that she could hardly see herself. But he didn't look away. He didn't smile, either. It was as if he stood on the edge of something he didn't want to fall into but found himself without any choice.

She understood. She'd felt that way when he'd held out his hand for her keys that morning.

Kenneth was nothing short of relentless upon his return. Tess watched as he nudged and pestered and badgered until John was sitting down again with one mic pointed at the lute and another staring him in the face.

"No need for perfection," Kenneth said soothingly, backing out of the room carefully, as if he feared to break the spell he'd been weaving. "He knows what you can do."

John shot him a murderous look, but said nothing. He took a deep breath. In fact, he might have taken a couple of them. He sat there for an excruciatingly long time, as if he wrestled with things he couldn't bring himself to face.

Tess understood completely.

He finally sighed, then tuned the lute as if he'd been doing it for the better part of his life.

Tess would have closed her eyes, but she was afraid she might miss something. She felt time begin to layer itself over her, over John, over the whole place, as if his past was colliding with her future.

She suspected that if anyone had touched her at that moment, she would have jumped out of her skin.

Kenneth popped into the production room and almost tripped over her. "Sorry, love. Didn't see you there. Guy, turn the tape on and leave it on. We'll edit out the profanity later."

"He's going to kill you," Guy said mildly.

"He won't," Kenneth said confidently. "Not today."

Tess wouldn't have been so sure of that, but maybe Kenneth was better at ignoring the rather pointed and vile warm-up of curses John indulged in than she was. Kenneth and Guy only watched, unintimidated.

John finally stopped, took another in that series of deep breaths, then was silent for a couple of minutes.

Then he began to play.

Tess lost her breath, then felt her eyes begin to burn when he

began to sing. The love song, sung in flawless medieval French—
and yes, she most definitely could pin down the accent—was
absolutely breathtaking. It was no wonder the mysterious Dave
wanted him on tape and Kenneth was willing to brave all kinds
of abuse to get him there.

And whatever else he was, John was a professional.

Or at least he was until he had finished with his song and
the final notes had died away. Then he stood up, shot Kenneth
another look of promise and left the studio, no doubt to look for
somewhere to stash the lute so he wouldn't have to see it again.
Kenneth killed the recording, flicked on the lights, then sat back
in his chair and sighed in contentment. He looked at her.

"Like that, did you?"

Tess could only nod.

"Couldn't understand a word of it," he admitted, "but he's
good, wherever he learned it."

She watched John return to the studio, retrieve his guitar, then
look at her through the glass.

"Let's go," he said shortly.

Guy laughed wryly. "The kid has no manners, but a helluva
voice."

Tess had to agree on both counts. She rose, thanked the men
for the chair, then let Kenneth open the door for her. She realized
only as she was standing in the lobby watching John study the
calendar on his phone while Kenneth was pestering him for more
time that she was having a hard time catching her breath.

Who *was* he? And why in the hell was he in her time and not
his family's?

She excused herself and looked for a loo to have a bit of privacy and see if she couldn't get ahold of herself. She realized
immediately that there was no hope for her; she looked every
bit as shell-shocked as she felt. She pinched her cheeks, put on
lip gloss, then put her shoulders back. She just had to get home.
Maybe she could sneak past John and bolt for the nearest Tube
station. Even if it took her until midnight to get back to Sedgwick, she would be better off than riding home with him. Then
she could get on with that stellar plan of avoiding him like the
plague.

She never should have come to find him. It had been a colossal mistake. What had she been thinking?

Well, she hadn't been thinking, that's what she'd been doing. She should have ripped up his card and run the other way.

Which she would do the first chance she had.

She walked back out into the lobby and eyed the exit. Unfortunately, she couldn't get herself there. That probably came from the renewed weakness in her knees she suffered when she realized John was watching for her while he was talking to Kenneth.

"Why don't you just move to London?" Kenneth asked in exasperation. "I have more work than you could handle."

"I don't like London."

Kenneth pursed his lips. "It's no worse than that no-man's-land you're living in right now."

John only grunted at him.

Kenneth threw up his hands in frustration. "There is no talking to you, is there?"

John shot him a look. "I'm two hours from London, not eight. It's the best I can do. And yes, I'm bloody grateful for all you've done for me. Now, will you stop with the nagging?"

"Just don't smash any fingers before Tuesday," Kenneth warned. "Our little miss won't do the day without you."

"I'll be here."

"Her father's *very* rich."

"I'll be here with fingers *intact*," John said with a gusty sigh.

"Leave your girlfriend at home," Kenneth suggested.

"I'm not—" Tess began, only to realize John had uttered the same protest.

Which was just as well. She pasted on her most polite smile, because she was nothing if not polite, and she certainly didn't want anyone to get the wrong idea. She had every intention of getting as far away from John de Piaget as possible and it was obvious he felt the same way.

All good, to her mind.

She continued to be polite as he escorted her from the studio. She stopped on the sidewalk and smiled politely.

"That was beautiful," she said. "Thank you for letting me listen."

He shrugged. "It was nothing."

"I'll pay you tomorrow for the rescue this morning," she said, taking a step backward. "Have a safe drive back."

He looked at her in surprise. "What?"

"Gotta go," she said, backing up another step.

"Don't be daft," he said with a frown. "I'll drive you home."

"I can get there on my own."

"It's ridiculous to take the train when I'm going the same way. I won't kill you on the motorway if that's what worries you."

Actually, that was the least of her worries. It was the thought of being in the same enclosed space with him for more than ten minutes that was about to give her hives. But before she could muster up the energy to run, she found herself shepherded in the direction of his car, then ushered into the passenger seat.

She knew she was an idiot to allow it, but maybe her imagination had been running away with her. She latched on to that thought with the tenacity of a drowning woman. Perhaps there was nothing at all odd about sitting next to her brother-in-law's brother. Her *medieval* brother-in-law's brother.

She tried to wrap her mind around that as he negotiated impossible afternoon London traffic. Even on a Wednesday, it was terrible. It reminded her of all the reasons she had been willing to live full time at Sedgwick.

Though she was more tempted than usual to take up a standing offer to come back and tutor at Cambridge.

"You play very well," she ventured, at one point.

"Thank you," he said in a tone that said he didn't want to discuss it further.

She was happy to oblige. She decided abruptly that not only had she had enough conversation with him for the day, she'd had enough of watching him as well. She concentrated on the scenery, didn't protest when he turned on the radio, listened for five minutes, then turned it off. She could understand. He played better than anything she'd heard and he was a far superior singer. She would have asked him why he didn't make a career of it, but she supposed she already knew the answer. If he was burying himself in a tiny shop in an obscure village in the south of England, he obviously didn't want any notoriety.

And she didn't care why not.

Not at all.

It was an excruciating ride back home. She was acutely aware of him sitting next to her, so close she could have reached out and touched him at any moment, but she wasn't attracted to him, no, not at all. He was grouchy, taciturn, and bossy. She wasn't altogether sure what she wanted in a man, but she had the feeling it would involve tweed. John de Piaget probably wouldn't recognize tweed if it wrapped itself around his head and suffocated him.

She'd never been gladder of anything than she was the sight of her castle rising up at the end of the road. She had her hand on the door latch before he had the car out of gear.

"Wait," he commanded. "I'll get the door."

"I can get it myself."

He shot her a look. "Wait."

She thought she might have had enough. "I am not your girlfriend," she said, doing her best not to grit her teeth, "so you have no right to boss me around."

"I don't boss around my girlfriends," he said evenly.

"I hate to think what you *do* do with them," she retorted.

"I'll get your door," he repeated.

She told him to stuff it. In not so many words. And not so politely.

He got out of the car. She did, too, and decided that a hasty retreat to the castle was the best course of action.

"Thanks for the ride," she threw over her shoulder, then she bolted for her drawbridge. She made it to the barbican gate before she realized he was right behind her. If she'd been able to drop the portcullis—any of them, or perhaps all three together—she would have. The best she could do was spin around and hold her hand out to hold him off. "That's far enough."

He leaned against the stone wall and nodded toward the courtyard. "I'll watch you get inside, if it's all the same to you."

"I couldn't care less."

He only lifted an eyebrow and said nothing.

She suppressed the urge to punch him. How was it a man she didn't like and never wanted to see again—odd how she had to keep reminding herself of that—could consistently and relentlessly bring out the worst in her?

Silence was golden, yes, that was the ticket. She nodded briskly to him, then turned on her heel and walked across her courtyard with as much dignity as she could muster. Fortunately, Peaches wasn't there to open the door and ask questions. She got herself inside her great hall, avoided her office, then continued on right upstairs to her bedroom.

If only the day could have ended there, she might have called it a wash. But no, she had to keep going until she had reached the roof. She stood just outside one of the guard towers and watched as taillights faded into the distance.

She stood there for far longer than she should have, hearing the song he'd sung echoing in what was left of her tiny little mind. She knew the tune, of course, because she had her PhD in Medieval Political Thought. To round out her education, she'd studied quite a bit about the music of the time, and the dancing, and the rest of the gamut of artistic endeavors.

Apparently John had, too.

She took a deep breath, then turned and went inside. She wouldn't see him again because he was obviously as unfond of her as she was of him, and that was a good thing.

It was a very good thing, indeed.

Chapter 6

J*ohn* stood in his garden with his sword in his hand, shaking
with weariness, and wished for nothing so much as one of his
brothers—preferably Robin—to grind him into the dust where
he might not need think any longer. He didn't want to think any
more about medieval things, things that seemed to be hedging up
his way everywhere he turned.

Which made it a bit ironic that he was training—if that's what
it could be called—with a sword, but he was happy to ignore the
irony.

It was safer that way.

He had, as it happened, been doing the safe thing for several
years now. He had never used his sword out of doors, preferring
to rent a large industrial space when he could and settle for ka-
rate or even the occasional stint in a gym when he couldn't. One
of the attractions of Grant's place for him had been the cottage
located behind the shop and a large, high-hedged garden behind
that that bordered nothing but pastureland. He had absolute privacy given that his shop was on the edge of the village and there
weren't any second-floor flats anywhere in the vicinity.

All of which had left him that morning rising before dawn

and marching out to his very luxurious excuse for lists in an attempt to ignore things that bothered him.

He dragged his sleeve across his forehead. What he needed, he had to admit, was something to train with besides dead air. Unbidden, and certainly unwelcome, came to mind the contents of Oliver's note. Ian MacLeod didn't advertise, which meant his school was either hideously expensive or terribly exclusive. John was betting on both, neither of which bothered him. He supposed it might be a bit of stretch to pit himself against a canny Scotsman, but it might be just the thing to cure his wee head of its ridiculous thoughts—of swords, and times not his own, and music that he had rattling around in his head that hadn't been preserved by others over the years.

And a certain dark-haired wench he couldn't seem to stop thinking about.

He turned back to less uncomfortable things, namely those MacLeods who seemed to have all manner of interesting tales following them. Now that he could allow himself to think a bit more on them, he remembered that he'd first heard of them, surprisingly enough, from the lad who had forged his passport and birth certificate and seemed not at all troubled by the fashioning of either. He'd advised John to seek them out if he needed anything, mentioning in passing that they had used his services now and again for the same sort of thing.

John had immediately filed that away with a list of other things he'd never intended to think about again.

Now, though, he was beginning to wonder if he'd been too hasty. It said much about his pitiful state of mind that he was riffling through the file of impossible minutiae. He could, with an unflinchingness that would have impressed even his father, safely say that he was losing it.

And he knew, again, at just whose feet to lay the blame.

But since thinking on unpleasant paranormal impossibilities was preferable to thinking about her, he'd readily turned to them. To go to Scotland, to venture into the Highlands where they would have once upon a time just as easily killed an Englishman as to look at him, was to acknowledge things about himself that he didn't like to think on.

Such as the fact that he had held a sword in his hand for hours a day for as long into his past as his memories stretched. And save for an impossible year when he had, with his brother, spent time at a castle half full of Scots, he had spent his life learning swordplay from his father, then having it polished by his elder brothers—no mean swordsmen themselves.

Perhaps he would be better off finding a local dojo and working out there. At least there he wouldn't be asked questions about his abilities with steel that would make him uncomfortable.

He stabbed his sword into the ground, dragged his sleeve across his forehead again, then turned to go into the house for a drink. He froze when he realized he wasn't alone.

Doris Winston was leaning against the wall, watching him.

He was flustered enough to swear, but he bit his tongue just in time. His mother would have been proud of him, but it did little for his level of comfort.

"You said you would play for me," she said, fumbling for her cane—which he was just certain was nothing more than a prop—and tapping it against the sidewalk. "Though I will beg pardon for intruding into your private garden."

"You weren't," he lied, because he'd been taught to be kind to old women. "I was just, ah, trying to keep from going to fat."

"Interesting way to do it."

"Isn't it, though," he muttered, half under his breath, starting across the garden so he could invite her in for tea and take her attention off things she didn't need to be looking at.

To say he was alarmed didn't begin to describe his discomfort.

"Don't forget your sword, lad. Wouldn't want it rusting in the rain."

John blew his hair out of his eyes, then turned and went to fetch his sword. He resheathed it, then rested it casually against his shoulder as if it were nothing more interesting than a rapier, not a medieval broadsword. It was, as it happened, his own sword, the sword he'd been given as a youth by his father. At least he hadn't been using the one he'd received at his knighting, or the Claymore purchased in the Future and generally kept hidden in the back of his closet. And he hadn't been fighting someone else. Doris could have seen much worse things than she likely had.

He stopped in mid-step at the look on her face. He took a deep breath.

"Just a hobby," he managed.

She only looked at him steadily. "I keep many secrets."

"A pity I have none to give you."

"Are you inviting me in," she continued ruthlessly, "to play your lute for me? I imagine it goes with the sword-fighting expertise, doesn't it?"

"Bloody hell, old woman, you're frightening me."

She laughed and took his arm, seemingly not put off by the aftereffects of his workout. "As I said, I keep many secrets for many people. I won't tell anyone what you can do."

"One could hope," he managed. He supposed his fate was sealed, at least for the next hour or so, so he surrendered without complaint.

Besides, England was full of reenactment lads. For all she knew, he had an unwholesome fascination with time periods not his own and had taken that fascination to an unhealthy level. There could have been nothing more to it than that.

He ushered her inside his humble cottage, saw her seated, then locked himself in his room and headed for the shower. He cleaned up, purposely keeping his mind empty, then stowed his gear behind his clothes where it usually rested. He considered, then sighed deeply and fetched his lute. He walked back out into the little living room to find that Doris had made a fire and tea.

"Thought at least one of us should be comfortable," she said.

"Good of you," he said sourly.

She sat down in his favorite chair, then looked up at him. "Well?"

He dredged up his best company manners, sat down, and took his lute out of the case. It wasn't an inexpensive reproduction, though it was indeed a reproduction. He'd had it made at great expense to suit his specifications. The mechanics were modern, but the sound was pure medieval.

He tuned the strings, then sang the song he'd recorded two days earlier for Kenneth, damn him to hell. It was one thing to play for himself—something he did quite often—and for old women who knew how to keep secrets, but it was another thing entirely to have anything of an antique nature associated with his name.

Not that anyone would have cared, surely.

He played for another quarter hour, then set the lute aside.

"Four?" Doris asked, disappointed. "That's all?"

"Three more than my usual limit," he said darkly.

"Then I'll be content," she said, rising. "Thank you, my lad. It was lovely."

"I'll take you home—"

She waved him away. "I need the walk." She paused at his door. "You know, they're having a little gathering up at the castle tonight."

"I didn't know," he said. Didn't know and didn't want to know.

"I'm surprised you haven't been more in touch with the happenings there," she said mildly. "Given your affinity for the past."

He forced himself to breathe normally because he had, he could admit modestly, iron control over himself. "I was still trying to settle in."

"You looked settled in now. You might have an opinion on how things are run. Given your affinity—"

"For the past," he finished for her. "Yes, you already mentioned that."

She only looked at him blandly.

He suppressed the urge to drag his hand through his hair. "I dabble in history. Nothing more."

"Young Tess does as well, which you know, but she might be in over her head tonight. I understand she's putting on a small party for *very* exclusive clients who are notoriously difficult to please. Her sister's in London and her caterer had a family emergency. I think she's all on her own up the way."

"A pity," he said. It was, but it wasn't his trouble so he felt no need to rush off to solve it.

"She doesn't look it, but I think she's fragile."

"She's dangerous."

Doris reached out and poked him in the chest with her cane. "You know, you little blighter, you *could* go offer her a bit of aid."

"'Tis hardly my responsibility," he said grimly.

"And how many times, my dear John, have you taken responsibility for troubles that were not your own?"

He scowled at her.

"They're arriving at seven for supper."

"I am not a chef."

"But you are an excellent lutenist."

He reached around her and opened the door for her. "A good day to you, Mrs. Winston."

She only smiled pleasantly, her dastardly duty apparently done for the day. She propped her cane up against her shoulder exactly as he'd done with his sword, then walked off with a spring in her step a woman half her age would have envied. John watched her go, then shut himself into his house and made plans for the afternoon.

Important plans.

Plans that didn't involve putting on a tunic and tights and masquerading as some sort of medieval reenactment nutter who had absolutely no bloody idea just how unpleasant the time period could be.

He wondered if there might be football on the telly.

He was still wondering that at quarter past seven as he pulled into the completely inadequate car park that huddled a safe distance away from Sedgwick's modern incarnation of itself.

He was wearing jeans.

That was the only thing that made him feel in the slightest bit in control of his own destiny. He spared a few dark thoughts for his damnable chivalry that he couldn't seem to control, then fetched his lute out of the boot of his car and looked at the castle with as much enthusiasm as he might have the welcoming maw of the Tower of London's dungeons.

He looked over the trio of cars alongside his. Two pretentious Bentleys and a Rolls. He wasn't surprised. He also wasn't at all certain why he was lowering himself to waste his evening on people who would likely spend it looking down their noses at him.

He shook his head and walked over to the keep. The place was wearing its best torchlight and actually looked quite lovely for a very rainy evening in November that threatened to turn to snow before the night was through. He could smell it in the air and wished, belatedly, that he'd driven something less ding-worthy. He should have brought the shop's Rover. Too late for that, he supposed. He would just have to press on and take his chances.

A bit like what he was doing with his life, actually.

He walked across the courtyard and avoided the great hall. He supposed he could, even after all the ensuing years, find the side door to the kitchens. He walked inside before he could stop to question his sanity—again—and found Tess up to her elbows in trying to simultaneously cook and direct staff who didn't seem to be up to the most menial of tasks.

She turned at the sound of his footstep and almost dropped a pot of something. She set it down on the Aga before he could leap forward and rescue it. She looked at the case in his hand, then back at him.

"I'm afraid to ask."

He pursed his lips. "You likely should be. Where are the snooty gits you're being tormented by tonight?"

The girls in the kitchen tittered. Tess frowned them into silence, then looked at him. "I don't think you'll help, if it's all the same to you."

He set his lute down and shrugged out of his jacket. "I can behave long enough to entertain them. What can I do to see dinner out on the lord's table?"

She closed her eyes briefly, then took an unsteady breath. "Can you stir white sauce?"

"Barely."

She didn't smile. She looked as if she just might break down and weep, which terrified him more than the thought of revealing more about himself to her and her guests than he cared to. He unbuttoned the cuffs of his only decent dress shirt, then rolled up his sleeves and moved to stand next to her.

"I'll tend the saucepans," he said. "You go play hostess. But fix your hair first. You're looking a little frazzled."

She blew fringe out of her eyes and glared at him. "I knew that."

He gently nudged her out of the way. "I think a glass of wine might do you good."

"I don't drink."

He gave her white sauce a stir, then went to rummage in the fridge. He came up with juice, which he poured into a glass and pushed into her hands.

"Imbibe."

She drank, but it didn't seem to be doing her any good. He took the glass away from her and set it on the worktable before she dropped it, then looked at her assessingly.

"Want me to go play lord of the castle?" he asked.

She looked momentarily horrified. "Ah—"

"I wouldn't snarl at them," he offered.

Her look of skepticism was priceless. He smiled to himself as he turned back to the stove.

"I'll confine myself to the kitchens for the moment," he promised. "If that will make you feel better."

"It will," she agreed, "because I very much need these people to leave happy. And the beef needs to come out in ten minutes."

"I have a watch."

She walked over to stand next to him, then reached out to give her sauce one last stir. Her hands were trembling, but he pretended not to notice.

"The veg is in the steamer and the bread warming in the back there," she said, her voice suffering from the same affliction as her hands. "I'll come back and put it together if you can keep it from burning."

"I think I can manage it."

She was silent long enough that he felt compelled to look at her. She was watching him gravely.

"I'm not trying to insult you," she said quietly.

He smiled grimly. "You don't have to like me, Miss Alexander."

"Maybe not, but I can be appreciative of your efforts. Which I am. Very."

He nodded over his shoulder at the passageway that wound up to the great hall. "Go see to your guests. I'll keep your supper from going up in flames, and I won't corrupt your staff."

"I'd appreciate that."

"I imagined you would."

She took a deep breath and walked away. He knew he shouldn't have, but he couldn't stop himself from turning a bit to watch her leave the kitchen.

He heartily wished he hadn't.

She pulled her hair free of her chignon and it fell in a cascade of irrepressible curls halfway down her back before she expertly caught it back up at the back of her head. She put her shoulders back and marched up the passageway, all business in a black skirt and sweater.

He turned back to his sauce before he looked any longer where he shouldn't have. Truly, he wasn't interested in her or her life or what she thought of living in a castle when she likely could have sold the thing and bought herself a quite comfortable country home. Perhaps she was a glutton for punishment. Perhaps she was another of those unrealistic souls who thought medieval times to be quite romantic.

Perhaps she was just a lovely woman doing the best she could with what she'd been given.

He supposed it would be wise not to speculate. He checked his watch, continued to stir, then followed Tess's instructions about removing things from the heat. He happily let her take over when she returned, did what she asked, then stood with her as the kitchen gels began to carry in supper. Tess watched the last one leave, then looked at his case in the corner for a moment before she looked up at him.

"Is that a guitar?" she asked finally.

He took a deep breath. "A lute, actually."

She closed her eyes briefly. "I'm not quite sure how to thank you."

He bit his tongue around an offhand remark about rescues and their limited number where she was concerned and instead settled for a nod. He walked over and took his lute out of its case, just to give himself something to do. He finally turned to look at her, because he couldn't put it off any longer. She was watching him guardedly, as if she thought he might just turn and bolt if she weren't careful.

A wise woman, that one.

"Is there a chair by the fire?" he asked.

"I'll find one."

"I'll fetch it," he said. "You hold this."

"I'm not sure I dare."

The truth was, he wasn't sure he wanted her to dare. She looked almost as unsettled as he felt. If she were going to drop something, 'twas better that she drop a chair. He looked at the stove a last time to make certain everything was off the fire, then nodded toward the passageway.

"I need something without arms," he said. "I'll just provide atmosphere, unless you've something else in mind."

"Would you sing?" she asked faintly.

"Only if your diners have been excessively courteous to you so far."

"Background music it is, then." She shot him a look. "Please be polite."

"Why would you think I would be anything else?" he grumbled, but she had already started for the passageway and perhaps hadn't heard him.

He caught up to her in a pair of strides, then contented himself with walking alongside her up the way to the great hall. In the end, he fetched his own chair, then set it next to the fire. He rolled down his sleeves, sat, then shrugged aside the unease he felt over playing things that spoke too loudly about what he was. Rich, spoiled Londoners were annoyances, not dangers. They likely wouldn't remember him or his music, so there was no reason not to simply play what he liked. With that in mind, he started at the beginning of his repertoire and worked his way through it to the last.

And whilst he did, he watched the goings-on in the hall. He didn't want to, but he unfortunately had a very good memory and didn't have to concentrate on what he was playing.

Tess's guests were miserable louts, every last one of them. The women were the worst, looking down their noses at their meals and rolling their eyes at their surroundings, which even John had to admit were spectacular. Whoever had restored Sedgwick had done a smashing job. The men were less conceited than the ladies, but just as critical. John would have thought his contributions to the evening to be of no worth at all if he hadn't caught out of the corner of his eye the looks he was having from a pair of the trio of women.

He suppressed the urge to send back looks of disdain. After all, he'd promised he would behave.

Tess endured it all with absolutely no taking of the bait being offered. He had to admit he was impressed. He wouldn't have managed it for ten minutes, much less three hours.

He played for most of that time, partly because he wasn't unaccustomed to practicing for longer than that, but mostly because it seemed to distract the would-be royals who seemed to think themselves very important indeed. He was quite happy to see the last of them.

He continued to toy with a tune until Tess finally collapsed in the chair opposite him. He looked up to find her watching him. He only lifted an eyebrow in question.

She let out a deep breath. "I'm not sure how to thank you," she said, with feeling. "I will pay you—"

"No."

She hesitated, then nodded slowly.

He played for a bit longer, then looked at her again. "Will the girls clean up?"

"They already have. They're gone. As are our guests, thankfully."

He considered her for a moment or two. "Why do you tolerate this sort of thing?"

"Because they're very rich," she said with a sigh, "and minor nobility. I needed to make a good impression." She lifted an eyebrow. "Didn't you recognize them?"

"I couldn't be bothered."

She smiled faintly. "I wish I could say the same, but I like to at least maintain some façade of graciousness, not having the luxury of telling them to take a flying leap. It keeps the lights on."

He imagined it did. He stood and put his lute into her hands. "Hold that."

"Where are you going?" she asked in surprise.

"To lock up."

"There are lots of doors."

"I imagine there are," he said dryly. "I think I can find the important ones."

He had to admit, as he started in the kitchens and worked his way up and back to the rear guard tower, that it was very strange to think of her all alone in such a place. On those very rare occasions when his father had left his mother at home alone, she had been protected by no less than two dozen very grim warriors with exceptionally sharp swords. She could have easily slept with her door unbolted and not spared a thought for her safety.

It bothered him that Tess didn't have that same sort of security system.

It bothered him even more that he now knew enough about her to have that even cross his mind.

He returned to the fire to find her plucking thoughtfully at his lute. She looked up and smiled wearily.

"It's a lovely instrument."

"It is," he agreed, sitting down across from her. "Do you play?"

"Very poorly," she admitted. She handed it back to him. "I would never play in front of you."

"I'm no critic."

"Still, no."

He shrugged, toyed with a melody or two for a moment or two, then looked at her. "I don't like it that you're alone here."

"I'm used to it."

He pursed his lips, then decided the very least he could do was sing for her. One song. It couldn't hurt.

He didn't watch her whilst he was about it, though he could feel her watching him. And he decided at that moment that the whole evening had been a very bad idea indeed. It had been useful to her, hopefully, but it had done nothing for him but convince him that what he should do was get away from her as quickly as possible.

He finished his song, then packed up his gear without delay. She walked him to the door without comment.

He walked outside, then turned on the top step and looked at her. "You bother me," he said bluntly.

She only watched him, silent and grave.

"I don't think we should see each other again," he added.

"I think you're right."

He chewed on his words for a moment or two, a novel enough occurrence that it should have given him pause. "You might still bring your car to my shop, if you like," he conceded.

"I'll come when you're not there."

He nodded. "Wise."

"I think so, too."

He shot her a look. "Lock the door, Tess."

"I will."

"Good night."

"Thank you, John," she said, very quietly.

He shrugged aside her thanks, because he could do nothing else. He nodded briskly, then turned and walked down the steps. He heard the hall door close and supposed she must have bolted it. He wasn't about to go check.

He put his head down and walked across the courtyard and out the front gates before his chivalry hung itself about his neck like a millstone and kept him from going on with the most sensible course of action. He ignored the fact that if Tess Alexander had been his, he would have lowered every damned portcullis the keep boasted and posted two dozen guardsmen with sharp swords and sour dispositions outside her door to keep her safe.

But as she wasn't his, he couldn't do any of that. He also couldn't bloody well camp in his car in her car park, either.

He cursed his way to his car, cursed some more as he backed out, then continued to accompany himself with foul words as he headed down the road back to the village.

He wasn't going to spend the night worrying about her, or pace until dawn because he was losing sleep over her, or think any more about how many times he'd fought the urge to pull her into his arms and hold her securely against him. She was not for him and he was not for her.

The sooner he accepted that indisputable fact, the happier he would be.

He would go home and make a list of all the reasons he didn't like her. Hell, he didn't know her well enough to dislike her, but he was certain that a list of that sort could be made with enough diligence.

And once he had done that, he would return to his very sensible, monotonous existence of being a mediocre studio musician, a modestly skilled restorer of expensive cars, and a compulsive watcher of stocks on his damned phone.

He honestly couldn't imagine anything more interesting.

Not at all.

Chapter 7

T*ess* leaned against a wall in an alcove leading into a courtyard in the oldest part of the second oldest university in
England and shivered. She wasn't one for leaning, but she was
just stretched too thin at the moment to do anything else but try
to keep herself upright.

She'd been in Cambridge for less than two days and to her utter surprise, she found she was ready to be finished and go home.
It was odd, that sensation, given that she'd worked the whole of
her life to get to where she was standing. From the time she'd
understood in what sort of unstable situation she'd found herself
in with her parents, she'd vowed that she would make something
different for herself. Her chance had come at fifteen, when her
parents had dumped her and her five sisters onto their aunt Edna
and vanished without a backward glance.

Her older sisters, Moonbeam and Cinderella, had been already on their way out the door by that point and hadn't been
subjected to the full brunt of the Victorian-era-inspired living
conditions. Her younger sisters, Pippa and Valerie, had had to
endure it longer than she and Peaches had, but she hadn't minded
it at all. She'd had her sights set on Cambridge from the begin-

ning and Aunt Edna's Victorian Institute of Arduous Study by Candlelight had suited her. She'd graduated from high school two years early, then blown through her undergrad and graduate degrees in just under six years. She'd just begun to work her way up the academic ladder when the offer of a castle had come her way and completely changed her life.

She looked out into the courtyard steeped in history and wondered why it was she wasn't still feeling that almost feverish urge to climb over everyone in her way to get to the top.

She put her hand briefly to her head. No fever. Maybe she was having a midlife crisis. She was tempted to call Peaches and see if that sounded reasonable, but she suppressed the urge. Losing a sibling was probably pretty high up on that Life Change list, so maybe she just needed to take it easy and roll with things for a bit.

She didn't particularly care for rolling, truth be told.

She was going to have to make a few life decisions very shortly, whether she wanted to or not. She wasn't sure she wanted to be teaching full-time, but she also wasn't sure she wanted to own a castle and simply host parties, either. The truth was, she missed the smell of old libraries and the visions of medieval glory she found safely lurking only inside them. She missed teaching bright-eyed students who were as nuts about the Middle Ages as she was. She missed spirited discussions with other academics who were as passionate about their opinions as she was about hers.

She was also getting a little tired of catering to spoiled rich people who talked through an evening of the most amazing medieval music she had ever listened to, played in the appropriate setting by a man who knew a thing or two about what he was doing.

She pulled her coat closer around herself. She wanted to go home, but home had become a place that didn't feel all that comfortable anymore. If it had been just continually wondering about Pippa and her life, she might have been able to put that behind her eventually. But now putting that behind her was impossible because ten miles away was a man who had moved into her village, a man she didn't want to see again—and not just because he'd suggested it would be best that they not run into each other. No, it was more than that.

It was that he was her damned brother-in-law's twin.

She wondered if it might be time to call Lord Roland's lawyer and get his number. Roland had told her that she could, if she liked, call him any time she felt overwhelmed. At the moment, she was tempted to ask him if he wanted the castle back so she could move back into a minuscule flat near Cambridge and hide herself away in the library where she wouldn't be troubled by shades of her sister, reenactment whackos, or the real deal driving a pricey black sports car.

She hadn't seen the real deal in four days, a fact for which she was enormously grateful. Truly. He'd played for the party on Friday, then disappeared. She'd holed up in her castle for the weekend, only opening her door on Saturday to the decorators who'd come to turn it into a Yuletide fantasyland for the next round of parties on the following weekend. She'd exchanged greetings with Peaches on Sunday afternoon as she'd picked her up at the train station, then sent her home while she took the train north. Crashing on a friend's couch had been a diversion, true, but only in that she'd had two days to try to work out the kink in her neck.

She'd spent the past two days working on a paper she was preparing for publication. She had been asked to give a lecture the following morning, then she would head back to dangerous territory to prep for the weekend festivities. She had nothing in front of her for the rest of the day but more time in the library where she could hide out and attempt to face things medieval.

Well, things medieval that had nothing to do with Sedgwick, its environs, or former inhabitants of the keep or their relations.

She briefly contemplated lunch, but decided that could wait. What she really needed was a hot fire and a nap, but that seemed destined to carry her along a path where she wasn't going to want to go. First she would start napping, then she would stop putting her hair up, then she would be spending her days in a ratty bathrobe and fluffy slippers. It just wouldn't end well, she was sure of that.

She pushed away from the wall and started across the courtyard, looking at the stones at her feet, already planning her assault on the library. That was a happy place full of things she was familiar with. It would surely cure what ailed—

She ran into an immobile shape before she realized she wasn't really watching where she was going. She looked up, an apology ready on her lips, along with a word of thanks for the steadying hands on her arms.

Then she froze.

Standing in front of her was John de Piaget.

He released her, but said nothing. She wasn't sure what to do with her hands. She felt one of them flutter up and fuss with the back of her hair self-consciously. She reclaimed control of it and put it and her other one in her pockets where their shaking wouldn't be noticed. It took her a moment before she could even manage to form words.

"What are you doing here?"

He shoved his hands into the pockets of his jeans, though she imagined they weren't shaking. It was such an unthinkingly modern thing to do, she almost lost her breath.

She realized suddenly that the question she wanted to ask wasn't, *What are you doing at Cambridge?* It was, *What the hell are you doing in the twenty-first century?*

Though she was curious about the first as well.

He looked profoundly uncomfortable. "I thought you might be hungry."

She was just sure she hadn't heard him right. Hard on the heels of wondering if she were losing her hearing was wondering how he'd found her and why he'd taken all the trouble to drive up from the village to tell her that he thought she might be hungry.

But, no, he hadn't driven that far. It was Tuesday. He'd been in London, recording things for that rich girl who didn't want him to have a girlfriend. Tess didn't need to check her watch to know it was just after noon, which meant he'd either worked hard or finished early. Or maybe the girl hadn't showed up and he'd been at loose ends. It just wasn't possible that he'd decided that in spite of his desire to never run into her again, he'd just meandered over to Cambridge, seen her stumbling across the courtyard, and decided that maybe she needed something to eat.

It occurred to her that she was frantically searching for things to think about, *anything* to think about besides the fact that just the sight of the man in front of her was enough to simply rock her very foundations. It wasn't his looks, or his background, or the fact that somehow, beyond reason, when she looked at him, she felt as if she'd been waiting her entire life to walk into her great hall and find him waiting for her there, in front of the fire, with a welcoming smile on his face.

It was all of those things put together.

He wasn't wearing a welcoming smile now. She nodded to herself over that, taking it as a sign that she was losing her mind. He didn't fit in at all with what she'd expected for herself. In fact, not only did he not fit in, he was completely wrong for it. She wanted a nice guy she could walk all over. She didn't want one who herded her and protected her and worried about whether or not she'd had lunch.

She had very vivid memories of Montgomery pulling Pippa behind him and reaching for his sword every time he'd smelled danger in the air, but she shoved those aside before she got lost in them.

"Tess?"

She focused on him. "What?"

"Lunch?" he prompted.

She grasped for the fast-disappearing shreds of coherent thought. "I thought you were in London today."

"I was," he said.

"Finish early?" she asked in an effort to deflect attention from the fact that just standing two feet from him was having a ruinous effect on her common sense and ability to not feel faint.

"The brat had a cold," he said, sounding faintly disgusted, "and couldn't be bothered to show up. I provided her with a practice track or two and left about ten."

"And drove here?" she asked, because she had to say something. Honestly, she didn't want to know what he'd done after he'd left the studio. She didn't want to see him. He said she bothered him, but that didn't come close to describing what he did to her.

He looked at her for a moment or two in silence, then nodded. "How did you know I was here?"

He looked slightly uncomfortable. "I saw your sister in the market yesterday."

"And you talked to her because she wasn't me," she said before she could stop herself.

She would have taken the words back if she could have, because she didn't want him to think she cared one way or another what he thought—because she had obviously been thrust back to junior high thanks to some weird quirk in the flux capacitor. She was beginning to think all time travel should be banned for those with any hearts to break.

He had the grace to look slightly . . . something. Sheepish wasn't it, nor was apologetic. He looked as if his conscience might have been giving him the slightest twinge of discomfort.

"Your sister doesn't bother me," he said, finally.

"Give her time," she advised. "She will."

The look he gave her almost singed on her on the spot. "I don't think I'm in any danger there."

Implying, perhaps, that he was in danger where she was concerned.

She almost turned and ran. It would have been the first sensible thing she'd done since she'd met him. Fortunately for her, she was very good at taking things only at face value, so she would assume he simply wasn't moved to lyricism by Peaches, which had no bearing on his opinion of her, and stay right where she was. Well, that and her shoes seemed to have become stuck to the flagstones beneath them.

"Your sister said she wasn't sure if you had either money or a hamper full of snacks," he continued, as if the words were being dragged from him by a team of calm but relentless horses. "And since that was the case, I thought perhaps it would be prudent to see to both."

"I have money," she managed.

He met her eyes. "Then since that's seen to, let's go find you something to eat."

"Is this a date?"

"Saints, nay—er, no," he said quickly. He took a deep breath. "You're too thin."

She clenched her hands in her pockets, stung from the vehemence of his denial. All right, so he didn't want to date her. Apparently he just wanted to drive through horrendous London traffic then lie in wait for her at University merely to torment her. For what reason, she couldn't imagine. It couldn't be because he wanted to date her, because he'd just said he didn't.

"You know," she said, when she thought she could speak without decking him, "a person can cross the line from politely protective to overly critical pretty quickly if one isn't careful."

He chewed on his words for a minute. "I talk too much."

"Yes, that is definitely your problem."

A corner of his mouth quirked up the slightest bit. "Are we going to stand here in the cold and discuss my failings all morning or are you going to let me feed you?"

"I hadn't begun to point out your flaws for your edification—"

She glanced behind him, on the off chance there might be someone standing behind him with a white board and markers, ready to take her list down for her. But there wasn't.

But doom was.

Doom, or maybe catastrophe, or the beginning of the end of John de Piaget's safe, comfortable life in a century not his own. She wasn't sure what to call it. She was even less sure how she was going to keep John's doom, who was dressed quite nattily in trousers and a tweed jacket with a cashmere scarf tossed carelessly about his neck, from blurting out something untoward—and the list of what those things could be was almost as long as her yet-to-be-made list of John's faults.

Or perhaps not. The man walking toward them with a smile was no one any more nefarious than a man whose class she had taken early on in her career at Cambridge. He had been a mentor first, advising her on academics and providing a listening ear for everything else. In time, he had become a friend. In the end he had become something of a brother.

The problem was, he also happened to be the eldest son of Edward de Piaget, the current Earl of Artane.

"Oh, I say, Tess," Stephen de Piaget said, walking up to her with a broad smile. "So good to see you. I've been in London all week, humoring my grandmother, and didn't realize you were here."

Tess would have held out her hands to stop the train wreck before it started, but she couldn't. She could only stand there and have complete sympathy for a deer caught in headlights. She watched, mute, as John stepped aside and turned to make a little triangle of disaster with the three of them. He looked at Stephen and froze.

Maybe he was experiencing that deer thing as well.

Tess looked from Stephen to John and back again, because she couldn't help herself. She also couldn't help but compare John's meeting of Stephen with the one Montgomery had had with his, ah, nephew if the branches of the de Piaget family tree could be twisted in the right way. The only difference between John's reaction and Montgomery's was that John's right hand only twitched instead of reaching for a sword as Montgomery's had done.

Stephen mastered his surprise no doubt thanks to generations of breeding and probably more poker games than he was willing to admit to.

He and John stared at each other, almost mirrors of each other, for several eternal moments before Tess managed to speak.

"Stephen," she said—well, she croaked, really, but she didn't suppose anyone was actually listening to her so how she sounded probably didn't matter. She cleared her throat and tried again. "Stephen, this is John de Piaget. He lives in the village near Sedgwick." She had to take a deep breath to finish. "John, this is a colleague of mine, Stephen, the Viscount Haulton and Lord Etham."

They shook hands like polite gentlemen—again generations of quality breeding and mothers who cared about manners, apparently. John, however, was wearing a look she was quite certain was a decent copy of the one she'd worn when she had first seen him. Odd that she knew him well enough to know that he was doing his damndest not to give any indication of what he was feeling. He suddenly took a step backward, checked his watch, then looked at her gravely.

"I'm afraid I've suddenly remembered an appointment I'd forgotten. If you'll excuse me?"

And without waiting for an answer, he turned and walked away.

Tess watched him go. He wasn't running, but he wasn't dawdling, either. She honestly couldn't blame him. He had come face-to-face with his past, his future, and his present all wrapped up in a man who would someday hold the title his father had initially wrested away from a medieval king of England.

"Good heavens," Stephen breathed.

Tess looked at him, but she could find absolutely nothing to say. She was afraid if she opened her mouth, she just might lose all the control over herself she'd been exercising over the past six weeks. Freaking out in the middle of a courtyard at Cambridge wasn't exactly how she wanted to carry on with her academic career.

Stephen took off his scarf and wrapped it around her neck. "Tess, love, you look as if you've seen a ghost."

"You don't look any better," she said pointedly.

He laughed rather uncomfortably. "Yes, well, I was expecting to see you. I wasn't expecting to see *him*." He took her backpack from off her arm and slung it over his shoulder. "Who was that?"

"Who do you think it was?"

"I'm not sure I want to speculate," he said carefully. "How long ago did you meet him?"

"Last week," she said. "I think."

His face was full of pity. "Ah, my dear," he said, reaching out and gathering her under his arm. "You've been through it, haven't you? Let's go hide in my office, and you'll give me the whole story."

She didn't argue—not that she had the chance to. He shepherded her toward his office without hesitation and without brooking any argument. Those de Piaget men: putting sheepdogs to shame for over eight centuries.

She walked into his office, then sighed a sigh she hadn't realized she'd been holding on to as he shut the door behind him. She let him see her settled in the most comfortable chair he owned, an overstuffed floral thing that he reserved for special company, accepted a cup of tea, then set it aside when she realized she wasn't going to be able to drink it.

Stephen sat down across from her and looked at her critically. "You've lost weight."

"I've been depressed."

"You have cause, I daresay." He rose. "Don't move."

"I don't think I can."

He returned in ten minutes with a full tray of things he badgered her into eating. She smiled and sighed.

"You are truly a good friend, Stephen," she said.

"'Tis fortunate I long ago gave up any designs on you," he said with an answering smile, "else that might have smarted a bit."

"I have no sympathy for you," she said, pursing her lips. "How many dukes' daughters are you dating at the moment?"

"Three," he admitted without a shred of embarrassment. "I'm bored to tears by them all."

"You need someone less stuffy."

"We'll discuss the sad state of my amorous adventures after we've dissected yours," he said, sitting back in his chair and propping his ankle up on his other knee. "Care to tell me a bit about your potential lover I obviously just frightened off?"

She sighed. "Don't make me give you details you already know. Haven't you been nosing around in your family's genealogy? Can't you guess who that was?"

He considered her for a moment or two in silence. "Montgomery's brother would be my first guess, but who's to say? Do you know?"

"I don't." She paused. "Not for certain anyway."

"Haven't you been to the library?" he asked, his face again full of pity.

"You know I haven't."

He only sighed. Then again, he knew what she'd been through. He'd watched her send her sister off to points unknown.

"And I'm not going to," she added.

"Tess, my dear, be sensible about this," he said sensibly. "You know—thanks to that rogue Kendrick—how Pippa's fairy tale goes. She lives a lovely, happy life with a man who absolutely adores her. Her children all survive to adulthood. All you would be searching for were details about Montgomery's brother. His twin, from all appearances."

She blinked, hard. "And despite all that, I don't want to find out something unexpected that I won't like. There, that's a piece of absolute honesty for you."

He rose and put a cashmere throw over her. "I'll go hunt. You sleep."

"I'm not tired."

"You look exhausted. Beautiful, of course, but exhausted. I'll be back in an hour."

Tess closed her eyes and sighed. She supposed she wouldn't sleep, though she was equally sure she needed it.

She woke to late afternoon shadows. She blinked and looked at Stephen, who was sitting across from her reading. The light sitting behind him on the table was lit, casting a warm glow along with the fire over an office fit for an earl. In Stephen's case, he had the academic credentials to merit it.

He looked up and smiled at her. "Feel better?"

"Not at all," she managed, trying to sit up. She groaned and rubbed the back of her neck. "How long was I out?"

"Three hours. I'm sorry. I should have put you somewhere else before you began your beauty sleep."

She shook her head and hid a yawn behind her hand. "What did you find out?"

She realized only as the question was hanging there in the air between them that she wasn't sure she wanted to know.

"Nothing but happy things about your sister," Stephen said gently.

"Really?" she asked carefully.

"Yes, Tess, really," he said, in a bang-up imitation of her accent, which was not far from his, actually. "Love, happiness, and hordes of children wielding sharp swords and no doubt saying things like *groovy* and *far out, dude*."

Tess didn't want to laugh, but she couldn't help herself. "My parents would have been proud, I'm sure."

"No doubt," he agreed. "And if you'll know what else I discovered, it would seem that Montgomery did indeed have a brother, a twin it would seem. His name was John and he died in 1233. He was all of nineteen."

"But he didn't," Tess protested. "He's here. Well, not here, but in our time." She paused. "I'm not imagining that, am I?"

"No, love," Stephen said gently, "I fancy you aren't."

"Then why would they say he's dead?"

"Well, it isn't as if anyone in the past could have said he popped through a time gate and landed in the future, is it?" he asked dryly, then he paused and looked at her with a frown. "I can scarce believe those words came out of my mouth."

"Life is weird."

"You ain't just whistlin' 'Dixie,' sister."

She laughed in spite of herself. "You've handled it all remarkably well."

"So, my dear, have you," he said. He smiled, then his smile faded. "I have the feeling our good John hasn't had such an easy time of it, though. Wouldn't you say?"

"He doesn't seem unhappy," she ventured, "but I honestly don't know him that well. He seems to divide his time between telling me he never wants to see me again and rescuing me. I'm not sure what to think."

"He's no doubt afraid if he draws too close, you might find out his secrets."

She pursed her lips. "He has good reason. If you only knew how many times I've had to bite my tongue already."

Stephen tilted his head and smiled. "The poor lad. I imagine there's a tale there we would both find very interesting, though I imagine you'll have it before I do."

"Not if he keeps running away."

"He keeps coming back, apparently, which is promising." He set his book aside. "Let me take you to supper, and we'll put off thinking about uncomfortable things for the evening. When do you lecture tomorrow?"

"Ten," she said, happily accepting his hand to be rescued out of the chair of no return.

"Then let's distract ourselves with a film as well as supper. There's a French indie piece I've been wanting to see."

"Can't talk any of your girlfriends into going with you?" she teased.

"Darling, if it doesn't involve Drury Lane and my Rolls, they have other plans."

"Do you have a Rolls, Stephen?" she asked with a disbelieving laugh.

"It's actually His Lordship's, stored cunningly in a garage downtown. I trot it out if I'm escorting Granny to tea or fear I'll be photographed with some society lass or other. It makes Father happy to see me carrying on with the trappings of my titles."

"You're such a snob."

He laughed easily. "That's me. Now, where are you staying? I would suggest you remove yourself to my flat, but that might cause eyebrows to raise."

"Don't worry about me," she said. "I'm crashing on Holly's couch."

"I'll drop you there—"

"No," she said quickly. "I need the walk. The nap about did me in."

"I'll call for you in an hour, then," he said. "Does that suit?"

"Only if you're bringing the Rolls."

He laughed and went to hold open his door. "Begone, gold digger."

She paused at the threshold and looked up at him. "Thank you, Stephen."

"What are friends for?" he asked with a heavy sigh.

She smiled and patted him on the cheek before she walked out of his office and down the hallway.

It took her twenty minutes to get to her girlfriend's street. She might have made the front door in twenty-one, but she was rendered momentarily motionless by the sight of a pricey black sports car parked illegally out in front of the gate of that particular house on the row.

She took a deep breath and continued on her way until she had her hand on the gate. She looked at the man who rose immediately from his perch on the front stoop. He walked over and opened the gate for her.

"I'm not stalking you," John began.

"I never thought you were," she said calmly, though she was feeling slightly less than calm. She looked up at him. "Did your appointment go well?"

"My wha—oh, that," he said, shifting. "Um, aye."

Tess almost felt sorry for him. Maybe he'd never come that close before to looking at his past while witnesses watched.

"I called your sister to find out where you were staying," he said.

"Did you?" she asked in surprise. "She doesn't have a listed number."

"Your business does, though, and she was good enough to answer the phone."

She shook her head with a weary smile. "Sorry. I'm not all here today."

He took a deep breath, then clasped his hands behind his back. "Might I take you to dinner?"

"Is this another non-date?"

He started to speak, then shut his mouth and simply looked down at her.

"Am I bothering you again?" she asked. She wasn't sure why she was so hell-bent on pushing him. There was just something terrible about knowing such a devastating secret about someone else yet keeping it to oneself. She wanted to blurt out that she knew it all, that he was no longer alone.

But she imagined if she did, he would hightail it out of there and she would never see him again. If there was one thing she was utterly certain of, it was that John de Piaget would never willingly divulge his secrets.

At the moment, she wasn't sure she wanted him to.

She took a deep breath. "I'm sorry. You drove a very long way to do something nice for me. I would love to come on a non-date with you tonight, but I already have plans."

"Do you?"

"With the Viscount Haulton," she said with as little emotion as she could possibly put into her words. She should have left it at that, but she found that she just couldn't keep her mouth shut. "I'm sure he wouldn't mind if we made it a trio."

John wasn't biting. "How about breakfast?" he countered.

"I have a lecture to give."

"Lunch tomorrow, then."

"I have a train to catch."

"I'll drive you home."

She looked at him seriously. "I thought we weren't going to do this."

"We aren't *doing* anything—"

She might have felt sorry for him that his life was full of nothing but his ridiculously expensive rocket on wheels, his unpleasant gig at a major recording studio, and his appalling good looks that no doubt felled every breathing female within a fifty-mile radius of himself at any moment, but she'd had enough of being good enough to take to lunch and for a ride in his car only so long as she knew her place.

Damn him to hell.

"Good-bye, John," she said curtly.

He caught her as she brushed past him.

She supposed there had been a few things in her life that had just about done her in. Pippa's leaving. The first time she'd put the key in the door of her very own great hall. Seeing John de Piaget on the street in her village.

Having him touch her hand.

Again.

"I'm . . . uncomfortable around nobility," he said, finally.

She just bet he was. She also imagined she could make a very long list of other things that he was uncomfortable around, beginning and ending with committing for any length of time to the same woman. She didn't look at him.

"Stephen and I were going to see a film. Too dark and public for any noble conversation." She paused. "You could take a date. I'm sure you wouldn't have any trouble digging one up."

He didn't move, but he rubbed his thumb over the back of her hand.

Just once.

"No," he said finally.

"No to the film, or no to taking a date?" she asked, because she was an idiot.

"No to taking a date," he said very quietly.

She pulled her hand away, though that about killed her, too. "I gave my word to him, and I don't break my word."

He took a deep breath. "Breakfast, then—nay, you have class. Lunch, then."

She turned to look at him, then. "Just lunch?"

He shot her a look. "A lunch *date*, Tess."

She discovered abruptly that it was much easier to deal with him when he was snarling at her. "That's Dr. Alexander to you, buster," she managed.

He looked at her in surprise, then seemed to realize she was teasing him. Some of the tension went out of him. "As you will, then, *Dr.* Alexander. I'll come listen in on your class, then we'll go find sustenance."

"I don't date students."

His mouth fell open, then he shut it with a snap and his eyes narrowed. "I'm about to let you take the train home."

"I've done it before."

He took a deep breath, then let it out slowly. "I know, but you won't tomorrow. I'll find you tomorrow after your class. And I'll wait now until you are safely inside. And tell that bloody *friend* of yours to pick you up and drop you off right here at your door else he'll answer to me."

"He's a gentleman."

"I imagine he is, damn him to hell," he muttered. He looked at her, then made shooing motions. "Go on, woman. Go inside."

"Are you always this bossy?"

"I'm protective."

"Awfully protective of someone you don't like."

He looked at her evenly. "I never said I didn't like you, Tess."

"You said I bothered you."

"Two entirely different things, love."

She was tempted to call Stephen and tell him to get lost, but she was afraid if she did, she would do something stupid, like throw herself in John de Piaget's arms and tell him that she now understood why her sister had fallen so hard for his brother in such a short time.

"Be nicer to me tomorrow," she advised.

He lifted an eyebrow. "I haven't begun to be nice to you."

And that, she could safely say, was one of the more terrifying things he'd ever said to her. She walked away while she still could, though she made the mistake of turning and looking before she shut the door. John was leaning against the wrought-iron fence with his arms folded over his chest, watching her.

Heaven help her, she was in trouble.

She shut the door before she got into any more of it.

Chapter 8

J^{ohn} walked into a building that was almost as old as he was, then frowned as he looked about him for some indication as to where Tess might be teaching. He supposed it wouldn't be one of the smaller chambers, so he made his way to what looked to be a lecture hall.

He wasn't unfamiliar with places of higher learning. He had, over the course of the past eight years, attended many lectures at various universities. It also wasn't that he hadn't had an excellent education at his father's direction, but there had been, he would readily admit, a few new things added to the body of knowledge since his father's day. Just becoming familiar with even a sketchy overview of all the history he'd missed had taken him a solid year of reading every chance he had.

He had, as the opportunity had presented itself, attended lectures at Cambridge along with many concerts. He was actually rather surprised he'd never seen Tess before. Then again, he likely wouldn't have taken a class from her given his determination to avoid all things medieval.

Ah, how the mighty were fallen, something he was especially cognizant of as he put his ear to the wood of the door, then opened it slowly.

The hall was larger than he would have expected, but that might work to his advantage. He would be able to slip into the back of it without being noticed.

Or, perhaps not. Tess looked at him the moment he closed the door soundlessly behind him, then went back to her lecture. That he could have borne, perhaps. It was looking for a seat at the back of the hall and finding only one empty one that unnerved him. Of course, that could have been because a man had removed his well-used briefcase from it and nodded encouragingly.

The Viscount Haulton, as it happened.

John would have looked for somewhere else to sit, but he'd been caught, and he was nothing if not polite. He supposed he might come to regret that at some point.

So he sat down next to the future Earl of Artane and suppressed the urge to pull his sunglasses down over his eyes. He supposed that would call more attention to himself than he wanted, so he refrained.

And aye, he knew bloody well whom he was sitting next to. He had a BlackBerry and knew how to use it. Not that he'd needed a quick search to figure out who the man was. A good look at him would have told John all he needed to know.

It was a paranormal oddity that would have sent his eldest brother Robin into fits they would have all heard about for months.

"Interested in this sort of thing?" Stephen de Piaget, future sitter on Rhys de Piaget's family seat murmured politely.

John only nodded. He didn't trust himself to speak and not blurt out something he would regret. In truth, it was all he could do simply to remain seated there and project an aura of calm.

He'd known it would happen sooner or later, that encountering someone from home. He'd just never expected it to be in conjunction with the pursuit of a woman he truly wanted nothing further to do with—

He took a deep breath and shook his head mentally at his ability to lie to himself. It wasn't that he didn't want anything to do with her.

It wasn't that at all.

He looked up at her standing behind the lectern, her dark hair pulled back in her usual business chignon, her too-thin frame clothed in a skirt and conservative dark sweater. All she lacked was a pair of librarian's glasses perched on her nose to look the part of a university fixture.

He wondered how old she was. His age, perhaps, or a bit younger. He also wanted to know where she'd been born, what her youth had been like, why she had decided to come to England where she had attracted the gaze of the Earl of Sedgwick, planted herself in that castle, then found her way to his shop where he had stood in the shadows, laid eyes on her, and found himself utterly and completely lost.

He'd never believed in love at first sight.

Before.

He turned away from that thought as quickly as possible and settled for simply watching the girl lecturing up there on the stage as if she truly knew what she was talking about—which, he discovered after only a few minutes, she most definitely did. She was discussing the politics of medieval England as if she'd been privy to the king's councils, dissecting the skirmishes of the time period as if they'd been a chess game and she a master of the art.

Very well, so he hadn't stopped to think that there was a reason she'd earned her degrees at such a young age. He had assumed they were of a less taxing nature. Humanities, perhaps, or music appreciation.

"She's brilliant," Stephen de Piaget said, "isn't she?"

John nodded, because he could readily hear that for himself.

"B.A. in art history," Stephen murmured. "Her masters in Old and Middle English, and her PhD in Medieval Political Thought. I have often told her she was born in the wrong century."

"If she'd been born in medieval times, they likely wouldn't have allowed her any education at all," John said, before he thought better of it.

"Sadly enough, I imagine that's true," Stephen agreed. "Unless perhaps she'd been born to a more enlightened sort of man."

John didn't dare comment. His father had certainly been that sort of enlightened man, for his daughters had been subjected to the same rigorous education his sons had. John merely nodded, hoping Stephen would take the hint and leave him alone. Whatever else they did there at Artane, they apparently still taught the lords' sons manners. Stephen sat back and remained blessedly silent for the rest of the lecture, most of which John didn't hear.

He was too busy trying to breathe normally.

'Twas madness. He had his life, his discreet, private life where he controlled any and all access to anything he could do and anyone he might have been. What he wanted was to go back to that life and—

He had to take another deep breath. Nay, as difficult to admit as it was, he feared going back to that safe life was becoming less possible by the moment. He had stepped out of what was comfortable, not the first day when he'd taken Tess her credit card, but the next day when he'd taken out a business card and written Studio Five's address on the back. Though he wished he could say otherwise, the writing down of that address hadn't been a random thing; it had been a purposeful, deliberate, absolutely deranged decision, but he'd made it just the same.

Because he'd wanted to see her again.

He couldn't blame Tess because he was uncomfortable. He was, after all, the one who'd opened the damned door and pulled her inside. In a manner of speaking.

But that didn't mean he was obligated to sit and converse with Stephen de Piaget any longer than he had to. The moment Tess finished and the applause died off, he rose, turned to Stephen, and inclined his head.

"Thank you for the seat, my lord."

Stephen rose as well. "We missed you at supper last night."

"I didn't want to intrude."

Stephen looked at him from gray eyes that were the mirror of his own. "I have no designs on her, old man."

"Neither do I," John said, though it sounded hollow to his own ears.

Stephen pursed his lips, then leaned in slightly. "Hurt her and I'll kill you."

"Thank you, my lord."

"And stop lying to yourself, you wee git," Stephen said in disgust.

John felt his mouth fall open. Stephen flashed him a brief smile that made him look so much like Robin, John almost flinched. He suffered Stephen's hand clapping him rather more firmly than necessary on his shoulder before Stephen picked up his portfolio and threaded his way through the remaining students to the front of the hall. John watched him shake Tess's hand very professionally, lean in and say something, then start toward the front door of the hall.

John found himself the recipient of a final look he didn't mistake for anything but warning. He nodded in acknowledgment of the threat, then happily watched the last of Stephen disappear through the door. He found himself a bit of wall to lean back against so he could wait until the last of the students had gone and Tess was alone.

He walked to the front whilst she was gathering her notes and stowing them in a backpack that had obviously seen a great deal of use. He would have mistaken her for a student if he hadn't known better. Or at least he would have until he was standing five feet from her and she lifted her head and looked at him.

Then he mistook her for nothing but a goddess.

His first instinct was to bolt. After all, despite what it meant for his future happiness, he had resolved never to entangle himself in any sort of permanent arrangement with a Future girl.

He suppressed the urge to sigh. He certainly wasn't in the market for a wife, but he also couldn't imagine beginning a relationship with the woman in front of him that ended with a casual word and a wave as he walked away. The saints pity him, he was a fool.

He woke to find her standing directly in front of him and he couldn't remember having seen her move.

"Too many deep thoughts, John de Piaget?"

"Only about lunch," he said, desperate not to talk about anything more serious. He stepped back and made her a little bow. "After you, Dr. Alexander."

She frowned at him, but said nothing. He followed her silently up the way between the chairs until they reached the doors. He caught her hand before she reached for one of them, then opened the door for her. She looked up at him.

"Your chivalry is showing."

He took a deep breath. "I'm trying to be nicer about it."

She leaned against the opposite door and looked up at him. "Why?"

He suppressed the urge to say something off-putting, though he supposed it would have been the safer course of action. He ruthlessly squelched the urge to flee. He was—or had been—a knight of the realm with spurs on his heels that hadn't been put there out of pity. He had faced sterner tests than simply being pleasant to a woman who stole his breath every time he looked at her.

But he also couldn't blurt out that he wanted to be nicer to her because he didn't want her to dislike him. He considered a bit longer, then leaned against the opposite doorframe.

"I'm trying," he said, taking another in an endless series of deep, steadying breaths, "because you deserve it."

"But you said you didn't want to see me again."

"I also said I could be a bit of an arse."

She looked up at him, smiled faintly, and walked away. "So you did."

He caught up with her and only had to stop her at one more door before she seemed willing to allow him to ply a bit of chivalry on her.

He saw her into his car, then took a fortifying breath or two as he rounded the boot. Perhaps it was just best to not think about anything at all unless it had to do with lunch.

He avoided the trendiest of the pubs near the university and headed instead for the most rustic. He supposed he was eventually going to give himself away as something he didn't want to if he didn't stop gravitating to things that were old. He found the nearest car park, then surrendered to the thought of dings on a car he should have left at home.

He ploughed through lunch, because there was literally nothing that put him off his food, then looked up and realized Tess was not as enthusiastic about her meal. He stopped with his fork halfway to his mouth.

"Not good?"

"It's delicious."

He frowned. "You're not one of those prissy women who won't eat something that's put in front of them just to impress a date, are you?"

"No, I'm one of those who doesn't like to waste the hard-earned money of men who take me out to lunch," she said shortly, "which is why I didn't order all that much."

"I was going to talk to you about that."

She started to glare at him, then she smiled, apparently quite reluctantly. "Is this the new you who's nicer to me?"

He finished the last pair of bites on his plate, then had a long sip of some nonalcoholic rot before he looked at her.

"I'm not off to a very good start with it, am I?"

"Oh, I don't know," she said with a shrug. "You've held open all the doors for me today."

"That seems a paltry offering."

She leaned back and stirred honey into her tea. "Then what else do you have in mind? The divulging of uncomfortable personal details?"

"Nothing so interesting," he said quickly, lest she think too much about the former. "Let's talk about you instead. How did you come by Sedgwick?"

She lifted a perfectly arched eyebrow. "Thinking to make me an offer for it?"

"Saints, nay," he said without thinking, realizing only as he'd said it that he'd blurted it out in French. He decided without hesitation that the only thing he could do was pretend he hadn't heard himself.

Coming to Cambridge had been a terrible idea.

"You aren't going to leave me here, are you?"

He blinked. "What?"

"Your keys are in your hand."

He realized with a start that they were. He took a deep breath, then let it out whilst he put his keys back in his pocket where they belonged. Then he looked for something to say to explain the action he hadn't realized he'd taken, but latched upon nothing but the truth.

She frightened the hell out of him.

She set her spoon down. "I was at a conference," she said, as if nothing untoward had just happened, "and Lord Roland came up to me after my presentation and asked if I'd like a tour of his castle."

"The bloody lecher," John managed.

She laughed a little. "He was—is, actually—every day of eighty, so I wasn't imagining he had anything lecherous in mind. I did take a friend, if you're curious—"

"I was," he said.

"And the minute I walked inside the front gates—" She took a sip of her tea. "Well, it was love at first sight. It isn't an enormous keep, I suppose, like Artane or Windsor, but I think it's beautiful. I understand Roland's ancestor, Lord Darling, did extensive renovations to it in the nineteenth century."

He flinched at the name of his father's hall, but he supposed she hadn't noticed it. "Did he?" he asked. "Clever man."

"Lord Darling had purchased it from the last of the Sedgwick family," she continued, "and for a song, or so I understand. Wrested the title to it away from the crown, as well. I don't think the seventeenth century had been particularly kind to the inhabitants of the keep. Politics and all that, I imagine."

"I daresay," he said. He couldn't have said he'd done any research into Sedgwick or its inhabitants, but he'd done more than his share of reading about the history that didn't concern his family. He could say with complete sincerity that he'd been more than happy to leap over the centuries and miss several unpleasant things. The Black Death, Henry the VIII, the absolute boredom of Regency manners and mores to name just a few. If he'd had to put on a cravat and limit his activities to hunting and drinking, he would have gone mad.

"And so the next thing I knew," she said. "I had the big brass key to the front door and knew the secret of dropping the portcullises."

"It seems a fitting thing for you to own," he said politely, "given your obvious knowledge of medieval England."

"Thank you," she said, blushing slightly. "I try to be as accurate as possible."

"You were—" He shut his mouth with a snap. "I thought you sounded as if you knew what you were talking about," he amended quickly. "For all I know about it."

"What's your degree in?" she asked.

"Life," he said without hesitation. "I was, ah, privately tutored for most of my youth. By the time I left home, I had other interests than University." He paused. "I read a bit now and then."

"Your time has been well spent, then."

"As has yours."

She laughed briefly. "You're being excessively polite. And don't say I had best enjoy it while it lasts."

He leaned his elbows on the table. He wanted to ask her why she found herself in England, but he suspected it might have been Fate getting involved, but he wouldn't have said that if tongs destined for his tender flesh had been warming in the fire. The thought that he could have ignored his first instinct and thereby passed on the garage, or she could have decided that French literature had been more to her taste and wound up in Paris—

He realized she was holding out her hand.

He reached out to take her hand only to find he was holding his keys in that hand. He met her eyes.

"Old habits die hard."

"Have you bolted often in the past?"

He opened his mouth to tell her it was none of her business what he'd done in the past, but the words disappeared almost before he could think them—certainly long before he even thought to blurt them out. He looked at his keys, then very deliberately put them into her hand. He folded her fingers around them, rested his hand on hers for an excruciatingly brief moment, then pulled away before he did something monumentally stupid. He wasn't sure what it would have been, but he supposed the list of possibilities was very long indeed.

"We could go," she said, very quietly. "If you need to."

"Nay," he said quickly and perhaps with a bit more force than necessary. "Nay," he repeated, then realized he was again falling back into habits he'd thought he'd long since rid himself of. Third bloody time was a charm, or so they said. "No," he managed. "I am well."

"Sure."

He looked at her. "You bother me."

"I'm not trying to."

"I'm not complaining, though that might not be as clear as it should be."

She smiled and put his keys on the table well out of his reach. "I won't ask you anything else personal today, which I'm sure will just glue you to your seat. Have I told you that I have a beauty queen for a sister?"

He had to agree that she hadn't, but he invited her to do so at length. He spent the rest of an hour, when he could do something besides stare at her by the light from the window and wonder why it hurt his heart to do so, asking her about herself. He heard tales of her five sisters, her parents who had stopped just short of tie-dyeing themselves, and her time at her aunt's house where she had learned to pull weeds with vigor and love the austere self-discipline her aunt distilled upon everything within her reach.

"Why England?" he asked finally, because she had his keys and he thought he could bear to hear how close he had come to never having clapped eyes on her.

"Castles," she said without hesitation. "Grooves in stairs where scores of feet have gone up and down them millions of times. Rocks that are covered with history."

"And the grubby leavings from fingers of Year Five boys on school outings," he said with a snort.

She smiled. "You're a cynic."

"Realist."

"Why are you in England?"

He blinked. "Because I am an Englishman."

She leaned her head back against the pub bench. "You are full of national pride."

"Do you have none?" he asked.

"Oh, I do," she answered easily. "I'm a Yank, through and through."

"Despite your rather crisp consonants and lovely vowels."

She smiled, one of the truer smiles he'd ever had from her. "Thank you. I've tried to mitigate the effects of a brush with a Midwest twang."

He felt himself relaxing—an alarming realization in and of itself—and thought that perhaps he shouldn't relax too much. There was no way to predict what sorts of perils he would plunge himself into if he did. He looked at his watch. "Shall we go?"

"If you like."

He didn't, but he *was* a realist. Too much more time sitting companionably with her and he would be letting things slip he didn't want to.

He walked with her out to the car, took his keys from her and saw her inside, then drove her to her mate's house where she collected her things. He put them in the boot of his car with his own he'd packed earlier from his hotel, then slid in under the wheel and was very grateful he was driving and not looking forward to several days' worth of travel to get to Sedgwick.

He was also happy to do nothing but drive until they were on the motorway. It never ceased to amaze him how easily a car with a bit of horsepower could accelerate to speeds he never would have dreamed of in his youth. More amazing still that he could be the master of that car and those speeds.

The Future was an amazing place.

And at the moment, it was made all the more pleasant by the addition of a beautiful woman sitting next to him, though that wasn't what drew him to her. It was simply that she was Tess and there was something about her that he couldn't look away from. She wasn't what he'd expected, but he realized she could have been nothing else.

He grasped quickly for the last shreds of his common sense. The truth was, it was too soon, he had too many secrets, she was too fragile—

Nay, the last wasn't true. She looked fragile, but he suspected that underneath that exterior that had recently suffered some sort of shock, she was tough as spring beef.

He wondered what sort of shock it had been.

Still, she looked tired. And she was too thin. He didn't mean the skeletal emaciation that he saw in films and on the covers of gossip rags. She was too thin for her frame, something he suspected came from whatever shock she'd endured. When he'd said as much the day before, he hadn't meant to be critical; he'd simply wanted to remedy the situation.

Which had driven her out on a non-date with the future Earl of Artane.

Lesson learned. He would keep his bloody mouth shut the next time.

The afternoon was waning by the time he walked Tess to her front door. He wanted to take her hand, or pull her into his arms, or say something meaningful. As it was, he could only stand there and look at her.

"Thank you for the day," she said simply. "It couldn't have been convenient to spend the night in Cambridge."

"It was nothing," he said with a shrug. But it wasn't nothing; it was something and far more of something than he was comfortable with.

"The gate's open."

He blinked. "What?"

"You're halfway toward it as it is. I just thought you might want to know it wasn't keeping you here."

He blew his hair out of his eyes. "I'm not sure we should see each other very often," he said bluntly, before he thought better of it. "Just to keep this thing from moving too quickly."

"This thing?"

He suppressed the urge to blush. "Perhaps I am venturing where I shouldn't have. I have presumed that you wanted to see me again, which perhaps you don't."

"I never said that," she said mildly. "And those were very nice rhetorical flourishes you just offered—no, don't glare at me." She attempted a smile. "It's been a very long fall and I'm not quite myself."

"Hence my desire to feed you at every turn."

Her smile faded. "Is that all you want to do with me, John de Piaget?"

"No," he said shortly, "it unfortunately isn't, which is why I think we shouldn't see each other very often."

"What's your definition of often?"

"Every day."

"That *is* often."

He didn't bother to say that by every day, he meant all day, every day. No sense in frightening off the poor wench unnecessarily.

"You're very comfortable dictating the terms of things," she remarked casually.

He clasped his hands behind his back. "Then you dictate."

"No," she said slowly, "I think I like it better when you do. Very chivalrous."

"And despotic."

"I wasn't going to say that," she said with a very small smile, "but yes, that, too. My oldest sister would be appalled by it, but I don't think I mind. What do you think?"

He thought that if he had to talk to her much longer, he would either attempt to kiss her senseless or drop to his knees and beg her to be his—neither of which he could do at present. He backed down a step.

"I think we should see each other next week, then." He said that because it sounded sensible. "On Friday."

"If you like."

He started to nod, then realized that was well over a week away. He frowned. "Thursday, perhaps."

"That's good, too."

"You could ring me sooner, if you like."

"I don't call boys," she said primly.

He shot her a look before he could stop himself. "I am not a boy."

She smiled. "Well, yes, I'd noticed, but I'm still not going to call you."

"Then I'll ring you. On Wednesday."

"Fine."

He grasped firmly at the shreds of his good sense, nodded briskly, then turned and walked down her handful of steps. He stopped on the courtyard proper, then turned and looked back up at her.

"Unless you're not doing anything on Friday." He paused. "This Friday."

"I have a reenactment group coming," she said. "You're welcome to come, if you like. If you're willing to put on tights. And bring a sword."

"Bloody hell, woman," he said, with no small bit of alarm, "what next? Curly-toed shoes?"

"Have any?"

"I most certainly do not."

She smiled. "Do you have my number?"

"I had it from your sister." He would have smiled, but he was altogether too unnerved to. "I thought it prudent. And I won't be using it until next Wednesday."

"I thought you said this Friday."

"Not if tights are involved."

She only smiled faintly.

He nodded briskly, then turned and walked away while he still could.

Wednesday. He would wait to ring her until Wednesday because any sooner than that was a way in which lay madness. Besides, he had things to do. Important things. Things that made him comfortable and anonymous and nothing out of the ordinary.

He could hardly wait to get back to them.

He supposed he was very fortunate that Stephen de Piaget wasn't there to point out to him that he was lying to himself.

He put his head down and left the castle whilst he still could.

Chapter 9

T ess checked her watch for the dozenth time that day, but time wasn't moving any more quickly because of it. It was, she could say with absolute certainty, the longest Friday she'd ever spent over the course of her life. She had already trudged through most of the afternoon working with her caterers, though that had perhaps been unnecessary. They knew the drill perfectly. The decorations had been done the previous weekend, so all that had been left for her to do was stand around uselessly, wishing she had something to think about besides what she shouldn't be.

He should have been easily forgotten, that John de Piaget. After all, he spent most of his time trying to get out of having anything to do with her. She fully expected him not to call her before Wednesday at the earliest, which meant she was safe for the next several days. She could forget about him and simply deal with the raucous crew set to arrive within the hour, and the truth was, she was going to have her hands full with them.

They had been the first large group she'd handled after she'd taken over the castle. The experience had been a bit like being thrown into the middle of a pitched battle. She'd survived the night, then spent the next day cleaning food off the walls and unearthing undergarments from behind tapestries.

When the club president had showed up that afternoon to collect things inadvertently left behind, she'd threatened never to let them through her gates again if she didn't have an apology letter bearing all their signatures in her hands within the week. Apparently they had enjoyed themselves enough that the embarrassment of obliging her in that had been worth it. The bash she'd thrown for them during the summer had proved to be manageable enough that she'd agreed to an early Christmas party for them.

At least there would be enough controlled chaos to keep her mind focused on her work and not on someone she shouldn't have been thinking about.

She wondered if she should have gone to the village earlier, just to pick up a few things at the market. Fortunately, she'd considered the quite likely possibility of running into John, which had seemed dangerous enough that she'd sent Peaches instead, who hadn't returned with any reports of any John sightings.

Tess had been relieved. Obviously he was a man of his word. He had said he wouldn't call her until the following week, and he'd obviously meant it.

She would have walked to the nearest tapestry-encrusted wall and banged her head against it to dislodge her normal good sense, but she'd just redone her hair. No sense in causing any stray curls to escape before the party started.

"What are you doing?"

She jumped a little, then put her hand over her heart as she turned around to see Peaches standing behind her, wearing a frown. "What do you mean?"

"I mean what are you doing? You're just standing there, holding a pencil."

"I was checking my list," Tess said weakly.

"You're not holding a list."

Tess realized that was true. She tucked her pencil behind her ear. "It's in my head."

Peaches reached up and pulled the pencil free. "You're losing it."

"You know, Peach, I think I just might be."

Peaches looked around the great hall, then back at Tess. "It's still empty, so why don't we have a little rest until your guests arrive?"

Tess realized that she didn't have any choice given that Peaches was pulling her toward her solar. First Stephen, then John, then Peaches. If she hadn't been so overwhelmed, she would have put her foot down. Repeatedly. Which she would do the moment she managed to catch her breath.

Peaches sat her down in a chair in front of the fire in her solar, then sat down in the chair facing her. "I haven't talked to you in almost a week. Why don't you take this opportunity to spill your guts?"

"Do I have to?" Tess asked wearily. "Can't you guess?"

"Probably," Peaches said, "but I think it would do you good to verbalize it."

"Turning to counseling, now?"

"It comes with the territory," Peaches said dryly. "People tend to let loose while pitching things languishing in the bottom of their sock drawers."

Tess couldn't help but smile. She opened her mouth to comment only to find she didn't know where to start.

It wasn't John, but it was him—and everything else. Her life had just turned out to be so much more devastating than she'd ever imagined it would be. She had intended to simply have her little piece of paper stating to the world that she knew all about medieval life. She'd never imagined that she would draw breath every day knowing that her younger sister was living that life, or that she herself might be actually, well, non-dating a man who had grown up in that time period.

"Life is weird, huh?" Peaches said gently.

"I don't want to have anything to do with him," Tess blurted out before she thought better of it. "He's not in my plans."

"I think you're in his," Peaches said mildly, "as casually as he might be going about it."

Tess jumped up and began to pace. "*You* go date him."

"He's not my type," Peaches said airily. "Too organized and bossy. I want a bearded guru who eats only raw food and has a potting shed that needs my expertise. Messy sock drawer is optional."

"No, what you want is a knight in shining armor to come sweep you off your feet," Tess said grimly, sitting back down, "which is absolutely what you deserve for your life of goodness and the miserable past week of putting up with me."

"Well," Peaches admitted, "that might do. But since I don't want *your* medieval lord down the street, you can date him freely and know that he looks on me like a sister. Which, as it happens, I am."

"And just what am *I* supposed to do with him?" Tess asked, throwing up her hands in despair. "Tell him what I know and watch him run? If he finds out our little sister is married to his little brother eight centuries in the past, he'll go and never look back. What do I do then?"

Peaches shook her head slowly. "I don't have a life plan for this kind of thing."

"Tell me she's happy," Tess managed.

"Pippa?" Peaches asked in surprise. "Of course she's happy."

"But she doesn't have us," Tess protested.

Peaches reached out and held her hands, hard. "Tess, she wouldn't have had us forever anyway. You'll get married; I'll get married. We'll start families of our own and make our own lives. I don't imagine we would have all been living here together in your gloriously restored castle forever."

"But we could have had reunions," Tess said, blinking back tears she hadn't realized she'd been close to shedding. "Girls' weekends on the beach. Shopping in Paris." She shook her head. "I don't know how you're dealing so well with this. I've been so wrapped up in my own grief—"

"Don't be an idiot," Peaches said gently. "I'm fine and you will be, too."

Tess took a deep breath. "Some days I think so. Other days, like today, I'm just not sure I will be. And every time I look at that man, I remember it all over again."

Peaches leaned back in her seat. "Tess, just take it as it comes. Date that gorgeous John de Piaget and wait for the time to come when you can talk to him. He's without his siblings, too, as you would remember if you could think clearly. He might feel better about his own life if he knew you were going through the same thing."

"Maybe he doesn't know he could go back," Tess whispered.

Peaches looked at her steadily. "Do you want to be the one to tell him?"

Tess shook her head. "I'm a coward."

"We could just make sure he was hanging around when we send Pippa another care package. I'm sure he'd enjoy watching us send it off into thin air."

Tess didn't like to think about that. She and Peaches had pushed a trunk through the time gate at the end of Sedgwick's bridge before Tess had sent Peaches back to the States. She'd been so shocked by the sight, she'd almost followed it into the . . . well, *void* was the only word she'd been able to come up with. She'd put up a historical marker over the spot the next day. Not a permanent one. Just one big enough to discourage too close a look unless one really wanted a quick trip to the past in which case the marker could be easily dislodged from its base.

And to think she'd assumed living with her parents would be the weirdest thing she would ever have to put up with.

"Just get through the evening," Peaches advised. "I can hold down the fort for you next week if you want to just get in your car and drive. Unless John is planning on monopolizing your time."

"He doesn't want to see me for a week. I don't think he wants this thing getting out ahead of him."

"Thing," Peaches echoed. "Is that what he calls it?"

"I think that was stretching his powers of commitment as it was."

Peaches laughed a little. "You can hardly blame him. The man is harboring appalling secrets and probably thinks you'd look at him as if he'd lost his mind if he dared share them." She looked at Tess calculatingly. "We could go on a double date. I could dig up some nice guy from the village."

"Or Stephen de Piaget."

Peaches pursed her lips. "When hell freezes over."

Tess blinked in surprise. "What happened? I thought you two—"

"No," Peaches said briskly. "And I don't want to talk about it." She rose and walked toward the door. "I have a couple of phone calls to make. You really should check your mail. Never know what's piling up."

As long as it wasn't long, rambling letters from Cinderella Alexander, beauty queen extraordinaire, wanting to come back and play Queen of the Fairies in her castle, Tess was happy to deal with it. Later, after the evening had been successfully navigated.

She watched her sister thoughtfully as she disappeared out the solar door, then set her questions aside for when she could wring the answers out of her more comfortably.

She took a deep breath, then walked out into the hall to find that the outriders for the evening's marauders had already arrived.

It was going to be a very long evening.

Two hours later, she realized she had grossly underestimated just how long an evening it would turn out to be. She'd reminded the president of the group that they were still on probation—their sedate solstice celebration aside—which seemed to have made an impression on most of them. The only trouble brewing seemed to be the well-dressed faux lords who were lingering just a bit too long near the punch bowl, which led her to believe that someone had spiked it already.

There were just some people who had known each other too long and dressed in tights once too often.

She supposed she might save all the ladies in the hall the necessity of keeping a few randy lads at bay if she saw to the refilling of that punch bowl. She pushed away from the tapestry she'd been gingerly leaning against and walked into the passageway leading to the kitchen only to feel someone take her hand and spin her around.

Her first thought was that it was John, but he wouldn't have manhandled her that way. She found herself abruptly backed up against the wall by a too-buff, sword-bearing blond man who had, unfortunately, not had too much to drink. He pinned her to the wall with his hands against her shoulders.

"You," he said distinctly, "are a very beautiful woman."

"And you," she said, just as distinctly, "are going to be without the use of your testicles if you don't take your hands off me immediately."

He grinned. "I like my women feisty."

"And I like my men chivalrous," she said shortly, "and you don't qualify."

"Give me a chance," he said, bending his head toward hers.

Tess tried to knee him in the groin, but he was, unfortunately, as practiced in the art of groping unwilling women as he was stupid.

Briefly.

She found him picked off her like a repugnant tick and held in the middle of the passageway by a fist grasping the back of his tunic.

"I say," a voice said with the utmost politeness, "I believe the lady said she wasn't interested."

Her would-be attacker squirmed and swore until he got a good look at who was holding him. Then he stopped, probably because the expression on John de Piaget's face was not nearly as friendly as his words had been. Tess felt a little faint, and she was the one being rescued.

"Just a friendly little embrace," the blond reenactment member squeaked.

"Well then, friend," John said coolly, "let me help you understand something that I'm sure will be of great benefit to you in your future *embraces*. When the lady in question threatens to geld you, it means she isn't interested. At that point, a gentleman apologizes, withdraws, and looks inward to discover what it is about himself that women find so repugnant. You, I believe, have many hours of such reflection to look forward to."

"Now, wait a minute—"

John released him and merely folded his arms over his chest, obviously content to wait for his opponent to make the first move.

Blondie blustered a bit, apparently thought twice, then quickly slunk off back to the great hall. Tess let out a shuddering breath.

"Thank you."

John turned a frown on her. "Are you hurt?"

She shook her head. "A little rumpled, but otherwise unharmed." She took a deep breath and looked at him. "I didn't expect to see you tonight."

He pursed his lips. "Wednesday was too far away."

"And yet you don't sound particularly happy to see me."

He took a deep breath, then let it out slowly. "It isn't that. I'm simply wrestling with my desire to go beat the bloody hell out of that lad for manhandling you."

"I would suggest a refreshing glass of punch, but I think it's the problem."

He lifted an eyebrow. "I would say your friend had already sampled more of it than was polite, but I don't think he'd been drinking."

"Too much time in tights."

"I didn't want to say as much, but you might have it aright." He reached out and tucked a strand of hair behind her ear, then dropped his arm quickly, as if he'd just realized what he was doing and regretted it. "Perhaps we should go police the punch bowl. Unless you'd rather dance."

"Can you dance?"

"It comes along as part of the lute playing." He nodded toward the hall. "Let's see if it will serve as a decent distraction for the both of us and save your would-be suitor my fist in his gut."

She didn't protest when he tucked her hand into the crook of his elbow, just as she'd seen Montgomery do a dozen times with her sister.

A devastating realization, actually.

She tried to concentrate on other things. She stole a look at John from out of the corner of her eye, grateful somehow that he wasn't wearing a sword or she might have mistaken him for someone else of a medieval vintage. She would have closed her eyes in self-defense, but she might have missed the view and that would have been a darned shame.

He was probably six foot three, maybe a bit taller, and somehow that height added to those broad shoulders added to long legs added to protectiveness he just couldn't seem to get past all combined to make her feet absolutely delicate when she was anywhere near him. She didn't consider herself particularly fragile, but she had to admit that there was something rather lovely about standing next to a man who made her feel that way.

"Oh, Miss Alexander!"

Tess sighed and turned to look at one of the catering staff who was running after her. "Yes, Karen?"

"You're needed," the girl said, looking at John with undisguised admiration. "Briefly."

John put his hand over hers. "I'll go guard the punch bowl."

She nodded and forced herself not to watch him walk away. She followed Karen back to the kitchen, solved a problem that didn't need her approval, then walked back up the way to the hall, hoping she wouldn't emerge to find it in a shambles.

Fortunately, it was simply full of dancers. She didn't see John immediately, which sent a little thrill of unease through her. She realized, however, that he was still there as she walked out into the middle of her hall, then turned to look at one of the hearths.

He was waiting for her, visible now and again when the sea of dancers parted.

She could hardly catch her breath. She'd watched her sister Pippa find herself facing Montgomery in exactly the same way, in the midst of a party of medieval reenactment aficionados—and watched the look on her sister's face.

The thought of it about did her in.

"Tess? Shall we dance?"

She took a deep breath, nodded, then put her hand in his and walked with him into the fray. She would have asked him, after a few minutes, what he thought of not only the music but the steps, but she was too distracted by the calluses on his right hand. Maybe they came from working on cars. Maybe they came from working with a sword.

She thought about that while she did her best to remember where to put her feet. She also thought about the fact that even though John was wearing the simplest garb there, he was the one who looked like a lord's son.

For some reason, that thought caught her heart and wrenched it, hard.

She lasted through three dances, three very formal, non-touchy, medieval dances before she looked over and saw Peaches watching her from a spot near the punch bowl. She looked away only to have her eyes full of John who looked so much like Montgomery that it left her with the unwholesome feeling that the future was again colliding with the past—and not just the past of two months ago when Montgomery and Pippa had danced in her hall, but the *past* past where Pippa and Montgomery had no doubt spent innumerable evenings dancing with each other just as she was dancing with John.

She shivered. The whole evening had become full of things she didn't want to think about. If she hadn't taken the castle, Pippa wouldn't have come to England, then Pippa wouldn't have fallen into the moat and into Montgomery de Piaget's arms, Pippa wouldn't be trapped in the Middle Ages, and she herself wouldn't be looking at her medieval extended relation who was loitering in the wrong century, but she was finding that she increasingly didn't want him to be anywhere else.

"I need a breath of air," she said, gulping down unwholesome amounts of the same. "I'll be right back. Make yourself at home."

He only frowned.

She shot Peaches a look she knew Peaches understood completely, then walked through the kitchens and out into the stables. She flicked on the lights, then paused in front of an empty box. She wasn't one to weep, but she was fast coming to the realization that she might not manage to avoid it.

She felt John come to a stop next to her. She wanted to offer a litany of excuses as to why she was so close to losing it, but she supposed that wasn't necessary. She took another gulp of damp, chilly December air, then gestured to the empty stall.

"Lord Roland kept horses," she managed. "I imagine all the lords of Sedgwick kept horses." She looked at him. "Do you like horses?"

"Love them," he said, then he bit his tongue. He was silent for a moment or two, then sighed. "I had one in my youth. I don't have room for any now, of course."

"I do, but I wouldn't know what to do with them," she said. "They're awfully big. And they bite."

He leaned against the stall and looked at her gravely. "Only if they're mistreated. Or you get your fingers in their mouths."

She nodded and attempted a smile. Unfortunately, and to her horror, she found that her eyes were filling with tears. She would have tried to brush them away as they fell, but she didn't want to draw attention to them. She looked at him and took a deep breath. "I don't cry very often."

"I was late in my rescue."

She shook her head and managed a small laugh. "It wasn't that, and it wasn't you—it *isn't* you." Well, it was him, but it wasn't as if she could tell him that. She looked up at the ceiling until she had control over herself. "I'm fine."

"So I see," he said. "What's bothering you, then, if it isn't my tardy rescue?"

"I'm supposed to tell you all my secrets yet have none of yours in return?" she asked with an attempt at levity.

His expression was grave. "I don't have any secrets."

She would beg to differ later, when she wasn't still reeling from dancing with him inside. She also wasn't about to tell him anything he wanted to know. It was one thing to talk to Peaches, who had so generously put off her own descent into grief so Tess could go first; it was another to describe her broken heart to the man who was so unwittingly mixed up in it all.

She wondered how his parents and siblings had managed to lose him to a different time, never knowing if he were alive or dead, never having even so much as a clue as to his happiness or lack thereof.

"I'm fine," she repeated, ignoring the way her eyes were still leaking. It was the remnants of hay in the barn, she was sure of that. Obviously she was allergic to horses and hadn't realized it over the years.

He reached up and moved a strand of hair back from her forehead. "Does Peaches know what ails you?"

She nodded. "She lived it with me."

"Lived what, Tess?" he asked, his expression even more serious than before. "What befell you?"

It was such a formal, old-fashioned way to put it, she almost smiled.

Or she would have, if she hadn't been so close to breaking down. She didn't know him, was sure she shouldn't get close to him, knew her heart wouldn't survive whatever path they walked together, but she couldn't seem to keep herself from blurting out the truth.

"I lost my younger sister."

He flinched. It was the last thing she saw him do before he reached out and pulled her into his arms.

"Is she dead?" he asked quietly.

That was the exact thing she just couldn't bring herself to think about. She wasn't even sure how to answer it. She knew that eight centuries in the past Pippa was still alive, but only if they were living in a sort of parallel universe, which she wasn't entirely sure wasn't the case. But if she was to look at things on a time line, then yes, Pippa was most certainly . . .

She let out a shuddering breath and nodded.

"Ach, you poor gel," he said, rubbing his hand over her back. "I'm so sorry."

She clutched the back of his tunic, which seemed altogether

too nice for a cheesy reproduction thing, and forced herself to get hold of herself. She wasn't a weeper, as a rule, preferring to look at things in a logical, rational manner and deal with them just as logically, but it had been a rather trying autumn. And she had held it together—poorly—when she likely should have wept with Peaches and gotten it out of her system. Which she would do, when she'd gotten over stifling her current batch of bitter tears.

That Montgomery de Piaget better have made her sister unbelievably happy, or she was going to go back in time, march up to his castle's front gates, and punch him in the nose.

John held her for several very long minutes in silence without a single complaint as she fought to keep herself from completely losing it. Maybe it would have been better if she had bawled her eyes out. Unfortunately, all she could do was stand there and shake.

"You know," he said finally, continuing to stoke her back, "you might weep fully, if you cared to."

She shook her head and pulled away—with a great deal of regret, but she didn't think she should accustom herself to being in his arms. It was hard to tell when he would want to run the other way again. Better that she at least put a little distance between them while she still could.

"I'm okay," she gulped. "Really."

He frowned. "There are times when it is understandable to shed a tear or two. I wouldn't think less of you."

She shook her head and put on a happy smile. Well, she attempted to put on a happy smile. She imagined it looked more like a grimace, but John was apparently too polite to say anything.

"Don't need to," she said firmly. "This sort of thing happens all the time and people get over it. Which I will do. And speaking of things I should do, I should probably go work on my face."

"If you work on your face any more, Tess Alexander," he said seriously, "I won't be able to look at it." He put his arm around her shoulders. "We should also rescue your sister from the louts inside, I daresay. I would like to believe your suitor was the only imbecile in the hall tonight, but I fear that isn't the case."

She would have smiled, but she realized something that had seemed just a little strange. "You're speaking French, you know."

If she hadn't been watching for it, she supposed she wouldn't have noticed that very brief look of panic that flashed in his eyes. It was gone immediately, which led her to believe he'd spent years—probably the last eight of them—perfecting the ability to listen to the most outrageous things and not react to them.

"Private tutors," he said.

The liar.

Tess shivered, and it wasn't precisely from the cold.

He tugged her—well, shepherded her along because he was a de Piaget lad, after all—back toward the hall. "How much longer are we to be enjoying these reenactment delights?"

"They're booked at least until midnight," she said. She looked up at him. "Sorry about the musicians."

"I've heard worse," he said politely. "I don't suppose you would care to dance a bit more."

"I've exhausted my repertoire of dances I know," she admitted, "but I think I can fake others if you don't mind a bruised toe or two."

He smiled, just the slightest bit. It almost knocked her over.

"'Tis a small price to pay for the view."

"The hall is lovely," she agreed.

"I wasn't talking about the hall."

She felt her mouth fall open, then she shut it with a snap. "Knock that off," she said with an uncomfortable laugh. "I think I like you better when you're snarling."

"Do you?" he asked, tilting his head just the slightest bit.

She walked away from him. "You bother me."

He caught up to her without effort. "In a good way or a bad way?"

She looked up at him. "Do you really want to know?"

He lifted his eyebrows briefly. "I'm not sure."

"I didn't think you would be. Let me repair the damage, then I'll dance with you. And now I won't feel bad if I step on your toes."

"It's why I wore boots."

She gaped at him only to feel the need to do so again when she saw his eyes were twinkling. He had a dimple, the lout.

She was in big trouble.

The next time he suggested they not see each other for a week, she was going to hold him to it.

Chapter 10

John leaned back against the wall in Sedgwick's great hall and found himself assailed by thoughts he couldn't seem to fight off.

First, it was altogether too ironic to find himself in a hall he'd frequented in his youth only to find himself in that same hall several hundred years later, no longer in his youth but dressed in about the same sort of clothing. All he was missing was his sword, but he didn't need it to, as they said in the Colonies, take care of business.

Second, there was something poetically just about finding himself in said hall because of a woman he had tried his damndest to forget.

Unsuccessfully.

He had danced with her as often as she would humor him, but for the most part, he'd simply stood with his back against the wall—a habit from his past he apparently hadn't managed to break, he supposed—and watched her. Watched *over* her, rather. She was an excellent lecturer, but he realized she was just as good at her current sort of thing. Perhaps managing college lads had been of more use to her than she could have anticipated. She moved effortlessly between keeping a few of the more exuberant knights under control and discussing more academic things with an ever-changing collection of admirers. John gave himself the task of managing the less well behaved of those pretend lords.

The evening should have seemed endless, but somehow it didn't. John supposed that was to be expected when one was spending most of his time trying to keep the past from intruding on the future.

He wondered, absently and after almost four hours of trying to fight off the speculation, who had taken over Sedgwick after Denys's death. Boydin, no doubt, unless he'd been done in by one of his siblings. No one from Artane would have been stupid enough to venture south and sentence himself to the place for the rest of his life. He was actually rather glad he didn't feel free to sneak off to Tess's library, else he might have been tempted to wander casually into it and do a little thumbing through her historical texts.

Nay, it was probably better to stay where he was.

He spent the next hour suppressing his yawns. He was, he could admit without shame, enormously glad when the last of the revelers had been escorted out the front door. Tess went off to see to the caterers, leaving him sprawled in a chair across from Tess's astonishingly pretty sister.

Whom he wasn't at all interested in, it should have been noted.

"It was nice of you to stay," Peaches said, smothering a yawn herself.

He wasn't at all sure how to respond. Did he tell her that there was no way in hell he would have trusted her and her sister to lock up properly, or did he tell her that he'd met lads like that blond fool before and hadn't wanted Tess to enjoy a second encounter with him?

"Where did you get your clothes?" Peaches asked with another yawn. "Costume shop?"

"Yes," he said simply.

"It's surprising how many there are here in the area, isn't it?"

"Very," he agreed.

She looked at him, then laughed a little. "Get talked out already tonight?"

He opened his mouth to protest, but didn't even manage a

single syllable before Peaches was popping up energetically to her feet.

"I'm teasing," she said with another smile. "Thanks for coming."

He could only nod and watch as she walked away, presumably to find her sister. He turned in his chair to have a better view of them as they met at the back of the hall. It was a little startling to see them standing there, mirrors of each other yet so unalike. No wonder he and Montgomery had received so many of the same sort of looks, never mind that those looks had usually been accompanied by some gesture to ward off evil.

Times had changed.

He rose when he realized Tess was coming toward him. She waved him back down into his seat and took the one across from him. He realized that he didn't much care for that, but he thought that moving his chair next to hers might have been a bit much.

She looked impossibly tired, which led him to believe the evening had been a bigger drain on her than he'd suspected.

"Have you eaten?" he asked.

"I can't remember."

He glanced at the front door to find it locked, then rose and reached out to pull her to her feet. He kept her hand in his and led her toward the kitchens.

And he tried to ignore that he felt as if he'd done the like countless times before.

He saw her seated at the worktable, then put a kettle on for tea. He rummaged about in an enormous refrigerator, but the best he could do was eggs. A traditional English breakfast it would be, then.

He cooked, then looked over his shoulder to make sure she hadn't fallen asleep on him. She hadn't. She was watching him with what a duller man might have suspected was tolerance.

Affection was, he supposed, something to hope for as time wore on.

"I could do that," she said.

"I imagine you could," he said, "but I'll do it instead."

"Bossy even in the kitchen."

He prepared two plates, then carried them over and set one down in front of her. "I like to be consistent."

She smiled, then looked at what was in front of her. "I think I'm too tired to eat this, but it looks wonderful."

"Force yourself."

"Pass the chilled toast, then."

He smiled and did so, then badgered and bullied her until she'd finished what he'd made for her. He washed up, put the Aga to bed for the night, then fetched his coat off the hook by the door and Tess from off her chair. He took her by the hand, then stopped in front of the fire in her great hall.

He handed her his coat. "I'll check the doors."

"They're fine—" She shut her mouth. "Don't say it."

He shot her a look. "I *will* check the doors of the keep, Tess, to make certain you're safe."

"You said it."

"You seem to need the reminder."

She only watched him, silent and grave.

He did a more thorough job of it than usual, only because he didn't trust any of the blighters who'd been lingering in her great hall. Apart from one tower door being propped open by a loose stone—something he found himself rather alarmed by—the rest of the hall seemed not to have suffered overmuch from the assault. He went so far as to look under what he assumed was Tess's bed, reminded himself that offering to sleep on the floor in front of her fire would be a very odd thing to do, then jogged down the stairs and out into the great hall.

Tess was asleep in the chair in front of the fire.

He stood in the middle of that great hall for far longer than he should have, allowing himself to entertain thoughts he shouldn't have for far longer than was wise. He never would have imagined during the last time he'd stood in the middle of Sedgwick's great hall with a sword at his side and his only method of transportation being his mount that he might one day be standing there in far different garb, admiring a woman who loved what he'd grown to manhood surrounded by but had no idea how well acquainted he was with the same.

Life was very strange.

He walked over to the fire and squatted down in front of her. He put his hand over hers, trying not to startle her. She opened her eyes, blinked, then looked at him.

She smiled.

He closed his eyes briefly, then attempted a smile in return. "All the doors are locked."

"Thank you," she said sleepily.

"Can you get yourself to bed?"

"That I think I can manage on my own."

"Just trying to be chivalrous."

She pursed her lips and held out his coat. "I wouldn't want you to use it all up."

He rose, then held out his hand for hers. She looked at his hand, then up at him, then hesitated again before she put her hand in his.

He understood why. It was rather earth-shattering.

But not so terrible that he couldn't bring himself to keep her hand in his as he walked across the great hall with her. It was madness, even thinking to start up any sort of relationship with her, but he was afraid he might have already crossed the line into lunacy.

He paused at the door, then looked down at her. "I suppose it would be unwise to suggest we see each other sooner than Wednesday."

"I suppose it would be," she agreed. "Though I appreciate the rescue tonight."

He leaned against the doorframe. "Another party tomorrow night?"

"A small one," she said. "Just supper for twenty."

He smiled. "After tonight, I can see why that seems small."

"And they're all very well behaved," she said. "Londoners entertaining out-of-town clients. I'll just welcome everyone at the front door, then spend the rest of the time in the kitchen, making sure the white sauce doesn't burn."

"It doesn't sound so taxing that you couldn't patronize a National Trust site in the morning," he said thoughtfully, "if you had sauce-stirring aid in the evening." He paused. "Knole House?"

She took a deep breath. "If you like."

"I'm more interested in what you would like."

"Accommodating tonight, aren't you?"

"You should probably take advantage of it."

"I love Knole House," she said with a smile. "It's a very luxurious place."

"They had no idea how luxurious, I'm sure," he muttered under his breath. He opened the door, squeezed her hand, then released it and walked out onto the top step. He continued down to the courtyard before he turned and looked up at her. He thought keeping those steps between them was a very circumspect thing to do, though it left her rather farther out of reach than he cared for. He put his coat on, then jammed his hands in his pockets. "I'll pick you up at ten."

She leaned against the doorframe. "All right."

He nodded, then paused. "Can I trust you would tell me to shove off if you didn't want to see me again?" He cleared his throat. "I haven't given you much choice about it in the past, just showing up as I have uninvited."

She wrapped her arms around herself. He could only hope that was because she would have preferred to wrap her arms around him but was being discreet.

"I would tell you."

He nodded, then shooed her inside. "Bolt the door, Tess. I want to hear you do it."

"How have I lived here so safely this long without you to make sure I locked the doors?" she asked lightly.

"I've only been here since the end of summer," he said seriously. "I would have come sooner if I'd known."

"That I needed my doors checked?"

"That, too."

She caught her breath, then managed a smile. "Go home, you awful man." •

Perhaps she was not as unaffected as he feared. "Am I bothering you?"

She rolled her eyes, then stepped back inside. "Thank you for the dancing and the rescue. Now, go away."

He kept his hands in his pockets and his feet on her courtyard, because it was safer that way. He waited until she'd shut the door, listened for the bolt to be thrown home, then turned and walked slowly across her courtyard. He didn't dare take as many deep breaths as he might have wanted to at another time, because he feared he might begin to hyperventilate if he did. So he simply walked slowly and ignored all the reasons that dating Tess Alexander was a very bad idea indeed.

If she had any idea who he was, she would—

He stopped in mid-step as the hair on the back of his neck stood up.

He looked up, but there were no lads on the battlements, no

glint of sword or spear in the moonlight, no beeping of a watch or mobile phone. He was tempted to go back inside and insist that he would be sleeping on Tess's floor, but he supposed that would only frighten the lady of the house unnecessarily.

He walked around the courtyard just the same, until he was sure it was empty.

It was late and his imagination was running away with him.

He had a final look about, glanced at the front door to make sure it was still locked, then took himself through the barbican gate and across the bridge. He continued to look about himself casually, but saw nothing untoward.

There were no additional cars in the car park and no modern torches flickering in the forest. Tess was behind impenetrable walls, and he was no more than a phone call away.

He took a deep breath, put his unease behind him, and walked out to the car park. It was empty save his Vanquish and Tess's little red Ford.

Still . . .

He took a deep breath and shrugged aside his unease. Tess's doors were all locked, and hopefully she would have the good sense to lock her bedchamber door. She would be safe enough for the night.

And he would be there perhaps earlier than he'd intended to on the morrow, just to see if there might be something inadvertently left behind that might explain his unease.

If not, Tess might find herself having an extra houseguest for the foreseeable future.

Chapter 11

Tess had always wondered what it had felt like to be in a pitched battle. She'd just never expected to learn while standing on her own property.

She clasped her hands behind her back, realizing only as she did so that it was what John did when he was trying to be unassuming. She was surprised to find she wished he were standing next to her at the moment. Not even Mrs. Tippets could possibly be immune to his charming smile.

Mrs. Tippets, however, was apparently not finding anything overly charming about *her* smile.

"Mr. Beagle," Mrs. Tippets said stiffly, "is the gentlest of beasts. He is beloved by all the young people in my neighborhood."

Tess looked at the small terrier baring his fangs and looking at her ankles as if he'd just bellied up to a tasty Texas barbeque. She looked at Mrs. Tippets and put on her best deal-with-crotchety-tenured-professors voice.

"I can see that," she said soothingly, "and I'm sure he's very loving in his home environment. I'm afraid, though, that here he might be less than comfortable."

"What can you possibly mean?" Mrs. Tippets demanded.

"He's chasing off customers," Tess said as politely as she could. "He does seem to like children, but not their parents. I'm having complaints about rips in trousers and stockings."

"Perhaps they're lingering a bit too long, looking at my wares," Mrs. Tippets said, her back ramrod straight. "I don't like lingerers."

Tess took a deep breath and waded into the breach, because she had no choice. "Mrs. Tippets, the truth is, these wares are meant to be sold. It's how I help keep the castle in the black. Mr. Beagle is getting in the way of that, so I must insist that you either keep him crated during your time here or leave him at home. I'm going to be faced with a lawsuit one of these days, or a hefty bill for emergency stitching and rabies shots."

"He does not have rabies!"

Tess glanced briefly around the shop. It was immaculately kept, true, but overstuffed with things that didn't seem to be selling very well. She had the feeling that was because Mrs. Tippets didn't *want* to sell anything very well. She didn't really want to fire the woman, but she was starting to think she didn't have a choice. At the moment, she had ample money to keep the lights on in the hall, but that might not always be the case. If there was money she could make in the gift shop, it didn't make business sense not to make it.

She looked at Mrs. Tippets pointedly. "Crate or home, Mrs. Tippets. With all due respect."

Mrs. Tippets sniffed. Tess wouldn't have been surprised if the woman barricaded herself into the shop and collected a stash of resin figurines to lob at her if she dared walk through the door. Perhaps she would leave that delight for another day. She nodded firmly, then walked out of the shop and back across her bridge.

She realized as she was halfway across it, that she wasn't dreading going inside.

The realization was so overwhelming, she had to stop and think about it for a minute. It wasn't that the pain of losing Pippa was any less, it was just . . . well, she had one gigantic distraction in the person of Pippa's husband's brother, that's what it was.

She continued on her way thoughtfully, then stopped on the edge of her courtyard, surprised at the sight that greeted her.

John was walking slowly around the courtyard, looking down

at the ground at his feet as if he looked for something in particular. If she hadn't known better, she would have thought he was looking for clues.

Odd.

She walked across the grass, but he was apparently very focused on what he was doing because he didn't turn around when she reached him. And since he was so busy being otherwise occupied, she thought it might be an opportunity to look at him.

Well, what she wanted to do was put her arms around him and not let go, but maybe that was premature. She honestly wasn't sure what he was thinking. He'd stood inside her hall door the night before and looked at her as if he might have wanted to kiss her. She'd fully expected his next reaction to be abrupt flight out of her courtyard. That he'd lingered said something, didn't it? And that he'd shown back up several days before he'd said he would said something else, didn't it?

She supposed it did.

She reached out to touch his shoulder—

And found herself with her clock not cleaned only because she had good reflexes and she ducked before he decked her. Or, rather, chopped her head off with a sword he fortunately wasn't holding in his hands.

He reached out and helped her straighten, then closed his eyes briefly and blew out his breath. "Sorry."

"You're on edge."

He looked as if he were—and not at all happy about it. He considered, then carefully gathered her into his arms. She closed her eyes and enjoyed it for not nearly as long as she would have liked. Cooler heads had to prevail, she supposed.

She sighed and stepped away from him. "Bad habit to start, probably."

He nodded and shoved his hands in his pockets. "Right." He looked at her gravely. "Ready?"

"Yes, after you tell me what you were doing."

"Nothing much," he said with a shrug.

He was a terrible liar, really. She would have pushed him on it, but she supposed it wouldn't be a good way to start her day. "I promised Peaches I'd look through my mail, but I can do that quickly." She paused. "You can keep looking out here for whatever you weren't looking for, if you want."

He pursed his lips. "I'll carry on my non-investigations inside, if you don't mind."

She didn't mind. She also didn't mind when he merely walked with her instead of taking her hand. It was hard enough to keep herself grounded when she was too close to him. Holding his hand might have been just too much.

She left him wandering around the great hall and went into the lord's solar to quickly dig through the pile of mail that had been staring at her resentfully for days. She was happy to find there were no bills—her accountant was obviously doing his job—and that the catalogs had been kept to a minimum. She set aside what she could see were inquiries about booking her hall, then found herself with a final letter in her hands.

A very official-looking letter, actually.

She opened it, read it, then had to feel her way down against her desk. She reread it again, then was almost positive she started to see stars. She looked up for help only to find John de Piaget standing in the doorway, leaning against it casually, watching her. He must have seen something he didn't care for in her expression because he pushed away from the door and walked over to her quickly.

"What is it?"

She realized to her horror that the reason she was holding what she held in her hands was because Roland of Sedgwick had somehow figured out how to prove she was related to one of the early lords of Sedgwick, no doubt through his wife.

Not exactly something she wanted John to see.

Unfortunately, he relieved her of her letter before she could hide it behind her back. She clapped her hand over her eyes and wondered if that was going to spell the beginning of the end for her just as meeting Stephen had likely signaled the same for John. She took a deep breath, then peeked at him through her fingers to see if he was wearing that look that said he'd come just a little too close to his past.

He wasn't. He was simply reading, a faint smile on his face. He finished, then turned to lean against the desk next to her. "Well, it looks as if the ranks of British nobility have been infiltrated by a dastardly Yank."

"So it seems," she managed. And it wasn't the first time those ranks had been breached, she could guarantee that.

"Tess Alexander, Countess of Sedgwick," he mused. "I like it. And an hereditary honor. I wonder how—"

"Don't know," she said briskly, taking the letter from him. "All I *do* know is that I'm going to be a laughingstock at school."

He smiled, a little smile that she had to pause in mid-rant to admire. "I don't know why. I'm very impressed. Now, if milady would permit me, I would be pleased to escort her to one of our national treasures. Perhaps you can flash your nobility card and earn us an entrance gratis."

She folded the letter up and counted herself well-escaped from a slew of questions she wasn't about to answer. She looked at him with mock disgust. "I'm not going anywhere with you if you don't knock that off."

He laughed a little, which was almost enough to do in what was left of her last vestiges of sanity, then took her hand. "Let's go. We'll just pay like regular rabble, and I won't poke at you about it."

Tess let him pull her across the solar, then shoved the letter at Peaches on her way by. "Read that." She shot her sister a very brief look of warning she was sure Peaches didn't miss.

There was silence as they walked the great hall, then a gasp.

"I'm not trading places with you anymore!" Peaches hollered.

"I wouldn't blame you," Tess threw over her shoulder, though she hoped Peaches wasn't serious. Having a double came in handy now and again. She looked up at John. "I don't want to think about this." Hopefully, he wouldn't want to, either.

"Perhaps today we could both put aside things that trouble us," he said gravely.

"Are there things that trouble you, John?" she asked, happy to turn the scrutiny away from herself.

"Besides you?" he asked with a grave smile. "Yes. A thing or two."

"Going to tell me about them?"

"Not yet." He nodded toward the door. "Let's be off on our escape before the thought overwhelms us both."

She had already left the hall in Peaches's care, so she concentrated on doing her best to not think about the complete improbability of walking through the courtyard of her keep with a man related to one of the early lords of Sedgwick. And now she found herself wearing the female version of that title.

She was definitely going to get in touch with Lord Roland and find out just what he'd been up to while sunning himself on some beach.

She settled herself in the absolute luxury of John's car and watched him as he got in, started it up, and backed out of her car park without thought. She continued to watch him as he drove away from the keep and turned onto the main road leading through the village. If he slowed down to eye his shop on the way by, she couldn't blame him. He frowned thoughtfully and continued on without saying anything.

Something was definitely up.

She didn't imagine she would have any answers about it, though, so she simply watched him and wondered how he felt about having left his own nobility card eight hundred years in the past. She imagined that somehow he just didn't care. Then again, he was driving a pretty nice car, so maybe he did care about a bit of status more than he wanted to let on.

He glanced at her, then did a double take when he realized she was studying him, apparently intently enough to make him nervous.

"What is it?"

"Just thinking."

"That, my lady, is a very dangerous activity."

"I thought you weren't going to poke at me about this," she said. "This thing that I'm not at all sure is legal or binding."

"The crown apparently thinks differently," he said mildly, "else Bess wouldn't have had one of her flunkies send you a letter. Best accustom yourself to the deference, I imagine."

"Are you going to be deferential to me?" she asked.

He only lifted an eyebrow and watched the road. "I thought I already was."

A noise of disbelief escaped her before she could stop it. He laughed a little, but said nothing. She settled into her seat more comfortably still and watched him, because she knew he knew she was doing it, and she knew it made him slightly nervous.

"You, woman, are about to earn an afternoon of *my ladys,*" he warned.

She smiled. "Why is it, do you think, that we just can't seem to keep ourselves from annoying each other?"

He shot her a look. "You don't annoy me."

"I bother you."

"Entirely different things, my lady."

She watched him a bit longer, wondering how it was he had such perfect teeth—then again, so had Montgomery, so at least Pippa wouldn't be regretting the lack of orthodontics in the thirteenth century—and had accustomed himself so well to the current day. She wondered how it was he decided which part of his past to allow anyone to see, and what his past had been like, and if he missed it. She wondered how he'd found himself in the future, if he'd known what to expect, if he'd been completely freaked out for as long as it had taken him to get a grip on things.

And she wondered why he hadn't tried to get back home.

For all she knew, he had, though Montgomery certainly hadn't said anything about it, nor had any of the usual suspects like Kendrick or Gideon. Did he miss his family, or wonder about them, or look them up in history books to see what had happened to them?

She wondered if, as Peaches had suggested, he was lonely.

"You're thinking entirely too hard," he said mildly, at one point.

"I'm curious about you."

"The saints preserve me," he said with feeling.

"French again, John."

He blew out his breath gustily. "My family spoke it," he said briskly.

She didn't bother to point out that his version of French wasn't exactly what she would have heard while slumming in Versailles. She also decided to refrain from further pointing out that it actually sounded a good bit like the medieval Norman French she'd studied at University. She shifted so she could watch him more closely.

"What do you do?"

He shot her a quick look. "What do you mean?"

"I mean, what do you do? You own a garage, yet you don't seem to work in it."

"I work," he protested. "Occasionally. I restore old things."

"At the peril of hands that make money playing heavenly music," she mused. "What are you restoring now?"

"A '67 Jag and an old MG."

"Even if you sell them, that's hardly enough to afford this, is it?"

"I'm not going to make you pay for lunch, if that's what's worrying you."

She smiled. "I wasn't worried."

He shifted and concentrated more fully on the road. Tess watched him draw stillness around him like a cloak, but since she'd watched him do that half a dozen times before, she wasn't offended. She was prying, which likely wouldn't have bothered anyone else, but she understood why it bothered him. She was only surprised that he hadn't pulled over and shoved her out the door to avoid any further discomfort.

She wasn't going to let the possibility of that stop her from posing a few more pointed questions while she had him at her mercy.

"And?" she prodded.

He didn't look at her. "And what?"

"I'm prying into your finances, which are none of my business."

"May I pry as fully into yours?" he asked pleasantly.

"I'm an open book, my friend. But let's read your chapter first."

He blew his hair out of his eyes. "I had a small inheritance from my father."

"Small?"

He paused at a traffic light at a roundabout and looked at her crossly. "Are you doing this on purpose?"

"To unbalance you?"

"Aye."

She had to admit, she was becoming altogether too enamored of the way he slipped into the native tongue when he was flustered. She had the feeling she might pay for that enjoyment someday, but since that day was probably safely in the future, she thought she would enjoy it while she could.

"I'm curious by nature."

"It is no doubt what makes you a good scholar," he said sourly as he pulled out into traffic.

"No doubt."

He passed a pair of cars, swore at them instead of doing what he no doubt wanted to do which was swear at her, then dragged his free hand through his hair. "Very well, it wasn't a small inheritance and when I converted—I mean, invested it, it turned into a staggering amount of sterling that I've stashed cunningly in Switzerland."

"I love Switzerland," she said with a happy sigh.

"So does my banker."

She smiled. "I imagine so." She paused. "Are you parents gone, then?"

He took a deep breath, then nodded.

She reached out and covered his hand on the gearshift briefly. "I'm sorry," she said quietly. "I won't go there."

He brought her hand to his mouth, kissed it just long enough to make her wonder if she would get over it anytime soon, then put her hand back in her lap.

"Let's talk about you and your title instead," he said, sounding a little hoarse, truth be told.

"Let's talk about you and your lute," she countered.

"Woman, you are relentless—and aye, I know. It comes with the territory." He shot her a quick scowl. "Curiosity is dangerous, you know."

"What's the worst that happens?" she asked with a faint smile. "You wouldn't drop me off on the side of the road, I don't think."

"I might," he muttered.

"You wouldn't. You could, I suppose, refuse to talk to me, but I've already enjoyed that on that trip back from London. I'd survive it again."

He was silent for a moment or two, then he reached for her hand. He put it palm down on his leg, then covered it with his own. "I was uncomfortable."

"With me?"

"Yes." He looked at her briefly. "I apologize for being impolite."

"You've made up for it since."

"Aye, by herding you and bossing you and forcing you to let me lock your doors," he said with a half smile. "Chivalry at its finest."

"Actually, yes," she agreed, "it was, and you're very good at avoiding questions you don't want to answer."

"I don't want to answer your questions."

"They aren't hard questions, John."

He frowned at the car in front of him, then managed to make a production of passing a few cars and a few motorway exits. Tess would have pulled her hand back while he was otherwise occupied with shifting, but he captured it before she could.

She was, she could safely say, in the very deepest of trouble.

"And?" she prodded after the silence had gone on a little too long for her comfort.

He sighed gustily. "My grandmother insisted that I learn the lute. I had lessons. There is all the answer you're going to have."

She wondered who his grandmother had been and from just whom he'd had lessons. For all she knew, it had been someone famous. He certainly played well enough for that to be the case.

"Will you play for me again?" she asked.

"The guitar?"

She shook her head. "No, the lute."

"For your guests tonight?" he asked.

"No," she said quietly, "some other night. Just for me."

He swore as he came near to rear-ending someone in front of him. He said nothing more until they had driven up the very small road to the car park and he had managed to get them safely stopped. He turned off his car, then took her hand in both his own and looked down at it for a moment or two in silence. Then he looked at her.

"If you like," he said.

"I like."

"I can play modern music as well, if you'd rather."

She considered. "I don't mind the occasional art song, or perhaps even the odd madrigal." She smiled. "I like medieval music best."

He leaned back against the door. "With all the music that came afterward, you settle for that?"

"Surprisingly enough, yes, but I'll happily enjoy whatever inspires you. Next week, when we see each other again."

"I'm not sure we'll make it to next week."

"It would be more prudent that way."

"Prudence be damned."

She fanned herself with her other hand. "A little warm in here, isn't it?"

He smiled a little, released her hand, then put his hand on the door. "I'll get your door for you."

"I wouldn't expect anything less."

"As a countess, you shouldn't."

"That does it—"

He caught her hand before she could get it on the handle. "I'll get your door, Tess. Wait for me."

She knew she was crazy to, but apparently she'd left her good sense back there in her castle along with the letter telling her about her newly acquired title. She only nodded and watched him crawl out of his car, a perfectly modern man dressed in jeans and a sweater. She wondered if Montgomery missed him. She wished there were a way to get word to his parents that he was alive and apparently not unhappy in the future.

She wished she'd known him for longer than just a pair of weeks.

He opened her door for her, helped her out of the car, then looked at her in surprise.

"What is it?"

"Nothing," she managed.

He considered, then shut the door, locked the car, and pocketed the keys. Then he drew her into his arms, as if she were the one who needed comfort. She put her arms around his waist again and stood there in his embrace until she thought she would either tell him she thought she might just be crazy about him or burst into tears. She took a deep breath, then stepped back.

"Not prudent," she managed.

He looked at her gravely. "Likely not." He reached out and tucked a stray strand of hair behind her ear. "And just so you know, that's the last of the embraces you'll wring out of me today."

She couldn't help a smile. "You are an awful man."

"Yet there you are."

"Here I am," she agreed.

He put his arm around her shoulders and turned her with him toward the entrance. "Let's go distract ourselves with some sixteenth-century grandeur. Just keep in mind I absolutely refuse to snog with you. I'm not even sure I can be prevailed upon to hold hands. We'll see."

"I was just going to say the same thing."

He laughed a little and tugged her along with him.

It was madness, absolute madness.

She understood, however, just how it was that Pippa had done the unthinkable and fallen for John's brother in such a short time.

She was very much afraid she was about to do the same thing.

Chapter 12

Johns wondered how it was that a man of medieval birth went about wooing a woman from the Future.

He had, over the years, wished he could have had a few minutes of conversation with his brothers, but he'd never wished for it more than he did at present. He'd watched Robin fall in love with his wife, but she'd been of their time and she'd had Robin's heart for years. Miles had wed himself a gel of unusual heritage, as had his brother Nicholas, but he'd been too stupid at the time to think he might hope for the same for himself. He supposed his father had foisted some wench of noble birth off on Montgomery who had no doubt already sired himself a handful of brats to be tormented by.

The thought was, John found to his surprise, a bit more painful than he'd anticipated.

He looked at his Future gel and wondered how it was he would go about winning her. She was currently trying to lean over a rope that separated her from Queen Elizabeth I's reputedly favorite bed without *looking* as if she were leaning over the rope that separated her from QEI's favorite napping spot. John smiled politely at the National Truster who was frowning severely in their direction, then did Tess the favor of hooking a finger through the belt loop of her jeans so if she pitched forward, she wouldn't bloody her nose.

"Thanks," she whispered conspiratorially.

"My pleasure, believe me."

She pursed her lips at his tone. "Scoundrel."

If she only knew. He released her trousers and reached for her hand when she'd finished her investigations, but he doubted she'd noticed. She was far too busy making mental notes of things she'd no doubt seen before. Why she was so interested in it all at present, he couldn't have said.

"Haven't you been here before?" he asked after the third chamber in which he'd had to cover for her nosiness.

"With Peaches, who doesn't have the patience for this sort of thing," she said, looking at him apologetically. "She would rather stand in the middle of the room, close her eyes, and take a reading on the feng-shui quotient of what she's seeing. I'm not entirely sure she doesn't have a paranormal meter running as well."

"Ghosts?" he said with a snort. "What rubbish."

She only lifted her eyebrows briefly and turned to focus on yet another bit of weaving.

He surrendered and resigned himself to holding on to her trousers.

It was a long morning.

"Lunch?" he suggested hopefully, when it seemed they had examined at least half the bedchambers and most of the common rooms.

"Briefly."

"I wonder what would happen if you studied me as intently as you have the tapestries?" he asked politely.

"If I subjected you to the same sort of scrutiny I have QEI's bedclothes," she said with a smile, "you would bolt the other way."

"I would not," he protested.

"Shall we test that?"

"Nay," he said, shifting uncomfortably.

She turned to look at him fully, which left him longing rather more than he would have suspected for those moments when she'd been studying tapestries and carvings.

"I thought you didn't want this thing moving too quickly," she said seriously.

He started to pull her into his arms, but he was interrupted by the pointed throat clearing of yet another National Trust do-gooder. He looked at Tess. "Never sell your hall to the government."

"I won't."

"At least there I can maul you without being harrumphed at."

She smiled and took his arm. "I think you need to be fed. You're starting to get a little cranky. And we don't have to look at all the rest today if you don't want to."

"The saints be praised," he said, though he wasn't entirely serious about it. He had to admit he enjoyed a good historical sight as well as the next Englishman, though if he were to be entirely honest with himself, he enjoyed the sight of Tess more. Traipsing through the past in jeans and boots was simply a decent excuse to have more of that last part.

What he ate for lunch, he couldn't have said. He consumed it without haste, but without tasting it, either—which could have been considered a good thing given its prepackaged nature. He was too busy watching Tess. She looked up from the notes she was making in the guidebook, froze, then blushed.

"Stop that."

"I'm not bolting," he pointed out.

She took a deep breath. "What *are* you doing, then?"

"Looking."

"And?"

He took his own deep breath. "Liking very much what I see."

She pushed the guidebook toward him. "I'm going to go powder my nose."

He watched her bolt—a novel occurrence in and of itself—and studied the book in front of him. It was interesting, but it was suddenly quite a bit less interesting than the sensation he suddenly had.

That he was being watched.

He would have said being aware of that was a habit he'd developed in the current century, but the truth was, the instinct was purely medieval. Learned from his father, honed by his brothers, perfected by himself in skirmishes he truly preferred not to think on.

Odd how that sort of thing came in handy in the present day.

He continued to feign interest in the book, but he was in truth taking note of everyone in the little outdoor seating area and wondering why he'd been stupid enough not to have done the like sooner. He saw nothing untoward, not even when he stretched and then used the excuse to carry the remains of their lunch to the rubbish bin to have a closer look around.

There were none in the little outdoor patio but a handful of tourists brave enough to venture out into the cold and a pair of pensioners and their wives no doubt determined to have their money's worth from their Trust pass.

"John?"

He was certain he'd jumped, but he ignored it. He turned around and smiled at Tess. "Nothing."

"I didn't ask you if it was something," she said slowly.

He took her hand. "Let's go find a darkened corner, shall we? Perhaps in the garden where we won't be pestered. I believe I have some sort of business with you that doesn't involve paneling and creaking wooden floors."

She looked at him as if he'd lost his mind. He wasn't entirely sure he wasn't well on the way to it.

He took a deep breath, then let it out slowly. "Let's walk, if you don't mind. I'm restless."

"Sure," she said easily.

He kept her hand in his, partly because he liked holding it and partly to keep her close enough to him that he could protect her if need be, though from what he couldn't have said. A disgruntled employee who'd watched them peer too closely at a sixteenth-century relic?

"I forgot my purse," Tess said suddenly. "I'll run back—"

"I'll come with you," he said without hesitation. He put on a soothing smile. "Because I want to."

"Whatever you say," she said, giving him that look again that said very clearly she wasn't at all confident in his hold on reality.

He wasn't about to explain himself. He simply walked quickly back to the loo with her, then waited for her whilst she went inside. She came back sooner than he'd expected, but empty-handed. He frowned.

"Find it?"

"No," she said slowly, "it was gone." She shrugged. "There wasn't anything in it. Five quid and some lip gloss."

"No identification?"

"I thought they could just look me up in Burke's Peerage if they needed to," she said lightly, but she seemed a little unsettled.

He was, too, actually.

"John."

He realized he wasn't paying her any heed. He had also pulled her behind him, which he hadn't realized he'd done until he'd been forced to turn around and look at her. "Aye?"

"You're acting a little suspiciously."

He blinked. "Do you think I nicked your purse?"

"Of course not," she said with a bit of a laugh. "I'm just wondering why it is that you seem to be looking over your shoulder."

"I'm not."

"You are. You also keep pulling me behind you."

"I'm trying to keep you out of the sights of those Trust busybodies."

"I don't think so."

He swore, because it was a bad habit, then took her hand. "I'm just wondering if that lad who tried to kiss you in your passageway might have been a little more irritated than he let on at my instruction."

She looked at him in surprise. "Really?"

"Really."

"John, maybe you just don't look in the mirror often enough, but if I were a jerk you'd come close to punching, I don't think I would be coming back for a second helping."

He put his arm around her and sighed. If she only knew just how dangerous a time she lived in. At least in the thirteen century, he could have protected her with a sword. Now, what was he to do? Swear and hope for the best?

"I might have an overactive imagination," he conceded, finally.

"And where did you come by that?"

"My misspent youth," he said, hoping she wouldn't ask him to elaborate. He kept his arm around her shoulders and walked with her back to his car. He opened the door for her, saw her inside, then shut the door and took a minute or two to look around him.

There was nothing.

He considered, then walked around to the driver's side and

slid under the wheel. He started up the Vanquish, half expecting it to explode, then sat back and let out a long, slow breath.

"John, you're starting to make me nervous."

He looked at her and smiled briefly. "Not enough sleep last night. Not to worry." He paused. "Would you mind if I did come and stir sauce for you tonight?"

She studied him in silence for a moment or two. His first instinct was to either deflect her obvious curiosity or shift uncomfortably. He chose to do neither. He was a knight of the realm, after all, and beyond squirming. Hedging, however, was another thing entirely, and he fully intended to engage in it when he'd caught his breath.

"Are you bringing your lute to play for me after the guests leave?"

He laughed a little in spite of himself. "You, Tess Alexander, are a difficult woman."

She reached out and tucked a bit of his hair behind his ear, then pulled her hand away quickly, as if she thought she shouldn't have. He caught that hand before it escaped too far, then kissed it before he released it.

"Aye, I will," he said easily. "If you insist."

"Very generous of you."

"It is, isn't it?" he agreed.

"You could play just for me while I stir, I suppose," she said thoughtfully, "but then you might draw all the guests kitchenward."

"And then I would be forced to share you with them more than I like," he agreed. "Let me get you home, then I'll run and fetch my gear. I'll see what instrument comes first to hand."

"And tights as well?"

He shot her a look. "Jeans, you hussy."

She smiled and buckled herself in. He supposed she was wise to do so. He didn't like the fact that someone had stolen her purse, no matter what it had contained. Perhaps she deserved nothing less for having been distracted enough to leave it behind, but that fact that it had been hers and he had felt someone watching them . . .

He shook his head and concentrated on getting them back to Sedgwick in one piece. Perhaps it was coincidence. Perhaps he had simply spent too many years listening for the crack of a twig or the glimpse of a shadow that might contain an enemy. The morning's events were nothing more than coincidence.

Surely.

Two hours later, he was standing in his bedchamber, looking into his closet, and feeling as if he'd been kicked in the gut by an enthusiastic stallion. In fact, he had to lean over with his hands on his thighs to catch his breath.

His sword was gone.

And there had been no sign of a break-in.

Coincidence? He seriously doubted it. He straightened and went to look about the cottage once more, on the off chance that he'd missed something. He checked both doors and every window—including the one over his bed that wasn't quite shut.

Which was not at all how he'd left it.

He looked on the bedspread and saw faint indentations, but nothing that he could have used to tell him anything except that his thief had rather large feet. He didn't even consider calling the bobbies. They would have wanted all sorts of details he wouldn't have wanted to give, beginning and ending with why he had a trio of swords propped up in the back of his closet.

Well, a brace of them only, now.

He stood in the midst of his bedchamber and folded his arms over his chest so he could scowl and think a bit. Nothing else was missing; he knew that from a cursory glance around. It wasn't that he had anything of value save his cars, and he'd had the priciest with him, leaving the others still safely tucked in their bays. The tools in his shop were worth something, but he wouldn't know if something were missing there without a serious search.

He considered, then walked into his closet, pulled aside the false front he'd built into the back and opened the man-sized safe he had there. His lute and two guitars were inside, untouched. He considered, then took his remaining medieval sword and stashed it inside. The fit was tight, which was why he'd never kept it in the safe, though now he wondered why not.

The Claymore was too tall to fit, so he supposed he had no choice but to simply take his chances with it. It was a reproduction, so the thought of losing it didn't trouble him overmuch. The realization that he'd been robbed of the sword his father had given him upon the occasion of his knighting, however, was substantially more gut-wrenching than he would have suspected it might be.

His father had given him his other sword as well, so perhaps he was being overly sentimental where he shouldn't have been. It was metal, nothing more, and the gems were useless to anyone who might have wanted to sell them. They were faceted with the tools of a medieval gemsmith. To recut them to modern standards would have radically diminished their value.

Nay, the worth to him was in the memories attached to the sword. He'd cherished the blade, even though his father had gifted it to him a year to the day before he'd thrown him out of his hall—

He wrenched his thoughts back to the present, which wasn't, as it happened, much more of a pleasant place to be than loitering uncomfortably in memories of his past.

Who would want a sword?

More curious still, why would anyone have thought he might possess one?

The only person who had seen him with a sword in his hands was Doris Winston, and he immediately dismissed her as a suspect. Even the lad who had accosted Tess might have fancied a more authentic-looking blade, but he wouldn't have known to look for it in a closet. If that fool had been bent on revenge, he would have likely trashed the entire cottage.

Nay, there was something else afoot.

He shut and locked his window again only to discover that the lock was broken. He cursed succinctly, then went and fetched a small crowbar from the shop. He wedged the window shut, hoping he wouldn't soon have a fire and need to escape. He collected his preferred guitar for classical pieces, then locked up the safe and replaced the false front. After a final look about his house, he locked the door behind him and walked away. The Claymore would either be there when he returned, or it wouldn't.

He thought that perhaps he should have taken Grant's suggestion to hook up the surveillance cameras. Too late now.

He wondered if Tess had them in her hall and if not, would she think him daft for suggesting she have them installed first thing Monday morning.

He drove to Sedgwick with less apprehension about the keep

and what it represented than great unease over what he might be drawing to it with his presence. He could only assume that whoever had nicked his sword was lying in wait for him, not Tess.

Though the loss of her purse couldn't be discounted.

He sighed, parked well away from potential door damage, then fetched his guitar and made his way across the bridge and into the courtyard. He didn't bother with the front door, though he did take the opportunity to look rather thoroughly about the courtyard for anything untoward. He saw nothing, but that didn't mean he wouldn't have another look later.

He walked into the kitchen to find Tess and Peaches up to their elbows in supper.

"Oh, good," Peaches said, sounding vastly relieved, "the cavalry has arrived."

John tucked his guitar into the corner, shrugged out of his jacket, and walked over to the stove. "What's amiss?"

Tess looked rather less serene than she usually did. Copious amounts of hair had escaped her clip, and she was slightly out of breath.

"The caterers mistook tomorrow for today, and we have nothing to eat."

"Bangers and mash?" he suggested.

She glared at him, and he held up his hands in surrender.

"What can I do?" he asked. "Run to the market?"

"They're closed," Peaches said gingerly. "Tess is whipping up some pasta, and we have enough salad things to make do. I'm working on dessert."

He considered. "I could go entertain them for a bit, if you thought that would do any good."

Tess closed her eyes briefly. "Thank you."

"Of course." He motioned for her to turn around, then he pulled out her clip and did his best to gather up all the hair that escaped from her chignon. He clipped it to the back of her head, kissed the top of that head, then went to fetch his guitar. "Are you sure you can manage, just the two of you?"

"Unless you have a catering staff hiding in your shop," Tess said, blowing the hair out of her eyes, "I don't think we have a choice."

John considered, then pulled his mobile out of his jacket and stepped outside to make two phone calls. He left the sisters to what would be a blessedly brief stint by themselves before true reinforcements came, then made for the great hall.

He looked at the guests milling around, apparently quite happy on their own, and set his guitar down near the hearth. He was in the process of fetching a chair when he heard someone call his name.

Dave Thompson, as Fate would have it.

It was a very small world.

He put on his best company manners and walked over to shake hands with one of England's most successful businessmen. The man had his fingers in so many pies, John half suspected he likely didn't remember them all. Then again, knowing Dave as he did, the blighter could likely recite on demand exactly where every shilling of his substantial fortune was residing.

"Dave," John said politely, "what a pleasant surprise."

Dave laughed at him. "Pleasant? Who are you kidding? Kenneth let me hear the raw track with all your warm-up vulgarity. I know exactly what you think of me."

John smiled deprecatingly. "I didn't want to ruin my reputation as a hard-bitten grunge-band bassist by letting anyone know I play the guitar, much less anything more esoteric."

"It'll be our secret."

"Until you spread it around," John said dryly.

Dave put his hand companionably on John's shoulder. "John, my friend, this might come as a bit of a shock, but there are people in the world who actually *want* me to produce their records."

"Bad manners are part of my charm."

Dave laughed. "So I've seen." He looked around the hall, then back at John. "This is a lovely place. What, may I ask, are you doing here?"

"Friend of the owner," John said easily. He paused. "How would you like to do me a favor?"

"Ah, you in my debt," Dave said, rubbing his hands together with an evil chuckle. "Ask away."

"Miss Alexander's caterers mistook the date and have left her doing all the prep herself. I called in a few locals to help out, but I don't suppose you could smooth things over with the rest of this rabble until we can set things right, could you?"

"Are you going to help by allowing them to listen to the finest jazz guitarist in all the UK?"

"He couldn't be here, so you're stuck with me," John said with a brief smile, "but yes, I'll do my best."

"Then I'll see what I can do for you whilst you consider just how heavy a price I'll exact from you when I'm at my leisure," Dave said pleasantly. "And you know, John, if it's too much trouble, we could just order takeaway."

"No need," John said. "Tess is a fabulous cook, though you may not see much of her as hostess."

"I'll put on an apron and do the honors," Dave said. "Go play, my boy, and I'll see to the rest."

John was happy to do so. He caught sight of Tess on the edge of the great hall and walked over to her. It was only as he saw her that he realized he'd forgotten what he'd seen at his house. He wasn't at all sure he would tell her about it, but he would most certainly make sure he had a closer look at her hall before he left her for the night.

He took her by the arm and pulled her down the passageway. He smiled.

"Not to worry. Dave, the blighter who left that lute for me at Studio Five, is one of your guests. He offered to pitch in and distract your guests until supper is ready."

"What sort of Faustian bargain did you make with him for that?" she asked breathlessly.

"He's still considering the price," John said dryly, "but I'll pay it willingly. And so you know, Adam's abandoning the pub to help out. Doris Winston is bringing a pair of her granddaughters to carry supper out to the table."

"You're a lifesaver," she said, with feeling.

"We'll see how grateful you are later, when I'm free to take advantage of it."

She took his hand and squeezed it. "Thank you, John."

He heard voices from the kitchen and knew help had arrived, and not just to save Tess from overwork in the kitchen but he himself from doing something stupid such as pulling her into his arms and kissing her. He settled for kissing her hand very briefly, then sent her off to the kitchen to supervise whilst he went about the purchase price of her peace of mind.

B_y the end of the evening, he had done his fair share of hobnobbing with the rich and cultured of London and watched Tess do the same. She was, he could admit without hesitation, very good at what she did. She gave Peaches all the credit for supper, praised village helpers for their aid, and effortlessly left everyone commenting on such a lovely evening. By the time the last of the guests had departed, Doris and her granddaughters were long gone and Peaches had finished tidying up the kitchen. He stood in front of the hearth with his hands clasped behind his back, just as he'd stood innumerable times in his father's hall.

He watched Tess stop just in front of him. She looked beautiful but exhausted. He smiled gravely, then reached out and drew her into his arms.

"We shouldn't begin this," he murmured.

"I couldn't agree more," she said, putting her arms around his waist and laying her head on his shoulder. She sighed deeply. "I'm not sure how to thank you."

"Breakfast tomorrow."

"Tomorrow isn't Wednesday," she said, the smile plain in her voice.

"I couldn't care—" Her phone rang, startling him. He pulled back and looked at her in surprise. "It's almost midnight."

She looked at her mobile. "It's Terry Holmes," she said, frowning thoughtfully. "He knew I had a party tonight, so perhaps he was waiting for it to end. It must be important for him to call this late."

"Who is Terry Holmes?" he asked.

"The president of the Tynedale reenactment group," she said. "The ones from the other night. Maybe he has bad behavior to apologize for."

"At least one of his club members certainly does," John said pointedly.

She shot him a quick smile. "I'll make it quick."

He watched her pace back and forth in front of the fire, stopping now and again when she apparently heard something that surprised her. John couldn't deny that he was curious about what that bloke might say. He didn't imagine he should hope for it, but he couldn't help but wonder if the man might have tidings about one of his members having acquired a fine new sword.

He finally sat down, then caught Tess's hand and pulled her down to sit on his lap. She was halfway there before she realized what she was doing. She shot him a warning look, then pulled away and went to sit in the chair across from him. He shrugged. Nothing ventured, nothing gained. He did, however, pull her chair close enough to his that he could capture her feet with his own.

"No, I'm not teaching next week," she said slowly. "When is the festival? Well, I suppose either Wednesday or Thursday would work."

John focused on what she was saying and had the words sink in. "No," he said firmly.

"Hang on, Terry," she said. She put her thumb over her phone and looked at him. "What's wrong?"

"I don't want you going alone."

She frowned. "John, it's a medieval faire at Warewick Castle. How dangerous can it be?"

"Go Thursday," he said firmly. "I'll take you."

"John—"

"Thursday, Tess."

She looked at him, clearly puzzled, then shrugged. "All right." She turned back to her call. "Terry, how about Thursday?" She listened for a moment or two, then smiled. "I'll be there. Thanks for the chance."

John watched as she ended the call and set her phone down on the floor. "What chance did he offer you?" he asked politely.

She took a deep breath. "He wants to introduce me to the president of the living history society that sponsors that faire. Apparently there's been some interest in trying to combine lectures with living reenactors."

He smiled at the light in her eyes, something he had yet to see in conjunction with her business of hosting parties. "A potent combination."

"And a very safe one," she said pointedly. "Are you going to tell me why I need a keeper?"

"Because I don't want you interacting with those fools unless I'm with you, and I'm in studio Tuesday and Wednesday," he said. "Or it could be that I just want to spend time with you."

"Why do I think there's more to it than that?"

He only looked at her.

"And why do I think you aren't going to tell me anything about it?"

Because she knew him already too well.

"You never know who might be in the crowd," he said carefully. "I don't want you caught in any dark corners."

"With anyone but you?" she asked with a faint smile.

He nodded solemnly.

She reached out and took one of his hands, put his palm against her cheek, then kissed that palm quickly before she smiled at him. "Play for me now, would you? Something you love?"

He thought he might be too winded to. He took his hand back, curled his fingers into his palm, then looked at the spot where her lips had touched his skin. He wasn't entirely sure she hadn't left some sort of scorching mark there. He met her eyes and saw that she was almost as overwhelmed as he was.

"I will," he managed, "play whatever you want."

Which he did. He got through half a dozen songs before he thought he might have exhausted his ability to play without blurting out some sort of sentiment he should have been saving for another time.

He left his guitar in her hands, checked the doors, had a little walk on the battlements just because he thought the chill might be useful in restoring his good sense, then went back downstairs to find Tess in the same place, trying out something on his guitar. She looked up when she heard his footstep and smiled.

He didn't stumble, but it was a near thing.

He forced himself to concentrate on packing up his gear and checking the kitchen door one last time. After that, he had nothing left to distract himself with, so he grasped for the last shreds of his good sense and walked with Tess to her front door.

"What are you doing tomorrow?" he asked.

"Church in the morning, naps in the afternoon," she said with a smile. "But we probably shouldn't see each other."

"I go to church," he muttered. "Now and again."

"Then we might run into each other."

"How long a nap?"

"Too long for you," she said easily. "Monday you should actually do some work in your shop, then you're in London through Wednesday. I'll be catching up on my mail and adjusting my tiara."

He smiled in spite of himself. "Very well, I'll limit my pursuit of you to phone calls and ecclesiastical sightings. Satisfied?"

"You made the rules," she said airily.

"I was an idiot."

She leaned up on her toes and kissed his cheek, then pushed him out the door. He went, because it was either that or stay and make bad habits out of several things. He turned on the bottom step and looked up at her.

"Good night, my lady," he said quietly.

"Thank you for the rescue tonight," she said, just as quietly.

He nodded, started to turn away, then looked back at her. "I might have to pop in for a moment or two now and again. Just to make sure your doors are locked."

"You might," she agreed.

He wasn't going to tell her just how thoroughly he intended to keep watch over several things, because there was no reason to unnerve her.

He smiled, wished her another good night, and bade her lock the front door so he could hear the bolt sliding home. He walked around the courtyard once, then out the front gates. He saw nothing, sensed nothing, heard nothing.

But he had the distinct feeling the games had only just begun.

Chapter 13

T ess wondered if the time had come for her to learn to use
a sword.

She wasn't unused to crowds, and she wasn't unused to people dressing up in costume, but having both combined into one
big medieval mob was almost more than she could take. If she
found herself jostled by one more guy in a tabard and tights, she
was going to do damage to him. She supposed, though, that the
men probably gave her a wider berth than they might have otherwise, given whom she was walking with. The women didn't, but
she honestly couldn't blame them. She would have been doing
the same thing in their places. John de Piaget was nothing short
of stunning.

She looked at him surreptitiously to find him watching everything around him with absolutely no expression on his face—a
sure sign he was on the verge of rolling his eyes or blurting out
some comment on the authenticity quotient of his surroundings.
He was dressed as she was in jeans and a sweater, and looked far
more modern than any of the somewhat scruffy men they passed.

She wondered how Karma felt about having time turned on
its head like that.

John glanced at her, then jumped a little. "What?" he asked.

"Just watching you."

"Why?" he asked, very uncomfortably.

"Because you're cute."

He blinked, then he smiled briefly. "And you're daft. I understand it comes from wearing a tiara that's too tight."

"I'll have to call my sister Cinderella and ask her how to mitigate the effects."

He squeezed her hand, smiled again, then turned back to his contemplation of their surroundings. She could tell he wasn't up to small talk, so she didn't push him. The fact that he'd come—albeit at his own insistence—to a medieval gathering was probably testing the limits of his tolerance anyway. She could honestly say she would be happy to get in, find Terry's friend and talk, then make her escape unscathed.

She had to wonder about John's willingness to come to a place that smacked so strongly of where he'd come from. There was something going on, something he wasn't telling her, something that seemed to worry him about her. She knew that because despite their pseudo-agreement to not see each other, she'd seen him every day since Saturday.

She'd sat next to him Sunday morning in church, then had a call from him in the evening, followed by a brief visit to check her doors. She'd had flowers on Monday, two phone calls on Tuesday, and a tiara on her doorstep Wednesday, all topped off by late-night visits every night to make sure the castle was secure.

She had begun to wonder if he thought someone might be trying to get inside when she wasn't looking.

But since she'd lived in the castle for a year without so much as a brochure having been swiped, she thought John might have been imagining things.

She had to admit, though, that she'd been happy to see him and his buff self that morning, leaning against the stone wall of her barbican gate, waiting for her—and not just because she had the feeling he could protect her.

The truth was, she was fond of him.

Which was perhaps a terrible understatement, but she wasn't going to examine it too closely. It was too soon, and there were too many appalling things that stood between them. Such as the fact that his brother was married to her sister, and she hadn't seen her way clear to tell him as much.

She realized he'd stopped only because he pulled her behind him exactly as she'd seen Montgomery do half a dozen times with Pippa. She looked around his shoulder, then suppressed the urge to swear. It was absolutely nothing he should get himself in the middle of, which she had every intention of telling him. She moved to stand next to him—

He pulled her behind him again.

"John," she began in exasperation.

"Don't."

Well, there was no arguing with him when he took on that very medieval tone. She wondered if he knew he'd said it in French. She sighed and wondered how Pippa had accustomed herself to being herded and protected and watched over as if she'd been something precious that merited absolute safety.

It was, she had to admit, quite lovely when looked at in that light.

She put her hands on John's back. He was tensed, as if he thought the entire French army was about to swoop down on them. She couldn't imagine the future could muster up anything close to that, but she'd been wrong before. She finally managed to lean a little more to her right and look around his shoulder to see just what was bothering him so.

The sight shouldn't have been anything out of the ordinary considering where they were. It was just two men carrying on with a little sword demonstration. They weren't very well matched because one of the men was substantially larger than the other, but the little guy seemed to be holding his own, for the moment.

There was something off, though, in the bigger man's eyes. Even from where she stood, Tess could see he wasn't doing what he was doing for sport; he was serious about it.

And then, as quickly as that, things took a definite turn for the worse. The smaller man began, perhaps, to sense that he was in over his head and no amount of bluster and no number of "take it easy, mate" entreaties were going to save him from embarrassment.

Or worse.

John looked over his shoulder at her. "Stay here."

Her mouth fell open before she could stop it. And before she could stop *him*, John had stepped between the very large, burly man with an obviously well-loved sword and that much smaller guy who had been trying to keep his opponent from forcing him to endure a whole slew of blunt-force traumas.

John looked at Mr. Burly, who announced loudly that his name was Bill and if John didn't move pretty damn quick, he was going to suffer a worse fate than little Gary who had since scurried to safety. John only folded his arms across his chest and looked Bill in the eye.

"Is that so," he drawled.

Tess would have done something, but she had no idea what to do. Putting herself between Bill, who was an idiot, and John, who looked perfectly capable of rendering Bill quite unfit for anything useful with nothing but his hands, would have been colossally stupid. She looked around herself nervously to find that quite a crowd had gathered, almost all of it comprised of men dressed in medieval gear and sporting swords.

None of them was smiling.

She couldn't decide if that was because they were irritated with John for ruining their entertainment or because they thought Bill was completely out of control and there might be a need soon for whatever doctor might be in the house.

"I believe," John said calmly, "that you may have had a bit too much to drink, friend."

"And I believe," Bill said, sounding perfectly lucid and sober, "that you have stuck your pretty nose precisely where it didn't belong. *Friend.*"

John looked at the sword in Bill's hands. "I suppose whilst we discuss that, you might want to put your blade down, lest you hurt yourself."

Well, that wasn't a very politic thing to say. Tess would have pointed that out to the edification of all, but she didn't have a chance. She was too busy being absolutely speechless with terror.

Mainly because Bill attacked John and no one seemed to care. John did an amazing job just keeping out of his way and avoiding being poked with a sword that looked a little sharper than it perhaps should have been. The point of that sword eventually caught the sleeve of John's jacket and put a spectacular rent in it. John considered that, shot Bill a look, then shucked his coat off and threw it across the little battlefield.

Tess caught it without thinking and decided that she'd had enough. She walked into the fray, as it were, fully intending to stop it.

John caught her by the arm and whirled her out of the way.

She went, because he hadn't given her a choice. And once she turned around to protest, she very wisely—to her mind—reconsidered her good intentions. She backed up, clutched John's jacket to her chest as if it had been a life preserver, and prayed blood wouldn't be spilt.

Bill shoved John suddenly. John tucked, rolled, and came back up to his feet with someone's sword in his hands.

And then she began to think that Bill might soon come to a different opinion about his own skills.

John threw away any pretense of being what he wasn't. She watched, openmouthed, as he schooled Bill in a little swordplay. She managed to tear her eyes away long enough to look at the men surrounding the combatants.

They were gaping as well.

She wondered how long things would go on, but she perhaps needn't have bothered. Bill was not up to the standards of sword-play at Artane. Tess could tell John was, methodically and mer-cilessly, putting him in his place. Bill finally watched, his mouth agape, as his sword went flying up into the air, hung there for a moment, then began its downward trajectory.

John caught it, then pointed both swords at Bill.

Then he seemed to realize just what he'd done.

She was sure no one else had noticed, but no one else knew what to look for: that little flash of panic in his eyes that was ruthlessly squelched and the way he stiffened his spine as if he prepared to deflect all inquiries by his posture alone. His face suddenly shuttered, as if he'd dropped a portcullis and slammed an inner gate home at the same time.

He turned and handed the sword he'd poached back to its owner without comment. He held Bill's sword in his hands and seemed to be considering just what to do with it.

"Bloody hell," Terry wheezed suddenly from beside her. "Where'd he learn to do that?"

"I wouldn't ask," Tess said, because it was hard on short notice to come up for an excuse as to why anyone but a perfectly trained medieval knight would make perhaps the best swordsman in the area look like a child with a plastic weapon. "I'm sure you can ask him later, after the little guy has finished slobbering all over him."

Terry shot her an uneasy smile, then went out to take Bill's sword from John and pry Gary from John's side where he was indeed heaping enormous praise on him.

Bill was still shaking.

And furious.

Tess thought it might not be imprudent to get herself and her very silent escort the hell out of Dodge, so she walked up to John and slipped her arm through his. She smiled easily at Terry.

"I just had a phone call from home," she lied, "and we need to dash. I very much want to meet your colleague, but perhaps another time?"

Terry only nodded, his eyes as wide as saucers.

Tess looked at John. "Peaches called and said the hall is on fire. I think we'd better get back."

He blinked, as if he couldn't wrap his mind around what she was saying. She smiled again at Terry, then pulled John away from the group without delay. That he was willing to come along perhaps said much about his discomfort. She hazarded a glance at his face and had no trouble reading there exactly what he was thinking.

He was kicking himself. Hard.

She couldn't blame him. He'd started out exercising a bit of chivalry and wound up revealing much more about himself than he ever would have if he'd been thinking clearly. She was fairly sure no one but she herself would have possibly thought him anything but a very dedicated living historian, but she also wasn't going to stick around to see if that was the case.

She also wasn't about to say anything about it to him or ask him any questions. He looked like he was going to bolt as it was, and she didn't want to get left behind.

In fact, to guarantee that, she pried his keys out of his hand and kept them herself.

He didn't seem adverse to leaving the celebration entirely, which she thought was a very wise decision on his part. She walked briskly but without running to the car park, then paused with him in front of his car. She looked up at him.

"I could drive."

"Well," he managed, "you do have the keys."

She looked at his car, then frowned. "How do I get in?"

"The saints preserve me," he muttered under his breath, in French. He took the keys, hit the unlock button, then opened the door for her. He paused. "Is your hall on fire?"

"Nope," she said cheerfully.

"Then you lied?"

She took the keys from his hand and sat down in the driver's seat. "I thought you might be mobbed by reenactment nutters if I didn't get you out of there posthaste." She smiled. "Go get in the other side, sport. I'll get you home in one piece."

"Sport," he repeated in disbelief.

She pulled the door shut and looked for her lock to keep him from pulling her back out. It wasn't necessary. John seemed quite willing to let her have control. It was a first, so she fully intended to enjoy it while it lasted.

She looked over all the bells and whistles until he put himself into the passenger seat. He sat back and let out a long, slow breath.

"Thank you."

"No problem. Where's the ignition?"

He made a noise that was something between a laugh and a groan. He apparently settled for something that sounded remarkably like a prayer before he reached around the steering wheel and pointed.

"Thanks," Tess said brightly. "I'll bet this thing goes really fast."

He leaned his head back against the seat and closed his eyes. "The saints preserve me."

"You already said that before we got in."

"I meant it twice."

She decided again that silence was golden at the moment, so she kept her mouth shut and concentrated on getting his car out of the car park without scratching it. She was extremely grateful that she'd driven in the UK long enough to not have to think about what side of the road to drive on. Trying to keep a half million dollars of machine going without killing it or speeding was going to take everything she had.

It did indeed go very fast, and there were a few dodgy moments at first when she wasn't altogether certain she hadn't made a grave mistake considering how touchy the gas was and how well it zipped along in just first gear. She glanced over at John while waiting at a roundabout light. His eyes were closed and he looked peaceful enough, but his left hand was clenched where it rested on his thigh.

She supposed she could predict how the rest of the afternoon would go. Despite how chummy he'd been over the past few days, he would draw silence around him like a cloak, drop her off at her castle, then tell her that they shouldn't see each other again for at least a week—though she imagined that now he might up the ante to at least a fortnight.

She honestly couldn't blame him.

She spent a good half hour dividing her time between making sure she didn't wreck his car and considering potential conversational topics. If she'd asked him where he'd learned that quite effective swordplay, he probably would ignore her. Then again, if she didn't ask him where he'd learned that skill, he would probably wonder why she wasn't asking him any questions and that might lead to all sorts of speculation about things she absolutely didn't want to discuss yet.

Then again, if she opted for the first and then kept her mouth shut when he ignored her, he might actually not run away, which she was finding she didn't particularly want him to do.

She finally decided that it was entirely possible she thought too much.

"You gave up your meeting," he said, finally.

"I'll reschedule," she said, keeping her eyes glued to the road.

He took a careful breath. "You can ask now."

"Ask what—"

"Watch the road," he said in a rather calm tone considering that she almost sent his car skidding by braking a little too hard. "You can ask whatever you want to ask me. You were thinking so loudly it was keeping me awake."

She shrugged. "I was just wondering where you learned to do that."

"Do what?"

"That thing with the sword."

He was very still. "My father taught me."

"Why?"

"To keep me out of trouble, I imagine."

She imagined Rhys de Piaget had taught John swordplay not only just to keep him out of trouble. She also suspected John had had a sword in his hands from the time he could walk. She had to concentrate for another few minutes to get them on the motorway, then she let out her breath slowly. "Who taught your father?"

"Not his father, surely," John said with a sigh. "Actually, it is a long, convoluted tale that isn't very interesting." He paused. "I actually never thought to ask him where he'd learned such an obscure and useless skill."

"I think it's an interesting thing to know how to do," she offered.

"Hmmm."

"I think that little guy was about to kiss you," she added, "or at least kidnap you and take you to dinner in thanks for his life."

"I had other plans."

"Did you?" she asked. "Football on the telly tonight?"

"Spoons and saucepans in your kitchen—bloody hell, Tess," he blurted out, "watch the road!"

"Sorry." She didn't even dare look at him. "You're the one who wanted me to drive."

"What was I thinking?"

"I don't know," she said weakly. "What were you thinking?"

"That I was too keyed up to do it properly," he said, "but now I'm beginning to wonder if I'd be less keyed up if I were behind the wheel."

"I could pull over."

He took a deep breath, then let it out slowly, as if he were deliberately calming himself down. He shifted a bit in his seat. "But if you do, then how could I admire you so freely?"

She shot him a look. "Stop that."

He smiled.

"Stop *that*," she said, with feeling, "or I really will plow your car into something. Growl at me until we get back to less busy roads."

He put his hand on her leg. "I don't want to growl at you."

She put his hand back on his leg. "You will, when I wreck your car. Keep your hands to yourself, buster, and your eyes on the road. I've got enough to do over here without any distractions from you."

He sighed deeply. "Very well. Wake me when we're home."

She looked at him quickly to find that he had indeed closed his eyes. And his left hand wasn't clenched any more.

A very good sign.

Her hands were not in such good shape. She wasn't too proud to admit her hands were sweating. Actually, she was sweating. She was very glad she had her hair up, but it wasn't comfortable to lean her head back against the seat. She finally pulled the clip out. Better sweaty than trying to drive with a kink in her neck.

"I'll take that," John said, holding out his hand. "Just know I'm not likely to give it back."

"I have others."

"I imagined you did."

She wiped her hands one by one on her jeans, then concentrated on the road. By the time they were half an hour away from the village, she thought she might have gotten the hang of things. She glanced at John to find him simply watching her. That gorgeous, valiant, impossible man was just watching her with a very small smile playing around the corners of his mouth.

"Frightened?" she asked.

He only shook his head slowly.

She wished she had his confidence. She turned off onto an A road, then looked behind her. She frowned. The same little brown Ford was behind her that had been behind her since they'd left Warewick Castle.

"What is it?" John asked.

"Nothing," she said. She frowned, then continued on. "I don't suppose you'd want to hum something to keep me awake, would you?"

"I don't suppose I would," he said, sounding startled.

She smiled. "Then turn on the radio and sing along. A little Puccini to pass the time."

He snorted, but turned on the radio anyway. It only took three tries at various stations before he popped in a CD. Vocal jazz with a lovely guitar accompaniment filled the car. She listened for a minute or two, then smiled at him.

"You?"

"Aye, braggart that I am."

She enjoyed his music for a good ten minutes before she

looked behind her. She ignored the car behind them, then turned off onto their own little B road.

The brown Ford followed.

"Enough hedging," John said, pausing the track. "What is it?"

"You're going to think I'm crazy," she began slowly, "but there's someone following us."

He shifted to look in the rearview mirror, then pursed his lips. "How long has that lad been behind us?"

"I think since Warewick, and you're assuming it's a man," she said. "It could be a woman, trying to figure out where you live so she can stalk you."

"Then I suppose you'll just have to hoist a sword in my defense," he said. He shifted back in his seat. "I don't suppose you could lose them, could you?"

"Are you crazy?" she gasped. "I wouldn't dare."

"Then pull in for some petrol, up the way there. We'll see what they do."

"Then you believe me?"

"I'm not attributing villainous motives to the poor fool, but I've no reason to doubt what you've seen. For all we know, some burly lad with a sword has decided that the lady of Sedgwick is greatly to his liking."

"Heaven help me," she said, pulling into the gas station. She pulled up to the pump, shut the car off, then leaned back against the seat and allowed herself to shake. "I'm not sure I want to drive this thing again."

"You did a splendid job of not crunching it."

She turned her head to look at him. "And you did a splendid job of rescuing that poor man this afternoon."

He rubbed his hands over his face suddenly, then shook his head, as if he tried to free himself from thoughts he didn't want to think. "Luck," he said apparently striving for a light tone, "and an intense desire to impress a beautiful woman."

"I didn't see her in the crowd."

He unbuckled himself, undid her seat belt, then turned to her and looked at her purposefully. She held out her hand to hold him off.

"This isn't a dark corner," she managed.

"But you are a very beautiful woman," he said, "and one I seem to be overcome with a desire to impress."

"And kissing me in your car is going to do it?" she squeaked.

He smiled, leaned over, and paused. "I was thinking to give it a go."

"Heaven help *me*," she managed.

He put his finger under her chin, turned her face slightly away from him, and kissed her cheek.

"I'll come get your door," he said, pulling back. "And see to our little brown Ford." He got out of the car, then leaned back down and looked at her. "What do you think?"

What she thought was that if he came that close to kissing her again and didn't, she was going to deck him.

"I think," she managed, "that I'm in trouble where you're concerned."

He smiled, a quick little smile that showed off his dimple to its best advantage, then straightened and shut the door. Tess leaned her head back against the seat and concentrated on not hyperventilating.

Five minutes later she was sitting in the other seat, watching John watch the road in front of and behind them with equal intensity. She didn't say anything. Either she was imagining things or she wasn't. She didn't like being in the middle of it, though. She much preferred studying things from the sidelines.

"Is he there?" she asked when they neared their village.

"Yes," John said simply. He glanced in the mirror once more, then whipped down a side street so quickly, she lost her breath.

The tires didn't squeal, though, not that time, nor the next time.

"You've been watching too many movies," she said breathlessly.

"A good driving school," he corrected dryly, then pulled the car over and waited.

She realized they were now facing the way they'd come. The little brown Ford seemed to realize the jig was up because it executed a rather poor three-point turn in the middle of the street and sped back off the other way.

"Told you," she managed. "Babes in bodices trying to figure out where you live so they can come ogle you."

He only tapped his fingers thoughtfully on the steering wheel, then looked at her. "I should have looked in your car park the night of that large party."

"It could have been Bill the Brainless."

"I don't think he could have fit under the wheel of that thing," John said. He studied the road for another minute or two. "How many more events do you have this week?"

"A family reunion tonight," she said, "but nothing for the rest of the weekend, but that's on purpose." She paused. "I have plans."

He stopped tapping. "Plans?"

"A non-date with Lord Haulton," she said. "There is, if you can believe it, a Regency-style house party at Payneswick. Stephen has been dragging me to it for five years now. I think he enjoys doing a Mr. Darcy impression."

He looked at her, then. "And you?"

"I enjoy trying to get into Lord Payneswick's library."

John smiled briefly. "A priceless medieval text?"

"More than one, actually." She hesitated. "I don't suppose you would want to come along."

He studied her. "You couldn't possibly be asking me out on a *date*, Dr. Alexander, could you?"

"What would you say if I were?"

He considered. She could see the wheels turning and imagined all that turning had a great deal to do with Stephen de Piaget. To be cooped up in close quarters with the man for an extended period of time might be just more than he could take.

He finally just frowned, put the car in gear, and drove on. She didn't press him. He was probably figuring out a good way to tell her no, which she supposed was for the best. They had seen more of each other over the past week than he'd wanted to or was good for her heart. A little break might be just the thing.

He was silent as he drove her home, silent as he fetched her out of the car, and still silent as he walked her across the drawbridge and up the steps to her front door. He opened it for her, looked inside, then stood aside to let her pass by.

She turned to look at him. "Well?"

He dragged his hand through his hair, then sighed. "I think it best I don't go."

"All right." She honestly would have been more surprised if he'd said yes. And after all, the world wasn't going to end before she saw him again the following week. "I'll see you when I get back."

"Nay, you won't," he said, "because I don't want you to go, either."

She blinked. "What?"

He chewed on his words for a minute. "That car was following us."

"It was following *you*."

"I don't know that's the case and until I'm sure, I want you tucked inside your castle with the doors locked where I know you're safe."

She would have smiled in disbelief, but she knew he wasn't kidding. And she was also absolutely sure that he wasn't telling her everything he knew and until he did, she was under no obligation to be not only herded but penned. Besides, she had the feeling this was her year to get into Lord Payneswick's private books. Stephen had been sucking up to the man all year long with that end in sight. She wasn't about to pass on the opportunity to be there.

"I appreciate the concern," she said honestly, "but Stephen has already paid for my ticket, as well as one for Peaches. We'll both be fine."

John was not a happy camper, that much she could say. She wondered, absently, what Montgomery would have done in his place. Probably drawn his sword and prodded Pippa back inside the hall with it. Poor John only had frowns to use, which he did without hesitation.

"Is Haulton coming to fetch you?" he asked curtly.

"What difference does that make?"

"It makes a great deal of difference," he said, through gritted teeth. "Now, is he coming to fetch you, or must I call him and insist that he does?"

"I think he's been at Artane this week," she said, finding that it wasn't all that difficult all of a sudden to dredge up a brisk tone of her own, "digging through artifacts for a paper he's working on. Peaches and I are driving north to meet him, and no, you absolutely can't call him and order him around like you do me."

He folded his arms over his chest, apparently the ultimate de Piaget pose of intimidation. "I don't like this."

"I don't care what you like," she said before she thought better of it.

The unfortunate truth was, she did care. It mattered to her quite a bit that he was concerned about her.

A bit more than she was comfortable with, actually.

"In spite of that," he said, looking as if he were making great efforts to be polite, "I would prefer that you remain here."

"And I would prefer that you stop telling me what to do."

He pursed his lips, then made her a low bow. "As my lady wishes," he said coolly.

"French again, John," she pointed out.

He glared at her, then turned and walked down her steps. He stopped on the courtyard floor, then turned and looked up at her. "Lock the door."

"It's the middle of the afternoon," she said incredulously.

"Lock the bloody door, Tess," he growled.

She started to slam it shut, then she paused and looked out the door at him. "Are we having a fight?"

"I believe so."

"Is it going well?"

He swore. Then he took a deep breath and cursed a bit more. He walked up the steps, pulled her into his arms, and clutched her to him.

"Tess, please," he whispered against her ear, "*please* stay home."

She had to take a deep breath, and not just because he was holding her as if he never intended to let her go. "Please come with me."

He held her for another very long moment, then released her without looking at her. He walked out the door and jogged down her trio of steps. He turned and motioned for her to shut the door.

She did, then turned and leaned back against it. The man was going to make her crazy. In fact, if she hadn't known how to take him because of what he was hiding, she wouldn't have taken him at all. Bossy, dictatorial, sheepdoggish.

Chivalrous, tender, fearless.

She had the feeling it was going to be a very long weekend without him.

Chapter 14

Jↄₕₙ stood in front of the small hearth in his rented cottage and forced himself to look at what was in front of him. He wasn't one to shy away from the difficult, but even he had to admit that what was going on in his life was becoming a bit much.

Things were much as he'd come home to find them the evening before. His table had been laid out for tea with his Claymore propped up conveniently against his chair. It had been rather unsettling, truth be told, and he had seen his share of unsettling things. He'd scoured the inside of his cottage, the garden, and his shop for clues, but found nothing, not even any tyre tracks that were discernible from those already there.

Someone was stalking him.

He was beginning to fear that he might be drawing Tess into danger by passing any time at all in her company.

And the thought of *that* about did him in.

He'd slept very poorly, then been up at dawn in his garden, putting that Scottish broadsword to good use. A pity he didn't have anyone to use it on. It certainly would have simplified things.

He'd spent the past two hours wrestling with himself. He

wasn't at all keen on the idea of Tess driving with Peaches all the way to Lincolnshire so she could put on Regency-era garb and have that damned Stephen de Piaget slobber all over her.

He took a deep breath. It wasn't Stephen who bothered him. It was whoever else was out there that he couldn't see and wasn't sure of. He could hope that 'twas only him the soul had in his sights, but he couldn't guarantee that.

And he didn't like that at all.

He had showered, tossed gear into a backpack, and wrestled with himself a bit longer. He wasn't sure what would be worse: dragging Tess into his unknown madness or sitting at home like a woman, wondering if she were being dragged into his madness just the same.

He pulled his mobile out of his pocket and dialed her number. It rang three times before she picked up.

"Yes?" she said coolly.

He wasn't at all surprised by her tone. She was, he suspected, easily as stubborn as he was and well versed in the strategies of warfare, even if in a purely academic way. He had fired the opening salvo, as it were, without apology or hesitation. She wasn't going to leave herself open to further attack. Obviously the only way to approach the battlefield and come away conqueror was to perpetrate a strategy she wouldn't expect.

"I apologize," he said without hesitation.

He could have sworn he heard the faintest huff of a laugh. "For what, you big bully?"

"For herding you," he said. "Is it too late to accompany you north where I might attempt not to herd you a bit more?"

"I'm leaving in ten minutes," she said, then hung up.

He snatched up his backpack and ran for the shop's Range Rover. He would have preferred the Vanquish for its ability to outrun ruffians, but Tess and Peaches couldn't share a seat, so the Rover it would have to be.

He pulled into their car park as Tess was putting her key into the Ford's door. He hopped out of his car with alacrity and relieved Peaches of her wee suitcase and plopped it in his boot before she could protest. He held open the back door for her and smiled pleasantly.

"Allow me to help milady's lovely sister into my carriage," he said with a small bow.

"I've already bought what you're selling," she said with an amused smile. "Don't waste any more time on me."

"I might still see to your lunch on the way," he offered.

"Done."

He shut her door, then turned to the sterner test. Tess was simply watching him. He walked around her car, then gently removed the strap of her overnight bag from her shoulder. He put it where she couldn't get at it without his keys, then returned for her. He started to clasp his hands behind his back in preparation for another bit of flowery sentiment, but only succeeded in dropping his keys.

It wasn't that he was nervous. It was . . . well, it was because she had him so turned around, he scarce recognized himself any longer.

Or perhaps it had been Fate.

He squatted down to retrieve his keys near her front tyre, then froze. It took no especial skill to recognize the faint smell lingering there, but he supposed he wouldn't have if he hadn't spent so much time under the bonnet of his own cars.

Brake fluid.

He considered for a moment or two, then took a careful breath and rose. He looked at Tess with what he hoped was less of a grimace and more of a pleasant expression.

She wasn't fooled. "What?" she asked immediately.

"Sore knee," he lied without hesitation.

"You were sniffing."

"I was trying to cover a grunt of pain," he said.

She pursed her lips. "You're not a very good liar, you know. In fact, you've been acting very strangely for more than just the last ten minutes. What aren't you telling me?"

The list was very long, but he put it aside and settled for the most innocuous thing he could come up with. He sighed heavily, then made a production of looking heavenward. "I didn't want to say anything before, but I'm honestly not sure I can manage it."

"Manage what?"

"Hose and heels," he said solemnly. "And short trousers."

Her eyes narrowed. "I'm about to pull my sister out of your car, you know."

He would have taken her hand, but she had her arms folded over her chest, no doubt to keep them out of range. The truth was, he would have put out his own eyes himself before he told her what had been happening to him—or what he'd just seen in her car park—but he supposed he couldn't lie to her any longer.

But he'd be damned if he'd tell her everything.

He sighed deeply. "Very well, the truth. I have very good reason to believe the little brown Ford was following me. I have no idea who it is or what they want, I just know I don't want whoever it is mistaking you for me and harming you."

She let out her breath slowly. "Really?"

He nodded. "Really. And that is why I didn't want you to go today."

"And why you've apparently mastered your fear of short trousers and cravats enough to come along?"

"The lengths I've gone to for you, Dr. Alexander, are truly appalling."

She was now hugging herself instead of trying to intimidate him, which he supposed was progress. "You could have told me all this yesterday."

"I didn't want you to worry."

"I can take care of myself."

He nodded as if he conceded the point when he most definitely had not. She had likely never in her life faced anything more intimidating than a feisty undergrad unhappy with his marks. Whoever was vexing him now had a very sharp sword—his sword—at his disposal. She wasn't going to find herself facing the business end of it as long as he had anything to say about it.

She walked around him suddenly. "Let's go. I want to get a good costume."

He didn't intend to argue with that. He saw her inside, shut her door, then pulled out his mobile phone and paused on the way around the back. Bobby, it seemed, was more than happy to hitch a ride to the castle and take Tess's runabout to the shop to see about brake lines, no car key necessary.

John would have smiled to himself as he ended the call, but he was slightly ill, truth be told. Tess would have gotten as far as London and been cruising along the motorway only to find that her brakes were absolutely useless.

He took a deep breath, then climbed into the driver's seat. He shoved his phone onto the dashboard, then wondered briefly if he shouldn't have checked his own brake lines.

Well, that was what a petrol station was for, which he would find as soon as would seem reasonable.

He looked in the rearview mirror, winked at Peaches, then wondered how long he should wait before he attempted to hold Tess's hand.

He stopped the first chance he had, had his surreptitious look at his own brakes, checked a thing or two under the bonnet as well, then got them back on the road without delay. If he continually looked behind them and watched the other cars they shared the road with more than he might have otherwise, who could blame him?

They were a pair of hours into the journey before he dared have a proper look at Tess. He was slightly surprised to find she was watching him. Gravely, but she was watching him. He attempted a smile.

"Plotting Regency torments for me?" he asked lightly.

"And what might those be?" she asked seriously.

"Dressing me as a servant and forcing me to attend you at all hours."

"Well, Brer Rabbit, we won't do that, then."

He smiled. "If you want the truth, I daresay the worst you could do was lock yourself off with the ladies and leave me forced to spend the weekend shooting and drinking port with affected fops. Or, worse still, chatting with noblemen whilst indulging in cigars and brandy."

"Does Lord Haulton count?" Tess asked mildly. "He called just after you did and was thrilled to know you'd be coming with us. I think he shares your aversion to whist and billiards."

"Good of him," John said grimly.

"He's also managed to get you a bed," she added. "He hopes that you won't mind bunking with him."

John supposed the only reason he didn't wince was because he'd had so many years of practice at not. *Real knights don't flinch* had been one of Robin's favorite axioms, one John had heard so many times, he was fairly sure it had been burned into the very matter of his brain.

"Of course not," he said, when he thought he could speak without any inflection in his voice. "He's very accommodating."

"Actually, I think he's just hoping to have you to himself for a bit so he can investigate your genealogies. He's fairly convinced you have to be related to him somewhere in the vast reaches of time. Distant cousins, no doubt."

John supposed he couldn't have expected anything else. He could, however, make damned sure he spent as little time privately as possible with the good viscount, lest they discover their genealogy was less distant than feared. Though how anyone could doubt the like, John didn't know. He and Stephen were certainly not twins, but they could quite easily have passed for brothers, something he imagined wouldn't escape the notice of quite a few people who cared to look.

He was beginning to wonder if he'd made a terrible mistake.

But since the alternative was letting Tess go on her own—and he now knew where that would have led—he had no choice but to carry on and keep a sharp eye out for escape routes.

He stopped for a bit of lunch when the furrow between Tess's brow grew pronounced and ignored her insistence that they go Dutch treat. He exchanged a look with Peaches, who he was quite happy to discover was still lingering on his side of the battlefield, then hastened around the boot of his car to stop Tess before she climbed inside.

"Tess," he began slowly, but found he couldn't say anything else. She was remarkably beautiful, which he'd known, but she looked less at peace than she had over the past pair of days. It almost made him wish he'd limited himself to seeing her but once a se'nnight. Perhaps then he would have simply thought his mysterious sword-thief was lying in wait just for him. The thought of Tess being involved—

She stepped forward suddenly and put her arms around his waist. He didn't hesitate to return the favor.

"You aren't angry with me," he said, hoping that by stating it as fact, it might be so.

"No," she said with a deep sigh. "I know it's just what you de Piaget men—I mean, what you men do."

He pulled back and looked down at her. "What did you say?"

She returned his look, clear-eyed, though he could see the pulse in her throat beating furiously. "Stephen herds me as well," she said easily. "You remind me of him."

He would have pressed her a bit more—or bolted, which was his first inclination—but she leaned up on her toes and kissed him on the cheek.

"I should be used to it by now." She opened her own door, then got inside the car and pulled the door shut.

John wondered if he might at some point in the future not find himself winded by the woman one way or another. He managed to get himself into his own seat with a minimum of fuss, then glance at Tess, but she was only watching him in the same grave, serious way she'd been watching him all morning. He looked in the rearview mirror, but Peaches had her nose in a book. He took a careful breath, then let it out slowly before he turned the Rover on and got them back onto the road.

"John?"

"Aye?"

"Thank you for coming with me."

"It is my pleasure," he said sincerely.

She put her hand over his resting on his leg. "It might do us both a bit of good to put all things medieval behind us. You know," she added, "reenactment crazies and castles and little brown Fords full of bawdy wenches wanting a closer look at your buff self."

He managed a smile. "I think, my lady, that you're simply trying to convince me that mincing about in high heels won't damage my enormous ego."

"Maybe," she agreed. "Or it might just be that we both need a break from ordinary life."

"Must it come thanks to eighteenth-century dress?" he asked, pained.

"You're halfway to Payneswick," she pointed out. "No sense in turning back now."

"Nay," he agreed, "'tis a bit too late for that."

Actually, it was a bit too late for that in several areas of his life, places he would have protected a bit more ferociously if he'd known just how easily his defenses would have been breached. His cottage, for instance.

His heart, for certain.

Though he had to admit he was less worried about the latter. If Tess were leading the charge, perhaps the siege laid to his poor self wouldn't be too painful.

He sincerely hoped he wasn't underestimating the danger to the rest of his life.

* * *

Six hours later, he was beginning to think he'd underestimated several things, beginning and ending with, as he'd suspected before, shoes that clicked as he walked.

He leaned against a handy wall and looked about the dancing hall. He saw nothing amiss, which should have reassured him, but he found he was too tightly strung for that. He attempted a pleasant expression as he scanned the hall, watching the dancers that marched about in precise formations, studying with even more care the servants who milled about or stood at attention as if they'd been extras in a film. At least it took his mind off the narrow misses he'd already had that afternoon.

They'd arrived shortly after two and been welcomed in grand style. Costumes had been assigned, and he'd found himself indeed sharing a bedchamber with his, ah, nephew. Fortunately for his peace of mind, Lord Haulton had apparently gone off to ingratiate himself with Lord Payneswick, no doubt in another attempt to pry the key to rare and interesting medieval texts from the poor man's hands.

John had put himself into clothing that had seemed less like a costume and more like properly fitting garments with the aid of a valet who had been assigned to Stephen but seemingly didn't mind tying the extra cravat. Properly dressed and well watered with a contraband glass of Lilt over ice, John had marched off into the fray, trying to ignore the fact that he felt as if he were tiptoeing.

He'd lost his breath when Tess and Peaches had come out of their bedchamber, absolutely resplendent in their finery. John had managed to bow to Peaches first before pointing out to her that she was going to leave every man in the house begging her to be his.

He'd turned to Tess and decided that there was no point in trying to cling to the notion that a man couldn't fall in love with a woman in such a short time. His brother Nicholas had taken one look at his lady wife and abruptly turned into a testy, unpleasant whoreson until he'd finally relented and admitted that his heart was lost. John hadn't been there to witness Miles's vanquishment, but he imagined it had gone much the same way.

But as he'd supposed dropping to his knees and begging Tess to be his—and securing her consent before he told her the truth about his past with the hope that she wouldn't have him committed to a Bedlam-like institution as a result—was premature, he'd merely offered his arms to both sisters and escorted them to supper.

Could he be blamed if he'd absconded with Tess's dance card and claimed an inordinate and improper number of dances?

And could he be blamed if he'd spent more time than he should have cursing under his breath as she ignored his name and danced with every other man in the room, including more dances than was polite with that damned Stephen de Piaget?

"This is the second time in a fortnight I've seen you in a century not your own."

John was certain he'd jumped half a foot. It was only dumb luck that he didn't fall off his shoes and land upon his arse. He took a deep breath, then looked to his left to find none other than David Thompson, nag extraordinaire, standing there watching him with a calculating smile.

John let out his breath slowly, then looked at the man's gear. At least Dave was trussed up as thoroughly as he himself was. There was some justice left in the world.

"Your wife's doing?" he asked politely.

"My daughter's," Dave said, looking slightly sheepish. "Too many BBC versions of the illustrious Miss Austen's offerings, no doubt." He looked at John assessingly. "What of you?"

"I'm here at the invitation of a neighbor."

"The lady of Sedgwick?" Dave asked shrewdly.

"As it happens."

Dave looked at him, then laughed. "I never thought I would see you in stockings, John, but stranger things have happened. She must have you twisted in knots."

"I'm afraid she does," John admitted.

"Which is why she hasn't danced a single set with you, obviously."

"We're in the middle of a row."

"Best of luck with her, then." He leaned closer. "I'll just warn you that it won't be that lovely woman to finish the job of breaking your heart; it'll be the daughters she gives you."

John was still feeling a bit as if someone had kicked him in the gut as Dave laughed again and walked off to join a gaggle of young ladies, some of whom John could easily see were related to him and his very lovely wife.

Daughters?

He was still trying to catch his breath when he realized Tess was walking toward him. He might have taken the fact that Peaches was giving her no choice a bit personally, but Tess had deigned to hold his hand most of the journey to Payneswick, so he supposed he shouldn't.

He couldn't help a frown, however, when Lord Haulton sauntered over, looking as if he fully intended to monopolize Tess for the rest of the evening. John took her hand and pulled her over to stand next to him before he thought better of it. It was only as Stephen looked at him with raised eyebrows that he realized he'd pulled Tess behind him.

He sighed deeply, then tucked her hand in the crook of his elbow and stepped aside so she was standing next to him.

"Sorry," he said.

She looked up at him, then at Stephen. "Buzz off."

Stephen considered, then looked at Peaches. "Will I receive the same treatment from you, I wonder?"

"I believe, my lord," Peaches said coolly, "that there's a duke's daughter across the room who's eyeing you. I'm sure you would be very comfortable with her."

Stephen frowned, then made her a stiff bow before he turned and walked off.

A rather dapper-looking lad appeared next to Peaches without delay and was accepted as a more suitable partner. John looked at Tess in surprise.

"Did I just witness something I should understand?"

Tess shook her head helplessly. "I'm as in the dark as you are. Peaches isn't usually that feisty, so Stephen must have really put his foot in it. Not that there was anything between them to start with."

John refrained from voicing the hearty wish that Stephen would put his foot in it where Tess was concerned and settled for making her a low bow. "A dance, my lady?"

"If you like."

He was grateful he'd taken the opportunity to have a lesson whilst Tess and Peaches had been at their toilette. At the very least, he might avoid treading upon Tess's frock.

"I believe we must have some conversation."

He realized Tess was talking to him, then he understood the

reference. He smiled. "Perhaps I could remark on the absolute delight that is your coiffure, my lady, or the loveliness of your gown."

They danced another pattern, then came together in a bit of marching.

"You look rather lovely yourself," she said quietly.

"It beats the bleeding hell out of tights."

She smiled, apparently in spite of herself. "You make it very difficult to stay irritated with you."

He pursed his lips. "You managed it all the way here, I daresay."

She looked at him seriously. "I told you before that I wasn't angry. I just needed a change of scenery, though not necessarily of society. This was my way to have it."

"Along with a peep at priceless texts."

"Well, that seems like something a serious scholar would be interested in, don't you think?"

He supposed so, but he had to admit he hadn't given it much thought. He nodded, but said nothing else, mostly because he was finding his thoughts going in directions he hadn't entertained before.

Was she unhappy where she was? He would have supposed that having a castle would have been a boon, given who she was and what she loved, but perhaps not. If she thought she had traded the glory of academia for nothing more than a pile of stones, then he could well understand her eagerness to embark on their current escapade. To make her feel as if she hadn't judged amiss in her current choice of ventures, if nothing else.

He understood that, actually. He had traded his birthright for the glories of the Future, but lost the rank and privilege of being his father's son, as well as the possibility of having inherited one of his father's estates and all that entailed. It had occurred to him, once or twice, that the bargain might have been badly done.

Then again, he was rather more content than he should have been with four wheels and some decent horsepower, but that was perhaps something to think on when he didn't have a mesmerizing woman almost within arm's reach.

He continued putting off thinking about things that unsettled him as, a pair of hours later, he walked Tess back to her bedchamber. He was quite sure the reveling would go on into the wee hours, but she looked tired, and he was frankly quite tired himself. He walked down the long gallery with her, then stopped and drew her over to a long window. He kept her hand in his and looked out over the darkened landscape. It reminded him abruptly that there were things out there he couldn't see, things he would have been prepared for had he chosen his birthright and remained where he'd been born.

But then he would have been without Tess.

"You think too much."

He looked down at her, standing there beside him, lovely and pale, and shook his head. "Just idle thoughts, in truth. But now that you have me considering other things—"

She looked at him in mock horror. "Surely not, good sir."

"It may be the only time I have you to myself," he said seriously, turning her to him and drawing her into his arms. "We are, it would seem, overrun by chaperons."

"That should make you feel better," she said.

He shook his head. "I will feel better when you're safely behind two-foot-thick walls and a door with a sturdy lock."

"John, you're paranoid," she said, sighing as she leaned against him. "This has nothing to do with me. I'm not even sure it has anything to do with you. After all, who in their right mind would wa—"

He supposed he was fortunate he'd grown to manhood looking for things out of the corner of his eye; it was the only reason he saw the end of the curtain rod that had loitered twenty feet above him coming down toward his empty head at such a rapid speed.

He jerked Tess out of the way and sent them both sprawling. He wasn't altogether sure he hadn't heard a rending sound, which he could only hope hadn't come from his trousers. He closed his eyes briefly, then looked up.

The Viscount Haulton was standing over him, looking down at him with a frown.

"I say," he said, sounding almost as unsettled as John felt, though perhaps for different reasons, "if you'd wanted a chaste embrace, you didn't have to indulge in it on the ground."

John sat up and glared at his nephew. "Does it occur to you that I might have considered that? Or that?" he added, pointing to where the heavy metal rod was dangling precariously by one end whilst the other swung and the heavy velvet draperies continued to flutter before they fell still.

Stephen looked back at him. "Pull that down yourselves, did you?"

"No," John said sharply, "we didn't."

Stephen chewed on that as he held out his hands to pull Tess up to her feet. Half of her skirt had been torn off, but the bodice was intact and she was quite fortunately wearing an undershift of sorts. John had no idea what the bloody thing was called in the current day. 'Twas for damned sure he hadn't undressed any Future gels to find out.

He crawled to his feet and looked at Tess briefly to make sure she wasn't bleeding—he would atone for bruises later—then walked over to look with Stephen at the hardware near the ceiling.

"Odd," Stephen mused. "Perhaps something that needed tending."

"Obviously," Tess said, from behind them. "A random accident if ever I saw one."

John exchanged a look with Stephen, then turned to Tess. He attempted a smile. "I daresay. Let's get you tucked up safely for the night, shall we?"

"John," she said with a long-suffering sigh.

"As you said," he said with a shrug. "Random."

And to anyone who hadn't been looking for mischief, it was. After all, what were the odds that he would have been standing in front of the only window with no curtains drawn over it? The rod could have fallen on anyone.

He walked with Tess to her bedchamber, then paused and considered what to say that wouldn't leave her thinking on tangles she shouldn't begin to unravel. He clasped his hands behind his back and settled for an apology.

"I'm sorry about your frock."

"I have another to wear tomorrow. I can sew this—"

"I'll see to it," he said without hesitation. "Surely there is a seamstress in the vicinity who needs a bit of lolly."

She smiled. "You don't have—"

"To," he finished, "but I will."

She sighed and leaned against the door. "Your chivalry is showing."

"I'm not sure you've begun to see it this weekend."

"More herding?"

"What do you think?"

She smiled, but that smile didn't quite cover the unease in her eyes. "I imagine I'll see you before breakfast. And I'll check all the locks in deference to you, Mr. Paranoid."

He leaned in and kissed her cheek, then pulled away before she could clout him in the nose, which he would have deserved. Or so he thought until she caught him by the lapels of his jacket. She looked at him solemnly, then pulled him close so she could put her arms around his neck. She leaned up on her toes and pressed her lips against his ear.

He shivered.

"I trust you."

"The saints preserve me," he managed, putting his arms around her before she could escape. "And aye, I know I'm speaking in French. 'Tis a terrible habit I can't seem to break."

She brushed her lips against his cheek, then sank back on her heels and looked up at him. "Where did you learn that particular version of it?"

"I can audit the odd class in medieval tongues as well as you can, my lady. And that," he said distinctly, "is your one question for the day. Actually, I think that might be the second."

"I should limit you to one bout of bossiness a day," she said darkly, "but I don't think you'd survive it."

"Likely not," he agreed. He released her, motioned for her to go inside, then made locking motions with his hand.

And he tried not to notice how the simple feel of her lips on his cheek about did him in.

Tess shut the door. John listened to her lock it, then turned to find Stephen standing five paces away, watching him silently. He tried not to be unsettled by the sight, though he supposed not even his father would have been able to suppress the slightest of shivers.

Time travel was, he could say with certainty, a very strange thing indeed.

"I think you should go find Peaches," John said seriously.

Stephen chewed on that for a moment. "She won't appreciate my pulling her away from the festivities."

"Resist being intimidated by a wench and do it just the same," John said shortly.

Stephen's mouth fell open, then he laughed a little. "I'm not intimidated by her."

"Then what are you waiting for?"

Stephen looked at him narrowly. "I'm waiting to see what it is you're planning in that wee head of yours, that's what."

"An equitable division of standing guard in front of this door," John said, "and speculation about how sturdy the lock is."

Stephen considered him for a moment or two in silence. "I'll go fetch Peaches, then I'll take the first shift."

John nodded. "Fair enough. I'll wait, then return in two hours."

"Six, you wee fool," Stephen said with a snort. "I slept last night. It doesn't look as though you did."

"Four, or nothing," John countered.

"Done. Make good use of it."

"Thank you, my lord." He paused. "If I might inquire—"

"My qualifications include several bouts of defense classes from a certain Scot named MacLeod," Stephen supplied without hesitation. "I think I can manage the odd, decrepit thug without overly exerting myself."

John sighed lightly. Obviously, he was destined to be haunted by MacLeods for the rest of his life. He also supposed that if Stephen had been dabbling with whatever Scottish mischief those MacLeods combined, he might be equal to guarding a door for an hour or two.

"I'll return posthaste," Stephen said, walking away. "We'll discuss the night's activities—or lack thereof—over Schnapps in Lord Payneswick's study tomorrow afternoon. I think between the two of us, we'll keep the ladies safe until then."

John watched him go, then looked up at the curtain rod hanging by its lone hook. Perhaps it had been a fluke. Short of fetching a ladder and climbing up to see, he didn't imagine he would know for sure. He supposed if anyone came to repair it, Stephen could put forth the pertinent questions.

He didn't like to leave Tess behind, but he wasn't fool enough to think he could be of any use to her without at least an hour or two of sleep.

He imagined he would have ample things to think on for the rest of the night to keep himself awake.

Chapter 15

T*ess* stood at the doorway to her bedroom and put her hand on the doorknob. She couldn't bring herself to turn it, though.

She took a deep breath and smoothed her hands down over her dress. The incident the night before had been a fluke, of course, nothing more. What had probably been the worst thing had been winding up on the floor with her skirts torn half off. Or perhaps that had been looking up, stunned, and seeing a heavy curtain rod having taken a trajectory that would have led through her head if she'd still been standing there.

She shivered, but that came from the flimsiness of her gown surely, so she concentrated on that instead of other things that bothered her. She honestly didn't know how Regency women had survived the winters unless they'd had better sartorial aid than she'd had. Her dress was long-sleeved, true, but better suited to a cool fall day than a chilly winter morning. She walked back to her closet and looked through what she'd been given to wear, hoping for some sort of sweater. The best she could do was a shawl, but since it seemed warm enough, perhaps she couldn't hope for anything more.

She passed on what Peaches had left her of breakfast and started toward the door. She shifted her shoulders under her shawl, then winced. She wasn't overly bruised, but she was definitely sore. She would have something to say to that John de Piaget sooner rather than later about his methods of saving her life.

She realized she had come to another stop in front of the door only after her hand started to ache from gripping the doorknob too tightly. She took a deep, steadying breath. There was nothing outside that she couldn't handle. For all she knew, there was still a de Piaget lad standing there. Peaches had been shut in with her the night before after having been herded back to their room by Stephen. Tess had had no doubt John would relieve him at some point during the night, to soothe his paranoid musings.

She had thought about those for far longer during the night than she likely should have, but the only conclusion that made sense was that something back in the village had spooked him and he'd gone into medieval mode.

That was understandable. He'd had a sword in his hands two days earlier, which had probably put him back in touch with his past in a big way. It was spilling over into his current life. The only problem was, his current life included her current life, and she couldn't seem to convince him that she wasn't part of his mystery. He was being stalked by some gal with medieval fantasies run amok. Nothing else seemed reasonable.

She opened the door and walked out into the gallery. She didn't run bodily into John, which gave her hope that he'd actually been sensible and finally gone to bed.

She refused to be unnerved because she was alone.

She took a deep breath, then started down the hallway. She looked up, but honestly couldn't tell which of the curtains had almost fallen on them. Everything was in its place; nothing sinister was lurking in the shadows. Just a normal, unremarkable day where she was wearing a gown made from a pattern designed over a hundred years ago. She didn't have murder and mayhem in her future; she had the potential sight of John de Piaget in a cutaway Regency coat and trousers to look forward to.

Whether he liked it or not, the man had been born to wear hose.

She continued on her way, trying to decide what to do first.

Peaches had left an hour earlier full of her own plans. Her sister could make friends out of potted plants, a talent Tess admired but had long ago resigned herself to never having. A fortuitous meeting with a London client, a gaggle of bosom friends made the night before, and a very long list of mesmerized men would keep Peaches busy far into the evening. That was wonderful for her sister, but it left Tess a bit at loose ends. She was quite sure Stephen would be well into Day Two of the assault on Lord Payneswick's reticence. That left her either pursuing her own flatteries of the man, or looking for John. Since she didn't imagine he would be far given his actions of the night before, she supposed she could just roam for a bit and eventually wind up with both.

She passed on a rowdy game of billiards, dismissed a serene roomful of stitchers, and settled for the library. There were women inside, so she supposed she wasn't breaking any taboos. She didn't dare hope that Lord Payneswick would keep anything of true interest out for public consumption, but she'd been surprised before. No sense in not having a good look on the off chance she was pleasantly surprised again.

She chose a random shelf and clasped her hands behind her back to study the titles there.

"Looking for anything in particular?"

Tess closed her eyes at the sound of that voice approximately three inches from her ear.

"Year Five and still no joy," she managed. "Hope springs eternal, though, when it comes to original manuscripts."

"Have you thought about just asking him?" John asked, leaning his shoulder against one of the bookcases and smiling gravely down at her. "Your credentials ought to at least get you a look at what he hides behind glass."

"Stephen's been trying for a decade without success."

"You're much prettier than he is."

"You would think that would count for something, wouldn't you?"

He wrapped one of the tendrils hanging down her neck very carefully around his finger, then let it slide away. "I'm convinced, even if Lord Payneswick isn't."

She laughed uncomfortably. "You're daft."

"Besotted, rather."

"Sleep-deprived," she countered, "especially since I imagine you didn't sleep any last night."

"Oh, I did," he conceded. "When Lord Haulton threatened me with bodily harm."

She looked into his lovely gray eyes and thought she just might have to find somewhere to sit down soon. something she should worry about. "I think you and Stephen have overactive imaginations."

"More than likely," he agreed, "and since that is the case, why don't you allow me to be your escort for the day out of pity, not unease?"

"Are you going to watch me look for books all morning?" she asked politely.

"I can imagine much worse things," he said seriously, "but I thought that since we are in this lovely little cottage with nothing but time on our hands, you might be interested in a little explore. If your shoes are up to the challenge, there is a very well-tended path through lovely gardens. Or," he said casually, "I understand Lord Payneswick keeps several private chambers dedicated to particular time periods."

She caught her breath. "Really?"

"Aye," he said, his eyes beginning to twinkle. "I believe he's out this morning on a pheasant hunt. We might have the morning at our disposal if we hurry."

She was horribly torn. "We shouldn't."

"Afraid?"

"Yes, that I'll be banned forever from his estate if we're caught."

He leaned closer to her. "I imagine he'll be gone at least three hours. You could thumb through quite a few texts in three hours, don't you think?"

She took a deep breath, then shoved the book she was holding back into its slot. If Pippa could brave the wilds of medieval England, she could venture a peek into Lord Payneswick's private books. "Let's go."

John offered his arm and wasted no time escorting her from the library and down the hallway. She wasn't sure she dared ask how he knew where he was going, but her curiosity got the better of her.

"Whom did you pay for the information?" she asked.

"I managed it all myself," he said easily. "I pulled up his website on my mobile and looked to see if there might be anything he was particularly proud of. Imagine my surprise at finding that that was indeed the case. It would appear that an entire floor of one wing of his lovely country house is a veritable treasure trove of history."

Considering how much history John had no doubt been gobsmacked by, she imagined his surprise was fairly extensive.

She also admired his technique of getting them past inquisitive staff and other guests. He might have been masquerading as a normal modern guy most of the time, but he could definitely pull out the lord's son stops when necessary. After he looked down his autocratic nose at a final pair of lads dressed in regimentals and sent them on their way, curiosity unsatisfied, she had to laugh a little.

"You are as autocratic as Stephen."

"It's the cravat," he said, sticking his finger between it and his neck and tugging uncomfortably. "Keeps me nose in the air, lassie, don't ye see?"

She smiled, because the man was utterly charming. She didn't even protest when he almost pulled her off her feet and hid with her behind a heavy curtain. He put his finger to his lips, then peeked around after the footsteps had passed.

"You're going to get us thrown out," she breathed.

"He has a harpsichord," he whispered back, "and I daresay it isn't a reproduction."

"You're going to get us thrown in *jail*."

"Not today," he said cheerfully, pulling aside the curtain and letting her duck under his arm.

"John," she began, prepared to make one last stab at reason and caution, "I think—"

"Payneswick will be gone for the whole of the morning?" he finished. "I'm not convinced of that, but I think we'll manage a couple of hours, at least." He smiled. "If we're caught, you dazzle them with your beauty and I'll plead insanity. We'll manage well enough."

She wasn't at all sure either would be enough, but John was already picking the lock with tools he had produced from somewhere upon his person. He made very quick work of it, which left her wondering just where he'd learned such a thing. He pocketed his tools, glanced at her, then froze.

"What?" he asked.

"You picked that lock," she managed.

"I've a bad habit of locking my keys in the car," he said as he opened the door. "Ah, Georgian from top to bottom." He glanced at her. "Lovely, isn't it?"

It was, which was just the distraction she needed from questions she probably didn't want to have answered. She was tempted to ask him which of the eras he liked the best, but she was afraid she wouldn't have been able to sound as casual about the question as she probably should have. She simply watched him hop over the rope that separated the room from the little vestibule where gawkers were no doubt contained, unsatisfied and tethered. He unhooked the velvet rope for her, then hooked it back into its brass stand. He looked around the chamber, then rubbed his hands together.

"What first?" he asked, his eyes bright with unwholesome excitement. "Books or music?"

"Whichever will be worth the humiliation of getting caught," she said darkly.

He lifted an eyebrow. "Have you never done anything dangerous, my lady?"

"I've kept library books past their due dates," she said defensively. "I've walked on the wild side."

He laughed at her, then reached out and pulled her into his arms. He held her close for a moment, then took her face in his hands and kissed her on both cheeks.

"I won't let him send you to jail. Go look around with your hands behind your back if you don't want to leave any fingerprints."

"And you?"

He flexed his fingers. "I'll entertain you whilst you're about your looking."

She would have said she didn't imagine that would calm the butterflies in her stomach, but she found she was wrong. He was only partway into a fugue before she found herself standing at the side of the quite lovely harpsichord, listening to him with her mouth hanging open. Apparently his unwholesome musical skills weren't limited to guitar-like instruments. Tess found herself torn between looking at his unwholesomely handsome face and listening in astonishment to his remarkably fine Bach. She found that with enough effort, she could do both.

He looked up at her as he finished what he'd been dancing through, then froze. "Not good?"

"Is there anything you *can't* play?" she asked.

"Things that blow, especially the pipes," he said with a small smile. "The rest?" He shrugged. "It's all rubbish, but I generally only torment myself with it, so I keep at it."

It was almost out of her mouth to ask him why he didn't play professionally—in any number of arenas, apparently—but she stopped herself just in time. He didn't, because he didn't want any more notoriety than he already likely had thanks to his studio work.

"What other eras do you specialize in?" she managed.

"I draw the line after Rachmaninoff," he said, toying with snatches of other things. "It has to sound like music." He looked up at her. "And you?"

"The same." She listened to him a bit longer. "John?"

"Aye, love?"

"What would you do if you could do anything?" she asked, before she gave the question too much thought and didn't dare ask it.

He shot her a look from under ridiculously long eyelashes. "I'm not sure you want to know the answer to that."

"Is it illegal?"

He smiled, a little smile that left her smiling in return. "Nay, but it is decadent and involves you."

"Cad."

He only winked at her, then turned back to concentrating on what he was doing. Tess watched him until she thought she might rather like to have somewhere to sit. She looked around, then found she couldn't move.

Lord Payneswick was standing just inside the door, watching them.

"John," she managed faintly.

He looked up, then stopped. "Ah—"

Lord Payneswick waved him on, then stepped over his velvet rope and sat down gingerly in a chair. He beckoned for Tess to come sit across from him.

She went, because she thought humoring him might be a good idea.

She listened to John, who seemed to have dredged up a new level of commitment to his playing, and watched Lord Payneswick, who didn't seem to be reaching for a phone to call the cops. Though she was tempted to make a few inroads into a relationship with him, she didn't suppose the time was right to be asking him for any favors. Better that he continue enjoying hearing Bach on the appropriate instrument and hopefully forget that she and John had ventured where they shouldn't have.

John played another pair of pieces, then stopped, dropped his hands in his lap, and turned to look at Lord Payneswick.

"My most abject apologies for trespassing."

Lord Payneswick pursed his lips. "I might believe that, Mr. de Piaget, if I didn't strongly suspect you were the sort who would pick the lock on any number of my other private salons to try your hand at whatever you might find there."

John smiled a self-deprecating sort of smile that Tess found was inspiring her to forgive him for things he hadn't done yet. She could only hope it would work on Lord Payneswick as well.

"Your instrument here is magnificent," John said sincerely. "The temptation was too strong."

Lord Payneswick looked at him sternly. "And the only reason you're still sitting at it, old chum, is because Dave Thompson convinced me not to call the authorities."

John took a deep breath. "Good of him."

Tess found herself suddenly the object of Lord Payneswick's scrutiny.

"I understand you're a colleague of the Viscount Haulton," he said sternly. "And the lady of Sedgwick."

"Guilty on both accounts," Tess admitted, holding out her hand and feeling quite grateful it wasn't trembling. "Tess Alexander. My specialty is the Middle Ages."

Lord Payneswick shook her hand with a gentleness that belied his fierce frowns. "I suppose you'll now tell me that you share Lord Stephen's interest in my medieval artifacts."

Tess smiled. "I can't deny that. Your collection is rumored to be extensive."

Lord Payneswick pursed his lips. "I'm beginning to feel a bit like a fox in a thicket." He looked at John. "I understand from Dave that you play the lute."

Tess forced herself to maintain a neutral expression. If John admitted to that skill, she might actually get a look at what she'd been trying to drool over for years. But she wasn't about to ask him to.

John met her eyes briefly, took a deep breath, then nodded at Lord Payneswick.

"If it means Dr. Alexander will have her look, I would be more than happy to play anything you like."

Tess didn't dare say anything. She imagined, however, that she was going to be humoring John in all sorts of herding activities as repayment.

Payneswick stood up and rubbed his hands together. "I'll look forward, then, to a little concert after supper. *If* you two can keep yourselves out of trouble this afternoon. Let me start you on that path now, shall I?"

Tess thought it might be best to agree quickly, before he changed his mind. It occurred to her that it might have been better to get inside on her own merits, but she shoved that thought out of her mind as quickly as it had come. Not even Stephen, with his impressive academic credentials and a couple of titles to augment them, had managed to convince Payneswick to let him in. If they both had to hang on to John's coattails to have what they wanted, so be it—and gratefully so.

Lord Payneswick showed them the door to the garden and advised them to use it. He looked at John before he walked away.

"Give her your jacket, lad, and show some chivalry."

John shrugged out of his coat immediately and draped it around Tess's shoulders. "Thank you, Your Lordship."

Payneswick looked at them both, then pursed his lips as if he strove not to smile. "Incorrigible."

Tess watched him walk off, shaking his head, then looked up at John. "That was close."

He blew his hair out of his eyes. "Too close, I'd say." He reached for her hand and smiled weakly. "Let's go have our turn about the garden, though I'm not entirely sure you won't be carrying me back to the house."

She stopped him before he started off. "Thank you."

He looked at her in surprise. "For what?"

"For playing the lute tonight so I can look in his private books." She paused. "I know it makes you uncomfortable."

"Tonight, the prize is worth it," he said seriously. "Consider it my pleasure." He looked at her with an eyebrow raised. "Are you already making plans for your assault on the inner sanctum?"

"That will all depend on how long you intend to distract him."

"You tell me how long you need."

She smiled in spite of herself. "You're a good man, John de Piaget, to make that sort of sacrifice for me."

"I am," he agreed dryly, "and you can thank my father for any chivalrous tendencies I have." He tugged on her hand. "Let's go, so Payneswick can see us making good use of his garden. We don't want him to change his mind."

Tess was relieved, several hours later, to find that Lord Payneswick hadn't changed his mind. She stood at the edge of a room that reminded her so sharply of her own solar—well, Montgomery de Piaget's solar, actually—at Sedgwick, she could hardly catch her breath. It was as if she'd stepped back in time hundreds of years.

There were a couple of bookcases, of course, tucked discreetly in a corner and filled with all manner of things that looked as if they were hundreds of years old. Tapestries lined the walls and were spread out over the floors. A modest fire burned in the hearth—just hot enough to keep them warm but not hot enough to disturb the delicate tempering of the amazing collection of period instruments residing inside what she was certain were climate-controlled glass cases.

She was joined by Lord Payneswick, of course, as well as Stephen and their earlier savior, the relentless Dave Thompson. Tess watched as John was allowed to remove what she could see from across the room was indeed an amazingly preserved medieval lute. If she hadn't known better, she might have suspected some plucky time traveler had brought it with him and plopped it down in Payneswick's private office.

"This ought to be interesting," Stephen murmured from where he stood next to her.

"Wait until you hear him play," Tess murmured back.

Stephen took her hand and pulled it into the crook of his

elbow. "Well, since you've already heard him, maybe you should discreetly take a turn about the room and see what you come up with. We'll both make lists of what we'll want further looks at."

She looked up at him and smiled. "Always the scholar."

"Darling, it flatters my enormous ego to be an expert in something," he said with an answering smile. "It's for damned sure that will never be swordplay—as Kendrick would tell you without being asked. I suppose that leaves me no choice but to pursue books."

"I'd be careful what you say," she warned. "Karma has big ears."

He patted her hand. "Go start at the other end of the room. We'll meet in the middle and compare notes."

She tried to, truly, but she kept finding herself distracted by the music. John shot her more than one look that said she should be keeping her nose to the grindstone, as it were, but that didn't help her much. She did manage to look over a good chunk of the titles in the bookcases and she did identify a few goodies locked in glass cases, but it occurred to her as she looked at them that she had been overlooking the true treasure.

She turned and looked at that treasure, sitting there on a chair with a lute in his hands, giving them all a glimpse into another world.

The thought was so staggering, she lost her breath.

She jumped a little when she realized Dave Thompson was standing next to her. That she hadn't noticed him getting up to do so said quite a bit about her mental state. She smiled weakly. "Hello."

He looked as overwhelmed as she felt. "I don't suppose you could use your influence on him to convince him to do all that in studio, could you?"

"With all due respect, Mr. Thompson, what do you think?"

He laughed quietly. "I think he has us all right where he wants us, you included."

"I'm afraid you're right."

Dave studied John for so long in silence, Tess found herself growing a little uncomfortable. She could see the wheels turning and suspected he was genuinely puzzled about where John had learned to play as he did. She was equally convinced it would never in a million years occur to the man that John was anything but what he said he was: a modern guy who knew a couple of songs on a medieval instrument. The only fly in that ointment was that Dave spent an equal amount of time looking from John to Stephen and back, as if he couldn't quite believe they looked so much alike but apparently didn't know each other very well.

That was going to have him asking questions John wasn't going to want to answer.

Tess caught Stephen's eye and tried not to look as uneasy as she suddenly felt. He sauntered over immediately to hopefully help her with a little diversion. He held out his hand to Dave.

"Stephen de Piaget," he said easily. "And you need no introduction, Mr. Thompson. Your business adventures are the stuff of legend."

"Are you and John related?" Dave asked bluntly, apparently content to ignore the flattery. "You could pass for brothers."

"Distant cousins, I believe," Stephen corrected smoothly. "I'd have to consult the earl's genealogy to be certain. My father's very keen on that sort of thing."

"I've met the Earl of Artane," Dave mused. "He's quite the patron of the arts, isn't he?"

"He is," Stephen agreed. "And he's always eager to see what sorts of productions you're behind."

"Has he heard John play?"

"I don't believe so," Stephen said slowly, as if he were truly trying to remember. "He likely should, though, wouldn't you say?"

Dave only looked at Stephen with a frown, then turned that thoughtful frown back on John. Tess didn't dare look at Stephen for fear some of her panic might show on her face. It was no wonder John didn't like notoriety. She could hardly stand it for him herself, and she wasn't the one in the hot seat.

It was with no small bit of relief that she watched John eventually hand the lute back to Lord Payneswick. He claimed no ability to play any of the recorders there and demurred when faced with the viols.

"Is your passion music only?" Lord Payneswick asked, locking up the case again and turning to look at him. "Or does it extend to languages?"

"I believe Dr. Alexander and the Viscount Haulton would be

better choices for that," John said promptly. "I've exhausted any pretense of expertise I have already."

The liar. Tess wanted to shake her head but she couldn't, because she was too unnerved to. Something was going to have to give—and soon. She couldn't pretend forever not to know who—and what—John de Piaget was. She found herself surprisingly torn between things she hadn't begun to think she might be torn by. The scholar in her didn't want him running off before she could ravage his mind for eyewitness accounts of things she had only read about in books. Rare books, but still not the real thing.

The rest of her didn't want him running off . . . well, because she didn't want him running off.

He glanced at her, then blinked in surprise. The next look he shot her was anything but casual.

Dave Thompson laughed suddenly under his breath and walked away.

Tess dragged her attention away from John to catch the tail end of an invitation from Lord Payneswick for Stephen to come back at his leisure and look at whatever paltry offerings were to be had. When Tess realized she'd been included in the invitation, she managed to grab for the last shreds of professionalism and thank Lord Payneswick profusely for the favor.

"And perhaps you'll prevail upon Mr. de Piaget to come along—"

Tess listened to Lord Payneswick stop midsentence and turn to look at the door. One of his aides stood there, looking rather unhappy at being the cause of an interruption. Tess was somehow not surprised to find John suddenly at her side, halfway to pulling her behind him.

She had to admit she was growing accustomed to it.

"I'm terribly sorry," the man said, "but it appears as if several of the bedrooms have been broken into. Our own security has investigated, of course, and nothing appears to have been taken." He paused. "But—"

"Whose rooms?" Lord Payneswick asked sharply.

"The Viscount Haulton's," the man said grimly. "Dr. Alexander's and her sister's. The rooms on either side as well, but those guests have determined that nothing was taken."

Tess found herself with her nose pressed to John's back. She sighed and rested her cheek against his coat. It was going to send him diving into new and heretofore unexplored depths of protectiveness.

"I'm sleeping with you tonight," he murmured over his shoulder.

"When hell freezes over, sport."

"I sense a chill wind blowing from the south."

Tess imagined he did, but she was equally sure the wind would blow itself out before any scandalous sleepovers became necessary. She didn't protest, though, when he reached behind himself and fumbled for her hand. She put her hand into his, his warm, strong hand, and thought she might be beginning to understand why Pippa had made the decision she had.

There was something profoundly attractive about medieval sensibilities.

Though she supposed she would have to deal with the reality of having had her room broken into soon enough—along with the fact that maybe John wasn't imagining things—which she wasn't sure any amount of herding could make any more palatable.

Chapter 16

J*ohn* shoved the last of his gear into the top of his backpack, then stood, supremely happy to be back in jeans and boots instead of high heels.

He wasn't sure how any woman ever chased after thugs with any success at all.

He left his pack at the foot of his bed, made certain all the costume paraphernalia was where it should be, then turned and walked toward the door, intending to go relieve Stephen and make certain Tess didn't run afoul of any trouble before he could get her safely back to her keep.

He was unpleasantly surprised to find his way blocked by none other than the dapper and perky Viscount Haulton, who most definitely should have been somewhere else.

He'd done his damndest to never be in a position to have lengthy conversations with the man, or to stand too near him lest someone find the courage to remark on the similarities in their features. He'd already had more than one person mistake him for his nephew. But none of that had anything to do with why he was so unhappy to see him standing there now.

"You're supposed to be guarding the girls," he growled.

"They're *women*, my dear John, with minds of their own. I delivered Tess safely to breakfast, then escorted Peaches—against her will, mind you—to her ride to London."

"My lord, I'm not sure you realize—"

"It was only breakfast, John," Stephen interrupted with a faint smile. "I'm sure Tess can manage that on her own. I must admit to being rather curious, however, as to why you've got your wee knickers in such a twist over this."

John could hardly believe his ears. "Ransacked chambers?" he said pointedly. "Falling curtain rods?"

"The second was a fluke and the first not limited to us," Stephen said, no doubt quite reasonably to his own mind. He studied John for a moment. "Is someone after you, lad?"

"I can take care of myself if they are," John said, trying not to snarl. "It's *Tess* I'm worried over."

"I think you're fond of her."

"Thank you for that, my lord," John said, gritting his teeth. "And please excuse me now before I say or do something I'll regret later. To you, as it happens."

Stephen only smiled as he stepped aside and allowed him to pass. John suppressed the urge to punch him on his way by. If something had happened to Tess, he knew exactly whom he was going to kill first, and it wouldn't be whomever had hurt her.

He strode swiftly down the hallway, then turned the corner and came to an abrupt halt. He wasn't one to eavesdrop, but he also didn't particularly care to intrude on women's conversations. At present, though, he thought a bit of the former just might serve him. Tess was standing on the edge of a window, apparently talking to someone—or two feminine someones if his ears hadn't failed him—who didn't sound particularly friendly. He looked up, just to make sure things were properly attached to the wall above his head, then took a step or two toward the little tête-à-tête. He stopped just behind an enormous vase on a table where he was fairly sure he wouldn't be noticed.

"So," some posh-accented woman was saying in a way that immediately set John's teeth on edge, "you're the party planner, aren't you, dear?"

"Well, yes," Tess said, sounding as if she might be at a loss for words. "I do hold events—"

"Events," the second woman laughed, her voice dripping with

scorn. "Yes, I suppose one could term them that, couldn't one? Do you *know* anything about the history of your castle, or is it just a pretty backdrop for your little costume dramas?"

John felt his mouth fall open. He had to admit he'd never been at his best when faced with a solar full of catty ladies' maids. He far preferred a battlefield where a lad's intentions were as clear as the sunlight shining on his sword. That business of words and double meanings and cutting remarks was just not for him.

But this was Tess out in the open, and he couldn't allow her to be harmed. He cast about for a useful—a *peaceful*, rather— resolution to his current quandary but found nothing coming to hand. It wasn't as if he could draw a sword and convince those harpies vexing her to behave better.

"I think, Alice, that you have to be fairly bright to actually represent the history of our country and its properties properly. I'm sure Miss Alexander is just the tour guide. After all, she certainly didn't ingratiate herself here at Payneswick without aid from Haulton—"

"Or from that luscious man she's with," agreed the second, "though I don't imagine she's more than a weekend dalliance for him."

John had heard enough. He emerged from behind the vase and walked over to Tess without hesitation. He hadn't a bloody clue what he intended to do, but perhaps a few cutting words would serve where swords could not.

He stopped next to Tess and smiled politely at her companions, a pair of middle-aged women who he didn't recognize but could tell by their very smart clothes were either rich or titled—or both.

"Good morning, ladies," he said with chilly civility. He turned and made Tess a low bow, but he didn't dare look at her. No sense in looking away from the peril.

"Ah, the man we've been admiring," the woman on the left said with something of a purr. "Sadly out of your Regency garb, however."

"Who are you?" the second woman asked with great interest. "I don't believe we've met."

"We haven't," he said, offering no remedy for that. "And if you'll excuse us, Dr. Alexander and I must go pay our respects one last time to Lord Payneswick. We'll need to thank him for the enjoyable after-dinner hour in his private collections, won't we, my lady?" he said, looking at Tess with his best smile.

Tess looked as if she'd just been slapped.

"Doctor?" one of the wenches said with another disdainful laugh. "Of what? Interior decorating?"

John lifted an eyebrow. "Hardly," he said calmly, "but I won't bore you with details you aren't clever enough to understand, though I will point out that she is also the Countess of Sedgwick. I would say that makes her something of an authority on her own home, wouldn't you agree?"

He didn't give them a chance to decide if they agreed or not before he walked away. Tess came with him because he didn't give her any choice. She was wheezing.

"Do you have any idea who those two were?" she gasped.

"Don't know, don't care."

"Wives of politicians, and potential clients."

"They'll go off and lick their wounds soon enough. Forget them."

Her hand that he'd taken was absolutely frigid. He would have stopped to blow on it, but he didn't want to draw any attention to any weakness on her part. He continued to tow her along with him, indulged in the humming of a cheerful melody he'd once heard one of Queen Eleanor's bards play, and kept a sharp eye out for ruffians and Lord Payneswick both, intending to address whichever of the two he found first.

"What is that song?" Tess said very quietly.

He looked at her. "Something I heard once. I'll do it justice for you—and only for you—later, if you like."

She let out her breath slowly. "I'm not sure what I would like right now. A stiff drink, perhaps."

"If only you weren't so puritanical about your liquor consumption, I might be able to provide you with the like."

"I haven't seen you knocking back much either, buster."

He smiled. "I like my wits about me and my liver intact, thank you just the same. I think eggs on cold toast might serve fairly well now, though. Unless you'd rather find something on the road."

"On the road, please," she said quietly.

He couldn't blame her. He also didn't fight her when she pulled her hand away from his and put it in her jacket pocket. She probably thought it hid the trembling better that way.

He would have turned around and headed back to fetch their gear, but he spotted Lord Payneswick standing at the far end of the hallway. There was no sense in not flattering the man a bit more whilst he had the chance, for Tess's sake.

And for his own, truth be told. Holding an amazingly preserved original instrument in his hands the night before had been a bit more overwhelming than he'd anticipated it might be. The chance to do that again was worth a bit of fawning deference. Perhaps the next time he was allowed the pleasure of playing it, he would ask just where Payneswick had come by it.

Lord Payneswick turned to them with a smile. "Ah, John and Dr. Alexander. Still recovering from your adventures yesterday?"

John smiled. "Near brushes with the authorities always leave a lingering something behind, don't they?"

"I wouldn't know," Lord Payneswick said, with an eyebrow raised, "and I'm assuming you're merely speculating. I can also assume you'll avoid dragging your lovely companion into anything untoward in the future, yes?"

He could only hope. John managed a smile. "I'll do my best, my lord."

"I'm afraid, Dr. Alexander," Lord Payneswick said, turning to Tess, "that you didn't have a proper look in my little solar last night. Perhaps you and our young rogue there might make a return visit after the new year. We'll discuss what rumors you've heard and if they might be true."

"That is very generous, Lord Payneswick," Tess said quietly. "The Viscount Haulton will be exceptionally jealous of my good fortune."

"Oh, I'll invite him, as well. Perhaps you two can restrain each other from fighting over my relics whilst I sit back and enjoy our good John's playing. John, I don't suppose your interest in all things medieval extends past music, does it?"

"Dr. Alexander is the expert in that field," John said without hesitation. "I just attend her lectures and admire the depth and breadth of her knowledge."

"She's free to add to that anytime she likes—as long as she brings you along to entertain me." He smiled and inclined his head. "A pleasure to have you both. I'll expect you sooner rather than later."

John made him a low bow out of habit, wondered if His Lordship thought it odd, then decided that there was nothing to be done about it. He waited until the man walked away, then looked at Tess.

Her stillness was tangible, and not a good thing. He fished her hand out of her pocket and tucked it under his arm.

"Let's fetch our gear," he said pleasantly. "I'll be polite to Lord Haulton if we see him instead of bloodying his nose as I should for leaving you alone."

"I told him to go."

"And more the fool was he for obeying you."

She sighed lightly. "The house is full of people, John."

"Exactly," he said distinctly, but he decided not to push her any further. He could see that she was thinking far too hard about something, and he suspected that something had to do with what those ridiculous wenches had said to her.

"Shall we be for home, then, my lady?"

She only nodded, unsmiling.

He supposed the sooner he got her there, the happier they would both be.

Several hours later, he shut off the Range Rover in Tess's car park, grateful to be off the road and close to having Tess back behind sturdy walls. He glanced at her to find her watching Sedgwick, as if she weren't sure she wanted to be there or not.

She'd been quiet the entire way home. He'd overseen a late breakfast for her, then an attempt at lunch, which she'd barely touched. He'd taken her apologies for her weariness with a grain of salt. He wasn't sure quite what had bothered her so, but he once again had the feeling it had all to do with the two women who had insulted her.

In a different lifetime, he supposed he would have followed his sister Amanda's example and cut both those wenches down to size with the weight of his father's name and a look or two of disdain. But he was in the Future where he was no one at all and those looks wouldn't have served him. He'd done what he could, which was take Tess away. He supposed time would cure the rest.

"I'm sorry," Tess said, looking at him with a sigh. "I've been terrible company today."

"It was a long weekend," he offered, "and a busy fortnight before that. Perhaps a good rest is what you need."

She smiled gamely. "The lord's solar has a decent hearth and a flat screen hidden behind a tapestry, if you're interested."

"As long as your DVD offerings don't include Jane Austen or any of that other girlish rot," he said with mock severity.

"Maybe you should settle for a book."

He smiled. "Quite possibly. Let's get your gear inside, then we'll see if we can come to an agreement on something." He shot her a look. "Wait for me."

She held her hands up. "I've given up fighting you."

He seriously doubted that, but he wasn't going to argue the point at present. He got out of the car, pocketed the keys, then went around to open Tess's door for her. He paused after he'd shut it up again.

"Was it worth it to you? The trip?"

She looked up at him. "Honestly, once I got in there, I realized I would rather listen to you play than look for priceless texts."

"Daft wench," he said, reaching out to tuck a stray lock of hair behind her ear. "I could play for you anytime."

She only nodded.

He decided that perhaps it was best not to try to read anything in her face at present. She looked terribly tired and more discouraged than he would have expected her to. She'd had the chance to look at what she'd wanted to, but perhaps it had been a bit of a letdown.

He left her where she was and went around to the boot to fetch her gear for her. He slung her pack over his shoulder, then started to shut the lid.

He supposed that at some point in the future he would have the stomach to reexamine that moment and understand why a cold chill had slid down his spine.

He pushed the lid back open, then reached in and pulled out a slip of paper just visible under his pack. He was almost certain it hadn't been there when he'd stowed their gear earlier. Where it had come from, then, was a bit of a mystery.

He unfolded it—noting the careless way it had been creased—
and began to read.

*Who were Rhys de Piaget and what's he to a particular
garage owner?*
*And if you're thinkin I've only to do with you and not the
pretty miss, you're sore mistaken.*

"John?"

John shoved the note into his pocket and stepped back from
the boot. He shut the lid, narrowly missing shutting Tess inside,
then pasted a smile on his face.

"Nothing," he said without hesitation. "Just daydreaming."

"You look like you've seen a ghost. What's wrong?"

What was wrong? He hardly knew where to begin. The list
was long and terrifying.

He knew at that moment and with a finality that made him
want to sit down, that he had gravely underestimated the danger.
He was not dealing with an offended reenactment lad; he was
dealing with the real thing.

Who were Rhys de Piaget . . .

He realized Tess had her arms around him. "I think you're
going to fall down. Here, put your arm around my shoulder and
lean on me."

"I've no need—"

"Don't be an idiot," she said, not looking any better herself
than he felt. "What happened to you? Something from breakfast?"

"Aye," he said thickly. "Bad eggs."

"You didn't eat eggs for breakfast, John."

"I poached some of Haulton's whilst he was admiring his
visage in the mirror. I've probably caught something vile from
him."

"English, John, please."

He closed his eyes and held on to her for a moment or two in
silence. He knew he was shaking, but then again, so was she, so
perhaps in the end, it didn't matter who held whom upright. He
looked around as much of the grounds as he could see from his
present position and wondered just what in the hell he was supposed to be looking for.

Someone who knew his father.

Someone who knew he loved Tess Alexander.

Someone who knew *he* knew he was being stalked.

So the sword theft hadn't been a random thing, nor had the rock propping open Tess's north guard tower door, nor the curtain rod at Payneswick, nor the slit brake line. He had to take a deep breath. The saints only knew where his enemy would strike next.

If it was at Tess . . .

Tess took her pack with one hand and kept her arm around his waist. "Lock your car."

He fumbled in his pocket for the key and did so, then put that arm around her shoulders and pulled her close to him as he walked with her across the grass to the bridge. He about fell into the moat when a ferocious barking started up behind him.

"Mr. Beagle," Tess shouted, "sit!"

The dog blinked in surprise, stopped barking, and sat.

"Go home," Tess ordered.

The dog took a final look at them, hopped up, then trotted back to the gift shop. John took a deep breath, then tried not to stumble as he walked with Tess across the bridge. He knew he was scanning the battlements for unfriendly souls, but he couldn't bring himself to stop. If he hadn't thought it would raise eyebrows, he would have dropped the damned portcullises and locked himself inside the hall with Tess until he'd determined who was stalking him. He didn't imagine Tess would mind if he pulled down one—or both—of the swords hanging crossed over the hearth in the great hall to help him with defenses. He imagined that with a little ingenuity, he could sharpen them up in a blink.

He locked himself in the great hall with her, then locked her in her solar as he checked every last door in the place. Nothing was amiss, but that didn't ease him at all. He went back into the lord's solar, built a fire, then stopped himself from forbidding Tess to go into the kitchen. If she wanted to eat, he wasn't going to stand in her way.

He left her holding a very sharp knife and supposed she could see to herself for as long as it took him to build a fire in the great hall.

It occurred to him, whilst he was about the task, that it might be time to call in reinforcements. His father wouldn't have hesitated, so John supposed there was no shame in it.

He waited until he'd seen Tess seated in front of the fire with a hot mug of tea before he excused himself and walked out the front door, pulling his mobile from his pocket as he did so. He dialed the number he'd had memorized for several years.

"Phillips," a voice said crisply from the other end.

John took a deep breath. "Oliver, it's John."

"John," Oliver said, sounding not at all surprised to hear from him. "How's the Vanquish?"

"Brilliant."

"Points on your license, mate?"

"Nary a one."

Oliver laughed. "That's because you take it to Germany every couple of months and get it out of your system. What can I do for you?"

John had to take a deep breath. "This is going to sound absolutely barking, but I need security."

"When?"

John dragged his hand through his hair. "No questions about why?"

"I work for Robert Cameron, John. I'm accustomed to not asking questions. How many lads and when?"

"A pair, perhaps," John said slowly. "And perhaps as soon as tomorrow."

"I'll be there tonight, with reinforcements."

John blew out his breath. "Name your price."

"Oh, it'll cost you," Oliver said, sounding as if he were smiling, "and Cameron will likely ding you as well for leaving me unable to fetch him his tea. I suppose you'll survive the blow."

"I could only hope." John hesitated, then supposed there was no reason not to be frank. "I think it's personal."

"It always is."

"You know," John said grimly, "you could sound a little less cavalier about this."

"You're not hiring me to stand in the corner and weep like a girl, are you?"

John smiled in spite of himself. "Nay, I'm not."

"Where's your flat?"

"I have a cottage behind the shop. I assume you can find that."

"Wouldn't be much of a snoop if I couldn't, would I?" Oliver asked. "Where will you be?"

"Tucking my lady up safely in her castle."

"Of course," Oliver said without so much as a hint of a smirk in his voice. "I might bring Ewan Cameron as well, just to keep her safe."

"I think I should be worried."

"I *know* you should be worried. Let me ring around a bit and see who's up for an adventure. I'll let you know when we're hiding in your hedge."

"I'd appreciate that."

He could have sworn Oliver muttered something about girls and castles before he rang off, but he couldn't be sure. He had little idea of what Oliver truly did for Robert Cameron, and he supposed it was probably better that way. He'd gotten himself out of a tight spot in a dodgy alley in Glasgow with Oliver at his side and was well aware of the man's ability to defend himself. A discreet inquiry or two about Oliver and his employer had produced absolutely nothing, which led him to believe that the Cameron's security was absolute.

He was beginning to suspect he should have been more careful about his own.

He walked back into the hall only to find it empty. Panic slammed into him like a fist until he caught sight of Tess coming out of the solar, her phone to her ear. She glanced at him but only smiled, so perhaps she didn't realize how loudly the blood was thundering in his ears. After all, he'd spent years perfecting the ability to be quaking with terror yet still look utterly bored. Montgomery had claimed so, at least.

His brother had best have had that aright.

"Of course," she was saying. "What time do you want me there?"

John frowned at her, but she was ignoring him.

"Terry, don't worry," she said soothingly. "Get me a topic later today and I'll have it ready by the time I get there. It isn't as if I'll have to research it from scratch."

"What are you doing?" John demanded.

It was possible that might have come out a little less politely than he might have wished.

She frowned at him, then walked away. "Are you kidding?"

she said. "I couldn't be more thrilled. A meeting is one thing, but this is a thousand times better."

"What is?" John said, following her across the hall floor.

She tried to shoo him away. "Four? Absolutely. Chevington isn't all that far away if I get an early start."

John felt his jaw hit his chest. Literally. "What?" he exclaimed. He might have shouted it. At the moment, he wasn't sure he was fit to judge.

Tess shot him a glare, then smiled into her phone. "Thanks, Terry. I really appreciate this."

"You absolutely won't—" John began.

She flapped at him and mouthed a very unladylike curse. John folded his arms across his chest and glared at her. She continued to walk away from him, as if she thought by that alone she might manage to get rid of him.

"Thanks, Terry. It's a terrific opportunity. Yes, see you tomorrow."

"Nay, you will not," John said loudly.

She shoved her phone into her pocket and glared at him. "Will you please knock that off?"

"Aye, when I'm convinced you're—" He cut himself off before he blurted out anything else untoward. "When we've both passed a solid fortnight without any incidents, then I'll knock it off, my lady. Until then, I most certainly will *not*."

She took a deep breath. "While I appreciate your concern, I am perfectly capable of seeing to myself. Terry managed to get me a slot at a living history faire at Chevington—"

"Nay," he said calmly. Well, he might have shouted that as well, but he was under a fair bit of duress. "Absolutely, unequivocally, no arguments, *nay*."

He supposed if she'd been a different sort of gel, she might have bloodied his nose at that point.

Tess only looked at him for a moment or two as if she had never seen him before. "Do you have any idea," she managed finally, "what an amazing opportunity this is? It's a chance—"

"To put yourself in danger where you need not," he growled, "which you absolutely will *not* do."

She gaped at him for a moment or two, then drew herself up and looked at him coolly. "I think you'd better go."

"Nay," he growled.

She walked across her hall to the front door, opened it, and pointed. "Beat it."

He stalked over to her. "I most assuredly will not, you witless—"

She shoved him out her front door.

He hadn't expected that, which was the only reason she managed it, to be sure. He stumbled down her stairs, but landed on his feet instead of his face, which she wouldn't have noticed because she'd already slammed the door shut. He stood there, his chest heaving, and cursed her. He dragged his hand through his hair and fought the urge to stomp off. She was an irascible, unpleasant, impossible—

She opened the door and peeked out.

He glared at her. "Come to finish the job?"

"I wanted to make sure I hadn't hurt you."

He closed his eyes and groaned silently before he managed to look at her again. Impossible, impossibly beautiful, dangerously courageous, absolutely, stunningly—

He had to take a deep breath. "What time does your train leave?"

She scowled at him and slammed the door shut again.

Well, as he had reminded himself in the past, he had a Black-Berry and knew how to use it. Assuming she didn't leave until the morning, and assuming she actually did take the train and not her car, he could have all the possible train times under his fingers within seconds. He would simply camp out at the station and follow her.

Perhaps he might even run into the lad who was following *him*.

"Lock the door!" he shouted, as a bit of an afterthought.

"Go to hell!" came the muffled response.

But she shoved the bolt home just the same. The sound ricocheted off the walls of the courtyard. John took a deep breath, glanced around him, and, finding no ruffians loitering where he could see them, took himself off toward the barbican gate. He stopped just inside the gate, had a final look about the courtyard, then turned and strode off toward his car.

He would go home, see if there was anything left of his cottage, then slip back to the castle. He wasn't as familiar with Sedgwick's grounds as he could have been—and likely should have been—but he could remedy that quickly. Once he knew the lay of the land, as it were, he would plan out a strategy. He would wait for his reinforcements, then put that plan in motion.

And at some point, he would hopefully stop wishing it was a battle he could have fought with a sword.

Chapter 17

T*ess* knew she was being watched.

The thought, when she said it aloud in her head, was absolutely ridiculous. Of course she was being watched; she was half an hour past a lecture that had been so full, people had been trying to listen from the hallway. She'd been meeting and greeting ever since, finally moving out to the great hall where she'd had more room to chat comfortably with men and women in medieval dress. Of course she was being watched.

Somehow, that didn't rid her of the shivers that continued to run down her spine.

She decided, as the line began to dwindle a bit, that her unease had less to do with an unknown watcher than it had to do with Chevington itself. She'd been to the castle several times before, because it was decently preserved and because there was a rich political history associated with it, but she'd never enjoyed any of the visits. She'd initially been able to ignore the paranormal oddities it boasted, though she'd been less successful at that on subsequent visits. She'd begun to have the feeling she was walking back into time—most often into the midst of a battle.

Today, that sensation had been impossible to ignore.

She continued to make what she hoped was pleasant and coherent conversation with the knight in front of her and forced herself to rationally examine the cause of her unease without wimping out by crediting it to being in one of the most paranormally active castles in all of England.

It couldn't have been because she'd given a bad lecture. She had stuck to basic, indisputable facts and presented them simply. No one was glaring at her for getting her facts wrong. She'd changed into appropriate clothing once she'd reached the castle, so the medieval gown and delicate if not precisely useful slippers on her feet shouldn't have garnered any especial notice. Terry had given her a terrific introduction, and she'd put on her best company manners after her lecture to leave the attendees with a good impression. There was no reason she should have stuck out in a castle full of medieval wannabes.

Still, she just couldn't shake the feeling that she was being *watched*.

She took the opportunity as it presented itself to glance around the keep and look for the looker. It was difficult, though, because no one seemed out of the ordinary. She recognized a few souls from Terry's group and took note of a few others who she was fairly sure she'd seen at academic conferences in different garb, but she didn't see any stalkers. She suppressed the urge to look behind her to see if anyone was going to come up behind her and clunk her over the head to carry her off.

Someone like John, for instance.

The thought of him left her with an entirely new reason to be uncomfortable. She had never in her life physically assaulted anyone. While pushing John down the stairs probably didn't descend quite to that level, it came perilously close in her book.

She supposed she could justify it in any number of ways if she tried hard enough. She had felt a tingle run down her spine the night before when she'd been talking to Terry, as if Fate had been breathing down her neck just to make sure she didn't miss the special significance of the moment. It had occurred to her as she was talking to him that maybe she could do that sort of thing at Sedgwick. In addition to parties, she could do seminars for those who truly wanted to step back in time and gain a feel for the Middle Ages. It might be a nice change from *events*. She supposed, with a fair bit of chagrin, that she was just as proud as the next academic, what with not wanting to look less than her degrees said she was.

But to attract the sorts of people who might want to attend those sorts of seminars, she needed to make a different sort of contact than the sort she had already. That was why she'd been so determined to get north, even if it had meant taking the 5:05 train that morning.

She might not have been so hell-bent on taking a different tack in her life if it hadn't been for the finish to her Regency adventure. Being belittled by women who wouldn't have known a trencher from a trowel had been very unpleasant. Needing a rescue had been galling, but having John try to thwart her subsequent march into the academic side of living history fray, no matter how well meaning it had been, had been the final straw.

Now, though, that her temper had cooled, she was unnerved, and she was half considering going back to the little guardroom where she'd left her stuff with the rest of the presenters and digging out her cell phone so she could call and ask for John to come herd her for a bit.

She had only four more people to talk to when a blond knight stepped up to her side and handed her a note. She glanced at it and felt her heart leap a little at the hastily scrawled words.

Meet me in the woods behind the keep. I have news.

It wasn't signed with John's name but it must have been from him. Tess looked up to ask the knight who had given him the message, but he'd disappeared. She frowned. It would have been just like John to follow her, then watch over her without letting her know he was watching over her. It would be even more like him to send a messenger who didn't want to be noticed.

She supposed an apology would be in order.

She finished her business, then briefly considered changing clothes before deciding to just go as she was. She had a cloak around her shoulders to ward off the chill, and her shoes would last for a quick trip outside and back. She looked for Terry to thank him, but didn't see him. He wasn't going anywhere before dinner, so she would just track him down later.

It was cold and rainy outside, which didn't surprise her at all. It only added to the supernatural atmosphere that seemed to slather itself over Chevington and its environs. No one followed her—she knew that from a quick look over her shoulder—and no one was waiting for her in the woods—she knew that from many other careful looks around herself. There was no reason to be spooked. She told herself that until she reached the end of the path that she suddenly suspected had been laid out just for her and saw what was waiting for her.

A sword, driven into the ground.

She stopped short of it, only because she hadn't expected to see it simply stuck there in the ground. Of course, that wasn't the only thing that gave her creeps.

It was that the sword was near a time gate.

She didn't want to examine how she knew that. She sure as hell wasn't going to do any investigating—

She stumbled forward thanks to someone's hands on her back, tripped, and felt herself falling toward the sword. If she managed to do something besides shatter her nose against the steel, she would consider Karma more of a friend than she ever had before.

She landed on her hands and knees but with her nose intact. She looked up and blinked.

The sword was gone.

She heaved herself to her feet and spun around. There was no one there, but that didn't make her feel any better. In fact, it was quite the opposite. Whereas it had been cold and rainy before, now it was absolutely bitter. She had the feeling that wasn't because she'd been overcome by a sudden bout of terror.

She took a deep breath, then began to run. The forest seemed thinner than it had before and the castle more easily reached. She looked up and felt her mouth fall open. It wasn't an eight-hundred-year-old castle covered in history standing in front of her; it was a squeaky-clean, recently built structure.

She turned and bolted back into the woods. She wondered, as she ran, what she intended to accomplish by that, but she conceded that she wasn't at her best at present. She needed a few minutes of peace and quiet to think. If she had indeed come through a time gate to another century, she could use that time gate to get back to her proper place. All she had to do was catch her breath, make sure she was safe, then retrace her steps. She would find her way home because she wouldn't give herself any other choice.

The forest ended sooner than she expected. She found herself facing not some useful B-road but a trio of poorly fed, poorly dressed reenactment wackos.

She looked over her shoulder and saw there another pair of men who looked to be about the same vintage as the three in front of her. They were scruffy, unwashed, and sporting several blackened teeth. That didn't seem to bother them any, though, because they were leering at her without embarrassment.

Tess decided that if she ever had the chance, she would tell John de Piaget that he was right. About it all. Well, mostly about the part where he'd told her to stay within arm's reach.

She kept her mouth shut, but it didn't do anything for the sudden bout of teeth chattering she was suffering. If those were living history types, they had achieved an entirely new level of authenticity. She wondered how in the world they'd managed to acquire that collection of blades without somebody kicking up an insurance fuss.

"If you'll excuse me," she said, taking a quick gander to both her right and her left to see what way might be more accessible, "I think I'll be going."

One of them leaped forward. She didn't think; she merely shoved the heel of her hand into his nose. The crunch might have been satisfying if she hadn't been so flat-out terrified.

He stumbled away, howling in a language she didn't recognize. His companions also began to babble in that tongue, angrily, as if they discussed things she wouldn't want to know about. And then she realized she had judged too hastily because she did understand them.

They were speaking Old English.

It was nothing short of astonishing to hear it spoken by guys who certainly didn't look as if they'd spent years at University learning the same thing. She watched numbly as the leader of the group—the one sporting the bloody nose—moved to stand in front of her. He wasn't smiling; he was glaring at her. She watched in abject terror as he lifted his sword high over his head. She gaped at it, openmouthed, watching a stray strand of sunlight attempt to reflect itself upon the blade that was most definitely not new and apparently not very well forged. She closed her eyes in self-defense, wondering if that sword would hurt when it cleaved her own stupid head in two.

The sound of metal on metal startled her into opening her eyes.

John de Piaget stood four paces from her, the end of his sword blocking her attacker's sword and keeping her face intact.

And then things took an even more medieval turn.

She found herself taken by the arm and invited to step backward—well, jerked really—with a directness she was just sure John wouldn't bother to apologize for later. She landed on her backside, then sat there for a moment trying to decide if her tailbone was broken or not as John went to work.

He exchanged a few words with her attackers in what she could easily hear was his own perfect Old English—his accent sounded a helluva a lot more authentic than her tutors' ever had—before he apparently decided unconsciousness could be dispatched without delay.

Too bad their new friends didn't seem inclined to agree.

Tess scrambled backward only because she was afraid she might be grabbed and used as a bargaining chip if she didn't. John killed the two men who rushed toward her, then turned back to the remaining three.

She wasn't one to throw up, but she was tempted. She clapped her hand over her mouth to keep not only her catered snack but her screams down where they belonged, then watched John take care of the rest of the crew. One was rendered blissfully unconscious thanks to a fist under his chin, a second courtesy of a roundhouse kick to his jaw, but the leader wasn't dispatched so easily.

He met his end finally on John's sword.

Tess watched John clean his sword on the man's tunic—and she had to wonder how it had been sharp enough to do damage, but perhaps that was a question better saved for later given that that was a sword she'd never seen before—then gaped at him as he turned and reached for her. There were drops of blood splattered on his hands.

She thought she just might lose it then.

"Save it for later," he said briskly.

She gulped and nodded, because that was the only thing that made sense in a sea of things that tossed her unmercifully about. He pulled her up to her feet, then towed her—well, dragged again, if she was going to be completely accurate—back with him into the forest. He seemed hell-bent on getting to a particular spot, which led her to speculate on all kinds of things she didn't want to.

Shouts echoed in the distance.

Those weren't the shouts of college professors looking for a missing colleague; those were the shouts of angry men cursing in the language du jour, which, again, was neither modern English nor twenty-first-century French.

"Damn it to hell," John said, searching the ground frantically. He muttered a few more things under his breath that she couldn't quite catch. She wasn't entirely sure he wasn't cursing in Norman French.

She was beginning to have a very bad feeling about things.

He stopped, listened, then cursed more viciously. The sound of things crashing through the underbrush was unsettling in the extreme. He grabbed her hand.

"Can you run?" he demanded.

"As if my life depended on it," she said, grasping desperately for something light to say.

"It will," he said shortly. "Let's go."

She didn't dare ask him where they were going, though she could tell it wasn't back toward the castle. She would have asked him why that didn't seem to be on his list of desirable destinations, but she soon didn't have the wind for it. The sun was setting, she was going into shock, and there wasn't a damned thing she could do about either.

So she just ran, as if her life depended on it.

She woke to the feel of a tree root in her back. It was hideously uncomfortable, but that wasn't what bothered her the most. What bothered her was not remembering when she'd lain down on top of it.

She sat up, shivering. She wasn't sure what sort of hellish place she'd reached, but she suddenly realized that she was there alone.

Or maybe not. John was standing ten feet away from her, leaning back against a tree with his arms folded over his chest, watching her. She noted the sword at his side and vaguely remembered his having poached a sheath and leather belt from one of the slain men as they'd fled out of the forest past them. That brought back a rush of memory she could have certainly done without but couldn't avoid. She smoothed her hair back from her face with hands that trembled so badly, she curled them into fists and hid them in her skirts.

"How long have you been up?" she managed.

He looked at her gravely. "I didn't sleep."

She started to crawl to her feet but had help. He walked to her, pulled her up, then drew her into his arms.

"I didn't mean to fall asleep on you," she managed, gritting her teeth to keep them from chattering.

"You didn't fall asleep;" he said solemnly. "You fainted. Conveniently near a bower of soft leaves so I didn't have to look far for a place to put you."

She put her arms around him and held on tightly. She didn't suppose there was any reason to mask her trembling. "What are you doing here?"

"I followed you."

She had to wait a few more minutes before she could speak without shrieking. "I should have listened to you."

"Aye, we should discuss that, I think," he said thoughtfully, "but perhaps when we're in front of a hot fire where I can shout at you more comfortably."

She pulled back far enough to meet his eyes. "You wouldn't shout at me."

"I most certain would—and will," he promised. "But not today. Today . . ." He took a deep breath. "Today I think we should make sure we don't meet any other unfriendly types."

"Who were those guys back there?" she managed.

"Unfriendly types."

She didn't bother to ask him if those were the ones he'd been looking out for back in twenty-first-century England, because she had the distinct feeling they weren't. The guys who John had taken care of the afternoon before were not—and she could hardly believe she was even going there—of a more current vintage.

She took a deep breath, stepped back, and wrapped her arms around herself. "I was told you wanted to meet me in the forest."

He closed his eyes briefly. "I'm not surprised."

"I was," she said frankly. "I was still a little dazed from

academic success and not thinking clearly. I hadn't realized
you'd come north with me, though I hoped you might have."

"I couldn't let you go alone."

She nodded, not a smooth motion by any stretch of the imagination. "Thank you. And I'm sorry. I should have listened to
you."

"Hmmm," was all he said. He reached out and tugged her
cloak up to her chin. "I take it you went to the forest."

"Yes, but only as far as the spot where the sword was stuck in
the ground." She paused. "That sword you have there."

He rubbed his hands over his face. "I found it in the forest as
well," he said, sounding impossibly tired.

"And you brought it with you? To . . . wherever we are?"

"It seemed prudent." He started to speak, then paused. It
was several moments before he seemed to find his tongue. "It's
mine."

"That sword?" she asked in surprise. "Then why was it in the
forest?"

He chewed on his words for a bit. Tess could see the wheels
turning but decided it was best not to either aid or impede him.
He finally took a careful breath.

"There's a reason for it, but I don't think this is the place to
discuss it." He paused. "Can you trust me?"

Though she really didn't have any choice at the moment, she
could safely say that she would have trusted him anyway. She
didn't want to think about what he'd already done to save her life
in the past twenty-four hours.

"Absolutely," she said honestly.

He looked up at the sky, considered, then looked at her.
"We'll have to go on foot."

"Where?"

"Not where we came from, that's for certain," he said grimly.
He took another deep breath. "My brother lives north of here."

"A brother," she echoed, praying he wasn't talking about
Montgomery. Then again, she might get to see Pippa—if they
weren't in the wrong point in time, in which case Montgomery
would meet her before he met Pippa, and who knew what sort of
havoc that would wreak. "How lovely."

"I have four of them, actually," John said, "and two sisters."
He paused. "'Tis another four days, perhaps, to his home."

She nodded, because saying anything would mean saying too much. She shivered again, because she couldn't keep herself from it. "Are we going to meet any more of those . . . well, those sorts of guys we saw yesterday?"

He looked like a man who had a terrible burden that he knew he had to bear alone. "I hope not," he said with feeling. He chewed on his words for a moment or two, then looked at her grimly. "I did what I had to."

"I wasn't condemning you for it," she said quickly. "I was just wondering what I should look out for."

"You should look out for where my back is," he said, "and stay behind it."

She nodded, because it was a very sensible piece of advice, given the current day. "If it will help keep us from any more of those encounters, I'm all for it."

"I was just trying to keep you—"

"Safe," she finished for him. "I know."

"And what else should I have done, Tess?" he asked wearily. "Pulled you in front of me and used you as a shield?"

"Of course not," she managed. "I wasn't criticizing you. You did what you had to."

He blew his hair out of his eyes. "Forgive me. I'm afraid I'm not at my best presently. And I can be a bit of an—"

"Arse," she supplied. "I know."

"As long as we're clear on that."

She stepped forward and put her arms around his waist and held on to him tightly. "You do what you have to, and I'll stay behind you if trouble pops up."

He held her tightly for several moments in silence, then released her and reached for her hand. "Let's go."

Tess wondered, after a bit, why he wasn't curious that she wasn't curious about their surroundings. Maybe he thought she was too flipped out to reason. Maybe he was so flipped out himself that he couldn't manage coherent thought. Maybe facing what he'd left in the past, for whatever reason, was weighing so heavily on his mind that he couldn't get past it.

She wasn't sure she wanted to know which it was.

Chapter 18

Day Two in the past wasn't going very well.

John fought currently with a pair of hungry, wild-eyed men who obviously thought he had something they wanted. He wanted to point out to them that they couldn't eat Tess so she was of no use to them, unless they intended other things, in which case he would skewer them on the end of his sword without hesitation. He wouldn't do them any good because he didn't have any gold. He supposed his sword was a bit of an inducement to keep at their labors, but he wasn't entirely sure they would manage to heft it even if they could kill him for it.

Tess squeaked.

John looked over his shoulder to find the extra man he'd suspected might be there but hadn't seen before stepping up behind Tess.

"Duck," he commanded.

She dropped to her hands and knees. John threw his sword and didn't bother to watch it quiver in the ruffian's chest as he stumbled backward. He turned back to his primary tormentors, rendered them unconscious in spite of their very sharp knives, then walked past Tess and retrieved his sword. He cleaned it, then resheathed it, grateful that he'd just about run bodily into it in Chevington's forest.

He was absolutely certain that hadn't been happenstance.

Nay, the entire thing had been planned. He'd known he was acting as someone's pawn as he'd stationed himself several seats behind Tess on the train and felt increasingly uneasy the farther north they'd gone. He'd had Oliver with him, true, and Ewan Cameron, who seemed to be canny enough in spite of his abundant good humor, but still he'd been profoundly uncomfortable. An afternoon spent with an entire keep full of living history aficionados when someone from the Middle Ages was stalking him—and Tess?

It had been nothing short of terrifying.

He'd managed, with help, to keep Tess and most of the attendees under surveillance for the better part of the day. He didn't suppose Terry of the Rowdy Reenactors could be considered a doer of nefarious deeds, but it was certainly his fault that John had lost sight of Tess, however briefly. By the time he'd caught a flash of her cloak, then had his way blocked by people watching a fascinating demonstration of hunting owls, he'd been past frantic. He'd sprinted into the forest, leaving Oliver and Ewan to keep potential thugs in their sights, only to find nothing there but a sword, randomly driven into an unremarkable spot in the carpet of moss and leaves.

His sword, as it happened. The one his father had given him at his knighting.

He'd stepped forward to reach for it only to realize as he made a hasty grab for it, that he was standing on a time gate. He'd allowed it to carry him wherever it would, thinking only that Tess had likely been caught in its vile embrace as well and with any luck, he would follow her.

None of which had left him with any idea who had been stalking him or if that soul had followed him back into the past. He didn't think so, for he hadn't seen anything but garden-variety medieval ruffians out for what they could steal.

Which was gobsmacking enough, he supposed.

He cleaned his hands on the grass in deference to Tess's white visage, then pulled her to her feet.

"We must run again."

She nodded, a faint, jerky movement that spoke volumes

about her weariness and fear, but stumbled along with him into a run that he was sure was wearing her down far too quickly. He didn't have any other choice. Walking left them too easy a target. Perhaps once he felt safe, they could slow down.

It had been two days of running, broken up only by tense stays in either haylofts or inhospitable patches of forest. Food had been difficult to come by simply because he'd had nothing but his labor to trade for it and the one innkeeper he'd encountered so far had been suspicious of his willingness to chop wood or muck out stalls. He supposed they thought him less a nobleman fallen on hard times than a ruffian of some sort who had stolen a nobleman's clothing.

Things were, as he had noted earlier, not going particularly well in the thirteenth century.

At least he he hoped it was the thirteenth century. The clothing he'd seen reflected it—give or take several hundred years. He wasn't sure he could bear arriving at Wyckham and finding Nicholas and Jennifer dead. The thought of finding them anything but young and hale was almost enough to keep him from traveling there in the first place.

Almost, but not quite. The truth was, he couldn't keep Tess out in the wilds of medieval England with nothing but his sword standing between them and starvation. He needed a place where he could think behind walls that would keep Tess safe.

It was remarkable how quickly a man could go from worrying about getting his car dinged to worrying about how soon he could get the woman he loved where a garrison of loyal men could help him keep her from getting more than dinged.

Only he couldn't help but wonder how willing she would be to go anywhere with him when she learned the truth about him.

He glanced up at the sky and frowned. He wasn't entirely comfortable traveling during the day, but at least then he could see his foes coming toward him. A pity he and Tess didn't look a bit more like peasants, for they would have traveled more easily that way. At least they were wearing period costumes and not jeans. It was one thing to be mistaken for nobility; it was another to be mistaken for witches needing to be killed.

Time wore on in a particularly unpleasant way.

By the time the sun had reached its zenith—which wasn't easily told thanks to the overcast sky—they'd reached an inn he hadn't remembered on the road from Chevington to Wyckham. It was so primitive, he found himself almost shocked by the sight. Admittedly, he hadn't managed very luxurious accommodations during his first few fortnights in the Future, but even the stables he'd mucked out for room and board had been far superior to what he was looking at. Well, he was willing to do whatever work was available. It wasn't as if he had any other choice. All he had stuck down his boot were his keys, his phone, and a credit card. Not exactly coin of the realm.

"We'll try this place," he said.

Tess was only staring numbly at the inn. She looked too exhausted to even manage words.

"Tess," he began slowly, "ah . . ."

How did one go about telling one's companion that they had apparently stepped back in time and were loitering sometime in the Middle Ages? Worse still, how did a man tell the woman he loved that he knew that because he'd been born during that time?

He wished, absently, that he'd taken the time to go to Scotland. He had the feeling those MacLeods might have had a suggestion or two for him, if the rumors about them were true.

He squeezed Tess's hand. "Let me do the talking."

That she didn't even nod worried him. She simply stood next to him whilst he made nice with the proprietor, found her a spot by a marginally hot fire, and went outside to add to the woodpile. He did an appropriate amount of labor, then joined a very shell-shocked-looking Tess for a meal that was just this side of inedible. He ate, because he'd eaten worse, and tried to give Tess the least disgusting of the offering. He thanked the innkeeper for his aid, then took Tess and pulled her away from the inn.

He had no doubts someone would come along behind them and try to rob them—at the very least—so he kept an eye over his shoulder as he shepherded Tess along with him quickly. Wyckham was, if he wasn't judging amiss, another day and a half of slow riding, which meant at least another pair for them with naught but their feet to use. He wasn't sure Tess would manage it, but he knew he didn't have a choice but to force her to. Perhaps if she had a few more facts at her disposal, she might have a bit more hope that the end of the road was worth the trouble of getting there.

He looked at her to judge her state of mind. She looked quite frankly terrified, which he thought a rather sensible reaction all things considered.

"Tess?"

She looked up at him. It took her a moment or two to focus on him. "Yes?"

"I have something to tell you," he began. He paused to judge her willingness to listen to absolute bollocks, but she didn't seem opposed to it. Then again, she didn't seem capable of reacting to much at all. Perhaps the time was right to spring a bit of truth on her, though he had to take a deep breath before he could do it. "This is going to seem fantastical."

"Does it—" she croaked. She cleared her throat. "Does it have to do with lunch?"

He attempted a smile. He supposed he hadn't succeeded. "Aye."

She only nodded. "All right."

"You might not believe me."

She shivered, once. "I have a pretty a good imagination."

She was going to need it. He attempted a reassuring look but wasn't sure it hadn't been more of a grimace.

"You needn't worry," he promised. "I'll keep you safe."

"You have so far," she managed.

"Roughly."

She winced. "Could we not discuss the fate of our would-be friends back there?"

He nodded, because he couldn't blame her for wanting to forget as quickly as possible what she'd seen. He was all for that. He was also all for holding her for a bit when she turned and put her arms around his waist. He imagined it was less for the sake of affection and more to hold herself up, but he wasn't going to argue. He held her for a bit, closing his eyes and hoping it wasn't the last time he would manage it.

A twig snapped and she jumped half a foot. John glanced in the direction of the sound but saw nothing.

"Not to worry," he said.

"Easy for you to say," she said breathlessly. "You have a sword." She pulled back and looked at him. "And you apparently know how to use it."

"My misspent youth."

"Interesting youth."

"Aye, well, that's part of what I need to tell you," he said gingerly. "I'm not exactly sure where to start."

"Try the beginning."

He reached for her hand laced his fingers with hers. "Don't run."

"I don't think I could, even if I had to," she said with a shiver. "Spew away. At this point, I think I'll believe anything you say."

It was more than she'd said to him at one sitting in two days. No sense in not plunging right in, then. He was tempted to simply find somewhere for her to sit, but they were too close to the last inn for that. "Could you walk?" he asked.

"Is it safer that way?"

He nodded, had a nod in return, then looked up and down the road before he started north with her.

"There are, if you can believe it," he said as they walked, listening to the words come out of his mouth and realizing how bloody daft they sounded, "little spots all over England, gates really, gates you can't see." He checked her expression. She was only watching him periodically, but mostly concentrating on the path in front of her. "This is the fantastical part," he said, attempting a bit of a laugh that fell rather flat. "They go from one century to another."

"Do they?"

"They do."

She looked up at him. "How do you know?"

"Because you and I just stepped through one to get where we are now, which, judging by what we've seen so far, isn't precisely the twenty-first century."

"And how would you know *that*?" she asked

He could hardly believe he was going to blurt out the truth, but he supposed there was no point in hiding it any longer.

"Because I was born in the Year of Our Lord's Grace 1214."

She didn't look surprised, which surprised him.

"Indeed," was all she said.

"Indeed," he echoed in surprise. "Do you believe me?"

"Have you ever lied to me before, John de Piaget?"

"I've hedged, damn it."

"Well, yes," she agreed, "that's true. But given our current surroundings, I think I'll just take your word on this one."

He could hardly believe his ears. "You can't be serious."

"There are strange happenings in the world. Why not this?" She studied their surroundings for a moment or two, then looked at him. "What year are we in now, do you think?"

"I have no bloody idea," he said, feeling faintly exasperated.

"Where are we going?"

"Wyckham," he said shortly. "My brother's keep. I have no idea if he's there, or even if we're in the right year for him to be there."

She walked next to him in silence for so long, he almost shouted for her to say something. But before he could muster up the rudeness to do so, she looked up at him.

"How long have you been in the future?"

"Eight ye—" He shut his mouth. "I can't believe you're taking any of this seriously."

She took a deep breath. In truth, she took several of them, but they seemed to be less frantic than the ones she'd been taking before so he wasn't going to complain.

"Those thugs we just encountered aren't exactly from the local reenactment troupe, are they?"

"They could have been crackheads."

"I suppose so, but I doubt it." She walked on for another few minutes in silence. "Here's the funny thing," she said finally, though she didn't look as if she thought whatever she had to say was at all humorous. "I have a few good reasons to take you seriously."

He supposed it was his turn to be surprised. "Which ones?"

She looked unaccountably nervous. "You know Stephen de Piaget, right?"

"Of course," he said, feeling a faint irritation at just the mention of the blighter's name.

"Well, I know him, too, as you're already aware. What you might not know is that I also know his younger brother, Gideon. Gideon happens to be married to a woman named Megan." She smiled again, but it wasn't a very good smile. "She has a younger sister named Jennifer. Yanks, the both of them."

He waited, but she didn't go on. He couldn't imagine what her genealogy lesson had to do with his tale, but he supposed Tess didn't do much without a reason.

"And?" he prompted, when she looked as though she might not continue.

She met his gaze. "Megan's sister Jennifer is married to your older brother Nicholas."

It took him perhaps five more paces before her words sank in. He stopped short so quickly, he almost pulled her off her feet. *"What?"*

She turned to look at him. "That isn't everything."

He released her hand and folded his arms over his chest. It served a dual purpose of keeping him from possibly doing damage to her hand in his surprise and allowed him to look more in control of things than he felt.

"What else?" he asked, more curtly than he'd intended. He couldn't take the tone back, nor was he sure he would be able to. How did she know he had an older brother named Nicholas? That would mean . . .

He put the brakes on thoughts that were too ridiculous to entertain. She couldn't possibly know anything about him. Perhaps she was confusing him with someone else, or making up a tale from whole cloth. He comforted himself with those thoughts and settled for a fierce frown, lest he look completely undone.

"I have something to tell you about my sister Pippa," she said. "The one I lost."

He only waited. Words were almost beyond at him the moment.

"It has to do with her husband."

John felt something slither down his spine. He would have said 'twas the cold, cruel breath of Fate blowing down the back of his tunic, but it wasn't Fate. It was the unpleasant realization that he hadn't been nearly as in control of anything over the past month as he would have liked.

"Nay, you didn't tell me about your sister's husband," he said, attempting not to grit his teeth. "An oversight?"

"No, it was a deliberate choice not to tell you an interesting story," she said, though she didn't look as if it were interesting. She looked as if she were close to sicking up that truly vile meal they'd just ingested. "You see, Pippa found one of those gates you were talking about—outside my bridge, as it happens. She went back in time, met the lord of Sedgwick, and fell in love with him."

"Denys?" he asked in disbelief.

She shook her head slowly. "Denys had already died and the

castle reverted to its proper owner." She paused. "Your father, Rhys."

John thought he might have to sit down. "And he gave it to . . ."

"Your brother Montgomery."

He had to lean over and take several breaths before the stars suddenly swirling around his head faded enough for him to see the ground again.

"I'm not sure I understand," he ground out.

"Your brother Montgomery is married to my sister Pippa."

He gritted his teeth. He couldn't help it. It took another moment or two before he dared raise his head to look at her. "How do you know?" he demanded.

"Because your eldest brother Robin's second son Kendrick, who just happens to be the Earl of Seakirk in the current day, told me so."

John could only look at her, speechless.

"I didn't need to hear it from him, though," she said, her visage very pale, "because I watched the way your brother looked at my sister. I listened to them agonize over where they would live. In which century, rather—"

"You *watched* him?" John asked incredulously. "When?"

"Two months ago," she said. "In my hall that used to be his hall—"

He walked away. He only made it ten paces before he walked back, took her by the hand, and pulled her along after him. He supposed he should have been grateful that she went along with him instead of punching him, but given how long she'd lived with her energy-analyzing sister, she probably knew he was about three words from absolutely losing . . . something. His cool, his temper, his sanity. He couldn't have said which. None of it was her fault, of course, and he wasn't the sort of lad to take out his anger on someone just because they were convenient.

But he could hardly believe what she'd just told him.

He took a deep breath. "I'm not sure I can manage speech right now."

She only looked up at him, her eyes full of sympathy and her own bloody great bit of grief. "I understand."

"Can you run again?"

"Yes."

He supposed he could have run for days and not outrun his past, which had now, it seemed, fully caught him up.

He'd known it would someday.

He'd just never expected to have it do so thanks to the woman he loved.

Chapter 19

Tess wasn't sure weariness quite described what she was feeling. She considered several other adjectives as she walked—stumbled, really—along with John toward a castle she could see rising up in front of them, but none of them could quite do justice to the bone-deep exhaustion she felt.

At least the end of the road was hopefully there in front of them. She'd been able to see the keep for quite some time, actually—no doubt the benefit of traveling on foot. It was a lovely, fairy-tale sort of castle that had first been shadowed by predawn darkness, then lit by a rare, clear-skied sunrise. She would have enjoyed it more, but she wasn't altogether sure she wasn't hallucinating it.

She'd long since stopped even wondering if John would ever indulge in polite conversation again. If he'd been taciturn when she first met him, he had descended into new and unfathomable depths of silence over the past two days. She couldn't blame him. Medieval England was probably the last place he wanted to be, much less discuss.

Not that he'd been unkind. The man was chivalry embodied, briskly though it might have been exercised. He'd found places for them to stay, chopped wood for their meals, and forced her to sit at least a handful of times a day so he could see for himself if she had blisters on her feet or not.

But he hadn't spoken beyond the most basic of conversation about the weather and her health. She couldn't blame him. She wasn't sure she hadn't limited herself to those same subjects during those first couple of weeks after Pippa had gone back in time.

To marry his brother.

She felt his hand catch hers suddenly. She turned and looked at him blearily. "What?"

His eyes were full of something another might have called anguish. At that moment, it occurred to her that perhaps he hadn't just stumbled accidently into a time gate eight years ago. Maybe something had happened somewhere along the line to *force* him to leave medieval England.

She wondered what it was costing him now to return.

He stuck his jaw out. "Don't look at me that way."

"What way is that?" she said hoarsely.

"As if you expect me to soon break down and bawl like a bairn."

She looked at him for another minute or two and wasn't entirely sure that he wouldn't do just that. He looked absolutely shattered. She closed her eyes, then stepped forward and put her arms around him. It took a moment, but she felt his arms come around her.

"You won't weep," she said. "But if you wanted to, I would understand."

He held her close, wrapping her in an embrace that was equal parts desperation, affection, and protectiveness. He bent his head and pressed his face against her hair.

"Thank you for understanding," he said, very quietly. "I haven't been pleasant."

"You can be a bit of an arse," she agreed, "as we all know."

He laughed a little, a rasping sound that sounded like it was indeed on the verge of something very emotional, then he pulled back only far enough to look down at her. "Your sister and my brother," he said, a little breathlessly. "Damn you, Tess, couldn't you have told me?"

"Why don't you look back over our volatile relationship, my hedging friend, and tell me just when I should have done that so it didn't send you scampering off the other way?"

He was silent for some time. "Did you want me to remain?"

"Oh, no, you don't," she said, pulling out of his arms. "You're not about to wring that sort of admission from me right now."

He reached out and gathered her back to him. "What I want you to admit was how deceitful it was of you to *date* me for so long without giving me a single bloody clue you knew all about me."

"I'm discreet."

He laughed, sounding pained. "I suppose you could call it that." He held her for several more, eternal moments, then released her only far enough to put his arm around her shoulders. "Let me escort you safely inside my brother's keep, see you fed and warmed, then we'll discuss it all at length. I'll attempt then to redeem myself from my pratishness."

She smiled, then felt her smile fade. "Don't ditch me."

"I wouldn't think to," he said in a very low voice. "Not here. Actually, not anywhere."

"And that's probably only because you don't have your keys."

"I have them," he said. "They're stuck quite uncomfortably down my boot. And nay, it has nothing to do with what I do or do not have. I would never leave you behind."

She closed her eyes briefly, then looked up at him. "Are we in trouble?" she managed. "Are we stuck?"

He took a deep breath. "Let's worry about that after we've seen who's at home here. And if I survive the encounter," he muttered.

"John—"

He nodded toward the keep. "I'm past thinking clearly, Tess. We'll seek shelter, sleep until we wake, then see what can be done."

"What if your brother's not home?"

"My father is at Artane," he said with a shrug. "That's a pass to quite a few venues not open to the average traveler."

She pursed her lips. "You're slipping back quite easily into the role of powerful lord's son."

He shook his head slowly. "If you only had any idea how unsettling that is, you wouldn't tease me about it."

"I like you unbalanced," she said pleasantly. "It gives me an opportunity to herd you for a change."

"You can herd me right back into your arms as soon as you've recovered from this miserable journey here—for which I apologize profusely. I would have done it differently if I could have." He looked at her briefly. "Your sister and my brother."

"Life is weird."

"It is indeed."

The gates were open, but guardsmen were loitering there. The man she assumed was their captain took a look at John, made him a low bow, then looked at her and frowned.

"My lord Montgomery," he said slowly, "and Lady Persephone . . ."

"Is my brother home?" John asked, not correcting him.

"Of course, my lord." He looked behind John. "But your guardsmen, my lord . . ."

"We've had a spot of trouble," John said easily, "but all is well now. What we need most, I daresay, is simply a place to sit and rest for a bit."

"Very well, my lord. Let me escort you inside."

Tess listened to the Norman French roll off John's tongue as if he'd never not spoken it. She expected him to release her hand, but he didn't. He merely laced his fingers with hers as they walked along behind the knight with a very bright medieval sword at his side. A page had been sent scampering ahead toward the keep to deliver heaven only knew what sort of tidings. She looked up at John in time to find him watching her.

"We might have a few things to discuss," he said very quietly.

She pursed her lips. "Yes, all that rubbish about your misspent youth. You're a terrible liar."

"I am not. I'm a very good liar. And I never lied."

"You withheld critical bits of truth."

"I didn't want you to think I was mad and lock me up where I couldn't look at your fetching self as often as I liked."

She would have blushed, but she was too nervous. Not for herself, but for John. "You're not going to manage to throw me off balance with that kind of thing."

"It won't be for a lack of trying, believe me," he said. He looked up at the hall, then caught his breath. "The saints preserve me."

"Want me to protect you?"

He shot her a look. "I don't hide behind women's skirts."

"They're *my* skirts, my lord."

He stopped suddenly, turned her to him, and pulled her into his arms so quickly, she lost her breath.

"I don't think he'll kill me if you're holding my hand," he whispered hoarsely against her ear. "So don't let go."

She hugged him quickly, then stepped back. "I won't."

"How's your French?"

"I'll manage."

He took a deep breath, then took her hand again and turned toward the hall. "Here we go," he murmured half under his breath. "A prayer at this point would not be unthinkable."

Tess knew she probably wasn't the first person to think it, but she couldn't help but wish she'd been able to sit back and watch from the comfort of time and distance a video of what was unfolding in front of her. She would have known from the reviews how the movie ended, and she would have spared nothing but a moment's worry over how things were going to play out. And while she might have felt some sympathy for the players, it would have been a more academic, removed sort of sympathy.

Instead, she was feeling her heart wrench out of her chest because she was standing in the middle of a family reunion that she thought might not go very well.

Nicholas—and it could have been no one else given how greatly he resembled John except for the fact that he was blond and not dark-haired—loped down the stairs with an easy grace that reminded her so much of John, she almost flinched. He looked slightly puzzled.

"Montgomery," he said, walking toward them, "and Pippa, of course. Where are your men? I thought you two were . . . for . . . ah . . . France—"

He apparently got a good enough look at her that he realized she wasn't her sister. He looked at John, then the blood drained from his face and he swayed. John reached out a hand and clamped it on his brother's shoulder to steady him. Nicholas looked at him, looked at her, then backed away and leaned over with his hands on his thighs.

John was completely still. Tess would have worried about him, but he still had hold of her hand and he wasn't breaking any of her fingers, so she supposed he was still hanging in there.

Nicholas simply breathed in and out for several minutes, then straightened. His color wasn't any better, but he hadn't passed out so she supposed he would count that as being good enough. He extended his hand to her.

"You have to be Persephone's sister."

"Tess," she supplied, then she realized he was speaking in English. "Her older sister, but not by much."

He bent over her hand with a formal sort of bow, then released it. He looked at her other hand in John's, then back at her.

"You might want to let go of him for this next bit," he said politely.

John's breathing didn't change, but she felt him stiffen. Nicholas wasn't wearing a sword, but she didn't imagine he needed it to do damage with. She looked at John, disentangled her fingers from his, then took a step away from him. He took a deep breath and looked at his brother.

"Hello, Nick."

Nicholas cursed him. Then he threw his arms around him and hugged him so tightly John squeaked. And he wept. Tess felt her eyes begin to burn at the sight. Nicholas pulled back, cursed a bit more, kissed John on both cheeks, then embraced him again in a manly way that included several rounds of backslapping that no doubt left bruises. He kissed him again, then slapped him on the back of the head before he released him.

"You bloody fool," he managed, dragging his sleeve across his eyes. "Where in the *hell* have you been? Wait, don't answer that." He shot John a dark look. "I can guess."

Tess looked at John. He looked no less affected than his brother. In fact, if she were to be completely accurate, his eyes were very red and he had to clear his throat before he could speak.

"I imagine you can."

Nicholas threw up his hands. "I'm not sure if I should embrace you again or take my sword to you. You bloody *fool*."

"You're repeating yourself," John said with the faintest of smiles. "Old age creeping up on you, is it?"

Tess found herself the recipient of Nicholas's look of disbelief. "How do you manage to endure him?"

"I ignore him a lot."

Nicholas laughed. "I daresay you would have to." He rubbed his hands over his face, blew out his breath, then took John by the shoulder and slung his arm around him. "You both look as if you've been running for a solid se'nnight. Before we think about anything else you need food and hot fire, then sleep. Separately, unless you have something you want to tell me."

"We aren't wed," John said, lifting his eyebrows briefly, "though I've been attempting to woo her. If I convince her to agree to anything else, it will be in spite of what she's been through over the last few days."

Nicholas grunted. "Obviously you've been without my useful influence for too long if you haven't gotten further than that with her. I'll aid you as I can in that endeavor. Tess, you might want to hold on to the other side of him as we go. He looks completely undone."

Tess had to agree, though Nicholas didn't look any better. For herself, all she knew was that trying to follow their rapid French—no matter how good she thought hers was—was giving her a headache. Or that might have been from trying to wrap her mind around the fact that she was walking through a medieval courtyard with a medieval lord and holding on to his equally noble younger brother's hand.

Talk about hands-on research.

"I'll have the whole tale when your lady doesn't look as if she'll drop where she stands. Perhaps you should be holding on to her instead of the opposite. Jennifer will find her a place to lay her head."

"Or perhaps Jennifer would rather talk about the fact that Tess knows her sister, Megan," John offered with an enormous yawn.

Nicholas's mouth fell open, then he looked at John and shut it. "I refuse to make comments on paranormal oddities."

"I would appreciate that."

"You'll hear enough about it from Robin when he learns you're home. I'm assuming you'll go to Artane."

John took a deep breath. "I hadn't thought that far, though I would like to see Father and Mother, aye."

"You'd have to go to France for that," Nicholas said. He looked at Tess briefly. "You won't regret that journey, I daresay. Montgomery and Persephone are there with them now, waiting for Sedgwick to be restored. That's one reason I was so surprised to see you—or, rather, who I thought you were—here."

Tess would have commented, but she found she could hardly keep her eyes open. She didn't protest when John put his arm around her. She realized he'd picked her up only because she found she wasn't walking any longer. She knew he didn't have any more energy than she did, but it wasn't as if she could carry him. She closed her eyes and put her arms around his neck.

"I didn't bring any money to go to France," she murmured.

"By the saints, John," Nicholas said in astonishment, "how have you been treating this poor gel? Forcing her to see to *you*?"

"I haven't," John said with an exasperated snort. "She just has these unpalatable ideas about independence and getting her own way."

"If you think you have troubles with her now, just wait until after she's spoken with Jennifer and become acquainted with all the subversive tactics she uses on me."

"The saints pity you," John muttered.

"A small price to pay, believe me."

Tess held on tightly so she wouldn't fall, then supposed that wasn't necessary. John wasn't going to let her fall. After all, he'd taken care of her for almost five days in very trying circumstances. He would have taken care of her for all the days before then if she had let him . . .

She promised herself a good think later, when she could open her eyes again.

"John?" she managed.

"Aye, love?"

"I don't think I can stay awake any longer."

"Don't try, Tess. You can sleep in peace here."

She hadn't realized before just what a luxury that was. She sighed deeply, then cast herself into the welcoming arms of insensibility. She could only hope she would awake in the same century as John.

She thought she just might be finished with anything else.

Chapter 20

John woke at dawn, shivering. It took a moment for his head to clear enough that he realized he was in one of his brother's guest chambers and not in his own cottage, but memory flooding back helped him with that soon enough. He stared up at the wooden canopy above his head, contemplating the absolute improbability of his current locale. He had never thought to return to his own time—which felt less like home and more like a tourist destination than he'd suspected it might—much less see any of his family again. It was difficult to remember he was no longer a green lad of nineteen winters, but a man of almost twenty-eight years who had seen things that would have turned his father gray overnight.

He rubbed his hands over his face, then threw back the covers and forced himself out of bed, cursing to keep himself warm. It was day, though he honestly had no idea what time it was. He pushed himself to his feet, then walked over to the hearth and kicked up the embers into something warm enough to serve him briefly. Morning, perhaps, since the fire had burned down to almost nothing. He yawned, grateful for the sleep and wishing he had the energy to have a bit more. But that would leave Tess possibly fending for herself and that he couldn't do, not even in Nick's hall.

He turned to look for water to wash with and found it on a table next to the hearth. That he had to break through a layer of ice to get to it was unsurprising but an unsettling reminder of just where he was.

He raised his eyebrows briefly in appreciation of the luxury of his brother's home—at least he hadn't had to brave a winter stream to wash or forgo washing altogether—then set to his morning's ablutions as if he'd never spent a day away from his usual routine in medieval England. He had his wash, shaved with a knife, then put on clean clothes and serviceable boots provided so thoughtfully by his brother. He reached for his sword and belted it around his hips, then stuck a pair of daggers down his boots, though he wondered why he bothered. It wasn't as if he would have to kill anyone to gain the breakfast table.

He dragged his hands through his hair and sighed deeply. Killing ruffians to keep Tess safe had been necessary but very unpleasant. He'd forgotten, living his soft life in the Future as he had, just how brutal medieval England could be. He wouldn't be unhappy to leave it behind. Assuming he could leave it behind.

He decided abruptly that *that* was something he could certainly think about later.

He walked out into the passageway, had to think for a moment or two about where he was in Nicholas's keep, then headed toward Tess's bedchamber. He supposed he could have found it easily enough by the sight of the guardsman standing just outside it. He paused and waited for the man to acknowledge him.

"Lord John," the man said, inclining his head immediately. "Sir Ranulf, at your service. And your lady's."

John almost smiled at the title, but supposed there was no reason in giving Nicholas's guardsmen more reason than they already had to speculate about him. He nodded toward the door. "Is Lady Tess still inside, then?"

"She hasn't left the chamber, my lord, and I've been here since the second watch."

"'Twas a difficult journey here," John conceded, "and I'm sure she's very weary. I appreciate your attending her. I'll happily relieve you now."

Sir Ranulf hesitated. "As you will, of course, my lord, but my lord Wyckham thought you might prefer to break your fast with him below and perhaps seek the lists. I've assigned a rotation of lads to keep watch here and escort your lady to you when she wakes."

John thought about balking, then relented. The truth was Tess needed a fortnight's sleep, which she wouldn't have if he poked his nose inside her door every quarter hour. She would be safe enough with his brother's guardsmen watching over her.

He nodded to Sir Ranulf, then thanked him again for his service before he continued down the passageway. He would have felt better if he'd known Tess's door was locked from the inside, but he knew it wasn't because he'd been the one to put her to bed the morning before—under the watchful eye of his brother, who was far too impressed with his own levels of propriety. He'd hardly been able to take off Tess's shoes without Nicholas harrumphing importantly. He'd had to leave Jennifer to help his very groggy love into a nightgown and tuck her into bed.

He jogged down the circular stairs, shaking his head a little as he did so. It was hard to believe any time had passed at all from his youth to his present, though he couldn't deny it had. The last time he'd been at Wyckham, he'd been a brash lad of eighteen, his spurs newly won and his ego colossal. He'd held his own against Nicholas in the lists—a feat he seriously doubted he would be repeating anytime soon—and strode across the world's stage sure in his ability to conquer anything that dared face him.

He sighed to himself as he walked across the floor and followed his nose to the kitchens. Obviously, he'd arisen too late to manage anything at the lord's table, but that didn't bother him. He was perfectly happy to attract as little attention as possible.

He walked into the kitchens and found Nicholas sitting at the worktable there, surrounded by his four sons. The boys looked up at him with varying degrees of astonishment, even though he'd been privileged to meet all his nephews the day before. Nicholas was only watching him, a faint smile on his face. John set his sword aside and pulled up his chair next to Nicholas's eldest, James.

"Well met, nephew," he said politely. "Again."

"Bloody hell," James blurted out. "You look just like Montgomery. Still."

"James," Nicholas said sternly, "we don't swear at table."

"But, Papa, this is just the worktable," said second son John, "not the *proper* table."

John was fairly certain the boy, who looked to be about seven, had been named after Jennifer's father, but he was happy to flatter himself that he could claim a bit of the boy for himself. The boy couldn't have looked any more like Nicholas. 'Twas obvious he had his father's ability to argue.

"Aye, it is, son," Nicholas said with a long-suffering sigh, "but we still don't swear at table."

"Well," John the younger said philosophically, "I suppose we should be for the lists then." He looked up at John. "We can say what we please there."

"I'm certain you can," John said, suppressing a smile.

"Are you coming along, Uncle John?" James asked, eyeing John critically. "Father said you'd been wallowing in unwholesome luxury for the last few years and might have forgotten how to wield your sword."

John shot Nicholas a look. "Did he, now?"

"He did," James said without hesitation. "He said he suspected even *we* could humiliate you without effort."

John smiled in spite of himself. He'd known James, of course, because Jennifer had fallen pregnant ten minutes after Nick had wed her, and he'd held the boy as a wee babe. He could only assume the others were approximately two years and ten minutes apart, which left young Connor a wee thing of about two summers. Thomas, who was apparently about four years old, looked to be canny enough that John thought he might indeed have a bit of trouble with him.

"Well," John said thoughtfully, "perhaps after I've eaten what your father's superior cook has masterfully prepared, you might lead me out to the lists and show me how 'tis done. Gently, of course, lest the humiliation be too much to bear."

"Swords, lads!" James cried, leaping up from the table and dashing for the door. "We'll await him in the hall."

John helped Connor off his stool, then found himself with the lad on his lap instead. He looked into bright blue eyes that saw already far too much.

"Uncle John," the lad said distinctly, "you home?"

"Ah," John said, utterly blindsided. "Well, aye, lad, I am. For the moment. I've been living very far away. I'm sorry to have missed your birth."

Connor looked at him again, turned and rested back against him, and popped his thumb in his mouth. John looked at Nicholas, who was only watching with a small smile.

"Well," John managed.

Nicholas shook his head slowly. "That one there," he said with a look at his son, "frightens us. He's been blurting out unsettling things for as long as he could put words together. Which hasn't been all that long, truth be told."

"Unnerving," John agreed fervently.

Nicholas looked around him, apparently to see if privacy might be had, then eyed John purposefully. "You know, I haven't begun to question you about your activities. You yawned too much yesterday for a proper grilling. I will want a particular set of answers about your past—and you know which ones I'm speaking of—before we carry on much further."

"Are you entitled to those answers, I wonder," John said grimly.

A muscle twitched in Nicholas's jaw. "I wonder why you would think I wasn't."

"Because the rub was between me and Father. It had nothing to do with you."

Nicholas cursed succinctly, apparently not finding the sanctity of the current table to be an impediment. "Do you have any idea, you bloody idiot, just how much your actions grieved us? We thought you were dead!"

John blinked. "But why? I left a missive for you—you, because I thought you might manage to blurt out what I'd done before Father killed you."

"A missive?" Nicholas echoed in surprise. "But I received nothing."

"But I entrusted it to Everard of Chev—" John's thoughts and words ground to a halt. "Everard of Chevington," he finished "I left the missive with him to give to you."

"And why in the hell would you trust him?"

"He wasn't my first choice, obviously," John said evenly. "But since he came upon me whilst I was preparing to step on a particular patch of ground—if you take my meaning, which I'm certain you do—I thought it best to give him something to do so I could leave without his noticing the manner."

Nicholas shook his head. "I never received anything."

"The bloody whoreson," John said tightly. "The saints only know what he did when he read what I'd written."

"You give him too much credit, for he could scarce scratch out his own name." Nicholas studied John for a moment or two. "I wonder why it was you intended to attempt such a foolish thing, no matter what sort of pretty note you intended to leave behind."

John didn't suppose servants were far away, so he didn't indulge in anything but generalities. "Haven't you considered the same thing?"

"Never."

John pursed his lips. "Honorable knights don't lie."

Nicholas glared at him. "Very well, I've thought about it endlessly, but I would never leave my family behind to indulge myself thus."

John suppressed the urge to roll his eyes. "I hadn't intended that it be a permanent thing, Nick. I simply planned a year of adventure, to see things I . . . well, to see things. I fully intended to come home afterward to regale you all with my tales of glory and leave you impossibly jealous."

"That sounds like something you would do," Nicholas said with a grunt. "And nay, I suppose I can't blame you. I might have done the same thing in your shoes." He frowned. "Why didn't you return?"

John had to take a deep breath. "I tried. The gate was—shall we say—uninterested in my wishes and refused to carry me home."

Nicholas closed his eyes briefly. "You poor lad."

John shrugged aside the memory of trying that particular patch of ground near Artane and finding it absolutely unresponsive to his pleas. He'd then gone to the second place he knew of only to find himself in what he now knew had been Victorian England. He'd been gang-pressed into service on one of Her Majesty's finest ships and only managed to escape because the terrain near Artane had remained familiar enough for him to know when to run. He'd thrown himself back into the depths of the time gate he'd come from and hadn't argued when it had carried him back to the Future.

"How did you know where to launch yourself from, as it were?"

John lifted an eyebrow. "Your map, though why a Scotsman should be making those kinds of . . ."

He wondered when his thoughts would cease grinding to uncomfortable halts. The mapmaker had been a certain James MacLeod. *James MacLeod?* It wasn't possible that he was related to Ian MacLeod, he of the discreet and exclusive sword school.

Surely.

"What is it?"

"Who is James MacLeod?" John asked, because he apparently couldn't stop his damnable curiosity.

"He's Jennifer's cousin, in a roundabout way," Nicholas said with a shrug. He shot John an amused glance. "Know him?"

"I don't, but I imagine that's my loss."

Nicholas laughed a little. "I imagine he would agree. He's been laird of the clan MacLeod in a pair of different centuries and, from what I understand, an incorrigible traveler through, ah, well, you can use your wee noggin to divine the rest. He is a compulsive mapmaker, it would seem, forever marking the spots he's investigated and found to be . . . unusual."

"And you would know."

"Apparently, so would you if you've seen one of his maps—in my private trunk, no doubt."

John couldn't help an uncomfortable smile. "My apologies."

"I need a better lock."

"Or less determined relations," John said. "I fear I did indeed have a quick peek at your map, but I only memorized two particular spots because I was stupid enough to think I wouldn't need more. I took my sword and my courage in hand, then decided that a journey might give Father time to cool his head."

Nicholas toyed with his mug of ale. "And what was the rub, John?"

John supposed there was no reason to put off telling Nicholas things he'd doubtless considered already. "Chevington," he said with a sigh, "as I'm sure you've guessed by now. I was fool enough to take Everard's side in his fight with his brother over the title. Father didn't appreciate my inserting my always nosey nose into business that wasn't mine."

"Is that all it was?" Nicholas asked with a pained smile.

"Isn't that enough? I was hotheaded and Father stubborn. I

had no intention of bowing to his commands, and he was determined to bend me to his will."

"You're going to have a son just like yourself, you know."

"The saints preserve me."

Nicholas laughed. "Aye, I daresay that won't be the last time you say that. Perhaps you'll be wiser as a father than you have been as a son." His smile faded. "They grieved terribly. Father himself searched for months."

John let out his breath slowly. "I never meant for that to happen. Surely you know that."

"I do—and I did." Nicholas shook his head. "I tried to convince Father that you had likely gone off and done something particularly foolish—and he knew exactly what I meant by that—but he didn't dare hope it had been just that. He felt terribly responsible."

"He would," John said with a sigh, "but he shouldn't have. I had been considering the journey for several months. He simply spurred me on sooner than I had planned." He finished his ale, then looked at his brother. "They're in France?"

"In the cottage on Grandmère's abbey grounds—though you know 'tis hardly a cottage. They needed a change, I suppose, and Father was happy enough to turn Artane over to Robin. There is a well-worn path between Calais and both Artane and Segrave, as you might imagine." He paused. "Joanna is fighting, but she's fading."

John had to simply sit and hold Nicholas's youngest son for a moment as the tidings sank in. He had thought about his grandmothers, of course, but never supposed he might see either of them again. "And the others?"

"Robin and Anne have four children, if that's what you're asking, though you know Phillip and Kendrick already. Mandy has three living of hers and Isabelle has two lads and a pair of gels. And Miles?" Nicholas laughed. "I can't bring to mind how many terrors he and Abigail have produced so far. They multiply in my eyes based on the mischief they combine whenever they come to visit."

John shook his head. "How much I've missed."

"And your younger brother's wedding, as well," Nicholas said pointedly. "He grieved most of all over your loss."

"As I would have his," John said. He looked at Nicholas. "And you? Did you shed no tear?"

Nicholas smiled. "Nary a one."

John laughed a little, knowing his brother was lying.

Nicholas pushed away from the table and rose. "I would send your charge there to his mother, but she needs her feet up for the morning. Let's bring him along to the lists with us, if you have the courage to face my three lads there before I grind you into the dust."

"I'll do my best," John said, rising with Connor in his arms. He turned him around and tried not to flinch at the feel of sweet small arms coming around his neck.

He'd thought time in the past might do him in. He just hadn't anticipated how quickly.

He spent an hour with his nephews, training with them until they were satisfied, then walked off the field to have a drink before turning to his brother, whom he was certain would be satisfied less easily. It would show him where he was lacking, though, and he couldn't be certain that that sort of preparation might serve him in some tight spot later on.

He drank, then glanced at Nicholas, who looked just as casually lethal as he always did. John had spent more time in his youth than he likely should have trying to decide which of his two eldest brothers was the more dangerous. Robin was, as Robin would have told anyone within earshot, simply the best swordsman England had ever produced. John had to concede there was a great bit of truth in that. Robin absolutely had the skill to back up his arrogance. But over the years, John had come to the conclusion that Nick was easily as skilled as Robin, he was just quieter about it.

In the end, all John knew was that he would have been greatly relieved to have had either of them guarding his back.

Nicholas set his cup down. "I'll be interested to see if there's anything left of your skill."

"Not having swordsmen of your mettle to train with has been a trial," John conceded. "Well, not having any swordsmen of any stripe, actually, has been something of a problem. You will no doubt have little sport from me today."

"You should have sought out James MacLeod or another of his family."

"So I'm beginning to think." John shook his head. "I can't tell you how many times I've heard that surname, though I knew nothing of James himself. I was beginning to think the clan was stalking me."

"Fate was, more likely," Nicholas said with a smile. "Well, you're here now and we'll do what we can with what you have left." He paused. "We should discuss Everard of Chevington further at some point, I daresay."

John sighed deeply. It wasn't possible that Everard had gone to the Future, though perhaps it was less impossible than he feared. In his missive he'd only told Nicholas that he'd intended to see where Jennifer had come from, knowing his brother would understand exactly what he was referring to. Surely Everard hadn't been canny enough to understand the meaning behind the words.

Though there was no guaranteeing that Everard hadn't watched him disappear through that time gate near Artane.

"Perhaps you should go to Chevington and call Everard a few names when you see him."

"I'll do worse than call him names," John promised.

Nicholas smiled, looking slightly satisfied. "I'm happy to see all that soft living of yours in the Future hasn't blunted your sense of vengeance." He paused, then leaned forward. "Do you have a car?"

"Four."

Nicholas scowled. "Gluttony, even with automobiles, is a sin, brother."

"So is speeding in a four-hundred-fifty-horsepower Aston Martin Vanquish," John said placidly. "I'll describe the sensation for you, if you like."

"If I ever come to the Future, you'll do more than describe it. I'll want the keys."

"You'll pry them from my cold, dead fingers with your sword."

Nicholas laughed. "We'll see where we stand after a few days in my lists. I won't work you too hard this morning. You'll want to see if your lady is recovered from the hell you put her through getting here. Couldn't you have found a horse?"

"And have bought it with what?" John asked with a snort. "My keys? My phone? A credit card?"

Nicholas's eyes were bright. "Do you have any of them with you?"

"All three, hidden cunningly in my boot. I'll give you a sight of them in your solar later, if you like."

Nicholas rubbed his hands together in anticipation. "Absolutely." He paused, then shot John a look. "I have to tell you, though, that this is all very strange."

John found he had absolutely nothing to say in return. He was about to step into his brother's lists, hopefully reach the other end of the encounter without finding himself impaled on the end of that brother's very sharp sword, then potentially spend the evening wooing his very modern love, and all the while contemplating showing that medieval brother all the apps on his mobile phone.

He thought he just might have to thank Fate for a change instead of cursing her.

Chapter 21

T*ess* woke, then froze.

Well, she froze partly because she was freezing, but mostly because she had no idea where she was.

Or at least she didn't for a moment or two. She looked up at the canopy over her head and remembered that she was in Nicholas de Piaget's castle. In the thirteenth century. In a night-gown she had only vague memories of being helped into by an extremely pregnant Jennifer de Piaget. Either her hostess was very near her due date, or she was about to have twins. Tess wasn't about to ask.

She found herself having to take several very careful breaths. It was one thing to go on vacation and experience a different culture or way of life. It was another thing entirely to be thrust back into a time period not her own with nothing more than the clothes on her back and her tenuous tie to a man of that vintage to keep her safe—

Not that she would worry about the last bit. John had promised to protect her and so he would. If she could count on nothing else in the world, she knew she could count on his keeping his word.

She was tempted to laugh, but she thought that might evolve into something that sounded less amused and more hysterical. There she was with a doctorate in medieval history, yet now she was actually *living* in a time that had been purely academic to her before. She realized abruptly that the only way she was going to keep from losing it was to look at things in a purely academic way. Obviously she was going to have to find pen and paper right off. It was the opportunity of a lifetime, and she didn't want to miss any of it.

She didn't allow herself to wonder if maybe she wouldn't need that pen and paper because she would never get back to her proper place in time.

She sat up, dragged her hands through her hair to encounter a rather unpleasant, greasy mess, then swung her legs to the floor.

She got up, made her bed that was actually not as uncomfortable as she would have suspected it might be, then walked over to the table under the window. There was a note there from Jennifer welcoming her and instructing her to make use of whatever she found in the room because it had been left for her. Tess walked over to the door, locked it, then quickly did the best she could with what was available. She braided her hair in hopes that it would disguise its condition, then dressed in the clothes Jennifer had left for her, feeling fortunate she and John's sister-in-law were close in size and height.

She took a deep breath, blew out the candle on the nightstand, then went and opened the door.

A man she didn't recognize was standing against the opposite wall. He made her a low bow, then straightened and smiled. "Lady Tess," he said politely. "A good morning to you."

"Morning?" she asked in surprise. She would have thought it was just evening, but perhaps she'd had a better nap than she'd thought. She nodded and hoped her French would be serviceable enough. At least she understood the offer of an escort to breakfast. She followed the man along the hallway and down the stairs, trying not to notice the newness of the place.

For some reason, that was very unsettling.

She walked out into the great hall, realizing she was hoping a bit more fervently than she was comfortable with to see John. He wasn't there, but Jennifer was, trying to chase after a two-year-old towheaded lad who was apparently determined to do something he shouldn't. His little boots were caked with mud, but then again, so were his hands and face. Tess didn't dare speculate on where he might have come by all that dirt, but she certainly wasn't above lending a hand when necessary. She caught the lad, swung him up into her arms, and looked at him seriously.

"Are you making mischief?" she asked, hoping it had come out as it should have.

He stopped squirming immediately and looked at her. "Lady Tess."

"Yes, I am. And who are you?"

"Connah," he said with a sweet smile. "Want John."

"I do, too," she said frankly. "Shall we ask your mama if we can go find him?"

He crawled out of her arms, reached for her hand, then tugged. Tess went with him and found herself deposited in front of the fire where Jennifer had taken refuge.

"Thank you," Jennifer said in English, with a grateful smile. "He's a bit much for me in my current state."

Tess cleared her throat. "I can do French, if you don't mind a few mistakes."

"Later, after you've given me a couple of details I might want to know," Jennifer said, looking at her with bright eyes. "How is Megan?"

"Happy, doted on, missing you," Tess said with a smile. "I spent a couple of weeks at Artane with her after—" She had to pause catch a breath she hadn't realized she would need before she could finish. "Ah, after Pippa . . . well, after Pippa left."

Jennifer's expression was one of sympathy. "I understand, believe me. If it makes you feel any better, she's deliriously happy. Missing you and Peaches, of course, but happy."

Tess nodded and attempted a smile, but wasn't exactly sure she'd succeeded. It had been difficult enough getting over having lost Pippa before; having to lose her again after potentially seeing her in her current situation—

Jennifer set Connor back down on the floor from where he'd tried to crawl into the chair with her. "Let's go find you something for breakfast, then Connor can take you out to the lists where he's apparently been all morning." She smiled. "You can call it research."

Tess suppressed a shiver. "It's giving living history an entirely new meaning, believe me." She stood up, helped Jennifer to her feet, then smiled in sympathy. "Are you due soon?"

"With twins, if you can believe it," Jennifer said with a game smile. "Girls, from what I understand."

Tess didn't want to pry, but she couldn't imagine Jennifer had a local clinic to frequent for an ultrasound. "How do you know?"

Jennifer leaned close. "My mother brought back a guidebook from Beauvois—that's Nicky's keep in France. Apparently we're not nearly done yet with having children."

"That sort of takes all the spontaneity out of it, doesn't it?" Tess asked weakly.

Jennifer laughed. "You would think so, but somehow it doesn't. I'll tell you what's really mind-blowing is to have your medieval husband quoting Shakespeare at you during labor or spouting in superior tones the odd Wordsworth quote. When he's feeling moody, he'll quote Yeats." She looked at Tess. "I suppose for you, the opposite is true. I can't imagine John has shed many of his medieval habits."

Tess shook her head. "He herds me, a lot."

"It's what his father taught him to do," Jennifer said with a smile. "Very chivalrous, if you look at it the right way." She linked arms with Tess. "I didn't know John as a child, but I'll tell you all about him as a young man, if you like."

"Was he terrible?"

"No," Jennifer said with a smile, "he was wonderful. Arrogant, of course, but very serious about his knightly virtues and making something of himself that his father would be proud of. He had a dry sense of humor that always killed Nicky." She looked at Tess seriously. "Does he laugh much anymore?"

Tess sighed. "I can't say he does, but the dry humor is definitely still there." She paused. "I think—no, I know he's spent the last eight years running from his past. I think he's still trying to deal with the irony of meeting me, though that's sort of a fluke."

"Some fluke," Jennifer said with a delicate snort. "It looks to me as though he has every intention of making it a permanent thing, though I'm not sure how you feel about it."

Tess shrugged as casually as she could. "I'm not sure that matters." She looked at Jennifer. "Now that he's home, that is."

Jennifer only looked at her with a pained smile. "I don't have

the answer for you, and I think I'll keep my speculations to myself for now. And we'd better switch to French or my kitchen
staff will think I'm crazier than they already do."

Tess couldn't imagine that because Jennifer was welcomed
into the kitchen with what she could see was true affection. She
was the happy beneficiary of the overflow of all that came Jennifer's way, as well as the pleasure of one Connor de Piaget who
seemed quite happy to sit on a stool next to her and watch her
with very wide blue eyes.

"That is Pippa's sister," Jennifer said. "They look alike, don't
they?"

Connor considered that while trying to take a few layers off
his thumb. Tess laughed a little, then turned back to breakfast
and a very basic conversation in medieval Norman French.

"Nicky has plenty of paper and ink if you want it," Jennifer
said, with a knowing look. "No sense in not making a few notes
while you can."

Tess agreed wholeheartedly because, again, putting herself
back in the role of scholar gave her a sense of security and purpose, which she realized she needed desperately. It was one thing
to look back on the Middle Ages and hunt for elusive surviv-
ing sketches of dress or spend hours translating and deciphering
crumbling texts for details that others might have overlooked. It
was another thing entirely to be sitting across from a woman who
moved easily in that world and seemed quite happy to carry on
without chocolate and a wireless Internet connection.

"John now?" Connor asked, popping his thumb out of his
mouth.

John.

Tess took a deep breath, then nodded. She hadn't seen him
yet, awake and moving about in his proper time period.

She only hoped she would survive the sight.

Half an hour later, dressed in boots and wearing a warm cloak
borrowed from the lady of the castle, she was walking with Jennifer's youngest son around the side of the hall itself and out to
the lists. There was a collection of young boys lounging on a
bench on the near side of the field, but they leaped up the moment they saw her. She was escorted over to that stone bench

pushed up against the castle wall and instructed politely to sit where they might watch over her.

She settled Connor on her lap, immediately forgot the names of the other lads who introduced themselves to her, and wondered why in the world she'd thought John had dredged up any of his sword skill that day at Warewick when he'd shown Bill how little he knew.

She let out a slow breath, because it helped her feel a bit less like she'd just fallen into a medieval movie. The bench was very cold under her despite Jennifer's cloak, and the boys crowded around her helped a little, but still she couldn't quite control her shivers.

Nicholas and John were sparring in tunics, hose, boots, and leather jerkins instead of chain mail. She supposed they knew what they were doing or they wouldn't have been so lightly protected, but still she jumped every time their blades crossed.

She grasped frantically for any shred of academic dispassion she possessed. So the guys in front of her—and not just them, but probably two dozen other men as well—were fighting with swords. It was what they needed to do to practice their survival skills. In fact, it was probably just a part of their normal day, like going off on a little ride or doing in the odd ruffian to keep their families safe.

She studied Nicholas for a minute because he was the lord of the castle, and she supposed there was a certain standard of swordplay he held himself to. An important point to verify for her next paper, of course. She could see why Jennifer had considered him capable of protecting her and her children in such an environment. He was, despite his obviously laid-back attitude and casual air, a master at his craft. If she'd seen him in a temper coming her way, she would have surrendered without hesitation. But he wasn't the man she was truly interested in watching.

She let out her breath slowly and set aside academics so she could look at the sight she truly wanted to savor.

John de Piaget, medieval knight.

She closed her eyes—briefly, so she didn't miss more than necessary. John was deliciously gorgeous, from the dark hair he kept shoving out of his eyes with a curse to the bottoms of his mud-encrusted boots. If he was out of practice with his sword, she couldn't tell. He was absolutely in his element, fighting with an intense concentration she had seen him use in other things, laughing periodically at something his brother would say that she was sure wasn't polite, cursing when Nicholas's blade came too close to his face or his ribs. It was as if he'd never passed a single day away from his normal routine, never been anything but the fourth son of one of the most powerful barons in medieval England.

"Lady Tess, your cheeks are red," one of the lads said, peering at her intently.

"I'm chilled," Tess said faintly. It wouldn't do to tell an impressionable young boy that she was lusting after his uncle.

She forced herself to tear her gaze away periodically to watch the other men training in the field, but they weren't nearly as interesting as the two in front of her—and she didn't think that was simply because she was fond—

She took a deep breath. No, she wasn't fond of John de Piaget. She was crazy about him.

She chewed on that realization for several minutes until she came to another one which was that *John* was crazy. His brother was obviously showing him no mercy, but he only laughed in the face of it. Hollywood producers would have killed to get their hands on either of the two men in front of her. Gorgeous, buff, and wielding swords as if their lives depended on it.

She leaned around Connor to see if he was impressed as well only to find him watching with enormous eyes and still working on his thumb. Answer enough.

She wasn't sure how much time passed before John held up his hand, then leaned over with that hand on his thigh to catch his breath. He was absolutely drenched. His brother was no less damp, so perhaps the workout had been spread around equally. She watched them exchange a few pleasantries—well, slurs, again, if her Norman French was anywhere close to accurate— laugh, then walk off the field toward her.

She prided herself on her composure, which at the moment was the only thing keeping her from embarrassing herself by either blushing or drooling.

John pushed his sweaty hair out of his eyes and smiled as he stopped in front of her. "I see you have a champion there."

She shivered in spite of herself. Norman French. *Medieval*

Norman French, which that gorgeous man standing in front of her had grown up speaking. That man who could likely just as easily participate in a tournament as hop in his Vanquish and zip up the M25.

And to think he'd been hiding it all under jeans, a sweater, and a demeanor that discouraged any and all questions about his true origins.

"I think," Nicholas drawled, "that your stench has rendered her speechless."

John elbowed his brother in the ribs with a good deal of enthusiasm. "Shut up," he suggested.

Nicholas eyed him archly. "Go bathe. I'll give your lady a tour of the lists. I would make haste were I you, though, before I convince her that life with you would be a misery."

John looked at Tess and shook his head in disbelief. "Did I *want* to see him again?"

She held up her hands in surrender. "I'm not going to comment. But I will wait for you."

"I'll hurry."

And with that, he was trotting back toward the house. Nicholas took his toddler, swung him up to sit on his shoulders, then smiled at Tess. "English or French?" he asked politely.

"French, if you have the patience for it," she said, rising. "I'm sorry to have taken such advantage of your guest room yesterday. I didn't realize I'd slept that long."

"Don't spare thought for it," Nicholas said dismissively. "I understand John ran you the entire way here from Chevington. I suppose he had no choice, but the distance isn't easy. You're justified in being weary." He smiled at her. "I understand you have a university degree in medieval history."

She found herself blushing. "Ridiculous, isn't it? I'm studying what you're living."

"I would say the subject is the only one worthy of study, but then I would sound like my brother Robin and that would make me queasy. Instead, let's take a turn about the keep, and I'll keep my thoughts to myself. If anything strikes your fancy, tell me of it and we'll discuss it."

She smiled. "You're very kind."

He studied her for a moment or two. "I think I can understand what it cost you to lose Pippa, who has made my youngest brother happier than he deserves to be. Consider it a poor exchange."

She nodded, though she found, to her horror, that it bothered her that he hadn't said anything about John being the exchange for Pippa—if such an awful exchange could possibly be contemplated without wincing.

She wondered, accompanied by a feeling that sat in her stomach like a rock, if John would want to stay in medieval England now that he'd found his way back to it.

"You're still weary."

She looked up at Nicholas quickly. "That isn't John's fault. He did the best with what he had."

Nicholas smiled. "I wasn't faulting him for it; just making an observation. We'll make this a quick trip. I think what you need is an afternoon in front of the fire."

Yes, where she could look at John and store up a lifetime of memories of the sight of him with the firelight flickering against his dark hair and his exceptionally handsome face. Then she would then go back to the future, find all the music he'd recorded, and sit with her collection in her solar and spend the rest of her days weeping over him.

"Tess?"

She blinked rapidly and looked up at Nicholas, attempting another smile. "I'm sorry," she said sincerely. "I think I'm more tired than I thought."

"Shall we go in?"

She shook her head. "I'm not about to pass up a chance to pry into the workings of Wyckham when I have the lord of the castle at my disposal."

She realized she was speaking English, but the French was beyond her. Nicholas only smiled.

"I don't know how long you're planning on staying, but my life is an open book for you for as long as that might be. Since you have on boots, let's start in the lists."

Tess nodded, grateful for the distraction.

So she walked with him, trailed by his other three sons who looked just like him, and tried not to pepper him with questions. She wasn't sure where she would have begun, because they were questions she could have asked of John without garrison knights listening and wondering why she was daft.

They made it to the stables and were admiring a horse before she hit upon the one thing she wanted to know that she hadn't been able to find in a book. She looked up at him.

"Are you ever afraid?"

Nicholas caught his breath, then smiled faintly. "A terrible question, which you doubtless know." He put Connor down on the floor, then studied the horse in the stall for a moment or two. "In my youth, I would have said to you nay without hesitation. I would have given my life for my family, of course, and grieved if any of them had been lost, but it wouldn't have inspired fear. But now?" He had to take a deep breath. "I don't think about it often, but aye, I suppose the fear is always there, waiting in the shadows. If something happened to Jennifer, or the lads—" He paused, then smiled at her. "If it eases you any, Montgomery feels that way about your sister. He is utterly besotted with her."

"And he'll keep her safe?"

"He is my equal," Nicholas said simply. "As was John, but he's gone soft, living in that land of yours with Lilt and chocolate and the saints only know what else. It wouldn't take him long to regain what little skill he's set aside for other things, though, if that eases you, though I'm not sure where he would use those skills."

"Not many sword-wielding ruffians where I come from," Tess agreed.

Nicholas shook his head slowly. "But there are other perils there that he must face that I never will." He nodded to his left. "I suppose he could tell us of those, if he cared to."

Tess looked to find the source of all her turmoil leaning against a post in the stable, freshly scrubbed and looking like a lord in his own right.

"Getting the tour?" he asked politely.

She nodded, putting on her best smile. "Your brother has been very kind."

"And now he can get lost," John said with an arch look cast that brother's way. "I can carry on from here."

Nicholas leaned against a stall door. "I think that perhaps instead I should offer my services as chaperon."

"When hell freezes over," John said with a snort. "I'm going to give Tess a riding lesson, so there won't be any mauling of her person unless she falls off her horse."

"Horse?" Tess echoed. She realized it had come out as more of a squeak, but it was too late to take it back.

"Every noblewoman should know how to ride," John said, looking at her solemnly. "My lady."

Nicholas put his hand briefly on her shoulder. "I think in this I can safely say that my brother knows what he's about. He's an excellent rider, and I think he has the good sense not to put you up on a horse that will fling you back into his arms. You'll be safe enough."

"Ah," Tess said, "I think I'll pass."

"And I think you won't," John said easily. "Tess, you must learn to ride. You cannot be in this—ah, I mean—" He dragged his hand through his hair. "You must learn to ride," he finished. "Nonnegotiable."

She wanted to argue with him that everything short of death and taxes was negotiable, but she knew she didn't have a leg to stand on—and since she would likely fall off her first horse and break both legs, maybe it was best she just get it over with. But she wasn't about to let John think he had the upper hand.

"Maybe," she said firmly.

Nicholas laughed and gathered up his sons. "Let's leave them to it, lads. Hands in plain sight all the time, Johnny lad. Don't make me take you out to the lists and beat you to a pulp because you didn't behave yourself."

John rolled his eyes. "Begone, my lord, whilst my tongue is still in check."

Nicholas flicked him on the ear as he passed, then continued on with his sons looking back longingly. Tess watched them go, then looked up at John.

"This isn't necessary—"

"It is," he corrected. "Critical, actually."

It occurred to her, with a startling flash that made her slightly queasy, that he might be entertaining the thought that not only did he want to stay in medieval England, he couldn't get out of medieval England.

Which meant she couldn't, either.

She felt her mouth go dry. "All right," she managed.

"Trust me."

"I do."

He smiled, a grave, serious smile that she'd never seen him

wear before, then found herself suddenly seated quite comfortably on a pile of hay while he went to put the appropriate gear on what was hopefully Wyckham's gentlest nag.

She tried to calm her racing heart and warm her very chilly hands.

She failed.

Medieval England?

She tucked her hands under her arms and hoped they would stop shaking by the time she needed them.

Chapter 22

John stood with his back against a tree, watching Tess look out over a panoramic vista that had been covered with snow the night before. He was profoundly grateful for a decent cloak, though he wouldn't have argued if some fairy godmother had waved her wand and caused his Vanquish—complete with its very serviceable heater—to appear behind him. A pity he wouldn't have been able to get inside it given that he'd left his keys, his phone, and his credit card locked safely in Nicholas's trunk.

He suppressed the urge to drag his hands through his hair. He honestly couldn't say what had been worse: leaving Artane for the first time or coming back to medieval England unexpectedly. Both had been wrenching.

Only then, he hadn't had a certain woman he would leave behind if he chose a century she didn't belong to.

He watched the woman in question and wondered what she was thinking. He'd actually spent quite a bit of the previous day watching her and wondering the same thing. He'd known she was sitting on the side of the lists, watching him as he trained. She had seemed a little shell-shocked, but he couldn't blame her for it. He was quite certain he'd worn that same look for the first few fortnights after his arrival in the Future. It was to be expected.

She'd seemed very uncomfortable at first with the horse he'd put her up on until she'd realized that he truly wasn't going to let go of the lunge line and leave her cantering off into the distance. She came by an excellent seat naturally somehow, and there had come a point where she'd actually smiled a time or two.

Her hands, though, had been positively frigid when he'd pulled off her gloves to see how they'd survived her first lesson. That had come, he'd suspected, from more than just the chill, as profound as it was.

He'd taken her inside and spent the afternoon and evening making sure she and Jennifer were well-fed and always sitting closest to the fire. The conversation in Nicholas's solar that evening had been carried on partly in French, partly in English, and had involved a wide range of topics that had been as innocuous as possible. Tess had mostly listened gravely. John had caught the single, questioning look Nicholas had sent him, but had only been able to shrug in return. Tess was thinking about something, but he was damned if he knew what.

That morning he'd marched out to the lists with his brother, indulged in a brief lunch with Tess, then announced that it was time for her to try a little ride outside the castle walls. She was plucky, he would give her that. Facing medieval times head-on instead of from the comfort of a library had to have been daunting, but she'd done it without hesitation.

Silently, of course, but without hesitation.

All of which left him where he was, leaning back against a tree with a sword at his side, freezing his arse off so he could have ten minutes of privacy with the woman he loved.

The woman who seemed to be about three heartbeats from bolting, truth be told.

She looked like something out of a painting, standing there in a deep blue cloak with its hood pulled up around her face and her stillness a tangible thing. Wyckham sat in a particularly lovely part of the country, which only added to the perfection of what he was seeing. He regretted having left his phone back at the keep. He would have happily taken a picture to remind him of the moment.

Tess turned and looked at him, and he lost his breath. He supposed he should have been accustomed to the sight of her, but he found he wasn't. She was beautiful, and brilliant, and courageous.

But she also looked still fragile enough that he reached out toward her without thinking. She looked over her shoulder at the guardsmen who surrounded them at a discreet distance, then shook her head at him.

"I'm fine," she said quickly. "I wouldn't want to ruin your reputation."

"I fear it would be the opposite," he said seriously, "so I will forebear." He took off his cloak and started to put it around her, but she balked.

"You'll freeze."

"We won't stay long."

He covered her cloak with his own, then fastened it at her throat. He hesitated, then put his hands on her shoulders.

"How are you?" he asked seriously.

"I'm fine," she said, nodding as if she strove to convince herself of it. "And since we have all this frigid privacy, you could see your way clear to telling me a few of the details about yourself that you couldn't seem to lay your fingers on eight hundred years from now."

He studied her in silence for a moment or two, then decided perhaps standing out in the middle of a winter wonderland was not the place to delve into thoughts and feeling she might not want to share. He couldn't imagine she wanted to discuss his past—either in the present or the Future—but perhaps it was the easiest thing for her to talk about. He looked for someplace to sit, but there was nothing that wasn't covered in four inches of snow. He looked at her.

"We'd best make this quick."

"You're the one talking."

He had to take a deep breath. "I think I might have to sit down in truth."

"You can't. It's snowing again."

To his surprise, he found that was indeed the case. "Very well. Ten minutes, then we go back."

"That will give you just about enough time to tell me how you went from 1233 to the Future without losing your marbles. I'll save the rest of my questions for when we're in front of a hot fire."

He suppressed the urge to shift uncomfortably. "I've never told anyone the particulars."

She closed her eyes briefly, then looked at him. "And you don't have to tell me," she said quietly. "Not really. I know it's a private thing—"

"No, I want to," he interrupted quickly. "Just don't bloody my nose if I hesitate."

She looked at him for several moments in silence, then sighed deeply. She closed the distance between them and put her arms around him. "I won't," she said, very quietly.

He wrapped his arms around her without hesitation. He wasn't sure if she was trembling from the cold or something else, and he didn't dare ask. Perhaps they could blame it all on the cold, for he was shivering as much as she was.

"How do you want this sordid tale?" he asked, trying to remove himself as far as possible from the emotions of it. "English or in the appropriate local vernacular?"

"English, since you have a choice. Just make it short. It's colder than I thought it would be." She took his cloak and wrapped it around as much of him as she could. "What were you doing that you shouldn't have been where you weren't supposed to be?"

He took a deep breath. "I was in Nick's solar, nosing about in his private trunk. There were rumors, you see, of things pertaining to Jennifer's dowry that Montgomery and I had speculated on, though I'll point out he didn't have the stomach to investigate with me. Likely afeared he would find a faery inside," he finished in disgust.

"Your brother has grown up," she said with a smile. "In case you were curious about that."

"Has he?" John mused. "I'm afraid he's fixed in my mind as a dreamy, tenderhearted lad of ten-and-nine."

"Stephen might have a different opinion—at least about his sword skill—but we'll leave that for later. So, you ventured where your brother feared to tread, then what?"

"I saw a map, with all manner of red Xs littering it."

"Time gates?" she asked faintly.

"I suspected the like. It was a poorly kept secret within my family that my sister Amanda's husband was from the Future and I suspected the same thing of Jennifer." He had to take another bracing breath of arctic air. "That isn't entirely true. I saw her simply appear out of thin air, so I knew, once I saw those Xs, just exactly what they meant. I had to investigate."

"Your poor parents."

"I daresay." He sighed. "I certainly wasn't about to tell my father that I intended to try one of those gates to see where it took me, so I simply informed him that since I had my spurs clanking so prettily at my heels, I was ready to venture off into the world and make my fortune and would he see his way clear to giving me a bit of my inheritance so I could."

She pulled back and looked up at him. "What did he say?"

"He told me to go soak my head until good sense returned."

"Did he know what you were planning, then?"

He smiled wearily. "I can't say for certain. All I know is that the conversation deteriorated rather quickly from there. I think my reply to him included the words *stingy* and *whoreson*."

"Oh, John," she said with a pained smile. "I imagine it wasn't a very pleasant afternoon."

"Oh, it didn't last all afternoon," he said easily. "He threw a bag of gold at me—a very heavy one, as it happened—then threw me out of his hall. Bodily."

She studied him for a moment or two in silence. "There's more to it than that."

"Aye, but it isn't interesting, having to do with, as it did, other men's lands and inheritances and things that were none of my business. I'll tell you all one afternoon when we've absolutely nothing else to discuss. Suffice it to say that I had no idea my father knew so many vile words or that he could use them as so many parts of speech."

"He must love you very much," she murmured.

"We are, I fear, very much alike," John admitted. "Bossy, unpleasant, short-tempered—"

"Chivalrous," she corrected, "loyal, protective."

He tightened his arms around her briefly. "All these medieval luxuries have clouded your vision, but I won't argue with you. My father is all those things, as well as absolutely relentless in the safeguarding of his children which is why, I suppose, his reaction surprised me so greatly. I assumed he would gently attempt to dissuade me from trotting off to be a part of some ill-fated Crusade or join myself to Henry's court, but . . ." He took a deep breath. "I didn't expect him to throw me out of his hall. I fair broke my neck rolling down the front steps."

"Maybe he thought it would bring you to your senses."

He sighed. "Looking back on it now, I would say you have it aright. He no doubt though a night or two sleeping in a ditch—without a horse or gear, mind you, which he refused to allow me to take—would bring me to heel. I was too furious to think clearly, which will no doubt come as a surprise to you knowing how tractable and reasonable I always am."

She only smiled and said nothing.

"I borrowed pen and parchment from the village alderman," he continued, "scribbled a note, then looked for someone to carry it to Nick. I knew he would understand where no one else would. I gave it to Everard of Chevington, but apparently he wasn't to be trusted."

She shivered. "Chevington is a creepy place."

"Isn't it? I wouldn't want to spend a night under that roof—what's left of it."

"What then? What did you do when you found yourself in the Future?"

"Found a job mucking out stables until I had enough money set aside—current pounds, of course, not the gold I'd brought with me—to stop mucking out stables. I bought a guitar and a bass, learned to play both, then bummed around playing bass in garage bands for a bit until I thought I'd had enough of the Future. I packed up my gear and started back toward Artane, fully intending to step on that very large X and make peace with my father."

She was very still. "And?"

"It didn't work," he said lightly, though at the time he'd felt anything but casual about it. "The gate was, well, turbulent is the only way I can describe it. I think if I'd stepped into it, I wouldn't have found myself in the right time. I tried another spot I'd memorized, was summarily gang-pressed into Victoria's British Navy and only escaped because they marched me through my backyard, as it were, and I knew where to hide."

She looked at him in shock. "You've got to be kidding."

He shook his head slowly. "I'm not. I suppose 'twas naught but luck I was able to escape to the Future with both my swords. After cursing myself for being too stupid to plan for more than just a main gate and a backup, I walked back to Edinburgh to settle for what had become my life." He paused. "I am, as you might imagine, not particularly keen on traveling through time. Apparently James MacLeod is, but he can keep the exhilaration."

She took a deep breath and pulled away. "I think I need to walk. It's too cold to stand still."

He nodded, then took her hand. He kept pace with her, but couldn't help but note her silence. Perhaps she was regretting having come with him—not that she'd had any choice in that—or regretting having met him in the first place.

But if she hadn't and she'd been thrust back in time on her own . . .

"And so there I was," he continued, because he couldn't stomach where his thoughts had been leading him, "leading a very quiet life in the village when into my shop came a dark-haired angel who seemingly couldn't judge the distance between her car and a brick wall."

"It was my oak, which you know," she said archly. "And I was knocking off mirrors on purpose, to give you business, which you also know."

"I've never been more grateful for a bout of altruism, believe me," he said with a smile.

She nodded, smiling in return, but there was something about that smile that didn't quite ring true.

Odd.

He pressed on. "All of that leads us to our current place, where you can continue to imagine the unpleasant surprise I had in finding out how much you knew about the Middle Ages. And whilst you're imagining that, I'll describe for you if you like in great detail the torment I was in, knowing that growing too close to you would force me to reveal things I'd spent eight years hiding."

She shrugged. "It wasn't as if you did anything particularly medieval, like play the lute or sing in Norman French, or know where all the important doors were in my castle."

"And if I hadn't been my brother's twin, would you have known?"

"I probably would have thought you just eccentric," she conceded, "though you might have given yourself away that first time you came face-to-face with Stephen."

"I suppose I must credit him with some discretion," John grumbled. "At least he didn't blurt out some sort of exclamation of surprise right there in a university courtyard."

"He's nothing if not discreet."

"I suppose so," John said, then he froze. One of Wyckham's guardsmen was signaling to him, as discreetly as Stephen de Piaget could have likely wished. John forced himself to breathe normally as he had a look around himself. He saw nothing, but they were perhaps closer to the forest than he would have wanted to be at another time. He nodded slightly, then smiled at Tess. "I can no longer feel my toes, so why don't we repair to a hot fire?"

"Wimp."

He laughed a little, then put his arm around her shoulders and walked with her to her horse. He boosted her up into the saddle, then put his hand on her foot. "We'll have another riding lesson tomorrow, if you like. You could consider it hands-on training."

"I'm not sure I can ever give another lecture again after this."

"It isn't as if you can use any personal anecdotes, is it?" he asked dryly. He paused and looked up at her. "Has it been so terrible so far? Well, save our journey here, which was hellish."

"No," she said seriously. "Your brother and his wife are wonderful hosts."

"And he's filthy rich, which helps," John agreed. "For the average peasant, the current time period isn't as lovely, though my father and brothers have gone out of their way to be good masters."

"I think I'm happy to be a peasant in my time."

"Which you aren't any longer, Lady Sedgwick," he said pointedly. "We'll discuss just what that means for your future when we have the time."

She nodded, but didn't look at him.

He put her reins in her hand, then walked over to his horse and swung up into the saddle. He realized then just how much he'd missed riding, though he'd indulged whenever the opportunity presented itself. Even so, it hadn't been often enough. Perhaps Tess wouldn't be opposed to stocking her stables with a bit of good horseflesh. He could teach her how to ride, then teach their children—

He put the mental brakes on that before the thought went any further. If he didn't find out what was amiss with her before long, he wouldn't be managing to get himself inside her stables, much less purchase beasts for their children.

He rode with her through Wyckham's gates, then jumped a little in spite of himself at the sound of the portcullis slamming home behind their guardsmen. He grimaced and supposed he would deserve every word of the lecture he was certain his brother would soon be giving him. He should have been watching their surroundings.

He'd been too long out of the appropriate century.

He dismounted, helped Tess from her horse, then handed the reins off to a stable boy without thinking. He froze when he realized Tess was watching him in a particularly serious way. Had she noted something amiss where he had not?

"What is it, love?" he asked.

"I was just watching you be the lord of the manor's brother and thinking that you'd done it a time or two before. Nothing more than that."

"If being that brother gets us a decent glass of wine and a hot fire, then it serves us well, doesn't it?"

She nodded, then walked with him silently to the hall door. She stopped him before he opened it. "I'm sorry," she said, very quietly. "About your father."

He latched on to that topic with alacrity. Perhaps that was all that bothered her. If so, he would talk about it until she was satisfied.

He shrugged. "It was many years ago, though I will admit I'm not sorry for the chance to set things right." He started to say he hoped the price wouldn't be too high, but he forbore. "You will enjoy talking to him, I think. He doesn't care for politics, particularly, but he's a master at the game. He's played it with both John and Henry, which you might find interesting."

She looked a little winded. "I can hardly wrap what's left of my mind around the thought of it."

He smiled and offered her his arm. "Perhaps you will have made a list of questions by the time we see him."

She looked a little green at the thought, but since he felt the same way, he couldn't fault her for it.

He could, however, frown a little over the fact that she wouldn't hold his hand. He made no especial note of it openly, but he noticed. There were thoughts she was entertaining that he suspected he might want to be privy to sooner rather than later.

The afternoon had passed more swiftly than he would have thought possible and with no chance to speak with Tess privately. He wished, rather more fervently than he likely should have, that he could have taken her by the hand, put her into the passenger seat of his car, and gone for a very long drive until he'd determined what sorts of thoughts were vexing her.

By the time evening shadows had fallen, he was limiting himself to conversation in his brother's solar, though he couldn't begrudge himself the pleasure of that. There was something very lovely about sitting with his family and carrying on as if no time had passed.

In truth, it was a joy—if he could unbend far enough to call it such a maudlin thing—to pass an evening with his brother and sister-in-law, enjoying their wee ones until the lads were put to bed, then speaking of simple things that required no especial effort. He had given Nick the most basic of details regarding his life the night before and had intended to save the rest for when his siblings arrived. At the moment, he was asked to do nothing more taxing than take a lute and sing things that didn't require him to look over his shoulder to see who might be listening.

Jennifer sighed at one point. "You play so well."

John shot her a look. "You, my lady Wyckham, are not without your own unholy set of skills, but I accept the compliment just the same."

"You should," Nicholas said with a snort, "considering that you can thank Grandmère for luring Queen Eleanor's best lutenist to Artane to give you lessons."

Tess made choking noises. "I knew it," she managed.

Nicholas laughed. "John, my lad, you picked a formidable woman to woo. I don't think you'll be keeping many secrets from her."

"I certainly haven't managed to yet," John said. He shot Tess a quick smile, then looked at Jennifer. "I would ask you to play for us, but perhaps not after you've spent the day chasing little ones."

"In the morning," Jennifer said, then she shifted uncomfortably. "And with that, I think I'm for bed. It was a pleasure, John. Sleep well, Tess."

He rose as Nicholas escorted his wife out of the solar, then put Nicholas's lute away. He paused and looked at Tess sitting there in front of the fire, staring into it gravely. There was no time like the present, as the saying went, to determine what was amiss. Though he supposed weariness might be troubling her, or trying to acclimate to a different time, that didn't explain why she was holding him at arm's length.

He pulled up a stool at her feet, sat down, and looked up at her. "Spill it," he said distinctly, in English.

She looked at him in surprise. "What?"

"You're chewing on something that's bothering you," he said bluntly, "and I want to know what it is."

"You're bossy," she said with a weary smile.

"You haven't begun to see bossy, woman, so out with it."

She shook her head. "It's nothing. A long trip here and some culture shock. I'm busily rewriting my dissertation in my head, that's all."

He rested his elbows on his knees, then held out his hands. He simply watched her until she put her hands into his. If he hadn't known better, he would have thought she was on the verge of a bout of tears.

"Is it your sister?" he asked carefully.

"Peaches?"

"Nay, but I imagine she will know where you've gone. I was speaking of Pippa."

"No," she managed. "I'm not worried about her."

"Then what?"

She looked at him, her lovely green eyes very red. "I'm just happy for you," she said very quietly. "That you have your family back."

He was, too, but it was nothing to weep over. Well, he supposed he already had and he suspected he would do it again in the future, but for the moment he was well. And it shouldn't have affected Tess save that she had a tender heart. Perhaps she was watching Jennifer and seeing her sister Pippa in that role. It couldn't be that she thought she would have to do the same thing.

The thought was so startling, he would have flinched if

he hadn't been so accustomed to masking his emotions. She couldn't believe that he would want to stay in the past.

Could she?

He had to admit that he'd entertained the thought—for exactly three seconds before his good sense had returned. He loved his family, true, and he was enormously glad to see them, but . . . well, how did he go about telling them that it had been a lovely visit, but he would rather go back to living in the Future?

Of course, it wasn't just the Future that drew him. If he'd had no reason to return save his material possessions, then aye, he might have considered other things. But Tess's life was there, not in the past. He couldn't ask her to give that up. And for what? The ugly truth was, his inheritance was tied up in Switzerland. Was he to keep Tess in the past and beg a piece of land from his father to work until his back was broken and Tess's fingers were worn to nubs?

He rose, pushed the stool back, then pulled Tess to her feet. He looked down at her.

"Would you," he asked very quietly, "permit me a chaste, though very lengthy, embrace?"

She hesitated, then nodded and allowed him to gather her in his arms.

But not before he saw a single tear fall to the floor.

By the saints, she *was* thinking exactly what he'd never thought she would. He rested his cheek against her hair and cast about for a decent way to tell her that there was no way in hell they were staying in 1241, not if he had any means at his disposal to get them home. He thought about several ways to phrase it, but nothing seemed to convey what he wanted. He finally sighed and blurted out the next thing that came to mind.

"I love you," he said, then he froze.

She did as well, then she pulled back far enough to look up at him. "What?"

He chewed on a backtrack, or a diversionary bit of blather, but couldn't quite muster up enough energy to give either a go. He took a deep breath.

"What I said," he managed. "Which I meant."

She closed her eyes. Tears rolled down her cheeks, which grieved him more than he would ever admit. He groped for a shield—he was a bespurred knight, after all—but found nothing there to protect his heart. All he could do was stand there and shake like a fool as she put her arms around his neck, leaned up on her toes, and held on to him tightly.

"I love you, too," she said, her voice as full of tears as her eyes had been.

"You don't sound too happy about it," he said gruffly.

"You don't, either," she said with a miserable laugh. "In fact, I think you're about ready to bolt."

He took a deep breath and let it out slowly as she sank back down to her heels.

"You know what I can be," he managed.

"It's part of your charm."

He attempted a smile, but failed miserably. "Actually, I'm afraid you're the one who's about to bolt."

She shook her head. "You have the keys, my lord."

He nodded, then took her face in his hands and brushed away her tears. "I think there's something else amiss, but I'm not sure you want to discuss it any more than I think I can bear to hear it."

"Probably not."

He bent his head and kissed her cheeks, one by one, then lifted his head slightly and looked at her. "Do you think you might set that aside for the next few minutes and concentrate on something else?"

"Something, or someone?" she asked.

"Let's determine that later—"

"Or now, which might be a much more appropriate use of your time than wearing down the resistance of an unwooed maid," a voice said distinctly from the doorway.

John lifted his head and glared at his brother. "I'm sorry," he said curtly, "I didn't realize you'd been invited to this conversation."

"It didn't look like conversation was what you had in mind," Nicholas said pointedly, "which is why my arrival could be considered so timely and fortuitous. Now, why don't you release your sweet lady, and I'll escort her to her bedchamber."

John considered objecting, but he caught sight of Tess's face. He had the feeling she was up for a right proper meltdown. He bent his head to whisper in her ear.

"Do you want to fall apart with me or without me?"

She patted his back. "I'm not sure you would want to watch."

He pulled back and looked at her seriously. "This once, Tess," he said quietly. "The next time, I'll be there to hold you."

She smiled gravely, then nodded as she pulled away from him. She dragged her sleeve across her eyes, then produced a smile. John supposed there was no sense in pushing her. It *had* been a long journey, and the change of venue was a bit abrupt. If she needed time to get her feet under her, he had no business interfering.

He took her hand, then looked at his brother. "In a different day, I would have kissed her just now."

"The saints be praised I'm here to help you determine when during the course of your wooing that would be appropriate. And I'm telling you that that moment is not now."

"I don't suppose you would tell me when that moment might be," John said carefully, "that I don't miss it."

Nicholas stroked his chin in a manner that was so reminiscent of Robin, John almost choked.

"I believe," Nicholas began slowly, as if he truly considered the matter, "that there must be dancing first. Perhaps a chaperoned walk or two. Flatteries and pleas directed toward her guardian at the moment, so that you might earn his favor."

John pursed his lips. "Don't tell me. That would be you."

Nicholas held out his arm. "Lady Tess—"

"Forget it," John said briskly. "*I* will escort her to her chamber. You may come along if you wish it." He didn't protest when Nick fell in on the other side of her. He supposed he'd spent enough time with his elder brother over the years to know when something was bothering him—and it wasn't just the thought of John pulling Tess into a darkened corner and kissing her senseless.

He walked Tess up the stairs, then embraced her chastely in front of her bedchamber door. He imagined, judging by Nicholas's enthusiastic clearing of his throat, that he'd stayed at the task a bit too long.

He kissed Tess with equal chasteness on the cheek, then released her reluctantly. She thanked Nicholas for the escort, smiled wearily, then closed and bolted the door.

John turned to his brother and scowled. "Do you care to tell me now what all that was about?"

"Just a bit of sport at your expense," Nicholas said with

an easy smile, "but also a chance to speak with what privacy is possible. Did you discuss with Sir William your outing this afternoon?"

"I didn't have a chance," John said, frowning.

"You should have," Nicholas said frankly. "He said there was someone in the woods."

John rubbed his hands over his face. "I feared as much."

"Is that why you ran all the way from Chevington?"

John looked at him seriously. "That, and I couldn't keep Tess out in the wild with just my sword between her and death. Would you have walked with Jenner?"

Nicholas shook his head. "You know I wouldn't have." He considered John for a moment or two. "You haven't told me all."

"I couldn't stomach telling you all," John said with a deep sigh, "but I will tomorrow. After I spend a pleasant night on my lady's floor, keeping her safe."

"Don't be daft," Nicholas snorted.

John shot his brother a look. "I'm sorry, did I ask your opinion?"

"*I'm* sorry, but aren't you old enough to know better?"

"I want her protected."

"Then wed her."

"I'm working on that," John said through gritted teeth. "And until that time, I'll do what I must—which includes sleeping on her floor this night."

Nicholas leaned back against the wall casually. "Let us consider my defenses, shall we? First we have the outer walls, manned by very canny lads with very sharp swords. Should some fool attempt the unthinkable—in the bitter cold, no less—and scale those walls, he would meet his end on one of those very sharp swords. Should he overcome those lads and drop down into the courtyard, he would meet not only braying hounds, but more lads with steel."

John sighed, but that didn't stop the deluge.

"The hall is secured and the great hall guarded by yet more men. Should some canny lad—which I can guarantee you couldn't possibly be a lad sired by Richard of Chevington—manage to get inside the hall, he wouldn't live to see your lady's bedchamber door."

"I'm not sure I feel any better," John said grimly.

"Then realize that my hall will soon be so overflowing with family and rambunctious children that you'll likely end up on a pallet on the floor in my chamber. If Tess doesn't mind sleeping with a blade in her hand, you might perhaps lay your head across the chamber from hers."

John closed his eyes briefly, then nodded. "You're right."

"We'll talk tomorrow about Chevington's get," Nicholas said seriously. "Montgomery had trouble with Everard."

John pursed his lips. "I'm unsurprised."

Nicholas clapped him on the shoulder, then turned him and pushed him down the passageway. "Her door is bolted, and there is Sir Ranulf come to keep watch. She'll be perfectly safe."

John stopped and looked at his brother. "She doesn't know the dangers."

"And that, brother, is something I understand perfectly," Nicholas said, "having considered the same thing with my bride."

John smiled faintly. "I suppose that's true."

Nicholas slapped him affectionately on the back of the head. "It is, dolt. Trust me."

John nodded, waited until Sir Ranulf was fully installed in front of Tess's chamber, then sought his own bed.

He would, however, be up before too many watches had passed. Everard of Chevington might have been a fool, but John was convinced he knew about gates through time, which made him a dangerous one.

He shucked off his boots and went to bed fully dressed, lest something happen and he be needed in a hurry. If Tess called for him, he certainly didn't want Nicholas trotting down the passageway in answer.

I love you.

He closed his eyes. The saints preserve him, but he did.

And if he ever talked her into loving him in return, he would make sure she didn't pay a steep price for it.

Chapter 23

Tess followed her guardsman—who appeared to be one of several—along the passageway and down the stairs to the great hall. She couldn't imagine why she even had guardsmen to begin with, but John was, as she could readily attest, a bit on the paranoid side. She would have thought that being inside his brother's hall would have made him relax a bit, but perhaps he knew things she didn't. The collection of men who were either standing at attention in various strategic spots in the great hall or pacing unobtrusively along the walls or up in the gallery didn't seem to be overly concerned, but perhaps they were used to humoring paranoid brothers of their lord.

She shook her head. She couldn't imagine being a medieval knight, either as part of a permanent or rotating garrison, and having one's life be taken up with protecting the keep's inhabitants during good times and whoever else could cram themselves inside the walls when times weren't so good. She supposed at least the weapons then were less devastating than during her time, though perhaps no less deadly in their own way.

Her trip with John north was certainly proof of that.

"My lady Jennifer is resting above and instructed me to offer you the run of the keep until she descends," Sir Ranulf said with a slight bow. "Shall you go to the kitchens?"

Tess shook her head. She wasn't much of a breakfast person anyway and while Nicholas's cook was indeed better than she'd dared hope, she didn't think she would be indulging in anything before lunch. Her stomach was in knots after spending the night torn between remembering that John had told her he loved her and reminding herself that she couldn't be the one to tear him away from his family.

And she'd been worried a medieval thug would be what would do her in. She'd never expected the danger to her heart would come from an entirely different place.

"I wouldn't mind just wandering, if possible," she managed, when she realized Sir Ranulf was still waiting for her answer.

He nodded. "Of course, my lady. Lord John is, I believe, with Lord Nicholas in the courtyard."

That sounded like an excuse to go outside and freeze. "I think I'll go fetch my cloak—"

"No need, of course," Sir Ranulf said. He beckoned for a page, then sent him scampering up the stairs.

Tess spared a moment of regret for the fact that she likely wasn't going to manage to hire any eight-year-old boys to run her errands for her at home, then accepted her cloak and walked across the hall, preceded by Sir Ranulf and followed by a cluster of guardsmen she didn't recognize. She couldn't imagine Nicholas was worried about her making off with any of his medieval relics, so she had no choice but to believe the men were there for her protection.

Weird didn't quite cover it.

But since she wasn't sure her medieval French would hold up to the scrutiny of a long conversation about the reasons for that, she decided to just go with things and see where they led. It was yet another in a very long line of academic distractions she indulged in purposely to keep herself from thinking about things she couldn't fix and didn't want to face.

She realized immediately upon exiting the keep proper that she wasn't nearly as flexible as she would have liked to have thought herself. The sight of a fully functional medieval courtyard was, to put it bluntly, shocking. Peasants were going about tasks that seemed to include caring for livestock, mailed men were either training or patrolling, and the sound of the black-smith's hammer was like a clarion call that screamed *not of your century, girlie*.

Or something to that effect.

Tess took a deep breath of bitterly cold air, coughed vigor-ously for her trouble, then held Sir Ranulf off when he peered at her to apparently make sure she wasn't going to swoon. She walked down the steps and decided that since there seemed to be a group of men standing just beyond the barbican gate and since two of the taller of those men were fair-haired and dark, there was obviously something interesting going on that might be of some educational value to her. It was a decent-looking distrac-tion, if nothing else.

She walked over to that little cluster of men, making furious mental notes right up until the moment she got a glimpse of what was lying there in their midst.

A lifeless hound.

Sir Ranulf stepped immediately in front of her. She was ac-customed to that sort of thing, so she didn't protest. Of course, she didn't let it stop her from trying to move to his left. She had a bit of a tussle with her other guardsmen bringing up the rear, but she finally managed to at least peek between shoulders and look at what was going on. There was something far too posed about what she was seeing there in front of her.

As if someone were sending a message.

John and Nicholas were standing together, almost mirrors of each other except for their coloring and age. They apparently realized she was standing there at almost the same time because John moved just before Nicholas's elbow caught up with his ribs. He stepped over the hound, walked through the sea of men who parted for him, and put his hands on her shoulders. He turned her around without comment and walked her forward, back through the gates.

She went, because he'd obviously trained her very well.

"What," she asked when he finally gave up herding and reached for her hand to tuck under his arm, "was that?"

"A not very amusing prank," he said with a shrug, "which we'll leave the mystery of to someone else. Now, what would you care for first: a walk on the roof or breakfast?"

"Are you distracting me?"

"I don't know," he said, frowning thoughtfully. "Is it working?"

"John," she began with a long-suffering sigh.

"A walk on the roof," he said, "after we have a moment or two by the fire. Having a bird's-eye view of the castle will be very informative, I'm sure."

She supposed that was better than either revisiting what they'd discussed the night before or wondering why someone would leave a lifeless hunting dog at Nicholas's front gate.

She went along and decided to save her questions for a more opportune moment. She agreed to wait by the fire—under guard, of course—while John went off to find bread and cheese and something to drink. She even humored him by eating more than she was comfortable with, which she was sure would lead to a mid-morning nap. She wasn't entirely sure that hadn't been his plan, catching sight as she did of the look on his face.

He was worried.

And he was subjecting her to an unusual amount of frowning scrutiny, as if he thought she might be thinking thoughts he wouldn't care for.

She put on her most untroubled smile, to throw him off the scent. Besides, what else could she do? If he wanted to stay, she couldn't order him to take her home. She might be able to get there on her own if she could get a peek at the infamous map in Nicholas's trunk.

It occurred suddenly that if his brother Robin was coming south from Artane, his brother would also be going home again. There was no reason she couldn't hitch a ride with him and use that big X near that castle to get herself back to her proper place in time. The current Earl of Artane would let her crash for a couple of days until she'd stopped bawling her eyes out over what she'd left behind in 1241, then she would get herself on a train and go home—

John rose to his feet suddenly and pulled her up to hers. "You think too much about things I don't think I like. Let's go walk."

She was wrapped in the exceptionally luxurious cloak loaned to her by the lady of Wyckham, then left to wait while John did whatever medieval lords' sons did when they were on edge about something. He had a couple of conversations with a pair of guardsmen while trying to look very casual about them, then looked around the hall with the same sort of carelessness. His eyes, however, were missing no detail. If someone had made a false move, she had no doubts that John would have reacted instantly in a way that would have rendered his foe quite unable to do anything else.

Tess shivered in spite of herself. Even with all the things she knew about medieval times, actually being *in* medieval times and enjoying its particular mores was almost too strange even for her strong stomach. All the things she had learned in a purely academic way had now become reality. Henry III was sitting on the throne of England, men were going to war, nobles were bickering, buildings were being built with heavy taxes.

She was surrounded by men carrying swords they obviously knew how to use.

John stopped his frowning and turned to look at her. All right, it was one thing to see the guy traipsing around in fake period clothing; it was another thing to see him in native garb. There were knives stuck down the sides of his boots, a sword belted around his hips, and hose instead of trousers. He looked as if he'd never spent a day away from the current year, never driven a car, never shopped at the local Tesco for crisps and fizzy drinks.

He looked at home, truth be told.

He walked over to her, stopped, then clasped his hands behind his back. "Lady Tess," he said with a very small smile.

She closed her eyes briefly, because it almost hurt her to look at him. "Lord John."

"Turnabout, is that it?"

"You seem to have latched back on to your title easily enough," she managed.

He leaned in close. "Are you kidding? It's absolutely barking, but I thought I would frighten my family if they saw me in a state. I was hoping you'd let me fall apart in your arms somewhere quiet tonight."

Heaven help her, that was the last thing she wanted him to do. She took a deep breath, then nodded, because it was easier than telling him that she was sure now that he would be better off in the past, and she intended to hitch a ride with his brother as soon as possible.

A throat cleared itself pointedly from behind him. Tess

jumped a little when she realized Nicholas was standing there, his ears perked up. She sighed in relief. The cavalry had arrived.

John turned and looked at his brother. "If I could, I'd kill you and not regret it."

Nicholas put his hand to his heart. "I'm wounded, John. Here I am, simply trying to save you from your sorry self and these are my thanks?" He looked at Tess. "Shall I thrash good manners back into him, Lady Tess? He's been out of my reach for too long, I fear."

Tess smiled at John's brother, then listened as he and John discussed the points where John might be lacking in quite a few things. John finally told his brother to shut up, promised his willing self to be grilled about a variety of subjects later in Nicholas's solar, then pulled her across the great hall with him toward the stairs. He paused at the entrance to the stairwell and looked at her.

"I'm glad you're here with me," he said very quietly.

She swallowed, hard. "I don't think you really need me."

"And that, my dearest Tess, is where you are absolutely wrong."

He might have a different opinion after she'd left him happily back in time with his family, but she wasn't going to argue the point at present.

"Let's go up on the roof," he suggested, then took her hand and pulled her along after him before she could protest.

She walked with him up stairs and down passageways until they exited a guard tower. She was absolutely not a fan of heights, but she had to admit the view was spectacular. John didn't seem to be bothered by their vantage point, but then again, he'd grown up with it. He looked thoughtfully over the landscape for several minutes, then glanced at her. He smiled, then his smile faded as he apparently realized she wasn't doing the same.

"I thought you'd be enjoying the view," he said.

I was—of you was almost out of her mouth before she could stop it, but she bit back the words. The truth was, looking at him in his native land, as it were, was killing her. If he went back to the future, he would trade family for . . . what?

Her?

He cleared his throat. "You know, my brother will thrash me if I pull you into my arms and distract you properly here where all can see."

She attempted a smile, but didn't think she'd managed it very well. "Just thinking."

"About what?"

"About what I saw there this morning," she lied. Among other things she wasn't about to divulge.

He tilted his head over his shoulder toward the east. "What's coming from that direction in a pair of hours is much more interesting, I guarantee it."

She looked behind him. She had to squint to see the company, but see them she could. She looked at him in surprise. "Who is that?"

"Robin, I imagine, with his wife, Anne, and their children." He looked at her steadily. "His second son is named Kendrick."

She took a deep breath and attempted to put aside her thoughts. The truth was, she couldn't do anything about returning home until John's brother arrived, and that was assuming he would be willing to help her. At the moment, her options were to mope, which she never did, or enjoy every moment possible with a man she was crazy about.

She chose the latter, because it was the only choice she could make.

She took a deep breath, then lifted an eyebrow. "So I know something you don't know. How convenient."

He folded his arms over his chest and leaned a hip against the parapet wall. "And if I demanded that you tell me?"

"I would tell you to stuff it."

He laughed, apparently in spite of himself. "You have very little respect for either my ego or my sword, my lady."

"Oh, I have a great respect for both, you bully," she said. "I'm just playing hardball." She frowned. "How would you translate that into your version of French?"

"I'll think about it and tell you after you've told me what I want to know."

"You go first."

He looked over his shoulder. Sir Ranulf was standing ten feet away, looking fierce. Tess didn't bother wondering who might be lurking in the guard tower behind her. She didn't suppose the walls were thin enough for that to make any difference. John sighed and moved to stand next to her. She wasn't about to make too much room for him, which he obviously noticed.

"Afraid of heights?" he asked in surprise.

"Just talk fast," she said, trying not to be too obvious about clutching the rock she was leaning against.

He turned to face her, then put his hand against the wall, keeping his arm between her and a fifty-foot tumble unto the courtyard floor. He smiled down at her. "Better?"

"Better," she said, her mouth dry. "And just for the record, the only reason I'm still up here is because I'm trying to go native."

He smiled. "And doing a smashing job. Now, whilst I have you at my mercy here, give me the details that I want."

"No."

He looked at her calculatingly. "Very well, we'll trade tidbits. You go first."

"The Kendrick I know in the future is your nephew."

He pursed his lips. "Very well, Nick and I think the hound was put there apurpose. 'Tis one of his, but the master of the hounds swears it had run off a fortnight ago."

"Meaning whoever killed it hadn't crawled over the walls?"

"Aye, my lady tactician, it means exactly that. Your turn."

"Kendrick has six children, including a set of triplets. I understand the boys are all just like him."

"His poor wife," John said, wide-eyed.

"I gave you two details," she pointed out. "This better be a good one."

He looked at her, suddenly serious. "I don't want to tell you any more."

"But you will," she said, feeling his seriousness become hers.

He kept his left hand where it was but fussed with her cloak for a moment or two with his right. "I will, but only because I fear these are details you should have in order to appreciate the seriousness of what troubles me." He paused, then sighed deeply. "A day or two before the medieval faire—I can't remember now how long before—I went home to find my sword missing. The sword I'm wearing now." He met her eyes. "My father gave it to me at my knighting."

"But you don't know who took it," she guessed. "Or why."

He shook his head. "Not yet."

"What else was missing?" she asked, afraid she already knew the answer.

"Nothing," he said, "just the sword. Unfortunately, that wasn't the end of it. After the medieval faire, I went home to find my Claymore propped up against a table that was all set up for tea."

A shiver ran through her. "That is terrifying."

"It was," he agreed grimly. "At first I thought I was the one being stalked, but after that reenactment party at Sedgwick—and aye, I know I'm convoluting the dates—I found one of your tower doors propped open. I might have thought nothing of it, but after we returned from Payneswick, there was a note in the boot of the Range Rover, something I certainly hadn't seen when we left, which meant the writer of it put it inside either as we stopped for breakfast or that terrible lunch neither of us could stomach."

She felt suddenly quite a bit colder than she supposed she should have. "And what did it say?"

"Oh, some rot about who Rhys de Piaget was and what I had to do with the man," John said dismissively.

She studied him. "And?"

He met her eyes. "The author, who wouldn't recognize decent grammar or spelling if it broadsided him, assured me I wasn't the only one he was keeping in his sights, as it were—Tess!"

She realized only because he had her by the shoulders that she had almost swayed right into the courtyard. She held on to his arms because he was suddenly the most solid thing she could find. "Me?" she squeaked. "And you didn't tell me?"

"I didn't want to worry you."

She took several deep, steadying breaths, then returned to clutching the rock behind her. "And I pushed you down my stairs."

"Feisty, aren't you?"

She pursed her lips at him. "You were getting in the way of potential academic triumph, but if it makes you feel any better, I've considered for several days just how thoroughly I would need to apologize for not having listened to you." She looked into his pale gray eyes that were quite a bit more troubled than she'd ever seen them before. "Do you think this person followed us here?"

"I have no idea," he said, but he didn't sound very convinced.

Tess blew her bangs out of her eyes. "Now that, my lord, is a flat-out lie. The very least you can do is tell me what you think and what you're planning."

He shook his head. "My time, not yours."

"But—"

"Nay. You can take notes from afar whilst I work this out, and *that* is nonnegotiable."

"Generous of you," she said sourly.

"I agree," he said pleasantly. "And in the meantime, what I think might be most beneficial at the moment to your next academic work is seeing a bit of medieval wooing. Up close and personal."

She had to take a deep breath, mostly because he was smiling that very small smile she loved so much, damn him anyway. Unfortunately, talking about the future, even in the context of things to fear in it, had reminded her of the relationship she'd been having with him in the present.

The same relationship she was certain she couldn't have with him much longer.

"John," she began slowly.

He caught her hand, then brought it to his lips and kissed it. "Aye?"

"You're going to ruin my reputation."

He apparently took that more seriously than she'd intended. He sighed and let her hand fall, though he kept hold of it. "You're right, of course."

"Well," she said, before she thought better of it, "I didn't mean to throw cold water on you entirely."

He looked at her from serious gray eyes. "What are you doing then, Tess?"

"Nothing much up here where I'm approximately three steps from falling to my death."

He laced his fingers with hers. "I won't let you fall."

He certainly hadn't so far. She looked behind him at the little company she could see in the distance. They would arrive, then she would have a built-in distraction for John. He would see what he had been missing, make his decision to stay, then she would take those riding lessons he'd been good enough to give her and put them to good use getting back to Artane.

She looked at him to find him watching her closely. She attempted a smile.

"I don't suppose it's time for another riding lesson, is it?"

He lifted an eyebrow. "It could be, if you like."

"It's a good skill to have."

"It is," he agreed, "but I'm warning you, Tess, if you are thinking to filch one of Nick's horses and go off to investigate on your own, you'll find yourself in my brother's dungeon approximately half an hour after I catch you."

"Are you going to put me there?"

"Damned right I will."

She laughed a little, uneasily. "You're a bully."

"Nay," he said quietly, "I am the man who loves you, and I'll keep you safe from your modern sensibilities if I have to lock you up to do so whilst we're lingering in this very brutal time. Is that clear enough?"

"Is this you being nice to me?" she asked a little breathlessly. "Or am I misreading you?"

He took her hand, then stepped past her and pulled her into the guard tower. He nodded briskly to the men there, then continued on, towing her along after him as if she'd been a very naughty fifth-grader on her way to the principal's office.

She followed him—well, she was given no choice about it, actually—into what turned out to be Jennifer's solar. He looked at his sister-in-law.

"We're borrowing your alcove for a bit of privacy," he said shortly.

Jennifer waved him on. "Don't mind me. I know how it is."

"At least she'll be able to hear me scream," Tess said with an uneasy laugh.

"You won't have breath for screaming."

Tess looked at Jennifer, who only laughed at her. She supposed there was no hope of help from that corner. She found herself soon standing in a little alcove that sported benches and a lovely window that was unfortunately too small to jump out of. She looked up at John only to find his expression one of concern. She rolled her eyes and sat down on the bench.

"All right. Go ahead with the lecture."

He sat down next to her with a sigh, then took her hand in both his own. "No lecture. And I wouldn't lock you in the dungeon."

"The solar instead?" she asked.

"It has a fireplace and comfortable seats," he said, leaning his head back against the stone behind them. He looked at their hands together for several moments in silence, then slid her a sideways look. "And to show you that I'm not a complete beast, you choose our afternoon's activity. We can stay here all afternoon and snog, or brave the chill and have a riding lesson."

"Snog," she repeated in disbelief. "What presumption."

He leaned over and kissed her on the cheek.

Mostly.

She realized her eyes were closed only when she felt his mouth on hers.

And then, in spite of her rather healthy sense of self-preservation, she just flat out lost track of time. She put her arms around John's neck at some point, because it seemed like the safest way to keep herself from embarrassing herself by falling off the bench. She also realized, at a certain point, that kissing him had been a very bad idea indeed.

She opened her eyes, looked at his mouth, then met his eyes.

"This isn't good," she said weakly.

"Not at all," he agreed hoarsely.

"It was *your* idea."

"It seemed preferable to throwing you in the dungeon to keep you compliant."

She opened her mouth to express her indignation, then realized his eyes were twinkling. She pursed her lips. "You're an awful man."

"But you love me."

"No more than you love me."

He slipped his hand under her hair and smiled sweetly. "Let's discuss that at length at another time. We have other business now."

She wanted to tell him that not only was kissing a very bad idea, it would only make matters worse when they had to say good-bye, but she quickly found that thinking was beyond her, much less trying to get in any decent conversation.

"Awfully quiet back there," Jennifer said at one point.

Tess heard John groan against her mouth, then he lifted his head and looked at her.

"I can't shout at my sister-in-law. I love her too much."

Tess fanned herself. "She probably saved you an encounter with your brother's sword. And while you're being relieved about that, why don't you open that window so I stop looking so flushed?"

He examined her critically. "You don't look flushed; you looked kissed."

"Even worse."

His expression was suddenly serious. "Is it?"

"Don't be daft," she said in her best medieval Norman French, but she shooed him away just the same. "We can't do that anymore."

"Can't we?" he asked, rising to throw open the shutters.

They most certainly couldn't, because it was going to be difficult enough to do what she needed to do. She made John sit on the bench facing her and wished she could do something besides simply drink in the sight of him. Gorgeous, medieval, chivalrous.

And apparently in love with her.

She took a deep breath and looked at him seriously. "I'm not sure I'll survive you," she said honestly.

He returned her look just as seriously. "Give it a go, would you?"

She studied him. "You're trying to distract me from other things, aren't you?"

"Nay," he said quietly "I just want to keep you alive so I can spend the rest of my life making sure you feel properly herded. There might be wooing involved as well. And if that wooing keeps you distracted from other things, so much the better."

She pursed her lips. "I'm not prone to the vapors, you know."

"Well," he said with a smile, "except for the other day when you fainted in my arms."

"I was under great duress."

His smile faded. "I'm afraid, Tess my love, that great duress might last a bit longer than we fear."

She nodded, looked out the window for a bit, then back at him. "What now?"

"Nick and I do a bit of nosing about, you stay safely inside the keep with my sister-in-law, her children, and a dozen very skilled guardsmen, and we see how the wind blows for a bit. And you and I snatch what brief moments together we can." He put his hands on his knees, rose, then reached down and pulled her up and into his arms.

Tess stood in that divine embrace for far longer than was good for either her peace of mind or her heart, but she couldn't bring herself to pull away. She closed her eyes and didn't protest either the occasional murmured endearment or the more frequent, sweetly stolen kiss. By the time the solitude of Jennifer's solar was breached by several young lads wanting their mother, Tess thought her heart might break.

But she couldn't talk to John about what weighed on her the most, which was whether or not he wanted to stay in the past.

She supposed she would find that out soon enough.

Chapter 24

Two days later, John stood in the lists, shaking with weariness and wondering what in the hell he'd been thinking to come anywhere near the Middle Ages.

He was in the lists because it was, as it happened, the only place he had any peace for thinking. That was saying something given that he was sparring with his eldest brother and being critiqued by the next one in line. He would have preferred to be inside, wooing Tess, but the inside of the hall was overrun by not only family—which he was happy to see—and a pair of very eligible medieval misses—which he was less than happy about. He wasn't sure how anyone had gotten wind of his presence at Wyckham, but he supposed Robin wasn't above putting the word out simply to annoy him.

Those gels were not at all what he was looking for even if he had been looking, which he wasn't. He wasn't sure why their mothers even bothered once they'd had a good look at Tess. She was well spoken, gracious, and so beautiful he could hardly look at her. Her French was even astonishingly good, though he supposed he shouldn't have been surprised. The slight accent she was still trying to iron out lent her a slightly exotic flair that he found quite riveting—

"You're not heeding me," Robin said in a singsong voice.

John dragged his attention back to his brother. "I was thinking."

"I won't ask about what," Robin said with an eyebrow raised. "And if you're curious, she's sitting over there with a gaggle of children piled atop her to keep her warm."

John realized that was true. That he wasn't precisely certain when that had happened said much about the quality of Robin's swordplay.

"I don't know why she finds you so interesting," Robin said with a yawn. "Your swordplay is dreadful."

Nick laughed and walked away.

John refrained from comment. He had enough to do to merely keep himself from becoming skewered on his brother's sword. It was, he had to admit, a little strange to be standing in Wyckham's lists, fighting Robin and feeling as if not a day had passed from the last time he'd done the same.

Only, things weren't the same. He knew too much about too many things.

That utter incongruity had only been exacerbated by having so much of his family arrive over the past two days. It was gratifying to know they'd all made the trip to see him in such haste, though finding beds for them all on short notice had been a difficult job in itself. He'd watched Tess help Jennifer, keeping herself as much in the background as possible.

He'd wondered about that.

But he hadn't had any time to find out the particulars because, again, he hadn't had a bloody moment alone with her since Robin and Anne had arrived three days earlier. He'd been besieged by family—which had been a joy—and interviewed by prospective fathers-in-law—which had been an utter waste of his time and left him limited to simply catching views of Tess only on occasion. The more he considered it, the more he suspected it had been Robin to issue those particular invitations. Why, he couldn't have said. Surely Nicholas had sent missives that had included tidings about Tess.

He remembered vividly watching Nicholas fight off their grandmother's efforts to see him wed to very powerful medieval gels with impeccable pedigrees instead of the woman he loved. He wished he'd taken notes to see how Nick had managed to rid himself of those lassies. The only thing in his favor was that at least Joanna wasn't there to orchestrate the whole fiasco.

Robin reached over suddenly and flicked him between the eyes. "Stop thinking so much."

John rubbed his forehead crossly. "I have many things to contemplate."

"Such as?"

"Life is perplexing."

"But love isn't." Robin tilted his head in Tess's direction. "Why haven't you asked her to wed with you?"

"Because when we were loitering in a time far, far away, she didn't know the details about me I thought she might need to," John said. "Well, that isn't exactly true. She knew who I was from the moment she saw me, having seen Montgomery, but I didn't know she knew until we were here. I've hardly had a bloody moment's peace with her since in which to even begin to woo her properly. Now, 'tis utterly impossible. How I'm to do it now with a houseful of twits—whom I'm convinced you brought along to vex me—I don't know."

"Me?" Robin asked, putting his hand over his heart. "You can't think I would want to grieve you. Not when I was so overjoyed to learn you hadn't fallen into a pile of manure and suffocated."

John glared at him. "I told you what happened."

"Which I'm not sure did anything to improve my opinion of your wits."

John put his sword point-down in the very hard ground and looked at his brother seriously. "'Tis done, Robin, and I cannot take it back, which you well know. You did your own share of foolish things in your youth, things I could remind you about, but I won't because *I* know when to keep my mouth shut."

Robin considered him. "Well," he said finally. "I suppose that's true."

John dragged his sleeve across his forehead. "Any other words of wisdom to offer?"

"Woo that lovely gel there."

"When?" John asked shortly. "Before or after I've thrown your pair of irritating wenches out the front gates? I'll never have a moment's peace until they're gone, you know."

"Well, you could teach Tess a bit of swordplay. That would give you some time to talk."

"She would only use that as an excuse to trot off into the gloom and vanquish ruffians."

Robin smiled. "She sounds a bit like Mandy."

"Nay, Tess looks before she leaps," John said. "And her assaults on my good sense are much more insidious."

Robin looked to his right. "I can see why you'd want her," he said frankly. "Not only is she beautiful and clever, she was perfectly willing to examine at length this morning a handful of maggots Kendrick unearthed from some cask somewhere. The children adore her already. Especially Kendrick."

"Your son's a menace," John muttered.

Robin only grinned. "Isn't he, though? I'm profoundly proud of him, if not a bit unnerved by his cleverness."

John wondered, briefly, if the Kendrick who loitered in the Future remembered Tess from having met her currently at Wyckham, or if those memories had been lost to him, or if time truly did fold back on itself thus.

Or maybe he was just completely losing whatever few wits he'd clung to over the years.

"Another hour," Robin said, lifting his sword with the ease and enthusiasm of a man who had spent an unwholesome number of hours doing just that every day of his life. "I'm not quite satisfied with your efforts this morning."

John obliged him, not only because there was something very satisfying about indulging in a little swordplay, but because he wasn't entirely sure that whatever time he spent at present honing his skills might be the difference between breathing and not breathing at some point in the near future.

For both him and Tess.

B_y the time he'd ingested a most excellent supper and planned out a decent way to have Tess to himself for a bit, she had volunteered to escort Jennifer upstairs and remain with her. He supposed he didn't begrudge Jennifer the company, but he was less than thrilled to have to make conversation with eligible maidens and their parents. He alluded several times to the fact that the lady Tess was a very good friend of the family and that he had always been of the opinion that wedding close friends of his family was the best alternative.

His declarations were met with blank stares.

He gave up after an hour of polite conversation and sought the refuge of his brother's solar. Robin and Miles were already there, having escaped the hall long before it was polite. Nicholas came later and announced the torture could begin. John accepted a cup of wine and sat back, steeling himself for the worst. Nicholas was the one watching him with the gravest expression, so he turned there first.

"What?" he asked wearily.

"I wasn't inclined to believe you at first," Nicholas said bluntly, "but I have no choice but to believe you now. You're assuredly being hunted."

"By whom?" Robin asked, with interest. "Someone we can humiliate publicly before we send him off to points unknown?"

"You're overly vindictive," Miles remarked calmly, "which I have always appreciated about you."

Robin smirked at him, then looked at John. "Well? Divulge the names, boy, so we can be about our plans."

"I haven't the proof to accuse anyone," John said slowly, "though I've been stalked by someone in the . . ." He had to take a deep breath before he could manage the rest. "In the Future."

Robin rolled his eyes heavenward. "That this rot is a part of my life is almost more than I can take. Very well, someone in the Future—which I'm not entirely sure isn't a place you've all made up to torment me—doesn't like you. That hardly merits more than a yawn, does it?"

"It does, when that soul relieved me of my knighting sword, then drove it into the ground near a time gate, intending that I should find it and no doubt embark on an unexpected journey. Tess says she was pushed into the same gate, no doubt by the lad who put the sword there."

"That sheds a different light on it," Miles agreed. "Who knew you had a sword?"

"No one," John said, though he wished he'd said as much with more conviction. "I was very careful in the Future when I first arrived, though I suppose some stable lad or other might have made note of my gear. In the years after that?" He shrugged. "No one that I can think of."

"No one who knew about the gates?" Nicholas asked carefully. "In either century?"

"No one," John agreed, "save Everard, but we've already discussed his flaws in detail."

"Everard can't read his own name," Robin said with a snort. "And aye, Nick told us about the missive you left behind. The only thing I'm surprised by is your witlessness in leaving such a thing with anyone from Chevington."

"I wasn't thinking clearly," John said, forcing himself not to grit his teeth.

"Obviously," Robin said. "And since Everard couldn't read, I wonder what he did with the missive? Whom would he have trusted?"

John shrugged. "His father, perhaps? It would have been a way to ingratiate himself with the man."

"Lord Richard isn't any more literate than his son," Nicholas said thoughtfully, "though Roland certainly is."

Miles shook his head. "Everard wouldn't have trusted Roland with such a task unless he had convinced his brother he had something Roland might be willing to trade his inheritance for—"

"Which wasn't his to relinquish," Nicholas finished for him. "Chevington belongs to Richard until he dies, but he only holds it in trust for Segrave's lord or lady. I can assure you that Grandmère has no use for any of those from Chevington." He looked at John and shrugged. "I can't imagine how either Roland or Everard is involved, though I won't discount them entirely. I'm just not sure I understand what this unnamed lad wants."

"He might want Tess," John said grimly.

"Nay," Robin said slowly, "I don't think so. She is enchanting, true, but if your lad had been in the Future and wanted her, he could have had her there. If he'd wanted your appalling number of automobiles, he could have slain you there and taken them. Perhaps he merely vexes you for his own perverse reasons, reasons that would seem foolish to us."

"Which doesn't make this mystery lad any less dangerous," Miles put in, "nor the need to find him quickly any less dire."

"Well," Robin said, rubbing his hands together, "I'm always up for a decent adventure. Let's decide how we'll begin this one."

And with that, they were off. John sat back and listened to his elder brothers discuss how to solve his problems, just as they had done from the time he'd been a child. In time, he'd been invited to join them in solving whatever traumas concerned their sisters. It reminded him so sharply of his youth, he almost caught his breath.

He had missed them.

Miles leaned over. "Maudlin gel," he said with a smile.

John looked at him seriously. "Do you blame me?"

Miles shook his head with a smile, then turned back to the fray.

John listened with half an ear to the spirited discussion of all those who might have wanted him dead, then stopped listening altogether and enjoyed the feeling of companionship he'd taken for granted for so many years. He realized at that moment just how lonely the past eight years had been. He'd always considered himself fairly independent, but being without family had been—

His thoughts ground to a halt.

Was *that* what was bothering Tess?

He leaned forward and waved at Robin when simply attempting to catch his eye didn't give him the results he was looking for.

"What?" Robin asked crossly. "You interrupted me during a very salient point."

"Has Tess talked to you about Artane?"

"Of course," Robin said, looking slightly confused. "Why wouldn't she? 'Tis a magnificent place with a rich and varied political history."

John rolled his eyes. "Did she ask you any details such as how long a journey there might be, or if you'd be willing to take her along with her when you left?"

Robin's mouth fell open. "How did you know?"

"What did you tell her?" John asked in astonishment, ignoring Robin's question.

"That I was sure you would want to show her your boyhood haunts, so you both could absolutely come back with me. I even offered to feed you, which I thought excessively generous under the circumstances."

John set his cup aside and rose. "I'll return later."

"We can carry on without you," Robin assured him.

He didn't doubt it. He caught Nicholas's amused look, shot his brother a glare, then left the solar without delay. He wasn't sure why it hadn't occurred to him before, because it should have. Tess knew exactly how painful it was to lose a sibling. Of course she would want to spare his family a second encounter with that pain. For all he knew, she might be thinking he would *want* to stay. And given what Robin had just told him, he had the feeling Tess hadn't planned on staying in the past with him.

The sooner he straightened that out with her, the happier he would be.

He ran up the circular stairs, banging his sword against the stone more often than he should have—the hazard of living so many years out of his proper time, no doubt—then jogged down the passageway and into his oldest sister, Amanda.

He caught her by the arms, then gaped at her in surprise for a moment. "When did you arrive?"

"Not a quarter hour ago," she said, then she threw her arms around his neck and hugged him tightly. "You great idiot."

He returned the embrace, squeezing her apparently hard enough to leaving her gasping out a laugh, then he pulled back and smiled at her. "I missed you, Mandy."

She dragged her sleeve across her eyes. "You *could* have come home, you know," she said sharply. "You could have found a way."

"I did, and here I am."

She rolled her eyes. "Earlier than this, John. Jake managed it; why couldn't you?"

He shrugged lightly. "Perhaps I was destined to remain where I was."

"And are you staying?" she asked bluntly.

Trust Amanda to cut right to the heart of the matter without mercy. He had to take a deep breath before he trusted himself to answer. "What do you think?"

"I think I don't want to think about it."

"Neither do I," John said with feeling. "Where's my lady?"

She took his arm and pulled him toward the stairs. It wasn't the direction he wanted to go, but she wouldn't release him and she was stronger than she looked. "Your exceptionally lovely lady is locked up more securely than the crown jewels—well, the new ones Henry's acquired given that John lost the last batch in the wash."

"Locked up where?" John asked suspiciously.

"In with the two gels and their dams," Amanda said, then she held up her hand to apparently stave off his protests. "I gave her a dagger. She promised she would use it if necessary."

"Amanda!"

She tugged on him. "She'll be fine. It will make her appreciate all your fine qualities all the more in the morning. I would see if you can't spirit her away sooner rather than later. For now, behave yourself and treat her as a proper medieval miss deserves to be treated."

He stopped in the passageway and looked down at her. "Do you realize I've scarce managed to kiss her yet?"

"That isn't what Jennifer told me," Amanda said, "but perhaps she misinterpreted all the silence in her solar a pair of days ago."

"Well," John amended, "I've been trying to be discreet. Unfortunately, I haven't had the chance to be even that of late, which is why I want to know where she is. I could at least exchange a few polite words with her before those silly twits leave her thinking I'm not interested in her."

"If you've left her any room to wonder that, my dear brother, then your work is obviously undone. You might reconsider your plans for the morrow."

"I think I might need to." He looked at her. "Any advice?"

She hooked her arm with his. "I wouldn't presume. You might consult Nicky."

"He annoys me."

Amanda pulled his head down where she could kiss his cheek, loudly. "I love you, you fool. Let's go see if Jake has anything to offer."

John stopped her before she could walk away. "They won't hurt her, will they?" he asked seriously. "She isn't lacking in courage, but she isn't accustomed . . . Well, you know what I'm getting at."

"They won't dare trouble her," Amanda said. "I told them she's my sister-in-law by marriage and I wouldn't look kindly on any insult. You *know* they won't dare incur my wrath."

John supposed that was true. Amanda's husband, Jake, was

a particular favorite of the king and few dared cross her for that reason alone. Her rather tart method of communication was famous—or infamous, rather—at court, which was another reason to remain in her good graces. He supposed those were reasons enough to leave Tess alone. All he could do was make sure she was well guarded from without and trust that Amanda's words would keep her safe behind the door.

"Jake is anxious to have speech with you," Amanda said, tugging on him. "Something about baseball."

"I don't follow baseball."

"Then you'd best have brought a peace offering."

He laughed a little. "Mandy, I didn't exactly plan this."

She stopped at the top of the stairs. "We've missed you."

He sighed. "I would have come home sooner, if I'd been able to. You know that."

She seemingly chewed on her words for a bit. "I think you'd best spend what time you have with us, then," she said finally. "To have to look back on later."

He wondered, quite honestly, if there would be anything left of his heart by the time his family and his love were finished with it. The thought of leaving his kin was about to do him in, but the thought of being without Tess was worse.

He knew only one thing for sure: when he returned to the Future, he was driving to Scotland and finding James MacLeod.

Then he was going to take a sword to the blighter.

Chapter 25

T**ess** decided that there was one place she could certainly
cross off her list of future vacation destinations and that
was medieval England.

It had been that sort of day. She'd had a little lesson in swordplay that morning from Miles de Piaget to the shock and dismay
of the pair of medieval misses who had apparently come to look
John over, and then a riding lesson from John's eldest brother,
Robin. He was Kendrick the adult, only more intense, if possible. She had struggled to divide her time between trying to
carry on a conversation with Robin about politics and war while
learning useful medieval skills and trying to commit everything
about Robin to memory for relating later to Kendrick.

Though she supposed there was no point in that. Kendrick
was still a child and likely would have his own memories to
draw on.

Supper had been no less of an adventure than it had been over
the past three days. Potential medieval brides preened, parents
attempted to look nonchalant, and Robin smirked. Tess might
have enjoyed the joke as much as he apparently did, but she
couldn't. It was one thing to think that John likely wanted to

stay with his family in the past; it was another thing entirely to think he might marry one of those girls, or someone very much like them.

She'd been actually quite glad to escape to Nicholas's solar, though she couldn't say she felt any more comfortable now that she was there. She was the only soul there who wasn't a part of the family, which she felt in a particularly keen way. She looked around her, noting the Future ex-pats, and began to think that time was less a strange thing than it was a cruel thing. It tore families apart, took loved ones away—

She realized that she was breathing raggedly only because Miles, John's next older brother, handed her a cup of something she didn't bother to identify. She drank it thankfully, then tried to get herself back together. She didn't dare look at John.

She couldn't make his life decisions for him. He would either, like Pippa, choose to go to a time not his own or he wouldn't. For all she knew, he would go back to the future, thank her for a few great dates, then be off on another adventure. He was easily as desirable a catch in her day as he was in the current day.

And those medieval misses were determined, she would give them that. After having spent two nights in the same room with them, even accompanied as she had been by Amanda's knife, she'd been grateful each morning to see the sun coming through the shutters. If it hadn't been for Jennifer having sent for her each morning, she was quite sure she would have been the last to use the washing water, leaving her feeling very grungy indeed. That was something she didn't need help with.

She studied the in-laws who seem to be perfectly happy in the Middle Ages and wondered if she could be that as well. She would have been near Pippa, though she wasn't sure as what. John had no keep of his own and all his money was tied up eight hundred years away. She wasn't a snob by any means, but the thought of scraping by as a medieval peasant was not a pleasant one.

But if it meant having John . . .

She looked up and found him watching her with that very small smile she loved so much on his face, and she thought she might not make it through the evening. How in the world would she get on a horse and ride off, leaving him behind? Worse still, how could she possibly ask him to leave his family behind now that he had them again?

•

He leaned back suddenly, scribbled something on a piece of paper, folded it up, and passed it to his sister sitting on his right. She watched as it was passed, unopened, from sibling to sibling, until it reached her. She looked at John, who was only watching her still with that very small smile.

She took a deep breath and unfolded the note.

I think you left white sauce on the Aga. You'll need help rescuing it before it burns.

She looked at him quickly. He only lifted one eyebrow. She closed her eyes briefly, leaned over and tossed the note into the fire, then looked at him again. Of course, she couldn't see him very well, but that probably had to do with the tears in her eyes.

"Nicky, vacate your chair," Jennifer said, "before John sticks you with something sharp."

"I just want it noted," Nicholas said, rising with a sigh, "that I tried to keep him under control. No one values the services of a decent chaperon these days."

Siblings changed seats without complaint. Tess smiled faintly at Nicholas as she passed him, then blushed at the look John gave her as she sat down next to him. He took her hand, kissed it briefly, then leaned close and put his mouth against her ear.

"Skiing in the Alps," he whispered. "A wee trip to Sicily during August to sample the local cuisine and the strand both. I'll even dig out my passport and brave crossing the Pond to see your Colonial treasures if you like."

"Do you have one?" she asked, looking into his beautiful gray eyes. "A passport, I mean."

"Absolutely," he said. "And I fully intend to use it for many years to come."

"I couldn't ask—"

"You aren't. I'm insisting." He considered. "Have you been thinking otherwise?"

"Yes," she said simply.

He looked at his brother briefly, then leaned forward and kissed her, long enough to leave Nicholas making noises of mock horror. He pulled back and looked at her seriously. "But in return, there is something I want you to do for me."

She suppressed the urge to fan herself. "What?"

"Love me," he said very quietly.

She took a deep breath. No sense in not ripping the plaster off right away. "For how long?"

"For forever."

She looked at his fingers laced with hers. "In a casual sort of arrangement?"

She felt him put his finger under her chin and lift her face up. "I am a knight of the realm," he said seriously, "and we do not indulge in *casual sorts of arrangements*."

"Then what do you indulge in?"

"Formal proposals sanctioned by parents, which means we're going to France to see mine before we go home and then to Seattle later to see yours, if they're still loitering there."

She had no intention of crying. She wasn't a crier. The wet stuff leaking out of her eyes was just, well, excess something.

John rose and pulled her to her feet.

"And just where do you think you're going?" Nicholas asked lazily.

"To find a darkened corner," John said, "so I can make decent inroads into the wooing of my lady."

Nicholas stretched his feet out and crossed them at the ankles, directly in John's way. "I think . . . not."

Tess looked at Nicholas, who was looking very paternal, then at Robin, who was only watching with his eyes twinkling and his finger rubbing over his mouth as if he hoped it might keep those lips from smirking unduly.

"I am," John said distinctly, "a score and eight. Old enough to—"

"Know better," Nicholas finished for him placidly. "Haven't we had this conversation before?"

"Aye, and I've no less desire to stick you for it now than I had before."

"You may not take an unchaperoned lady of breeding and kiss her senseless in my hall," Nicholas said sharply. "For reasons you can divine using your own wee brain if you stretch yourself."

"And if she were a lady of breeding who was betrothed to a lord's son?"

"A quick peck on the cheek," Nicholas conceded. "In plain sight."

John glared at him. "Father said just that same thing to you, didn't he?"

"Aye, and I was a score and eight as well," Nicholas said, reaching for Jennifer's hand. "And not too stupid to listen. Though we might be having a slightly different conversation if you were to now make certain this wasn't a casual sort of arrangement."

Tess watched John kick his brother's feet out of his way, then turn to her purposefully. He took both her hands.

What are you doing?" she managed.

He tugged her closer. "Making headway, I hope."

"You aren't going to kiss me here," she blurted out in English. "In front of everyone?"

"Isabelle and Montgomery are missing."

"John!"

He looked at her in silence for several long moments, then took a step backward.

And then he sank to one knee.

The room was absolutely silent. The fire cracked and popped in the hearth, which Tess supposed had been happening all evening though she only noticed it at the moment. She felt her face flaming as well, but perhaps that was to be expected.

John looked up at her seriously. "I had hoped to do this in a more private setting"—he shot Nicholas a pointed look, then turned back to her—"but at least we'll have witnesses."

She supposed that was true, but she wasn't going to say as much. All she could do was concentrate on keeping her mouth from hanging open.

Jake leaned forward and tapped John on the shoulder. "You'll need this."

Tess watched John accept a ring, then look at his brother-in-law in surprise.

"You're prepared."

"I was a Boy Scout," Jake said dryly. "And to answer what you haven't had the chance to ask, I was thinking about you a while ago for some odd reason. It occurred to me that you might need a ring for a woman charitable enough to rescue your sorry self from eternal bachelorhood. I thought it was a ridiculous idea at the time, but apparently it wasn't."

Tess looked down at the ring. Emeralds, rubies, sapphires— she lost track of the colors of stones set into the band. The only thing she knew was it looked absolutely medieval.

"I'll pay you for this," John said hoarsely.

"Yes, you will," Jake agreed cheerfully.

John looked at the ring in his hand for a moment or two, then up at her. She tried to drag her sleeve across her eyes, but he wouldn't let go of her hands. She was already shaking, so maybe the tears running down her cheeks wouldn't be as noticeable as they might have been otherwise.

John took a deep breath. "Tess," he began slowly, sounding a little more nervous than she'd ever heard him sound, "I have little to offer you—"

"Besides a Vanquish," Jake put in, sounding disgusted, "and no doubt numerous Swiss safe-deposit boxes overflowing with cash."

John shot his brother-in-law a warning look, then turned back to her. "I have a few quid," he conceded, "which means nothing in either century except that I'll be able to provide for you as you deserve. I vow I will shield you with my name, protect you with my sword, and sheepdog you until you beg me to stop." He paused, then looked at her seriously. "I want forever, Tess."

She blinked rapidly, because she had to. "John—"

He shook his head quickly. "I'm sure," he said. "The question is, are you?"

She couldn't see him any longer. She also couldn't deny the fact that the thought of leaving him behind, or even being in the same time with him and not having him be a part of her life, the most important part of her life, was devastating. She also knew what it would mean to his siblings if she said yes.

She had a level of sympathy for Montgomery de Piaget she'd never imagined she might.

She didn't dare look at his family, so she looked just at him. "I'm sure," she said quietly, "and I want forever, too."

He slipped that lovely ring onto her finger, then rose to his feet and pulled her into his arms. "I'll take that as a yes," he whispered against her ear.

She threw her arms around his neck and held on tightly. "It absolutely is a yes," she said. "Forever yes." She pulled back, then looked at Nicholas. "Have you an opinion on my kissing him?" she asked.

He put his hands behind his head. "We'll judge how well you do it, if you like."

John unhooked her arms from behind his neck, then pulled her behind him. She was somehow unsurprised, so she went. She rested her cheek against his back and looked at Jennifer, who was smiling through her tears. She returned the smile, because she knew Jennifer understood that her yes was about more than just a proposal of marriage. She took a deep breath, then wrapped her arms around John's waist, just to keep him from doing something he might regret later.

"You, Nick," John said distinctly, "are three words from finding yourself sporting my blade in your chest."

"And what three words would those be?" Nicholas asked politely. "Go to hell? Keep your hands to yourself—nay, that's more than three, so I'll try another trio. You ridiculous boy?"

Tess kept John from starting forward only because she supposed when it came right down to it, he had some hesitation at the thought of killing his brother.

"I will see you in the lists," John said curtly, "at dawn. Arrive prepared to depart speedily into the next life."

"Will you rob my children of their father?" Nicholas asked plaintively. "My lady wife of her husband? How hard-hearted you've become in that future of yours."

Tess felt one of John's hands come to rest over hers.

"And if you were me and had a stunningly beautiful and frighteningly clever woman who wanted to pull you into a darkened corner and kiss you senseless, what would you do to the brother who stood in your way?"

"After I thanked him for the concern, I would have clipped him under the jaw and stepped over his insensible body to follow after my lady wherever she led."

"Thank you," John said pointedly.

"Five minutes," Nicholas said pointedly in return. "Find a corner, thank her properly for agreeing to take your disagreeable self in the bargain, then hurry back before we come looking for you."

Tess found her hand taken and brotherly feet removed from the path. John stopped and looked back over his shoulder at Robin.

"Nothing to add?"

Robin held up his hands. "I wouldn't presume."

Tess found herself shepherded out of the solar without delay.

She stopped John before he pulled her too much farther along the passageway, because despite everything, she had to know for certain that he knew what he was getting into.

"Are you really sure?" she asked. "Your family—"

"Is thrilled I finally met someone who'll endure me," he finished. "Why would you think anything else?"

"You know why." She had to take a very deep breath. "I was caught up in the moment inside there, but now I'm not sure—"

"About me?"

"Of course not," she said without hesitation. "But I don't know that I can take you away from your life here."

He wrapped his arms around her and looked down at her seriously. "Tess, you can't imagine I want to remain in the past."

"Well, of course I can *imagine*," she blurted out. "Your family is here."

He looked over his shoulder and apparently found the hallway empty enough to suit him. He held her close with one hand, slipped the other under her hair, and proceeded to kiss her until she thought he might have made inroads into convincing her he meant what he said.

"My family, my love," he said against her mouth, "is wherever you are, which family you just agreed to be since you accepted my proposal of marriage." He lifted his head and smiled faintly. "Though I think I've gotten slightly ahead of my wooing here."

"You and your medieval sensibilities," she said, feeling a little breathless.

"You can expect nothing else." He gathered her close and sighed deeply. "Unfortunately, those medieval sensibilities tell me I shouldn't maul you in public until you're properly wedded and bedded else our reputations will suffer. But I think a brief foray into some secluded spot wouldn't be beyond the question. Then I'll tell you what I find most appealing about your time period."

"If you tell me it's the Vanquish, I'll punch you," she warned.

He laughed a little. "Of course not. I meant you."

"Who are you kidding? You wouldn't last two weeks without bangers and mash. And jazz. And your mobile phone."

"Nay, just you, and thankfully you are portable. But," he added, "that doesn't mean that I want to carry you off to the past." He paused and looked at her seriously. "I think you would rather teach medieval niceties, not live them. Or am I wrong?"

She smiled and it came more easily that time. "Honestly, the only medieval nicety I'm interested in is you. And if you want the whole truth, I don't care what century I have you in."

He looked slightly winded. "You just earned yourself a quarter hour in my brother's darkest corner."

"He'll come after us."

"Let him try." He took her hand and pulled her back the way they'd come. "Let's go before he comes trotting along after—"

She realized he wasn't saying anything else because he'd run bodily into his brother. She looked around his shoulder to find Nicholas standing there, lute in hand.

"I have other things in mind besides playing for her," John said pointedly.

"I'm playing for *you*," Nicholas said cheerfully. "We decided that perhaps an impromptu bit of dancing might save you from yourself."

Tess watched John sigh, then found herself with his arm around her shoulders.

"I suppose it isn't ideal," he said heavily, "but I'll endure your generosity. Then I will escort my lady to your solar where she will take her ease without the twin horrors of unwanted maidens and their mothers."

"I'll consider it," Nicholas conceded.

John waved him off. "Tess needs better shoes. We'll follow posthaste."

Nicholas turned and walked away, shaking his head. Tess didn't have a chance to ask John what he meant—she was wearing the only pair of shoes she had that weren't gifts from Jennifer—but she realized quite quickly she needn't have bothered. She found herself pulled into a very light-free alcove and drawn into familiar arms.

"A brief kiss," John announced, "lest I not be able to dance."

"A peck," she agreed.

By the time he let her up for air, she wasn't sure either of them would be dancing. She put her arms around his waist and rested her head on his shoulder.

"Are you sure?" she asked.

"Are *you* sure?" he returned. "A lifetime of being herded,

bossed about, drawn into darkened corners, and thoroughly kissed?"

She leaned up and kissed him softly. "I'm sure."

"Thank you," he whispered against her ear.

She laughed a little. "No, thank you."

He pulled away and took her hand. "Let's go argue about who is more grateful: me, that you said me aye; or my family, that you're ridding them of me."

She stopped him before he walked away and looked up at him seriously. "I can't make light of that, John."

He turned, winced, then gathered her into his arms again. "I'm sorry," he said, holding her close. "It isn't fodder for jest. My family *is* happy, though. And I'm ecstatic."

"Why?" she managed.

"For dozens of reasons I'll begin to explain tonight as we pass each other in what I'm sure will be a score of very chaste, very sedate dances where I won't be allowed to touch you."

"At least you're not wearing heels," she pointed out.

"For you, I might even be persuaded to wear them again next year at Payneswick." He pulled away and smiled. "Let's go have this over with. I have plans for you later."

She followed him back to the great hall, sure she wouldn't take a step that she didn't feel uncomfortable for what had just transpired in Nicholas's solar, but she found she was wrong. She was swept into a family circle, the likes of which she'd enjoyed only with her sisters.

And after John had whispered to her *stop thinking* for the dozenth time, she found that she could.

Though she imagined she would weep over it later just the same.

Chapter 26

J*ohn* stood on the steps with Nicholas and bid farewell to the trio—for their numbers had increased briefly—of disappointed gels and equally unfulfilled parents as they trudged off toward the front gates.

"None too soon," Nicholas said under his breath.

John smiled in spite of himself. "Thank you for the aid in helping them see clearly my attached status."

"I wanted them gone because they were about to eat through my larder." He looked at John and shook his head. "Why is it these arranging of marriages tend to include so damned much food in the bargain?"

"To test your stamina, no doubt," John said, "which, thankfully, was apparently not up to their standards."

"Or that might have been you walking up and down the passageways last night and announcing in stentorian tones that you were engaged to that lovely Lady Tess of points unknown so they'd best shove off this morning and look for more accommodating ports."

John lifted his eyebrow briefly. "Just making it so you have enough to eat this winter."

"Normally I wouldn't worry about it, for we would be in France, enjoying the bounties of land and sea," Nicholas said with a sigh. "I suppose you're fortunate Jennifer is so close to her time, else you wouldn't have found us here at all. You would have found shelter, though, of course."

"Without bursting into tears and terrifying you," John said seriously, "I will say that I was profoundly pleased to see you."

"And I you." He looked out over his courtyard for a bit, then turned back to John. "And for your future?"

John looked around himself casually to see who might be within earshot. Finding the coast clear, as the saying went, he decided the opportunity was before him to speak freely. "I'm going home." He looked at his brother frankly. "It makes me sound a perfect bastard, doesn't it? To trade you all for a different time?"

Nicholas shrugged. "As I admitted before, I've been tempted to have a wee visit myself, but Jennifer won't let me. Not until we're finished with bairns."

"And how many more will you have, do you think?"

"I understand we have ten who live. How many don't, I don't know. Perhaps we'll be spared that grief." He lifted an eyebrow. "Have you been poking around in my genealogy?"

John shook his head slowly. "I couldn't bear to. As far as I was concerned, I had no past. Certainly no past *in* the past."

"How interesting for you, then, to encounter a woman whose specialty is the past."

"Trust me," John said dryly, "the thought has occurred to me more than once. I looked for every possible reason not to see her again."

"Unsuccessfully, apparently," Nicholas said with a smile, "and fortunately for you, I think."

"Do you like her?"

"Very much," Nicholas said without hesitation. "I think she might be the single person in the Future who could live with you and not think you completely mad." He studied John for another very long moment. "Would you stay?" he asked finally. "If we begged you to?"

John shifted uncomfortably. "The thought of you down on your knees makes me slightly ill."

Nicholas laughed. "I was going to advise you not to expect *me* to be the one begging, but that would have sounded too much like Robin." He sighed. "I wouldn't ask it of you. This will sound as daft as anything you could possibly say, but I think you belong in that time of yours."

"I'll make sure we have guest chambers enough that you might make a visit in your hoary-headed old age."

"By the saints," Nicholas said with a shiver, "what a thought." He shot John a look. "But don't think I haven't fondled your keys already just the same. And your phone."

"How did you know how to work it?" John asked in surprise.

"I can find the *on* button as easily as the next medieval lord," Nicholas said archly.

John laughed in spite of himself. "I can't believe we're having this conversation."

"Neither can I. We'd best head for the lists. I'm sure a morning of swordplay will ground us in the proper year."

John wasn't opposed to that, for a variety of reasons. The first was because he wanted to be prepared, but perhaps even more than that, he wasn't going to pass up a morning spent with his brothers.

By the time Nicholas, Robin, and Miles had taken their turns with him, he was so wrung out, he wasn't sure he would make it back to the house, much less back to the Future. He stumbled off the field and looked for a place to sit only to find the bench by the wall occupied by Tess and an extensive collection of nieces and nephews. She was holding Robin's only gel Mary on her lap whilst others had piled onto the bench next to her. Kendrick and Rose, Amanda's eldest, were standing in front of her, arguing the merits of investigating things better left uninvestigated if the speed with which they bit back their words on his approach was any indication.

He folded his arms over his chest and looked at them severely. "Plotting naughtiness?"

"They are," Amanda's eldest son Jackson said without hesitation. "I can tell you—"

Rose sat down on her brother and robbed him of his wind. She smiled up at John innocently. "Nothing untoward, Uncle John. Just expanding our minds in useful ways, as Father always instructs me to do."

"I can just imagine," John muttered. He looked at Tess and smiled. "At least they're keeping you warm."

She looked perfectly serene. "Warm and entertained. A lovely combination."

John looked at the collection of the eldest lads there, sons of Robin, Nicholas, Jake, and Miles, and tried not to let the sight of them make his heart ache. If he could have, he would have taken a few pictures of them with his phone, just to have in the Future.

"I'm going to clean up," he said to those same lads. "See to your future auntie Tess for me until I return."

Chests were puffed out and weapons checked for proximity to young hands should something dangerous occur. John smiled at Tess, then walked away whilst he still could without it breaking his heart further. His siblings he could live without—especially Robin—but the bairns?

He walked into Robin before he realized what he was doing. He had to take a deep breath as he steadied himself.

"I'm maudlin."

"Aye, you always have been."

"Nay, you're mistaking me for Montgomery," John said, pursing his lips. "I'm the hard-hearted one."

Robin shook his head slowly. "You hid it well, but your heart was tender. You haven't changed."

"Shut up, Robin," John said with a sigh.

Robin laughed a little and slung his arm around John's shoulders. "I'll do this for you, because I love you so much. I'll have Jake paint a portrait of all the wee ones every couple of years and hide them up somewhere in Artane. You can dig them out of the wall when you go home. Surely the current Earl of Artane won't mind you nosing about in his artifacts."

John cleared his throat. "Likely not. And that's very generous of you."

"I didn't say I would pay Jake to do it, just that I'd needle him. You'll have to work out his price yourself."

John shook his head and walked on with his brother. Things didn't change. Robin took delight in tormenting his brothers, doting on his wife and spawn, and grinding every swordsman in the area into dust whenever and for however long possible. He supposed he and Tess could attempt another trip at some point in the future and find Robin at three score just the same—

He turned away from that thought because he wasn't at all sure he trusted any time gate in England, no matter how easily

James MacLeod seemed to use them. His own experience had been so terrible, he was hardly willing to take the risk for himself alone. The thought of risking Tess for a lark of that sort, or any children they might have . . .

Nay, he would make peace with his father, kiss his siblings and their progeny good-bye, then he would take Tess home and wed her. Explorers and pilgrims of all stripes had done the same over centuries of the world's tale, leaving behind the hearths and homes of their childhood and knowing they would never see them again.

He wondered how they'd borne it.

The cuff on the back of his head had him turning with his sword half drawn. He glared at Robin. "What?"

"Nothing," Robin said cheerfully. "Just dislodging a bit of good sense."

John rolled his eyes and carried on with getting himself cleaned up and back downstairs where he could join Tess in keeping warm with those sweet children his siblings were fortunate enough to call their own.

H_e spent a good part of the afternoon entertaining those sweet children with French translations of all the modern children's music he could bring to mind whilst keeping a close eye on Kendrick and Rose. The saints only knew what mischief those two would combine, though perhaps less than they might have if Jackson the Fifth hadn't been watching them with a frown.

John spent quite a bit of time smiling to himself as well.

He had just sat down next to Tess at supper, envisioning a long, lovely evening stretching out in front of him, when a man burst into the hall. John was standing in front of the table with his sword drawn before he realized he'd leaped over the table to do so.

The messenger held up his hands quickly. "Not war," he blurted out. He walked swiftly to Nicholas and bowed low. "From Joanna of Segrave's steward, my lord."

Nicholas took the missive, read it, then sent the messenger off to the kitchens for something to eat. He turned around and swept them all with a look.

"Grandmère has sent for us. Well, not for me because she

doesn't want me to leave my lady so close to her time." He exchanged a brief look with Jennifer, then continued. "She wants the rest of you to go to Segrave, as quick as may be. Leave what children behind you will and I'll see to them. My mother-in-law and her mother will be arriving any time, so we'll have extra hands enough."

John resheathed his sword, let out his breath slowly, then walked around the table to drop down in the chair next to Tess. He looked at her seriously. "Care for another journey?"

"Of course," she said, just as seriously. "Do you think this is why we're here?"

"Perhaps," he agreed, though he couldn't imagine time would have brought him back to the past merely to see his grandmother shuffle off her mortal coil. She could have haunted him—and likely had been but he'd been too stupid to realize it—in the Future without much effort. He smiled at Tess. "Perhaps. I imagine we'll leave at dawn. Robin likes to get an early start on these sorts of things."

She nodded. "Will we just camp, do you think, or stay in inns?"

"I imagine both," he said, "and I believe, my lady, that I *will* be sleeping on your floor, and the critics be damned. Or I could just wed you tonight and solve that problem."

She smiled, looking substantially more at peace than she had before. "And here I thought you promised me medieval wooing, up close and personal. I wonder if it will involve something besides herding."

"That's all I know how to do," he said, only half jesting. "Though I suppose I could save you a tumble off your horse if the opportunity arose."

"That's very romantic."

'Tis better than a broken neck was almost out of his mouth, but fortunately the filter between his brain and mouth was functioning as it should. He smiled. "I'll stretch myself and see what comes to mind."

She took his hand. "I'm sorry about your grandmother."

"She's ancient," John said with a sigh, "and long overdue for a new adventure, I daresay." He smiled. "You'll like her, I think, given that she is, as you know, the one who forced me to learn to play the lute."

"It was well done, by both of you," she said. She looked at him carefully. "And then we'll go to France?"

"If you wouldn't mind."

She looked a little green, truth be told. "I'm not sure about how I'll do with your parents, but I would like to see Pippa. How will we get there?"

"I'll borrow gold from some brother or other," he said with a shrug. "The journey isn't easy, but we'll manage."

She nodded, then turned to answer a question Amanda had asked her from her other side. John leaned back in his chair and watched Nicholas and Robin making their plans. It was how things had gone for as long as he could remember, though his father had always been a part of that very small circle, and Jake had joined it years ago. He had still been too green at nineteen to be invited, which he supposed had been part of the reason he'd taken his own fate in his hands and marched off toward points unknown.

He realized Robin was trying to get his attention. He excused himself and walked around the table to find himself now part of that exclusive circle of planners that now included Miles as well.

He supposed he was too old for it to please him as much as it did.

Robin rolled his eyes. "Stop daydreaming and concentrate. This might be an excellent opportunity to see what hunts you."

John blinked. "Whilst Tess is there? Are you mad?"

"I don't think you want to leave her here, do you?" Robin asked, no doubt quite reasonably to his mind. "You could try, of course, but I don't imagine she'll stay."

John exchanged a look with Nicholas, then glanced at Jake. Jake only held up his hands in surrender.

"Amanda won't stay behind, but that won't come as much of a surprise. Your Tess is very much like her, I'm afraid. I think between the four of us, we can keep our ladies safe."

"I brought my own guardsmen, of course," Robin put in. "Though I'll leave most here to see to Anne, Jason, and Mary, I'll bring enough with me that no one will dare assault us."

"I don't like this," John said grimly.

"You would like it even less if Tess wandered off without you because you allowed fear to rule the day," Robin said sharply. "I'm bringing Kendrick, for pity's sake. You don't think I would put my son in danger, do you? Well, I left Phillip with Montgomery when he still had holes in his walls, but that has nothing to do with this. *I* have perfect confidence in my ability to vanquish anything that might be hunting you, even if you don't."

Unless that soul had acquired a modern weapon, then Robin would be rapidly reassessing his prowess. John sighed, dragged his hand though his hair, then nodded, because he could do nothing else.

"Go pack," Robin said briskly, "and say your good-byes, all of you. We'll leave before dawn."

John watched him walk away to consult with his own guardsmen, the steely eyed, supremely capable looking lads who were interspersed within the ranks of Nicholas's garrison, and supposed his brother had things aright. Jake and Miles would bring a contingent of their own men to add to Robin's, and it wasn't as if he and his brothers couldn't attend to any stray threats.

But what convinced him was the thought of Tess taking matters into her own hands—and he was quite sure Nicholas would be unable to control her.

He could only hope that taking her with him wouldn't be worse.

Chapter 27

T *ess* stood in the courtyard before dawn and honestly wished herself anywhere else. She wasn't a coward, though, so she made herself witness a parting she wished she didn't have to.

Robin was leaving Anne behind because of the swiftness of their prospective journey and something to do with Anne's leg that she didn't seem to want to talk about. Amanda and Jake were coming, as were their two eldest, Rose and Jackson the Fifth. Miles was bringing a pair of his sons, but leaving the rest behind with his wife, Abigail.

Nicholas was staying behind as well, though she imagined both he and Jennifer were unhappy over missing his grandmother's last days.

She realized he was standing next to her, and she couldn't help but jump a bit.

"Sorry," she said. "I didn't realize you were there."

"You were lost in thought."

She looked up at him. He was every bit as gorgeous as the rest of his brothers and had charm to spare. She could see why Jennifer had readily left the future to itself to remain and camp with him for the whole of her life. She cleared her throat.

"Do you always do what your grandmother tells you to do?" she asked.

He smiled. "We were there visiting in the spring, and aye, I always do what she tells me to do. She pinches my ear if I don't. And were I to disobey her edict, she wouldn't be at all pleased to see me, and the trip would have been wasted."

"She sounds formidable."

"She is. She'll be thrilled to see John, though she'll remind him that I am her favorite grandson. I don't know that John isn't next in line, though. She grieved enormously when he went missing."

"I understand," Tess said, because she did—at least in part. At least she'd known what Pippa had intended to do and she'd had a day or two to get used to the idea and say her good-byes.

"Jennifer's family came to our wedding," Nicholas said, as casually as if they were talking about the weather. "And her mother and grandmother have come for the birth of each of our children. They should be arriving soon."

"Brave women," Tess said faintly.

"They are," Nicholas agreed, "but they didn't have John's experience with the gate near Artane. I daresay, if I might offer an opinion, that he was meant to stay in the Future. I would imagine that most souls are likewise wedded to their places in time. My mother-in-law and her mother are the only ones I know who seem to be scampering about out of Fate's sights, as it were."

"At least they can see Jennifer now and then," Tess said, then she realized what she'd said. She took a deep breath and, it had to be admitted, blinked rather rapidly a time or two. "Her siblings must miss her. I know Megan does."

"I'm sure they do," Nicholas said quietly. "But 'twas her choice, wasn't it?"

She looked up at him, pained. "Why are you telling me this?"

"Because I stood in your shoes," he said simply. "Jenner stayed for me."

"And you think John is going for me?"

"He's certainly not going for those four damned cars he has plunging him into the sin of gluttony."

She couldn't even attempt a smile. "And how did you survive it?"

"The responsibility?" he asked. He shrugged. "I spend every

moment—well, almost every moment—trying to make sure she doesn't regret her choice. You needn't do the same. Adoration is for my brother to see to. Your task is to keep him in line, which is far more difficult."

"I'll try to make sure he doesn't regret it."

"I don't think you'll have to do much more than breathe to see to that," Nicholas said dryly. "You might allow him to herd you now and again, just to make him feel more manly."

"He doesn't give me much choice."

"He wouldn't," Nicholas agreed. "He loves you very much. And I imagine he's also feeling rather fortunate that you understand his past."

She managed a smile. "I suppose that's true. At least when his right hand twitches, I know he's reaching for a nonexistent sword."

Nicholas laughed uneasily. "Please keep him out of your modern dungeons for me, won't you? I don't think I could rescue him there." He hesitated, then smiled. "And keep Megan apprised of your happenings, if you would, so her mother might bring us those tidings."

"I will," Tess agreed.

"And send the occasional thing to Montgomery, will you? He is unwholesomely addicted to all manner of future snacks."

Tess promised him she would see to that as well, all the while trying to find her linguistic bearings in the rush of medieval French and modern English that Nicholas seem to toss about with abandon. She continued to make polite conversation with John's brother until she found herself pulled away by John's nieces and nephews. By the time she'd said good-bye to all of them, John was coming to fetch her.

He looked at her, then closed his eyes briefly and pulled her into his arms. "Let's go," he said hoarsely. "Before I break down and bawl like a bairn."

"John, maybe—"

"Tess, nay," he said firmly, then he blew out his breath. He pulled back and looked at her. "I'm sorry. My distress speaks." He managed a smile. "I could have been hit by a bus a fortnight ago and not had any of this. I'm grateful for an unexpected pleasure."

Which he could have for the rest of his life if he wanted it, but she supposed there was no point in saying as much any longer. He knew it as well as she did. She couldn't make his choice for him. All she could do was try not to imagine the hole that would be left in her heart if he decided to give her a firm push through a time gate while remaining on the far side of it.

He took her face in his hands, looked at her seriously, then bent his head and kissed her softly.

"By the saints, none of that!" Robin bellowed. "There are *children* being subjected to the spectacle!"

John pursed his lips. "He is one sibling I will *not* miss."

"Liar," she said breathlessly. "But don't do that again. I'm supposed to stay on my horse today."

"The first dark corner I find," he said, looking at her purposefully. "You're coming with me."

"Of course, my lord."

He laughed a little, hugged her tightly, then led her over to her horse and helped her up into the saddle. Tess took the reins from him and prayed she wouldn't fall off.

Considering how floored she was by the very briefest of kisses from a man who had turned her around from the moment she'd seen him, she didn't hold out much hope for it.

And damn him if he didn't know it.

He winked at her, then swung up onto his own horse. He looked back only once, as they rode through the front gates. Then he put his face forward and was very quiet. He did look at her and attempt a smile after a bit. She couldn't say anything.

She appreciated Nicholas's words, but the reality of John's situation was very difficult to watch. She knew he had made his choice, and he didn't regret it, but that didn't make watching it any easier.

She put her face forward and tried not to join John in a few discreet tears.

*M*edieval travel was, she could readily admit three days later, hellish.

Riding was better than walking, but not by much. She was never again going to complain about her little runabout. If she ever rode in John's car again, she was going to spend half of every journey thinking kind thoughts about the absolute luxury of his seats.

The journey hadn't been without its unexpected pleasures, despite the difficulty of it. Having the chance to get to know Amanda had been one of those. John's oldest sister was the sort of medieval girl Tess would have wanted to be if she'd been born in the era. She was absolutely fearless, terribly outspoken, and full of her own very strong opinions. Tess rode next to her as often as possible—actually between Amanda and Robin—just to get an earful—in stereo—of current day happenings. Tess wished she'd had a tape recorder or a photographic memory. Robin told her not to worry, that John had the same thoughts running through his wee brain, but she couldn't take much comfort in that. She had tried not to chew on decisions already made, but she honestly wouldn't have blamed him at all if he had . . . well, if he changed his mind.

Though he didn't look like he was contemplating that. She glanced at him to find he was watching her with a small, affectionate smile.

"You're going to run into something," she managed.

"Never. I can admire you all day and still remain in the saddle." He shrugged. "It's a gift."

She laughed a little, then caught her breath as he reached over and took hold of her hand. She was wearing gloves, but that didn't stop her from realizing he had put his thumb over her fourth finger, over the ring he'd given her.

"Stop thinking so much," he said seriously.

She let out a deep breath, then nodded. He squeezed her hand very gently, then released her. She smiled briefly at him, then turned back to concentrating on that spot between her horse's ears.

She realized, quite a while later, that they had stopped only because she woke from her stupor of too many thoughts she shouldn't have been entertaining to find that her horse was no longer moving. She looked around her to try to figure out where she was only to realize she was somewhere she definitely didn't want to be.

Chevington.

The place shouldn't have given her the creeps. After all, it was the scene of her most recent academic triumph. It was also fairly new so there wasn't any of that pesky paranormal activity to worry about.

It was also the place where she'd launched her journey into her current locale, so perhaps that was reason enough for a few shivers.

She realized with a start that John was holding up his arms for her. She had grown accustomed to simply falling out of the saddle into them, so she did it again, with apologies to her mount. He put his arm around her shoulders and pulled her close, then looked at his eldest brother.

"I'm still not sure this is wise."

Robin looked at their company with a thoughtful frown. Besides the adults of John's family, there were a handful of children and at least thirty guardsmen. Hard-eyed, hard-bitten warriors with swords and attitudes, not all of whom apparently belonged to Robin, but all of whom called Robin *my lord* in near worshipful tones. Robin shrugged.

"And just what, my dear brother, is it you think the hapless Richard of Chevington is going to do? Heave his equally useless son Everard over the parapet and hope he lands on one of us?"

"I sincerely doubt Everard is here," John said grimly, "based on what Nick told me of his recent escapades. Roland, however, is another tale entirely. I'm not sure we have any idea where he is."

"Roland is about as likely to slip a dagger through your ribs as I am," Robin said with a snort. "I wouldn't be surprised to find he'd gone south to Segrave to pay his respects to Grandmère. He's no doubt hoping to fawn over her so much that she forgets that Chevington is part of Segrave's holdings. Or perhaps he simply wants to arrive early to flatter his new overlord."

Tess blinked in surprise. "Is that how it is, then?"

"Aye, 'tis complicated, isn't it?" Robin said with a pleasant smile. "I'll admit it gives me pains in my head trying to remember who holds what, but there you have it. Richard continually indulges in thinking he is more important than he is. Roland isn't a bad sort, but I wouldn't give you a damned shilling for Everard. Why Montgomery has endured his company for so long, I don't know."

"He's a tenderhearted sap," John said.

Robin looked at him knowingly. "Cross blades with your wee brother and see if you don't think differently now. As for me, I'm only interested in a bed. We'll eat our own stores, I believe, instead of risking a taster."

Tess thought she might start to hyperventilate soon. She forced herself to take slow, deep, even breaths until she thought she might have even the tail end of the impulse under control. John pulled her into his arms and wrapped his cloak around her, as if he strove to shield her.

"I agree about supper," John said in a low voice, "but I'm not convinced we shouldn't bed down in the stables."

Robin considered. "The bairns would brag about it endlessly, true, but I'm not sure 'tis wise, simply because there is too little between us and the outside world."

"And we're better off inside his hall where we might be pinned in chambers?" John asked sharply.

Robin reached out and put his hand on John's shoulder. "You don't actually think his garrison is capable of overpowering us, do you?"

Tess felt John sigh, then tighten his arms briefly around her before he released her.

"I suppose not," he said heavily. "And I suppose being inside his hall might provide us with clues we might not find elsewhere."

Tess supposed that was true as well, but she shivered in spite of herself just the same as she walked to the front gates with John. They were surrounded by a collection of very fierce men, but that was somehow less comforting than she would have thought. She had the feeling that a few of the things Chevington might have to offer were things that couldn't be bested with a sword. To say it was spooky to be walking over the same ground she'd walked over in a different century was understating it badly. She looked up at John, but it had grown too dark to see his expression clearly. She couldn't imagine, based on his unwillingness to enter the forest, that he wasn't thinking the same thing.

The castle was lit not by floodlights but by torches. She could see the glint of something occasionally along the walls. Swords, perhaps. Chain mail and helmets, definitely.

"We're expected," John said quietly. "Robin sent word ahead."

"So they're planning on us?"

"For better or worse," he agreed.

She wondered if he noticed that she moved closer to him. For the first time in their rather tumultuous relationship, she could safely say she wouldn't argue if he pulled her behind him.

She wasn't sure she would be able to describe with any precision the procession of events from that point on. They were welcomed inside, she did her best not to gape at the lord of Chevington, and they made noises about not putting Richard to any trouble. He didn't seem to find their having brought their own supper to be anything out of the ordinary, though he balked at allowing them to sleep in the great hall. The ladies, at least, would have decent chambers.

Tess found herself escorted upstairs with absolutely no chance to talk to John about what she'd just discovered. She was given the courtesy of her own room, which she wasn't sure she appreciated, but there was nothing to be done about it. She didn't even dare undress, so she simply sat in front of a completely inadequate—even by medieval standards—fire and fretted.

And as she fretted, she considered yet again just what had bothered her so much about their very brief bit of conversation with Richard of Chevington. John had to know what she'd seen. She jumped to her feet and went to open her bedroom door.

John was standing there with his back to it. He turned around and frowned. "Why aren't you abed?"

"Why aren't you?"

He shot her a look she didn't need words to decipher.

"You'll fall off your horse tomorrow," she predicted.

"And you'll be alive to catch me," he said pointedly. "Go to bed, Tess."

She shook her head. "I need to talk—"

"Tomorrow."

"But—"

He scowled. "Woman, my time—"

"And in my time," she said, exasperated, "Richard is Roland. Well, he isn't Roland, but he looks so much like him, they have to be related."

He stopped scowling. That could have been because his mouth had fallen open. "What?"

She reached out and took hold of the front of his tunic and pulled him closer. "I'm telling you that Roland—Roland, the last

Earl of Sedgwick who gave me my castle—looks almost *exactly* like Richard of Chevington, the Richard I just saw downstairs. They aren't the same person, I'm sure of that, but they have to be related somehow."

He put his hand on the wall, apparently to steady himself. "Richard has no brothers, and his father's name was Stephen," he managed. "There is no other Roland in his line that I know of save his son." He drew his hand over his eyes. "So, are you telling me you think your Roland of the future is somehow our Roland of the past?"

"I don't know," she said helplessly. "I just know they look too much alike for it to be a coincidence."

"Why didn't you tell me sooner?"

She looked at him in disbelief. He laughed a little, then smiled at her. "Very well, I didn't give you a chance. I apologize." He considered for a bit. "How long had you known Roland in the future? *Your* Roland?"

"Only a couple of months before he gave me the castle. I don't even know how long he'd lived there." She let out her breath slowly. "I never thought to investigate it."

"You wouldn't have had any reason to," he agreed. "A pity, though, for knowing that would answer a few questions for us."

"I think there's only one question," she said slowly, "and I imagine we can speculate on the answer to it without any help."

"You're talking about the note I wrote for Nick?" he asked, leaning against the doorframe. He was speaking in English, which gave her a very good idea of how adverse he was to being eavesdropped on. "You think Roland may have read the missive and understood it where Everard couldn't?"

"Or they both could have read it and both tried the gate."

"Everard can't read."

"And if he'd had help—in either century? What would he have done then?"

John blew out his breath. "The saints preserve us, I can scarce think on it."

"Well, if it makes you feel any better, I think Roland's harmless," she offered. "He's been very generous to me."

"Where I can guarantee Everard wouldn't have been," John said grimly. He rubbed his hands over his face suddenly, then shook his head. "Let's sleep on it, then give it more thought tomorrow." He made a twirling motion with his finger. "Turn around and walk on, gel."

She turned because he gave her no choice, but she turned back around and put her hand on the door before he pulled it shut. "You have to sleep," she said seriously.

He smiled very briefly. "Another hour and I'm off to bed as well, I promise."

"I wish your BlackBerry worked so we could do a little quick search on the history of Sedgwick."

He laughed a little, then reached out and pulled her into his arms. He smiled down at her as he slipped her hand under her hair. "I'm afraid we're on our own, but oftimes that can work to our benefit."

"You unscrupulous kisser of maidens in distress," she breathed.

"And at such a time as this," he agreed, just before he rendered her quite incapable of speech.

By the time he finally lifted his head and looked at her, she had been reduced to clutching the doorframe. It seemed a little more stable than John, actually.

"You should stop that," she managed. "You need a clear head."

"And that won't lead to it, I assure you."

She leaned up and kissed him primly on the cheek. "That might. Go to bed when you're supposed to." She started to shut the door, then paused. "Be careful."

"Always." He leaned in, kissed her very briefly, then pulled back and motioned for her to shut the door. "Bolt it. Please."

Well, that wasn't the first time she'd heard that, though she appreciated the added bit of politeness. She bolted her door, then turned and looked over her accommodations. The bed was full of bedbugs—she'd already looked—and the floor was filthy. She hated to lie down on it in Jennifer's dress, even one that was, as Jennifer had protested as Tess had insisted on it, fit for the rag bag.

But better dirty than itching, so she lay down in front of the fire and hoped she would see John and the sunrise both in the morning.

Roland? The Earl of Sedgwick?

She closed her eyes in an attempt to block out the thought,

but that only led to others. It was conceivable that he'd left her the castle out of altruism, but it was equally possible he'd had a more sinister motive.

She only hoped she could divine what it was before it was too late.

Chapter 28

John reined in just outside Segrave's gates with his company and waited for Robin to sort the gate guards. He was grateful not only for the chance to sit still, but to wonder about a few things that puzzled him still.

Such as why Roland of Chevington would have gone to the Future.

Well, perhaps there was no mystery there. Roland had always been a quiet lad, but a thinker. If he'd even been able to imagine another world, he might well have mustered up the courage to go have a look at it. John understood that, given that he'd done the same himself, but he'd had the benefit of having watched siblings wed souls from that era. Roland would have known nothing of it, would have had no idea what to expect, and surely had no good reason to go farther than a dozen paces from his father's coffers.

But if he had, the ramifications were truly stunning. The thought of Roland of Chevington actually being the Earl of Sedgwick, bought title though it must have been, made his head spin in ways he wasn't entirely comfortable with. Roland couldn't have known Tess in the past, and he surely wouldn't have gone to the Future with the express purpose of meeting her and giving her Sedgwick.

Surely.

John supposed that if he'd been a more romantic sort of lad, he might have entertained the idea that perhaps Roland had used the gift of Sedgwick for Tess to bring them together, but that seemed altogether too fanciful, even for him.

Everard, however, wasn't above any number of schemes, impossible or not. He had never been in his father's favor, never had gold in his hand for longer than it took him to find the nearest inn, and would have happily plundered his father's coffers if he'd had the chance. If he had, eight years ago, understood the missive he'd been given and precisely what it meant, he would have no doubt used the time gate then and there, hoping to find more accessible coffers to delve into. The thing was, though, if Everard had managed to find himself in the Future, he never would have left it. The riches were too tantalizing and the marvels, even for a lad of as little true wit as Everard, too mesmerizing to trade again for the simplicity of medieval England.

Besides, Everard was still in the past, a thing John knew because apparently Montgomery had dealt with the lout not two months earlier.

Unless Everard had forced the gate to bend to his will. If that was true, then he might have used it time and time again, accustomed himself to future mores, then decided to come back to the past to annoy Montgomery.

John drew his gloved hand over his eyes. That made no sense, but he wasn't sure making sense was anything any of those from Chevington did on a regular basis.

At least he could say with certainty that there was no possible way Roland would have suspected that he and Tess would travel back in time, never mind the irony of their having done so from the forest near Chevington.

Though the only reason he'd found a time gate in the forest at all had been because his sword had been driven into the ground right next to it.

That was another mystery that gave him a sharp pain between the eyes. Whoever had stolen his sword had obviously placed it cunningly next to a time gate, but the question was why. Merely to send him back in time? To what end? If Roland had wanted him dead, there was little point in stealing his sword, then sending him back to the past. If Everard had wanted him dead, he could have slain him at any point in time with a bullet to his head.

Why either of them—if they were his only suspects—would have wanted him back in medieval England where they had to have known he would be surrounded by his very intimidating brothers was something he simply couldn't understand.

He sighed deeply. Perhaps 'twas nothing more than coincidence. He wondered how many other poor souls had stepped on an unassuming patch of forest ground and wound up where they hadn't intended to go. At least at Artane, the gate made the hair on the back of one's neck stand up. That spot at Chevington hadn't done more than make him slightly ill, though he fully intended to use it again. At least that way he and Tess would be able to collect their gear from the castle and get themselves on a train back home.

The thought of that was enough to leave him feeling slightly disembodied, as if his soul wasn't quite sure which century it should cling to. He hadn't had that sensation all that often in the Future, but then again, he'd done his best to forget his past, and he'd avoided like the plague any medieval historical sites.

A consideration of that irony took him inside Segrave's gates where he found he was having a bit more trouble remaining unaffected than he would have suspected he might. It was difficult to remember he was a man of almost a score and eight, not a lad of ten winters as he rode beneath the barbican and was assaulted by the sights and sounds of a place he had loved to visit in his youth.

He thought he might have been rather glad not to have gone to Artane, truth be told.

He looked at Tess sitting beside him and smiled as best he could. "How are you?"

She returned his smile, albeit weakly. "Segrave is very impressive. I had no idea."

"I think that means I don't dare ask what it looks like in the Future."

"I don't think you do," she agreed slowly, "though you'll be glad to know the National Trust has done a tremendous job with the grounds."

He winced. "Then I'll assume the castle hasn't fared so well. At least at Sedgwick, I can keep you safely tucked behind three portcullises."

"Can you live in a castle for the rest of your days?" she asked with half a smile.

"If you're mistress of it, then aye," he said pleasantly. "Especially if it boasts running water and a lovely Aga in the kitchens. I think we'll manage to make do."

"I imagine we will," she agreed quietly.

She didn't look completely convinced, so he sent her a look that made her sigh lightly. Obviously, his work was undone.

But that would have to come later, when he had a bit of privacy for it. He concentrated on not looking affected by his surroundings. It was, fortunately, not quite dawn, which at least gave him the cover of darkness for his rampaging emotions. He managed to get off his own horse without incident, help Tess down from hers, then keep her hand in his as he waited for his family to gather themselves together. He was happy to let Robin lead the way into the keep, make polite conversation with the steward, then see them all shepherded upstairs to Joanna's bedchamber.

It was something of a surprise to see his grandmother looking so frail, given that he'd never seen her doing anything but leading whatever charge she'd decided upon. She was lucid, though, and didn't seem to be in any pain. If her time had come, he could only wish for her that her passing would be peaceful and easy.

He waited until the rest of his siblings and Jake had greeted her before he took Tess's hand and a deep breath, then went to kneel down by his grandmother's bedside.

She sat up and looked at him in surprise. "John," she croaked. "You dratted rogue, where have you been?"

"Ah—"

"I can see by the looks of your lady—who must be somehow related to my darling Persephone—that your time has been wisely spent."

John smiled. "Grandmère, should you be using so much breath for speaking?"

She leaned over and put her bony but surprisingly strong arms around him, then hugged him tightly. "I want the entire tale, when I've recovered from this shock. I wept over you, you terrible boy."

"I'm sorry, Grandmère," he said sincerely, attempting a smile as he helped her lie back down. "I was detained."

"I won't ask where." She gestured toward Tess. "Introduce us, if you have any manners left."

"My betrothed," John said, shooting Tess a quick smile. "Tess Alexander. And she is, as you guessed, Persephone's sister."

"I would be very interested in the circumstances of your meeting, but I'll have that from your lady. From you, I'll have a song or two. Go fetch a lute, John my lad, and let's see if you've forgotten all I paid so dearly to have pounded into your wee head."

John rose to do just that, but Robin waved him off and left to apparently see to it himself. Joanna patted the side of her bed.

"Come and sit with me, Mistress Tess, and tell me of yourself and how it was you met my Johnny. He's my second favorite grandson, you know. *All* my great-grandchildren are my favorites because 'tis impossible to choose between them. A fine brood, aren't they?"

"They are indeed, my lady," Tess said, sitting down and taking Joanna's proffered hand. "I don't think I could choose, either."

Joanna regarded her shrewdly for a moment or two, then nodded. "My tale, gel, if you please. Spare no details, however shocking. "

John could hardly wait to see what Tess would come up with, but he had the feeling his bad behavior would figure prominently. The best he could hope for was to provide a little musical distraction before Tess had to provide other, more startling details about things his grandmother surely wouldn't believe.

*I*t was late in the morning when he found himself released from his labors and that only because Joanna had fallen asleep. He laid the lute aside for future use, then rose and stretched.

"A walk, Tess?" he asked.

She nodded and rose to leave quietly with him. John pursed his lips at the warning look from Robin, then took Tess's hand and left the bedchamber. He looked at her.

"Food?"

"Your grandmother's been feeding us all morning," she said with a smile. "Gracious even while not feeling her best."

"Any redeeming qualities we have, we can thank her for," John agreed.

He walked with her down the stairs and through the great hall, realizing only as he put her cloak around her shoulders that she was trembling. He turned her to him and looked at her in surprise. "What is it?"

"I'm just nervous. I've never had future in-laws before. Parents-in-law, actually." She took a deep breath. "I'm not sure they'll like me very well, especially considering that I'm taking—"

"I'm going," he corrected. "Home, with you. And they will love you, not just because I love you. My father will be thrilled to have someone to argue politics with and my mother will love you because you've agreed to put up with me. If we make our home a bit farther away than their other children, then so be it."

She looked up at him seriously. "You know, you might find someone here to love."

"So might you."

She blinked, then smiled. "I'm not looking."

"Neither am I," he said, "and since that's finally settled, let's go watch the sunset, such as it is. From the ground, in deference to you."

"Good of you."

He laughed and opened the door for her, then walked outside and into a solid shape that almost had him bouncing backward. He looked at the man, an apology on his lips, then he froze.

It was Montgomery.

"Tess!"

He found himself shoved out of the way by a dark-haired beauty who he could only assume was Pippa, given how much she resembled Tess. He regained his balance in time to watch Pippa throw her arms around his future wife.

Tears were shed.

John stepped backward to allow the sisterly reunion to go on in comfort, then looked at his brother, who was gaping at him in much the same manner as he suspected he himself was using.

"Bloody hell," Montgomery gasped, then he stepped forward and tried to choke the life from John.

John would have laughed, but he was too close to expressing a different sort of emotion. So he returned his brother's embrace, exchanged several rounds of manly backslapping, curses, and the occasional kiss on the cheek. At least it was more dignified than what was going on to his right, which was a supremely feminine display of overwrought emotion.

He found himself eventually standing shoulder to shoulder with his brother, watching the sisters fall apart. He looked at Montgomery.

"Embarrassing."

Montgomery laughed. "Isn't it, though? I would suggest we retreat somewhere for a bit of privacy, but I'm not sure we should interrupt them." He looked at John assessingly. "I hesitate to ask where you and Tess met."

"You'd hesitate even more fully if you knew that she'd had the title of Countess of Sedgwick bestowed upon her not a fortnight ago."

"Wedding your betters?" Montgomery asked with a smirk.

John laughed in spite of himself. "Aye, and you've been spending too much time with Robin, apparently." He shook his head. "I vow I can hardly believe you've grown so much."

"I can wield my sword, too," Montgomery said solemnly. "Astonishing, isn't it?"

"I would say we should step outside and test that, but I fear you would find me gravely lacking—despite Rob and Nick's attentions to my poor swordplay over the past few days. I'll indulge you later, if you like."

"Agreed," Montgomery said. He looked at Pippa and Tess. "We should perhaps sequester those two in Grandmère's solar sooner rather than later. And I should pay my respects."

"Joanna's sleeping, but Robin promised to alert us when she wakes." He paused. "It would give us time to talk for a bit. I have a tale to tell you."

"I imagine you do," Montgomery said dryly. He looked at John, then shook his head. "I will tell you, if you care to hear it, that I never thought you were dead. I find myself now quite unsurprised to assume that you were loitering in Tess's time."

"It was a happy series of coincidences," John said.

"I imagine so. You can tell Father all about them tomorrow. He would be here now, but he was caught in London and had to flatter the king. I doubt that will last very long."

John shook his head. He couldn't have been further away

from the throne in the Future yet here his family interacted with the king more often than they were happy about.

Montgomery put his hand on John's shoulder. "Let's collect our ladies and find somewhere comfortable to sit. I have the feeling it's going to be a long afternoon." He shot John a look. "I'm happy to see you."

John could only nod, because if he'd said anything else, he likely would have displayed more emotion than he cared to. He stood slightly apart and watched his brother brave the sisterly bit of tumult still going on. Montgomery hugged Tess and inquired—in modern English, no less—how her journey had been so far and if John had been behaving himself. Tess provided him with very brief answers, but promised more in return for copious details about his and Pippa's marriage. Montgomery offered his arms to the sisters, then started across the great hall with him.

Tess smiled up at Montgomery, then stopped and looked over her shoulder. She held out her hand and waited. John took a deep breath and walked forward to take that outstretched hand.

"Still have battery on your phone?" she asked.

"Aye, enough. Why?"

"I wonder what Robin would do if we asked him to take a picture of the four of us," she said. "For posterity's sake."

John could imagine very well just what his brother would say, but since it would give him something to shake his head over for years to come, John was all for it. He brought Tess's hand to his lips, then smiled at her. "I'll ask him later. For now, you might want to . . ."

"And you might want to as well," she said quietly.

He took a deep breath, because she obviously knew he was talking about spending time with Montgomery and Pippa. He had no doubt that when the time came, he would leave medieval England behind without looking back over his shoulder, but until then . . . well, there was no sense in engaging in maudlin displays when he could instead be mocking his brother for having been talked into taking on Sedgwick.

He would also have to give serious thought to what he would say when his father arrived. He knew if he thought the most difficult part of his journey was behind him, he was deluding himself. First his father, then a frank discussion with Montgomery about Everard of Chevington and what mischief he'd been combining.

He wasn't sure which of those conversations would be more difficult.

"Are you all right?"

He dragged himself back from uncomfortable places, smiled at Tess, then nodded. He squeezed her hand and continued across the floor with her, happy for the moment to put off difficult things for a bit longer.

Chapter 29

Tess sat in Segrave's solar, holding her sister's hands and trying not to weep.

Well, she actually wasn't trying very hard only because she'd already lost it there in the great hall and gotten it mostly out of her system. She'd known, of course, that she would be running into Pippa eventually; she just hadn't expected it to be so abruptly. She couldn't deny that Pippa was absolutely glowing with happiness, which eased her heart quite a bit. Obviously being married to a de Piaget lad agreed with her.

She glanced at John and Montgomery sitting there laughing together as if they'd never spent a day apart. She had known her fair share of twins over the years, but somehow she'd never been as startled looking at them as she was looking at her brother-in-law and her, well, her fiancé. She watched them for a bit more, then looked at Pippa.

"Is this killing you like it's killing me?"

Pippa shook her head. "I'm not sure I can talk about it, so let's talk about something else. Tell me how you met John."

Tess was happy to distract them both with less heart-wrenching details. "I knocked off a mirror a while back, just to give the local mechanic something to do, and walked into the shop only to find the owner not exactly who I'd expected him to be."

Pippa smiled. "John?"

"Yes," Tess said, feeling suddenly a little breathless at how easy it would have been never to have crossed paths with him. If he'd been interested in something besides cars, or she'd never taken Sedgwick, or—

"What did you do when you saw him?"

"About fainted," Tess said, dragging herself away from unproductive thoughts. "I didn't say anything about knowing who he was, of course, especially since he kept telling me he didn't think we should see each other again."

"Self-defense," John put in, in English.

Pippa laughed at him. "Did she make you crazy?"

"Absolutely," he said without hesitation. "Still does. In a *good* way, of course."

Tess smiled wryly at him, then turned back to her sister. "I won't give away all his secrets. Let's just say it was a little improbable to watch a guy walking around in the twenty-first century when I knew he'd been born in the thirteenth. Especially when he was doing everything he could to make sure no one knew what was going on. I wish you could have seen his face the first time he met Stephen."

"I would have loved it," Pippa said cheerfully. "So, when did you tell him what you knew?"

"About three days into our excellent adventure in medieval England." She paused. "I don't think he was happy with my revelations, but what else was I going to do? I couldn't bring myself to tell him what I knew while we were in the future, but I didn't have much choice here in the past."

"I understand, believe me," Pippa said. She smiled at Montgomery, then turned back to Tess. "What now—" She stopped abruptly. "Never mind."

"A visit," Tess managed.

Pippa smiled faintly. "I wish you'd make more of them."

Tess had to take a deep breath. "We'll try. And I'll bring Peaches next time."

"How is she? Still rescuing people from their junk drawers?"

Tess nodded, then happily filled her sister in on the things she'd missed over the past couple of months. It was as if no time at all had passed, no grief, no traipsing through time that belonged within the pages of a book instead of in her life. And once she was finished with all the details she thought Pippa would want to know, she listened to what her sister had been doing eight centuries in the past. She even found it in her to laugh a time or two at the vagaries of medieval life.

Pippa paused and looked up as the door opened. Tess did, too, expecting to find Robin there, having come to call them back upstairs.

Only it wasn't Robin.

It was an older version of him who was followed into the solar by a woman who could have been no other than Amanda's mother. That meant that the man who had come to so sudden a stop that his wife had run into his back was none other than John's father, Rhys de Piaget.

Montgomery rose immediately. "Father," he said, surprised. "I thought you were caught in London."

"Escaped early," Rhys said, his tone garbled.

Tess watched John shoot her a look she didn't have any trouble deciphering—he was about three seconds from coming undone—before he rose and turned slightly to face his father.

Tess wasn't sure what was harder to watch: the look of absolute shock on Rhys's face, or the tears that suddenly streamed down Gwen's. Before John could even move, his mother had pushed aside her husband rushed forward to throw her arms around him. Rhys swore, then stepped forward and wrapped both of them in an embrace Tess wasn't sure he would ever break. She looked away out of respect, but she had no trouble hearing the grief that all three of them indulged in.

It went on just as long as she'd suspected it might, ending only with Rhys pulling back and greeting John with loving words.

"You bloody fool," he said hoarsely. "What in the bloody *hell* were you thinking?"

John took a deep breath. "I left word, but it was . . . diverted."

"And you couldn't have found another of those . . . those *things* to use to come home?" Rhys demanded. "You didn't look?"

"I did look, Father," John said patiently. "Things went awry."

"I don't doubt that, but why you couldn't have found another way to leave that accursed place behind I surely don't—"

"Father," John said in a low voice that was nonetheless full of warning.

Rhys seemed to realize suddenly that he wasn't alone with his son. Tess watched as he dragged his sleeve across his face and took a deep breath. He greeted Montgomery properly, then walked over to pull Pippa up out of her chair and embrace her. He took her face and kissed her forehead.

"The journey here wasn't too taxing, daughter?" he asked with a smile.

"Nay, my lord," Pippa said, in perfect medieval French. "Montgomery, as always, made it a pleasant excursion for me."

Rhys released her and paused. Tess stood when he turned to her, because it was the thing to do, though she wasn't exactly sure her knees would hold up under the strain. Rhys's assessment of her was quick and brutal, but his subsequent smile was no less charming than it had been for Pippa.

"A sister," he mused. "Either Tess or Peaches, I would say, but I'm not sure how to tell. Then again, I couldn't tell my lads apart half the time, so I'm not the best judge of these things."

"I'm Tess," Tess managed. "'Tis a pleasure to meet you, my lord."

Rhys considered her, then stepped back so he could look at John as well. "I sense something going on here that I wasn't informed about."

John looked at his father gravely. "I had the great fortune to meet Tess . . . well, we met because of a fortuitous set of circumstances. And aye, there is something between us as you'll notice if you'll mark her left hand."

"I wonder if you've wooed her properly up to now," Rhys said with a frown, "or if I should be taking matters and this sweet girl under my protection until you display all that chivalry I instilled in you."

Gwen laughed a little, then elbowed him out of the way and embraced Tess warmly.

"Ignore my husband," Gwen said, pulling back and smiling at her. "It bothers him when his children go on to lead useful, productive lives without his aid."

"It doesn't," Rhys protested. "I just like to have a say in the timing of those lives. And since this lovely gel here is indeed wearing one of Jake's rings on her finger, I fear I've arrived too late to see that she's been properly courted. Fortunately we have come in time for me to remedy what I can."

"Find a chair," Gwen suggested. "I think you'll have nothing at all to say about this save *congratulations*. John is old enough to choose his own bride, and I daresay Tess can decide where her heart has led her."

"We aren't wed," Tess offered.

"But we will be soon," John said pointedly.

"Excellent," Rhys said, rubbing his hands together. "That will give me a chance to dower her properly since I don't see her father here." He shot Tess a look. "Your sister has told me quite a bit about your parents."

Tess nodded, finding herself rather happier than usual that she'd taken the trouble to become fluent in modern French. It made navigating the medieval Norman version of it quite a bit easier. She imagined her efforts wouldn't necessarily make John's parents feel any better about losing him yet again, but at least they would know she could understand him should he feel the need to fall back into the native tongue.

Rhys unclasped his cloak, helped Gwen off with hers, then tossed both over a chair. "I think we'll have some refreshment, children, then assess the battlefield and see what must be done from here. John, help me find the kitchens. I won't even say anything vile about your grandmother's propensity to starve me every time I visit, but not being able to now. I imagine she left instructions behind for my care and feeding."

Tess exchanged a brief glance with John, who looked as if he were contemplating a trip to the gallows, then watched him leave with his father. She imagined it might take a bit longer to fetch snacks than Rhys had let on.

She turned to Gwen once the door was shut. Gwen smiled.

"Tell me of him," she said, her eyes glistening. "It shouldn't be difficult to think of him as a man, but I find it is. Are his manners acceptable?"

Tess was happy to launch into a recounting of John's finer points for his mother, grateful that Gwen was being so gracious to her even though she had to know Tess was what would take her son away from her again.

She wished Nicholas had come along for the ride. She might have found it necessary to pull him aside and ask for a few pointers.

She'd barely gotten through the story of her meeting John and a decent recounting of subsequent incidents of medieval behavior before the solar door was thrown open again and Robin stood there, slightly out of breath.

"Grandmother calls for us all—oh, hello, Mama. I didn't realize you were here, but none too soon, I'd say." He held out his hand and helped her to her feet, then tugged her across toward the door. "She has pronouncements. I don't mean to be too blunt, but she's hanging on just to make them, if you want my opinion."

Gwen let out a shuddering breath. "Give me your arm, Robin. I find I'm not as prepared for this as I thought I would be."

"Mama, she's outlived Eleanor by a year and still boasting of it. I'm not sure you can ask more of her than that."

Tess hung back as Pippa and Montgomery walked toward the door. Pippa looked at her in surprise.

"What are you doing?"

"This is family," Tess said, feeling altogether uncomfortable.

"Which you are," Montgomery said. "Come along with us, Tess. I guarantee she'll call for you also."

Tess couldn't imagine that, but she supposed it was less obtrusive to go upstairs than it was to remain behind. She walked behind Montgomery and Pippa, trying not to dwell on the absolute improbability of following her medieval sister and that sister's husband down a hallway that wouldn't survive the ravages of time.

She went inside Joanna's bedchamber but pressed herself back against the wall and tried to be inconspicuous. John came in only a handful of minutes later, looked for her immediately and lifted his eyebrows briefly. He looked as if he'd been through something, but his father looked undamaged where he stood next to him, so perhaps they'd gotten through it without incident.

Joanna was propped up on pillows, ordering everyone into places as if she were a field general and they her loyal troops. The great-grandchildren were called first, kissed, admired, and instructed what of hers they were to have. Tess didn't pay too much attention to it besides Joanna telling Rose she would have left her the keep if she'd been able to and instructing Kendrick to keep hold of the gold she was giving him to make repairs to whatever mechanics of familial keeps he destroyed.

She bid farewell to her grandchildren in what seemed to be no particular order, giving them instructions as well, and gifts that they received with reluctance but bowing to her wishes. She looked at Gwen, who sat on the far side of her bed.

"You'll tell Isabelle that I loved her," Joanna said. "I know she was near her time. And you'll do the same for Jennifer. She's a lovely gel, and I'll miss listening to her music. Tell Nicky he's still my favorite."

"Of course, Mother," Gwen said, tears streaming down her cheeks. "Whatever you wish."

"What I wish is that you would stop feeding your husband such rich food. Look how he stands there and glowers at me."

"I'm trying not to unman myself by weeping," Rhys said dryly.

Joanna scowled at him, then took a deep breath. "I suppose that leaves me just a thing or two more to do before I go. You all seem to be very well settled in lovely keeps. Well, save my wee Johnny, so I suppose that means he should come and sit by me."

John perched on the edge of her bed and took her hands. "I don't need anything, Grandmère—"

"Of course you do," Joanna interrupted him, "for more reasons than to provide your bride with a decent life." She looked around John. "Rob, love, go fetch the priest and a scribe."

"Priest?" Robin squeaked.

"Make haste," Joanna said sharply. "By the saints, whelp, think you I have all day for this business? I've a marriage to witness, then I think I'll sleep. I'm very tired."

Tess watched John look at his mother. "Marriage?" he mouthed.

"Yours," Joanna said distinctly, "to that very lovely gel huddled against the wall where she shouldn't be hiding. Come over here, Tess. You'll have to humor an old woman this afternoon."

Tess went, because she didn't dare do anything else. Joanna looked at her closely.

"Want him, do you?"

"Aye, my lady," Tess said, because it was true. "Though I live very far away—"

"Aye, I know all about that," Joanna said, waving dismissively, "though I won't talk about it in front of the bairns. I pried Jennifer's details from her one afternoon, though I'll admit it was during the midst of one of her labors and her resistance was a bit weaker than it might have been otherwise. If you're of her ilk, then I know all about where you live. I can only assume John's been loitering in the same place."

"Aye," John managed. "I have been."

Joanna pursed her lips. "Well, this will put a bit of a crimp in your plans, but you two will work things out, I imagine. Where is that lazy priest of mine?"

"Here, my lady!" a man said breathlessly, bursting into the room. "I'm here with my scribe."

"Robin, recount everything," Joanna said, sounding truly weary for the first time that afternoon. "But be quick about it."

Robin ran through the list without hesitation, the scribe scribbled, and Joanna nodded.

"Witness it," she said. "Whoever wants to contest it can fight with you, Robin, after the fact." She looked at Rhys. "Roland of Chevington was here last night, trying to convince me to leave Segrave to him. I understand that Richard disowned him a fort-night ago—again. He was very keen to be his father's overlord, which I can scarce fault him for."

"He's a cheeky whoreson," Rhys said cheerfully. "Though he learned that from his sire. I wouldn't be surprised to watch Rich-ard go to the king and try to have Chevington and Segrave both."

"Which is why I fully intend to see both thwarted myself, lest your generous heart overwhelm you and you lose your senses long enough to make him a present of my hall." She looked at Robin. "Assure yourself that the scribe takes this down properly. The bulk of my gold your father can see distributed as he wishes, but your grandsire's title and the keep go to John."

Tess had to sit down on the bed.

Joanna looked at her. "You needn't live here, gel, but I want him to have the title. Second-favorite grandson and all. 'Tis his reward for all those years spent at the lute." She glanced at John shrewdly. "Well? Nothing to say?"

John cleared his throat. "Grandmère," he said slowly, "I'm not sure how—"

"You'd best determine *how*, hadn't you, whelp?" Joanna said briskly. "Now, I'll see you and your lady wed, then I want another round of kisses and sweet embraces whilst earthly breath remains me. Father Edward!"

The priest leaped forward. "Aye, Lady Joanna?"

"Wed these two here," Joanna said with a languid gesture. "But be quick about it."

Tess watched John rise, then turn and hold out his hands for her. She put her hands into his, faintly reassured to find his hands were not quite as steady as they looked.

"Well," he murmured.

"I'm not about to argue with her," Tess said, feeling slightly breathless.

"It's best not to," he agreed. He turned to the priest. "As for a recounting—"

"Skip that part," Joanna instructed. "Rhys, give this sweet girl some of my gold and a pair of horses. John no doubt has enough of his own to see to her comfort in the future. John, wed her and bed her so I can go to my rest peacefully."

Tess found that she was blushing as she knelt next to John in front of the priest. She looked at John and had a smile for her trouble.

"Want to change your mind?" he asked.

"No," she said without hesitation. "You?"

He shook his head with a slow smile. "At least Pippa will get to watch."

That was something, at least. Tess supposed someone would tell her later what the priest had said. She understood the Latin, of course, but she was slightly distracted by the fact that she was marrying the Earl of Segrave, who would have a keep eight centuries in the past that he was responsible for while he would be concurrently carrying on an ordinary life in the future.

And then John kissed her and she couldn't think at all.

She only realized that the noise bothering her was feet pounding down the passageway instead of blood thundering in her ears because the bedchamber door was thrown open.

"We're under assault," a man exclaimed.

Rhys turned immediately. "By whom?"

"Chevington colors."

John pushed himself to his feet, swearing. He was joined in his opinions by several of his closest relations, most notably Joanna, who obviously had no use for anyone from Chevington.

"John, you'd best lead the charge," she said firmly, "carrying the title as you do. I'll stay here with the gels whilst you lads go see to the annoyance. Gwen, find me a dagger. Amanda, I'm assuming you have a blade or two tucked into your boots?"

Tess thought it best to get herself out of the middle of the fray, as it were, though that made her lose track of John sooner than she would have liked. She finally managed to push through the press of people and get herself out into the passageway. She made a grab for his arm before he ran off.

"Where are you going?" she asked, feeling slightly terrified by the prospect of his taking a sword and using it in a pitched battle.

"Out to keep you safe," he said. He shrugged. "Not to worry."

"Not to worry?" she echoed incredulously. "But, John—"

He pulled her into his arms and kissed her briefly. "Stay," he commanded.

"John—"

"Stay behind, Tess," he said seriously, "as a good medieval wife should."

"But—"

He smiled. "You don't think I'm about to wed you and be too dead not to fulfill the rest of my grandmother's commands, do you?"

"I don't know what to think," she managed, feeling light-headed. "John, this isn't a movie scene—" She shut her mouth abruptly at the look on his face. She put her arms around him and held him tightly. "You don't have to say it. I know you've done this before. At least I think you've done this before."

"I have, and come away unscathed." He took her face in his hands and kissed her briefly. "Go back inside that bedchamber, sit with my mother, sisters, and nieces, and wait for me. I'll be back when I'm finished outside. If someone tries to break down the door, clout them over the head with a fire iron."

She knew he was trying to make her laugh, but she honestly couldn't. The realities of his former life were staring her in the face, and she didn't like them.

"My time period," he said quietly. "My rules."

"And when do my rules apply?"

"We'll negotiate that later, when we have the leisure to do so. I'll tell you right now, however, that there will never be any negotiation where your safety is concerned." He kissed her again, then turned and walked away. "Go back inside," he called over his shoulder.

She started to, then stood with her hand on the door. He turned at the top step.

"I love you," he said quietly.

"I love you," she managed.

He held up his hand, then disappeared down the stairs.

Tess turned and walked into the bedroom only to walk bodily into her sister. She didn't protest when Pippa took her by the arm, then shut the door and bolted it. It was all she could do to get herself over to a chair and sit down before her knees gave way. She looked up at her sister. "How do you stand this?"

"All part of the territory, sister dear," Pippa said gently. "You can still play the lute, can't you?"

"Now?" Tess asked incredulously. "And yes, I play, but very badly."

"Play for Joanna anyway. She'll love you for it."

Tess soon found she didn't have any choice. She dredged up the two things she knew, played them very badly indeed, then toyed with a few Renaissance things she'd learned to pad her repertoire. She was quite happy eventually when Amanda's daughter Rose volunteered to demonstrate to her grandmother the things she'd been learning. She waited until everyone was resettled before she drew her sister aside and prepared to grill her quietly about the Chevington boys and what they'd been up to.

She had the feeling knowing that might mean the difference between John's life and death.

Chapter 30

J *ohn* wasn't sure if chain mail was going to be a help or a hindrance, but he didn't protest when his father helped him into it. He wasn't unused to battle, but he had to concede that eight years of being away from it left him feeling rather less prepared for it than he would have been otherwise. No sense in not being protected against an attack he might not see coming.

Rhys put his hand on John's shoulder. "We'll finish our conversation later, after this annoyance is seen to. And after that conversation, I intend to have a goodly bit of speech with your wife. I'm sure she'll provide me with details of yours I'll be most interested in."

"She's a scholar, just so you know," John said. "Her specialty is medieval political thought."

Rhys blinked in surprise, then laughed. "You're not serious."

"Oh, I am. She has her degree from Cambridge."

"Does she, indeed?" Rhys asked in surprised. "I can scarce believe the place still exists. I assumed the windbags there would blow it over somewhere in the fifteenth century."

"It wasn't for a lack of trying, I'm sure," John said dryly. He stretched, but there was no hope for finding any comfort from that. "That damned Everard. What is he thinking?"

"You're assuming 'tis Everard who vexes us," Rhys said. "For all we know, 'tis Roland behind this idiocy."

"Nay," Montgomery said, walking up to them and shaking his head. "Everard wants Segrave much worse than Roland ever did. I'm quite sure he's been loitering in the area like a carrion bird, waiting for the spoils. " He smiled. "Canny of Joanna to thwart him by giving the keep to you, wasn't it? You might have to come back now and again to see how your crops are coming and keep Everard out of your larder."

John blew out his breath. "I can't think about that right now. Let's go rid ourselves of this plague, then discuss it later over a decent supper."

"And then to the standing up," Robin said cheerfully from behind him. "And to think I feared I might miss out on that joy with you."

John turned around. "Have you managed it with *any* of your siblings?"

"Nay," Robin admitted with a grin, "but hope, as they say, springs eternal."

"Not with me it doesn't," John said. "So wipe that smirk off your face before I must see to it myself."

Robin only smirked once more, then laughed as he walked away with their father. John scowled at his back, then looked at Montgomery, who was standing next to him, watching him with a faint smile.

"You aren't going to echo him, are you?" John asked in disbelief.

Montgomery smiled more deeply. "Of coure not. And if it makes you feel any better, he tried the same thing with me. I left him with the aftereffects of my fist in his mouth. Miles finished the job whilst I went off to more pleasant labors."

"The saints be praised for brothers with sense." He shrugged his shoulders again to adjust his mail, then blew out his breath. He wasn't unaccustomed to a case of nerves before a battle or a tourney, but in the past all that had been at stake had been either his honor or his own life. Now . . . now he had much more to worry about.

He shoved his worries aside. He had been in enough battles over the course of his youth to believe he could emerge from one more unscathed. His sojourn in the Future had added eight years of learning to fight with his hands and feet, something no medieval knight would expect. If he found himself in true danger, he would toss aside his honor and do what was necessary to keep himself alive.

He looked up at the sky that threatened rain, then back at his brother. He wished he'd had the chance to talk to Montgomery in more detail before, but there was nothing to be done about that now.

"When did you see Everard last?" he asked, settling for a question that wouldn't require aught but a brief answer.

"A pair of months ago," Montgomery said. "I cast him from my hall, though I'll admit I have wished since that I'd kept him close a bit longer. He had rallied a handful of my garrison knights to his banner, but I imagine they soon realized that they had made a grave mistake in following him." He paused, then looked at John seriously. "I've been curious about his activities, especially given that he watched Pippa come through the gate at the end of my drawbridge."

"Do you think he had any idea what he was seeing?" John asked unwillingly. Though he would have liked to have believed that Everard was the fool his brothers thought him, there was simply no guaranteeing that the man hadn't watched eight years ago as John disappeared into that gate near Artane. If he had subsequently watched Pippa do the same near Sedgwick, then . . .

"I doubt he had any idea what he'd witnessed," Montgomery said. "Besides, if he had gained the Future, why would he have returned to our time?"

"To make a spectacle of himself?"

Montgomery smiled. "This is a great deal of trouble for that, don't you think? Nay, I suspect 'tis nothing more than it looks. He wants Segrave and thinks that an attack at this moment, when we're likely caught up in our grief over Joanna's impending passing, will win him what he wants."

John was willing to try to believe that—at least until he could prove otherwise. He looked up to find his father coming back toward him. "Who leads the charge?"

"Some burly lad wearing Chevington colors who isn't Everard," Rhys answered, "though I imagine Everard is lurking somewhere in the company. Why do you ask?"

"Just resigning myself to a pair of hours spent schooling the whoreson in manners when I find him," John said with a sigh. "I'm for having that over with as quickly as possible."

Rhys nodded, clapped him on the shoulder, then went to take the reins of his horse from a squire.

John swung up onto the back of his borrowed horse and rode through the gates, then found himself back in a medieval frame of mind without having to try. The battle began without fanfare, but with a desperation on the part of Everard's lads that was unusual. Perhaps Everard had inspired his men more successfully than Montgomery had supposed he might.

Not that it would matter, in the end. His father and siblings were still formidable, their men terrifying. John was profoundly relieved to be fighting with them, not against them. It was almost as if no time had passed since the last time he'd stepped out into a fray with Montgomery on his left. He hardly had to give thought to what he was doing, which provided him with the opportunity to look for Everard. He didn't see him, but then again, chainmail coifs weren't precisely made to reveal who the wearers might be.

Or, he realized with a start, perhaps not, for there was at least one lad he recognized.

Roland of Chevington, loitering uselessly at the rear of the press.

It was at that moment that something else occurred to him, something that left him feeling as if he'd taken an enthusiastic fist to his gut.

If Tess had it aright—and he had no reason to think otherwise— and Roland of Chevington was in the Future Roland of Sedgwick, then the man who was fighting feebly with his sword was in a great bloody bit of danger at the moment. All it would take was a stray bolt from a crossbow, or a purposeful sword between the ribs to render him quite dead. And if he were dead—

"John?"

John looked at Montgomery who was still beside him. "What?"

"You look as if you'd seen a ghost," Montgomery said with a frown. "What is it?"

"Tess thinks that Roland is the man who gave her the keep in the Future," John said hoarsely. "Your keep, I mean. And if he dies now without going to the Future, then—"

Montgomery blanched. "Pippa never falls into my moat, and you don't meet Tess."

"Exactly."

"Bloody hell," Montgomery managed.

John left his brother to a renewed enthusiasm for his work and cut his way across the field over toward Roland. Perhaps he was imagining it, but it seemed as though things heated up in direct proportion to how close he came to the key to his future. Perhaps Everard's lads had been told there was treasure inside Segrave and Roland was the one to help them procure it. It was odd that they were fighting so fiercely with no one to lead them, but perhaps those tales of spoils had been rather more embellished than they should have been.

Or so he thought until he realized that they weren't leaderless.

Everard of Chevington stepped out from behind a group of very large soldiers and looked at John with a smirk.

John realized with a start that Everard had a pair of sunglasses hanging around his neck. It was without a doubt the most ridiculous thing he'd ever seen on a battlefield. He would have wasted the breath to mock him, but he suddenly didn't have any breath because the ramifications of what he'd seen hit him.

Everard was sporting sunglasses, which meant he had gone to the Future. He had made sure John saw them so *John* would know he had gone to the Future. And for the final blow, he looked at Roland, looked back at John, then lifted his eyebrows briefly before he began to move purposefully toward his brother.

John would have bet his life it wasn't to keep that brother safe.

In fact, he was certain it was quite the opposite. He swung down off his mount, because he felt more comfortable on his feet, then fought furiously with men who had obviously been instructed to concentrate solely on him. He would have called for aid, but he was too busy trying to keep his body unpierced by half a dozen well-wielded swords. He looked for Roland out of the corner of his eye, then swore viciously.

Roland was cowering, holding his sword over his head and using it as a shield against his brother's relentless attack.

Everard finally cursed, then simply reached out and took the sword away from his brother. He slapped him with it, then tossed it aside in disgust. He looked at John.

And he smiled.

John fought as if his life depended on it because, as it happened, it just might. He cast aside his honor and any pretense of fighting fairly. He slew half the men facing him with the sword, then used dirty street-fighting to render the rest of them senseless. If Roland died . . .

He shoved the last man out of his way, then sprinted across the distance that separated him from the brothers, hoping he would get there before Everard's falling sword cleaved Roland's skull in twain. He slew the final man standing in his way, then flung himself forward again.

He stopped Everard's sword with his own approximately three inches from Roland's empty head.

He shoved Everard backward by means of a foot in his belly, then put himself in front of Roland. Everard regained his balance, then stepped back, accompanied by a look of utter boredom.

"It seems unsporting to slay your brother," John said, his chest heaving.

Everard only shrugged carelessly. In his eyes, though, there was a callousness that was chilling.

John looked over his shoulder at Roland and jerked his head toward the keep. Roland took the hint and decamped for safer environs. John watched him run bodily into Jake who seemed happy enough to take him in hand. John nodded his thanks, then turned back to the fool in front of him. He watched as Everard lifted his sunglasses up and frowned thoughtfully at the blood spattered on them.

"Buy those at Boots?" John asked pointedly, suppressing the urge to reach out and make a grab for them so he might strangle the whoreson with the strap.

"I did, actually." He allowed his sunglasses to drop back down to his chest, then patted them affectionately. "I'm finding your adopted time to be much to my liking."

John rested his sword against his shoulder. Roland was safe and most of Everard's men had been rendered unable to aid their leader, so he might as well have a few answers for his trouble. "How have you managed?"

Everard shrugged. "I threw my lot in with a group of fools pretending to be knights. One of them was willing to ferry me about in his car after I told him I would share with him the hidden treasure only I knew was lying in Sedgwick's cellar. As for anything else, 'twas simply good fortune to drive through the village near Sedgwick and see you standing outside your shop."

"Then you're the one who took my sword," John said flatly.

"Of course," Everard said pleasantly. "And I did a smashing job of laying out tea, didn't I?"

John pursed his lips and decided that didn't merit an answer. "Why vex me?"

The change in Everard's mien was swift and unsettling. "Because I loathe you," he spat. "My bloody father held you and your unholy shadow of a brother up to me every day of my bloody life as perfect examples of chivalry. I failed to strike out at Montgomery, but I had every intention of succeeding with you. And I knew just how to do it."

John imagined he did. "Then you slit Tess's brake lines," he said, "and you wrote the note—nay, you couldn't have written the note I found in my car because you can scarce sign your name."

Everard's look was murderous. "I had my servant do it, of course, because it was beneath me. I also left your sword in the forest and arranged it so your little wench would have to stop on a particular piece of ground to avoid running into it. And I sent you after her, because I could."

"It seems a fair bit of trouble," John began evenly, "to use slaying your brother as a way to strike out at me."

"But he doesn't want to kill Roland," said a voice suddenly from behind him.

John whirled around to find Tess standing there, dressed, damn her to hell, in lad's clothes. "What?" he demanded incredulously

"He doesn't want to kill Roland," she repeated. "He wants to kill—John, look out!"

John shoved Tess away from him, out of danger, then spun around. The only reason he hadn't been skewered on the end of Everard's sword was because Tess had shouted out a warning. He managed to keep himself alive after leaping aside only because he'd spent most of his life honing his skills with his father and brothers. Everard was hardly his equal, but he was apparently dredging up previously untapped reservoirs of desperation. John, had he been a lad with a weaker stomach, might have thought himself in a bit of a spot once or twice.

But since he could see out of the corner of his eye that the men of his family were watching him, their arms folded over their chests, and he could hear Tess behind him, making little sounds of distress, he collected every ounce of skill and strength he possessed and fought as if his life depended on it. Everard feinted to the left, then, to John's absolute surprise, kicked John's sword out of his hands. He followed that up with the heel of his hand under John's jaw.

John went sprawling backward in the muck. He looked up through the stars spinning around his head, then rolled to avoid Everard's sword stabbing where his own empty head should have been. He rolled again to avoid another thrust, pulling a knife free from his boot, then rolled to his knees and shoved his blade upward.

Everard gasped, then looked at the haft of John's blade protruding from his belly. His sword fell from his hands.

"I'm dead," he said in surprise.

John leaped to his feet and watched as Everard stumbled backward over the body of one of his men and went down hard upon his arse.

John glanced briefly over his shoulder to find Roland standing there, gaping at him. The future Earl of Sedgwick looked suddenly quite green, then turned and lost whatever he'd eaten that day. Tess clapped her hand over her mouth, presumably to keep herself from joining him.

John strode over to Tess and started to pull her behind him, then thought better of it.

"What did you mean back there?" he managed, feeling as if he were on the edge of falling into an abyss. "He wanted to kill whom?"

"You," she said breathlessly. She was splattered with the filth of the battlefield and looked absolutely terrified. "If Everard had wanted to kill Roland, he could have done it at any time, either here or in our day. But he left his brother alive. The only reason that made sense was because he didn't want anything Roland had—"

"I want what *you* have," Everard gurgled. "There, in that other world. And I'll have it yet." He lifted his head and glared at John. "And your wench, too, if she knows what's good for her."

John handed Tess off to Montgomery who had taken his bloody sweet time about sauntering over to offer aid, then walked back over to where Everard was now lying back in the muck. He checked again for weapons he might not expect, then looked at him.

"But why here?" John asked. "Why not slay me in the Future?"

"No body," Everard gasped, "no proof. I leave you here . . . and escape to there. Don't you watch . . . telly? Some snooping bobby . . . would . . . have . . . caught me up . . ."

John watched as Everard's eyes closed and he breathed his last. He sighed deeply, then bent and pulled his knife free of Everard's lifeless body. He found his sword and resheathed it, turning over in his mind what he'd just learned. He supposed Everard's plan made sense. Why not lure him back to medieval England, slay him, then return back to Future and take over all his affairs? It wasn't as though he had any close associates, no one who would have known the difference between him and someone pretending to be him. Everard could have gathered up all John's assets and disappeared into any number of luxurious locales.

He wasn't sure how Everard had thought to win Tess over, but perhaps he simply hadn't thought that far. Tess would not have gone quietly, John could say that much with certainty.

He scanned the battlefield quickly, but the skirmish was ended. His father, his brothers, and their men were simply milling about, making certain the threat had been eliminated. John took a deep breath, then looked behind him. Roland was now standing ten paces away, watching silently. John pursed his lips.

"And why are you here?" he demanded.

"I wanted to see what my brother was combining," Roland said with a shrug. "And to give you a few answers I thought you might want."

"Well, 'tis for damned sure you didn't come to save my life," John muttered. "I assume you've been doing a little traveling?"

Roland shrugged, but apparently couldn't help a smile. "Everard couldn't read the note you left him, and he was too stupid to imagine I might poke through his things whilst he was otherwise occupied. So, aye, I've been using your gate, when I've had the urge to roam. I stumbled by accident upon the one that lurks in my father's forest, though I'm afraid Everard saw me at it. I began to suspect over the past pair of months that Everard might understand its use, so I've nipped back home now and then to keep tabs on him."

John realized Roland was speaking English. "Interesting way to pass your time."

"It is," Roland agreed. "I've tried several centuries. Can't quite decide on what suits me the most, but I can name a couple I didn't particularly fancy."

John turned slightly to look at Tess, who was leaning heavily against his brother's shoulder. John reached over and caught her hand, then pulled her over to stand next to him. "I should introduce you to my lady wife. Tess Alexander, this is Roland of Chevington."

"I know," Tess said faintly. "Or I will know, I should say."

Roland frowned. "I'm not sure I understand."

John took a perverse pleasure in enlightening the man. "You, it would seem, have a few things to do that you haven't thought of yet. I would simply suggest that you do them properly."

Roland frowned. "How does that work?"

"Don't ask," Tess said, a little breathlessly. "And, John, don't torment him. We owe him quite a bit."

Roland shifted uncomfortably. "I'll go have a think about that, shall I? Unless you've any hints to give me before I do."

"I don't think I should," John said seriously. "I don't want the Future changing because of something I blurted out. Just carry on. You seem to have done a smashing job all on your own." He paused. "I suppose we'll let you get back to your jet-setting ways, unless you'd care to come inside for supper."

Roland tilted his head and looked at him. "I assume you're preparing to be lord of the manor."

"How did you know that?"

"The lady Joanna told me she wished she could leave the place to you but since she had no idea of your whereabouts, she would be forced to find someone else suitable. That someone would not, she assured me, ever be anyone from Chevington. After making certain I understood that, she instructed me quite

politely to go to hell and take my brother with me." He laughed
a little. "I'm not sure she wants me in her gates again, though I
must declare that my motives were pure." He looked at Tess. "A
pleasure, my lady. I hope we'll meet again."

"I do, too," Tess said gravely.

Roland made them both a small bow. "Well, I'll see to cleaning up what's left out here and perhaps beg a meal in the garrison
hall. Then I think I'm for France." He laced his fingers together
and stretched his hands over his head. "Post-revolution France,
though. I've had enough of bloodshed for the day."

John watched him walk away, then sighed deeply, wondering
why he was so unsettled. It wasn't that Roland might not manage to do what he was supposed to have already done—from
a certain perspective, of course. He frowned, looked about the
battlefield, then his gaze fell upon just what it was that had left
him feeling as if things weren't as they should have been.

"And just what in the hell," he asked the miscreant politely,
"were you thinking?"

Well, he might have been a little less than polite, but he was
covered in blood, so he thought he might be permitted an enthusiastic question or two.

Tess put her hands on her hips. "Don't yell at me."

"Tess, this is a damned battlefield!" he exclaimed. "Of *course*
I'm going to yell at you. You're bloody lucky I don't take my
sword to you!"

She ducked behind his brother, but Montgomery only laughed
and moved out of the way.

"I'm not about to get between you two," he said frankly. "I've
trained my lady to stay at home with the doors bolted. Obviously, John, you have some work still to do."

Tess glared at her brother-in-law, then walked forward until she was standing toe-to-toe with him. "Your sister Amanda
found the clothes for me," she said, sticking her chin out.

"A messenger would have sufficed," he said with a scowl.

"Are you having your first row?" Montgomery called back
over his shoulder.

"We already had that," John said shortly. "This is the second,
I daresay. Perhaps the third."

"She helped save your life, you fool," Robin said as he walked
by, covered with muck and other substances John didn't care to

identify. "If I were you, I would take her inside and indulge in a little wooing. She's liable to bolt her door against you otherwise. Not that I ever give my lady any reason for that, but I am, as many have noted, a perfectly chivalrous knight."

"Yeah," Tess said, nodding. "What he said."

John realized he was becoming the center of attention for the rest of the men of his family, none of whom he was particularly interested in hearing from at the moment. He nodded briskly to them, took Tess by the hand, and marched off the field.

"At least you put your sword away," Tess said breathlessly.

"I can draw it again, just as easily."

"Are you serious?"

He realized she had stopped only because she was stronger than she looked and she'd almost pulled him off his feet. He looked at her, fully prepared to enlighten her about all the things that could have happened to her, then he realized she was holding it together by a very tenuous thread.

His first instinct was to pull her into his arms, but he was covered in blood and filth. The last thing he wanted was for her to be wearing any more of the battle on her than she already was. Then again, it was probably the first and last time she would ever march out onto a medieval battlefield, so perhaps it didn't matter. He pulled her into his arms and held her tightly, hoping as an afterthought that he didn't pinch her with his mail. He wasn't at all sure that some sort of unsettling noise didn't escape him.

"I'm sorry," she said with a gulp. "I didn't know what else to do." She pulled back and looked up at him, her face covered with dirt and filth. "I was afraid you wouldn't be looking in the right direction."

He closed his eyes briefly, then ran his blood-caked hand over her hair. "Let me have a wash, then we'll borrow Grandmère's solar and I'll go to pieces in front of you. The sight of what's left of a man after he sees the woman he adores standing behind him in the midst of a war will be very educational, I imagine."

Her eyes were full of tears. "Your grandmother told me to come."

"As you were pulling on hose, no doubt."

"Actually, yes." She took a deep breath. "She passed on before I finished dressing."

He closed his eyes briefly, then looked at her. "At least we were able to see her a final time." He let out his breath slowly. "I must make certain all is clear on the field, then see to arrangements for her. But then, my lady, we will have some privacy." He paused. "Though I don't agree with your methods, I am most grateful for the warning."

"So am I," she said fervently.

He managed a smile. "I think you just might love me."

"You have no idea."

"Tell me later?"

"I will, in detail."

He smiled, saw her back to the hall, then returned to take care of the duties that fell to him as lord of Segrave. He supposed there was no shame in admitting that a good deal of what held him together was the thought that he could indeed take the woman he loved, find a private chamber somewhere, and hold her close whilst he shook.

She would understand, he was sure.

Unfortunately, it was quite a bit later than he wanted before he managed to see the castle settled, his family occupied with tasks pertaining to the necessary burial arrangements, and himself and Tess trudging up the stairs to a guard tower. He invited the men there to step outside for a moment or two, drew Tess inside, then locked the door.

He turned and leaned back against the wood, then looked at Tess who was standing in the middle of the small room, rubbing her arms and looking absolutely shattered. She turned around in a circle, presumably looking at what wouldn't be intact in her century, then stopped and looked at him.

He held open his arms.

She walked over and into his embrace without hesitation.

He held her close as she wept. He honestly couldn't blame her. He had, after his first battle, puked his guts out, then wept in private where his brothers hadn't been able to see. His father had known, of course, but he'd only offered a quiet embrace, then absolute silence on the matter thereafter.

"I *am* sorry," she managed, finally, pulling back to drag her sleeve across her face. "I just didn't know what else to do. I was honestly terrified that I wouldn't get to you before Everard did."

He dabbed at her cheeks with a handkerchief his mother had handed him at some point during the afternoon, then handed it to her so he could take her face in his hands. He kissed both her cheeks, then looked down at her.

"I'm just sorry that you needed to," he said quietly.

She shook her head. "I don't imagine I'll be asking you to apologize for yelling at me."

He managed a bit of a laugh. "That's probably very sensible. Words spoken in the heat of battle can't be used against a man after the fact."

"Is that in Robin's knightly code?"

"My father's, actually, inspired no doubt by my mother's propensity in her youth to pick up a sword and attempt to wield it in his defense."

She smiled a little. "She didn't."

"Oh, she did, imperiling all those around her, friend and foe alike. I have the feeling my father might have expressed his disapproval of her actions in less than dulcet tones on more than one occasion. Hence the addition of his no-apology rule. He would have been at it endlessly otherwise."

Her smile faded. "I don't ever want to do that again, John. Ever."

"Thinking of changing your academic discipline?" he asked lightly. "Victorian England, perhaps?"

"Believe me, I'm tempted. Especially since it would mean you'd have to wear heels and hose more often."

"Thank you, but nay," he said with a half laugh. "I'll remain comfortably in boots, if it's all the same to you."

She looked at him seriously for a moment or two, then pulled his head down toward hers.

John decided, after she was finished almost bringing him to his knees, that she had abandoned most of her worries about his wanting to stay in the past.

"Did that ceremony count?" she asked breathlessly.

He was very happy to have a door to lean against. "Definitely."

"I'm not sure it's good to begin a honeymoon the night before a funeral."

He smiled and pulled her close. "My grandmother would have approved, actually, but you might have a point. Besides, I haven't wooed you very well yet."

"Outside of threatening to take your sword to me, you haven't wooed me at all."

He raised his eyebrows briefly. "You should have concentrated a bit harder on your brief lessons with Robin, then you wouldn't take the threat so seriously."

She pulled out of his arms. "I'll go see if he's busy—"

"Nay, you won't," he said with a laugh, catching her before she escaped. He wrapped his arms around her, then looked at her gravely. "We will mourn my grandmother, take care of certain formalities pertaining to titles, then I believe we'll have a proper ceremony in the chapel." He paused. "Do you mind being chatelaine for a few days until we have this all sorted?"

She shook her head. "Of course not."

"We'll turn for home soon enough, I hope."

She was very still. "Are you sure you don't want to stay?"

"How can you ask?" he asked, pained. "After all that's befallen us over the past day?"

"Because you now have a keep," she said very quietly.

"So do you. I like yours better."

She met his eyes. "But you're now the lord of Segrave, John. I'm not sure you can walk away from that."

He snorted. "For all the good that title will do me in the Future. I doubt it will even earn me a free entrance to a Trust site. Nay, Tess, my grandmother left me the keep for her own perverse reasons, but she didn't intend I live here. She knows where my heart is."

"What are you going to do, then?" she asked, relaxing a bit.

"We'll put someone in charge, promise Montgomery all manner of prepackaged snacks to inspire him to check in on the steward now and again, then wait for one of our nephews to grow up and claim it."

Tess considered. "How about Rose?"

He smiled. "It would serve her right, the hellion. A perfect idea. I'll put it in trust for her until she comes of age. She'll have to see if she keeps it on her own or not." He rubbed her back for a moment or two, then pushed away from the door. "Let's go find a hot fire. My father has been itching all evening to talk to you about politics. I've just gotten back into his good graces; I don't want to fall out of them by keeping you up here where we'll get into all sorts of trouble."

She caught his arm before he pulled away. "Will you play for me?" she asked quietly. "Your mother and I will sit and weep together while you do."

He gathered her close for another eternal moment, then put his arm around her shoulders and opened the door. He couldn't do anything but nod. He hadn't played for his family in years, so he wasn't entirely sure he would get through it without a few stray tears of his own.

He wondered, along with his rules of knightly behavior, why his father had never told him about all the bittersweet things he would face in his life.

He took a deep breath and led his lady wife down the stairs. He would sort it all in the morning, decide what in the world he was going to do with a keep he was responsible for eight hundred years in the past, and make plans for his future.

And he would be very grateful to have those he loved around him whilst he did so.

Chapter 31

Tess stepped off the train in her own station and took a deep breath. It was one thing to walk from medieval England through a time gate to modern-day Chevington and see the castle wearing the ravages of time. It was another thing entirely to get off the train near Sedgwick, look over at the departure board, and see the appropriate date.

She felt a warm hand wrap around hers and looked up to see John standing next to her. She smiled.

"Almost home."

"If Oliver saw his way clear to leave the Vanquish for us instead of poaching it for himself," John said with a snort. He looked around, then took his own deep breath. "This is very strange."

"It's been that sort of month."

He laughed and leaned over to kiss her. "So it has been, my love. Let's go home, and we'll discuss it over a traditional English breakfast cooked for supper by yours truly."

She hesitated. "Are you really okay living at Sedgwick?"

"Unless you want to move into my cottage or set up a tent at Segrave, I think that's the only option open to us," he said dryly. He lifted an eyebrow. "Can you stomach the thought of me there?"

"Let's go home and I'll see if you suit."

"Elitist snob."

She laughed and hugged him before she walked with him out of the station. His car was indeed waiting for them there. She had to admit, there was something rather pleasant about the seat of a sports car as opposed to the back of a horse. She was very glad they'd managed to shower at an inn near Chevington station. She wasn't sure John would have let either of them into his car otherwise.

She put her hand on John's leg and closed her eyes as he drove back. She waited until he pulled into their car park, shut off the engine, and sighed before she looked at him.

"You look tired," she said with a weary smile.

"I think I could sleep for a solid se'nnight," he agreed. "Well, for the most part."

She blushed, though she knew she should have been well past that. They had spent almost a fortnight at Segrave, first mourning Joanna's death, then celebrating her life, then turning to their own celebration. She had soaked up every moment possible with Pippa, spent copious amounts of time with John's mother and sister, and happily served as a medieval lord's wife the rest of the time.

The partings hadn't been particularly joyous, but she'd had the distinct feeling they hadn't been final. She wasn't sure she would be using any gates again anytime soon, but she certainly couldn't say the same for others in John's family.

She considered, then looked at John. He shook his head slowly.

"Don't ask."

"I have to."

He sighed deeply and looked at her. "Tess, my dearest love, I do not want to go back and live in 1241. I do not want to go back to the Middle Ages and be lord of Segrave. I will miss my family, 'tis true, but I'll hazard a guess we'll see them now and again. Until that time, we'll make do with each other, your sisters, my nephews and other assorted extended connections. Do you believe me now?"

"I don't know," she said seriously. "Lord of Segrave and all."

"Earl of Sedgwick and all," he retorted.

She laughed a little. "And you think I'm sharing my title with you?"

He leaned over to kiss her. "As I said before, you're an elitist snob. Now, take me inside your lovely hall, woman, and be at your leisure whilst I make you supper. I don't know about you, but I want something to eat that I didn't have to slay myself earlier in the day." He started to open his door, then looked at her. "Wait for me."

"Forever," she said with a smile.

He kissed her again, then crawled out of his car. Tess waited for him to open her door, then found herself helped up to her feet and into his arms.

"I love you," he said seriously.

"And I love you," she said, putting her arms around his neck. She took a deep breath. "I just don't want you to regret your choice."

"I never will," he said seriously.

"Because I understand your past?"

"Because you are my future," he corrected. He tightened his arms around her briefly, then pulled away and took her hand. "We're exhausted. Let's eat, go to bed, then wake up in our proper time and place. And then we'll get on with our lives as my siblings have in the past. We'll work, raise our family, and have glorious family reunions where we'll share all the things that have bound us together."

"And life will be sweet," she said softly.

"It will, my love."

She nodded, because she supposed there was nothing else to be said. She took his proffered hand, then walked with him across the grass, stopping in surprise at the sight of Mrs. Tippets standing at the end of the bridge. Even more surprising was to find Mr. Beagle sitting at attention with nary a snarl in sight. Mrs. Tippets inclined her head.

"Lady Sedgwick."

Tess suppressed a smile. "Mrs. Tippets. And how nicely behaved Mr. Beagle is."

"Obedience school," Mrs. Tippets admitted. "And you'll be pleased to know we turned a tidy profit in the shop whilst you were away. Your sister, Miss Peaches, said you'd gone off on a research holiday and thought you might like to see things humming along as they should after you returned."

"It was a rather unexpected trip," Tess said, trying to latch on to something reasonable to say. "I assume the events went on as planned?"

"Miss Peaches took over without so much as a hitch in her step," Mrs. Tippets said. "Enlisted my aid now and again with a few things."

Tess wondered why she hadn't thought to do the same thing. "A very wise choice, of course," she managed. "Is my sister at home?"

"She went to London this morning to meet a client," Mrs. Tippets said. "Promised to be back tomorrow. She's been chatting with Lord Roland quite often over the past fortnight."

Tess suppressed the urge to look at John. At least Peaches would have known where they went. Tess made a bit more polite conversation, introduced John as her husband to complete shopkeeper approval, then walked with him across the bridge. She realized as she did so that she was looking up to see who might have been loitering on the battlements. She looked at John and smiled uneasily.

"I've been corrupted."

"I do the same thing every time, if it makes you feel any better," he said wryly. "Habit."

She walked with him across the courtyard and up to the front door. She found it open, which was just slightly unsettling. John, true to form, set their backpacks down on the ground and pulled her behind him.

"And just what are you going to do?" she asked in a frantic whisper. "Your sword's in the boot of your car!"

He pulled up his jeans and pulled a knife from his boot. "I think I can manage with this."

She looked around his shoulder. "I wasn't insulting your skill, you know. I just don't want to lose you to a bullet between the eyes."

He leaned over and kissed her softly. "You won't, I promise. But stay behind me."

She wasn't going to argue. She'd been on a medieval battlefield and *never* wanted to repeat that experience.

She waited for John to ease open the door, then peek inside, his knife in his hand. He straightened abruptly, then fumbled for her hand.

"We have company," he said.

He didn't seem overly stressed, so perhaps the guest wasn't an unwelcome one. He didn't protest when she moved to stand beside him. She looked at the man sitting in front of the fire, then gasped. She knew him, of course, from the future. She also had just seen him not a fortnight earlier looking fifty years younger.

"Lord Roland," she managed.

He rose and made them a low bow. "Lady Sedgwick," he said politely. "Lord Segrave."

John resheathed the knife in his boot, retrieved their gear from the front stoop, then set it inside the door. He took Tess's hand and walked with her across the hall to stop in front of the fire.

"Roland," John said with a huff of a laugh. "What a surprise."

"I'm sure it isn't," Roland said with an answering smile. "A surprise, I mean. I'm pleased to see you both back from your rescue mission in the past."

Tess sat down in the chair John pulled up for her, then put her hand in his. "I think I'm very glad you worked out a few details over the past few years."

"I imagine you are," Roland agreed.

"I would like to know how you did the same," John said politely. "Since you're here to give them to us."

"It's why I kept a key to let myself in," Roland said with a smile, "though I'll leave it behind now that my work is done. And to answer your question, I'll just say that your parting words to me on the field in front of Segrave haunted me for quite a while until I began to see what they meant. You perhaps won't be surprised that I've had a hand in a few things. John buying the shop was a gift I didn't arrange, though I would have found some other way to have you both meet. You, my lady, being here at the castle, though, was something I definitely saw to."

"How many times over the years have you made the trip from the past to the future?" John asked. "And how did you become so bloody old?"

Roland laughed. "Since I have you to thank for the opportunity to have all these gray hairs, I'll answer that happily. As I told you all those years ago, I'd been traveling back and forth quite a bit in my youth. As time went on and I understood what I needed to do, I lingered for a few years in Victorian England, directing the activities of a certain Lord Darling. After that, I settled on modern England, waiting and watching for Tess to arrive at Cambridge."

Tess shook her head. "It's just beyond strange to think you knew about us together before we knew about it ourselves." She paused, then looked at him narrowly. "You didn't influence me to choose medieval history somehow, did you?"

"Oh, nay," Roland said with a shiver. "That would have been too much, I think. You love what you love, my lady, simply because you love it. I can't say, though, that I didn't contemplate the irony of your encountering our good John there from time to time. And I did interfere just the slightest in John's musical career."

"Did you?" John asked. "How?"

"Nothing too dire," Roland assured him. "I had heard you play in Edinburgh once which had been completely a matter of happenstance. I put a bug in Dave Thompson's ear, that's all. It seemed a small thanks for my life."

"Damn you," John said weakly. "I knew that couldn't have been coincidence."

Roland smiled. "It actually was, if that eases you. He was there at the Festival listening to you with his mouth agape in a most unattractive fashion. As I knew you and recognized him, I simply told him your name, which of course meant nothing to him save something to plug into his diary and save for later use. Of course, I had no idea how it was you and Tess would meet given that you'd told me nothing of it in the past, so I will admit that I was fully prepared to orchestrate that if need be. I knew old Grant from my own loiterings here at Sedgwick, so when we encountered one another in a market in Provence and he told me to whom he'd sold his shop, I supposed all I needed to do was leave the rest of it up to Fate."

"Dangerous," John said wryly.

"Well, I didn't leave *everything* to Fate," Roland amended. "I can't say I've been honest with very many people, but Doris Winston knows all about me, the lovely old bird. I hoped if things went completely awry, she would help me out."

"But what if John hadn't wanted anything to do with me?"

Tess asked faintly. "What if he'd meant it when he told me that he thought we'd do better not to having anything to do with each other?"

John kissed her hand. Then he turned her hand over and kissed her palm. "Somehow," he said with a slow smile, "I imagine that was the least of Roland's worries. How could I not have fallen for you at first glance?"

Tess wondered if there would ever come a time where just the touch of his hand on hers didn't leave her looking around to see if someone had thrown another log on the fire.

Roland laughed. "I believe I'll leave you to your honeymooning."

Tess tore her gaze away from her husband. "You won't stay the night?" she asked. "We have rooms enough."

"Well," Roland said slowly, "if it wouldn't be too much trouble. I'll head back to France in the morning." He rose, then paused and pulled something from his trouser pocket. "I forgot this. Since I gave you the castle, Tess, I started to feel guilty that I'd given nothing to your husband who had done such a smashing job saving my life." He handed John a piece of paper. "Enjoy."

Tess watched him walk across the hall, humming a jaunty medieval tune, then looked at John, who was watching her instead.

"You know you're speaking French," he said with a smile.

"I didn't, no," she said in surprise. "Habit, I suppose. What did he give you?"

John handed her a piece of paper. It looked quite a bit like the one she'd had from the crown, only John's announced that the title of Earl of Segrave had been formally bestowed on him. Apparently, someone had done enough research to prove he was related to a certain John de Piaget, lord of Segrave in 1241. Tess looked at John in surprise.

"Well," she said, nonplussed. "What goes around comes around, I guess."

"For all the good it does me," he said with a snort, "though my grandmother would be pleased. But I won't be wasting any gold restoring that pile of stones, in case you were wondering."

"Or buying it back from the crown?"

He shook his head. "There's no land attached to that title any longer. In truth, Bess could have the land and title as well, but I won't spurn the gift. We'll picnic there every now and again and flash Burke's Peerage at them to see if they'll waive the entrance fee—which I doubt they will."

She smiled. "What a cynic."

"Realist," he said dryly. He rose, folded the letter and put it in his pocket, then reached for her hand. "Let's go have supper."

Tess was happy to sit at the worktable in her kitchen and watch John putter around in jeans and a T-shirt. He made quick work of making them dinner, then sat with her and tucked into more saturated fat than they would have seen in medieval England in a lifetime.

"You know," he said at one point, "we haven't really had a proper honeymoon."

"Where do you suggest?"

"I think there's a particular keep on the edge of the sea in the north I might like to take you to."

She smiled. "Will they let us in, do you think, or will they charge you a fee?"

"When Artane is your father, you find doors open to you that aren't open to the average traveler," he said with a wry smile. "Even the Artane of the current day."

"And if not, you have a credit card?"

He laughed a little. "I didn't want to say as much, but aye, I do."

"You'd better call Gideon and let him know we're coming," she advised. "Kendrick as well, I'd imagine. I'm not about to." She studied him. "Do you think he knows about us?"

"Tess, my love, he was at our wedding."

"He was ten."

"I imagine he has a very long memory. And he was inordinately fond of you. You're the only aunt who would look at bugs with him. A lad doesn't forget that sort of thing."

She rested her chin on her fist. "He certainly didn't say anything to me when I saw him several weeks ago."

"He knows when to keep his mouth shut," John said with a shrug, "being his father's son and all."

"What will Rose do with Segrave, do you think?"

"I shudder to think," he said with a shiver. "That one . . . she frightens me."

"I imagine she won't hit sixteen without several hours of

self-defense training under her belt, along with the appropriate amount of swordplay," Tess said with a bit of a laugh. "Being her father's daughter, as she is."

John nodded, then rose, stuck their dishes in the sink, and held out his hand for her.

"We'll do those in the morning," he said purposefully. "Since we'll be here to do them."

"That's why I put a stone over the gate at the end of the bridge."

"We'll uncover it in a couple of months and shove a care package through for Montgomery," John said with a snort. "He was very disappointed I hadn't brought anything tasty along for him."

"Pathetic."

He laughed. "He is, but you can hardly blame him." He pulled her into his arms in the passageway and smiled down at her. "Come wait by the fire, my love, and I'll make sure the doors are locked."

"And then will you play for me?" she asked. "I have a lute in the solar. It's nothing compared to yours, but it might do."

"Later," he said. "I believe I have business with you first."

"Locking the doors?"

He smiled. "Nay, love, not locking the doors, but I'll do that first."

Tess sat in front of the fire in the great hall and waited for him. She supposed she wasn't much for maudlin displays, but she couldn't help a few unsteady breaths as she thought about how fortunate she was. Modern conveniences, a castle she loved, and a text message waiting for her on her phone letting her know she'd been a hit at Chevington and would she be interested in doing that sort of blending of academics and atmosphere in her own keep.

But most of all, a medieval lord walking across that hall toward her in jeans and boots, a man who loved her not in spite of who she was and what she knew, but because of it.

It was so much more than she ever could have hoped for.

TURN THE PAGE
TO LEARN MORE ABOUT THE MacLEOD
AND DE PIAGET FAMILIES.

family lineage in the books of
LYNN KURLAND

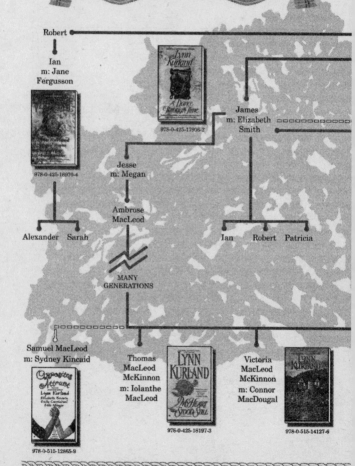

Robert

Ian
m: Jane
Fergusson

978-0-425-16970-4

978-0-425-17906-2

James
m: Elizabeth
Smith

Jesse
m: Megan

Ambrose
MacLeod

Alexander   Sarah

Ian   Robert   Patricia

MANY
GENERATIONS

Samuel MacLeod
m: Sydney Kincaid

Thomas
MacLeod
McKinnon
m: Iolanthe
MacLeod

Victoria
MacLeod
McKinnon
m: Connor
MacDougal

978-0-515-12865-9

978-0-425-18197-3

978-0-515-14127-6

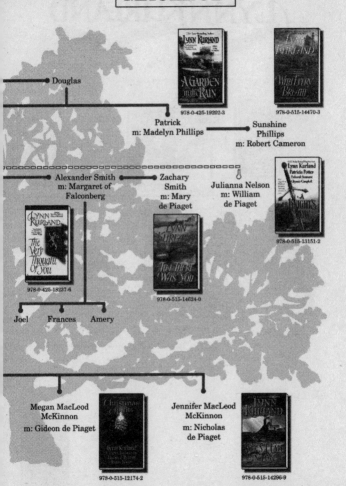

MACLEOD

Douglas

Patrick
m: Madelyn Phillips ━━━▶ Sunshine
Phillips
m: Robert Cameron

978-0-425-19202-3

978-0-515-14470-3

Alexander Smith ◀━━▶ Zachary
m: Margaret of
Falconberg
Smith
m: Mary
de Piaget

Julianna Nelson
m: William
de Piaget

978-0-425-18237-6

978-0-515-14624-0

978-0-515-13151-2

Joel   Frances   Amery

Megan MacLeod
McKinnon
m: Gideon de Piaget

Jennifer MacLeod
McKinnon
m: Nicholas
de Piaget

978-0-515-12174-2

978-0-515-14296-9

PA-6060

family lineage in the books of
LYNN KURLAND

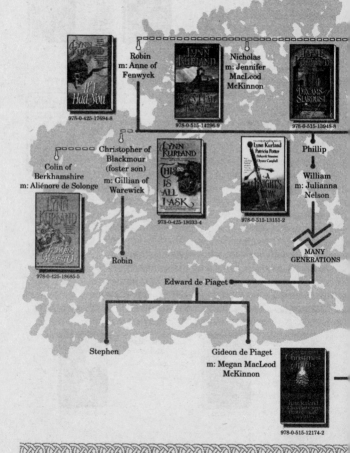

Robin
m: Anne of
Fenwyck

978-0-425-17694-8

Nicholas
m: Jennifer
MacLeod
McKinnon

978-0-515-14296-9

978-0-515-13948-8

Colin of
Berkhamshire
m: Aliénore de Solonge

Christopher of
Blackmour
(foster son)
m: Gillian of
Warewick

Phillip

978-0-425-18685-5

978-0-425-18033-4

978-0-515-13151-2

William
m: Julianna
Nelson

MANY
GENERATIONS

Robin

Edward de Piaget

Stephen

Gideon de Piaget
m: Megan MacLeod
McKinnon

978-0-515-12174-2

DE PIAGET

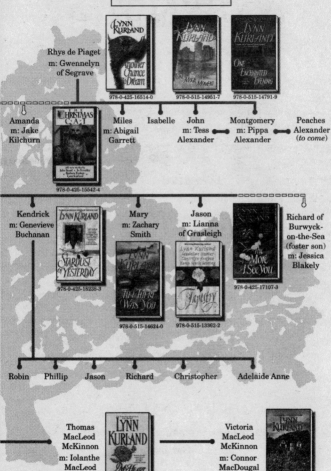

Rhys de Piaget
m: Gwennelyn of Segrave

Another Chance to Dream 978-0-425-16514-0

This Is All I Ask / The Very Thought of You 978-0-515-14951-7

One Enchanted Evening 978-0-515-14791-9

Amanda
m: Jake Kilchurn

A Christmas Cat 978-0-425-15542-4

Miles
m: Abigail Garrett

Isabelle

John
m: Tess Alexander

Montgomery
m: Pippa Alexander

Peaches Alexander
(to come)

Kendrick
m: Genevieve Buchanan

Stardust of Yesterday 978-0-425-18238-3

Mary
m: Zachary Smith

Till There Was You 978-0-515-14624-0

Jason
m: Lianna of Grasleigh

Tapestry 978-0-515-13362-2

Richard of Burwyck-on-the-Sea
(foster son)
m: Jessica Blakely

The More I See You 978-0-425-17107-3

Robin   Phillip   Jason   Richard   Christopher   Adelaide Anne

Thomas MacLeod McKinnon
m: Iolanthe MacLeod

My Heart Stood Still 978-0-425-18197-3

Victoria MacLeod McKinnon
m: Connor MacDougal

978-0-515-14127-6

PA-6761

**Praise for the novels of *New York Times*
bestselling author Lynn Kurland**

One Enchanted Evening

"Kurland presents another triumphant romance . . . Readers unfamiliar with her works will have great joy and ease in following the story of Montgomery and Pippa, and longtime readers will exult in having more familial pieces fall into place." —*Fresh Fiction*

"A perfect blend of medieval intrigue and time-travel romance. I was totally enthralled from the beginning to the end."
—*Once Upon a Romance*

"*One Enchanted Evening* is another of the de Piaget series woven with magic, handsome heroes, lovely heroines, oodles of fun, and plenty of romance . . . a typical Lynn Kurland book—beautifully written with an enchanting, entertaining, and just plain wonderful story line." —*Romance Reviews Today*

"Montgomery and Pippa were a delightful hero and heroine. Humorous, touching, and full of fun, this tale was really entertaining." —*The Romance Dish*

"This latest installment of the de Piaget romance series will not disappoint Ms. Kurland's fans." —*Smexy Books Romance Reviews*

"Readers will be entranced with *One Enchanted Evening* as much as I was." —*A Romance Review*

"Humor is always a big factor in Kurland's delightful tales, and that holds true for this one. Enchanting!"
—*Romantic Times Book Reviews*

Till There Was You

"*Till There Was You* proves Kurland's mastery of time travel, and has forced this reviewer to impatiently wait and see who she will write about next." —*Romance Novel TV*

"A fantastic story that will delight both readers who are familiar with the families and those who aren't."
—*Romance Reviews Today* (Perfect 10 Award)

continued . . .

"This is an amusing time-travel romance starring a terrific, fully developed hero whose good intentions, present and past, are devastated by love."
—*Midwest Book Review*

"One of those feel-good romances that expertly mixes past with present to prove that love endures all things and outlasts almost everything, including time itself. With an eye to detail and deliciously vivid imagery, this paranormal tale of matchmaking comes fully to life . . . Spellbinding and lovely, this is one story readers won't want to miss."
—*Romance Reader at Heart*

With Every Breath

"As always, [Kurland] delivers a delightful read!"
—*Romantic Times* (4 stars)

"Kurland is a skilled enchantress . . . *With Every Breath* is breathtaking in its magnificent scope, a true invitation to the delights of romance."
—*Night Owl Romance*

When I Fall in Love

"Kurland infuses her polished writing with a deliciously dry wit, and her latest time-travel love story is sweetly romantic and thoroughly satisfying."
—*Booklist*

"The continuation of a wonderful series, this story can also be read alone. It's an extremely good book."
—*Affaire de Coeur*

Much Ado in the Moonlight

"A pure delight."
—*Huntress Book Reviews*

"A consummate storyteller . . . [Kurland] will keep the reader on the edge of their seat, unable to put the book down until the very last word."
—*ParaNormal Romance*

"No one melds ghosts and time travel better than the awesome Kurland."
—*Romantic Times*

Dreams of Stardust

"Kurland weaves another fabulous read with just the right amounts of laughter, romance, and fantasy." —*Affaire de Coeur*

"Kurland crafts some of the most ingenious time-travel romances readers can find . . . wonderfully clever and completely enchanting." —*Romantic Times*

A Garden in the Rain

"Kurland laces her exquisitely romantic, utterly bewitching blend of contemporary romance and time travel with a delectable touch of tart wit, leaving readers savoring every word of this superbly written romance." —*Booklist*

"Kurland is clearly one of romance's finest writers—she consistently delivers the kind of stories readers dream about. Don't miss this one." —*The Oakland Press*

From This Moment On

"A disarming blend of romance, suspense, and heartwarming humor, this book is romantic comedy at its best." —*Publishers Weekly*

"A deftly plotted delight, seasoned with a wonderfully wry sense of humor and graced with endearing, unforgettable characters." —*Booklist*

My Heart Stood Still

"Written with poetic grace and a wickedly subtle sense of humor . . . romance with characters readers will come to care about and a love story they will cherish." —*Booklist*

"A totally enchanting tale, sensual and breathtaking." —*Rendezvous*

continued . . .

If I Had You

"Kurland brings history to life . . . in this tender medieval romance."
—*Booklist*

"A passionate story filled with danger, intrigue, and sparkling dialogue."
—*Rendezvous*

The More I See You

"The superlative Ms. Kurland once again wows her readers with her formidable talent as she weaves a tale of enchantment that blends history with spellbinding passion and impressive characterization, not to mention a magnificent plot."
—*Rendezvous*

Another Chance to Dream

"Kurland creates a special romance between a memorable knight and his lady."
—*Publishers Weekly*

The Very Thought of You

"A masterpiece . . . this fabulous tale will enchant anyone who reads it."
—*Painted Rock Reviews*

This Is All I Ask

"An exceptional read."
—*The Atlanta Journal-Constitution*

"Both powerful and sensitive . . . a wonderfully rich and rewarding book."
—Susan Wiggs

Titles by Lynn Kurland

STARDUST OF YESTERDAY	A GARDEN IN THE RAIN
A DANCE THROUGH TIME	DREAMS OF STARDUST
THIS IS ALL I ASK	MUCH ADO IN THE MOONLIGHT
THE VERY THOUGHT OF YOU	WHEN I FALL IN LOVE
ANOTHER CHANCE TO DREAM	WITH EVERY BREATH
THE MORE I SEE YOU	TILL THERE WAS YOU
IF I HAD YOU	ONE ENCHANTED EVENING
MY HEART STOOD STILL	ONE MAGIC MOMENT
FROM THIS MOMENT ON	

The Novels of the Nine Kingdoms

STAR OF THE MORNING	A TAPESTRY OF SPELLS
THE MAGE'S DAUGHTER	SPELLWEAVER
PRINCESS OF THE SWORD	

Anthologies

THE CHRISTMAS CAT
(with Julie Beard, Barbara Bretton, and Jo Beverley)

CHRISTMAS SPIRITS
(with Casey Claybourne, Elizabeth Bevarly, and Jenny Lykins)

VEILS OF TIME
(with Maggie Shayne, Angie Ray, and Ingrid Weaver)

OPPOSITES ATTRACT
(with Elizabeth Bevarly, Emily Carmichael, and Elda Minger)

LOVE CAME JUST IN TIME

A KNIGHT'S VOW
(with Patricia Potter, Deborah Simmons, and Glynnis Campbell)

TAPESTRY
(with Madeline Hunter, Sherrilyn Kenyon, and Karen Marie Moning)

TO WEAVE A WEB OF MAGIC
(with Patricia A. McKillip, Sharon Shinn, and Claire Delacroix)

THE QUEEN IN WINTER
(with Sharon Shinn, Claire Delacroix, and Sarah Monette)

A TIME FOR LOVE